**The lantern flame fluttered, and Milo noticed
the greasy smell of the oil.**

He didn't want to be caught in the darkness of the temple,
trying to find his way back to old Kirot in the inky black. He
rose, but he couldn't bring himself to leave. There needed to
be something more. Some gesture that came from him, that
made all of this his own.

"I will guard this secret," he said, his thin voice echoing
through the chamber. "No man alive will take it from me."

He had a feeling of acceptance, almost of gratitude, radiating from the still stone before him. It was an illusion, of
course, no more real than the voice of the water, but its unreality didn't seem to matter. He would carry this moment
with him, buried under the world with the sea at his back
and the dragon before him, forever.

A sound came like the thunder of a gigantic wave, and
Milo fell back. The great statue shifted, ripples passing
along the expanse of its side, dust sheeting down. It shifted
its foreclaws, raised its head, the vast mouth opening in a
massive yawn. Within, the flesh of its mouth was wet and
black, and the hot breath stank of oil and bit the air like the
fumes from distilled wine. The massive head drooped, took
a new position on its folded claws, and went still again.

Publications by Daniel Abraham

THE LONG PRICE QUARTET
A Shadow in Summer
A Betrayal in Winter
An Autumn War
The Price of Spring

Leviathan Wept and Other Stories

Hunter's Run (with George R. R. Martin and
Gardner Dozois)

THE BLACK SUN'S DAUGHTER
Unclean Spirits (as MLN Hanover)
Darker Angels (as MLN Hanover)
Vicious Grace (as MLN Hanover)
Killing Rites (as MLN Hanover)
Graveyard Child (as MLN Hanover)

THE DAGGER AND THE COIN
The Dragon's Path
The King's Blood
The Tyrant's Law

THE EXPANSE
Leviathan Wakes (with Ty Franck as James S. A. Corey)
Caliban's War (with Ty Franck as James S. A. Corey)
Abaddon's Gate (with Ty Franck as James S. A. Corey)
(forthcoming)

THE
TYRANT'S
LAW

BOOK THREE OF THE DAGGER AND THE COIN

DANIEL
ABRAHAM

www.orbitbooks.net

Orbit
Hachette Book Group
237 Park Avenue, New York, NY 10017
HachetteBookGroup.com

First Edition: May 2013

Orbit is an imprint of Hachette Book Group, Inc. The Orbit name and logo are trademarks of Little, Brown Book Group Limited.

The Hachette Speakers Bureau provides a wide range of authors for speaking events. To find out more, go to www.hachettespeakersbureau.com or call (866) 376-6591.

The publisher is not responsible for websites (or their content) that are not owned by the publisher.

The characters and events in this book are fictitious. Any similarity to real persons, living or dead, is coincidental and not intended by the author.

Library of Congress Control Number: 2013930150

ISBN: 978-0-316-08070-5

10 9 8 7 6 5 4 3 2 1

RRD-C

Printed in the United States of America

To Katherine and Scarlet

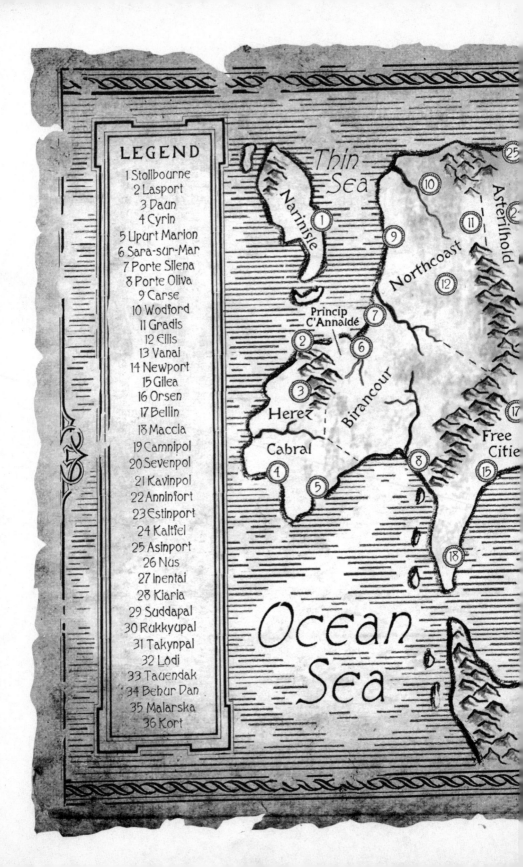

LEGEND

1 Stollbourne
2 Lasport
3 Daun
4 Cyrin
5 Upurt Marion
6 Sara-sur-Mar
7 Porte Silena
8 Porte Oliva
9 Carse
10 Wodford
11 Gradis
12 Ellis
13 Vanai
14 Newport
15 Gilea
16 Orsen
17 Bellin
18 Maccia
19 Camnipol
20 Sevenpol
21 Kavinpol
22 Anninfort
23 Estinport
24 Kaltfel
25 Asinport
26 Nus
27 Inentai
28 Kiaria
29 Suddapal
30 Rukkyupal
31 Takynpal
32 Lodi
33 Tauendak
34 Behur Dan
35 Malarska
36 Kort

Thin Sea

Narinisle

Asterilhold

Northcoast

Princip C'Annaldé

Birancour

Herez

Cabral

Free Citie

Ocean Sea

Prologue

Milo of Order Murro

Milo slipped in the darkness, falling to one knee. The stones of the beach cut his skin, and the blood darkened the oiled wool of his leggings. The old fisherman, Kirot his name was, paused and looked back at him, lifting his lantern and one white eyebrow in query. *Are you coming, or staying here?* To the north, the waves cracked with ice. To the south, the deep darkness of the village waited for their return. Milo forced himself to stand. A little more blood would do him no harm. He'd lost enough, God knew. Kirot nodded and turned back to the long, slow trudge along the shore.

The rhythm of their steps sounded against the waves like the complex patterns of a marriage dance. Milo could almost conjure up the thrill of the violins and the tapping of the shell drums. He had heard it said that of all the thirteen races of mankind, the Haaverkin had the most exquisite sense of music. In fairness, he'd only heard this said by other Haaverkin. A woman's voice rose in the music, ululating in a sensual harmony with the strings, and Milo recognized that he was hallucinating. The voice of the water, his father called it. He'd heard it before sometimes when he'd been out on the boats in the dim light before dawn or limping back in to shore after a long day on the cold northern waters. Sometimes it was music, other times voices in conversation or argument. Some of the very old or very young claimed that the sounds were real, that they were the Drowned calling out to their brother race. Milo's father said that was rot and piss. It was only a man's mind playing tricks on itself, and the roar of ice and water to give it ground to play on. And so that was what Milo believed.

The coast nearest his village was ragged. Cliffs and stony beach, fat green crabs and snow-grey gulls. Some nights the aurora danced green and gold in the sky, but tonight it was low dark cloud and the smell of snow coming. The moon struggled now and again through the cover, peeping down at the two men and then looking shyly away. No, not two men. Not yet. One man and one nearly so. Milo had been a boy that morning, and would be a man before he slept, but he was still in the dangerous place between places, neither one thing nor another. It was why he was here.

He knew that the best thing was not to look directly into the glow of Kirot's lantern. The tiny light would blind him. Better to stare into the shadows and leave his eyes adapted to the dark. But without his willing it, his gaze slid toward the flame, and he didn't have the will left to pull it away. Of the hundreds of small fishing villages along the Hallskari coast, each had its order, its ritual, its secrets and signs and mysteries. Bloody battles had raged between some for generations over disagreements whose origins were lost in the dark waters of history. Order Wodman, their faces tattooed in blue and red, sank the ships of the green-faced Order Lûs, and Order Lûs burned Wodman salting houses until the elder clan came from Rukkyupal to force a reconciliation. In some orders, to become a man meant a monthlong voyage in a boat of your own design. In others, the boys would fast until the great rolls of Haaverkin fat were reduced to thin folds of skin. For Milo and the boys of Order Murro, there was the initiation. A night of songs and coddling, a last chance to sleep in the women's quarters, and then from dawn to dusk a series of ritual combats and beatings that left Milo's back raw and his knees shaking-weak.

And after the last of these, the secret initiation about which no boy knew and no man would speak. Even now, all that Milo could say for certain was that it involved walking along the shore at low tide on the longest night of the year.

Kirot grunted and stepped to the left. Milo's hazy mind failed to grasp why until he trod into the freezing puddle between the stones. The cold bit at his toes. Any of the other races—Firstblood, Tralgu, Yemmu, even the oil-furred Kurtadam—would have been in danger of death with a wet leg on a night like this. The dragons had made Haaverkin to survive the cold, and Milo only felt the wet as another insult to his dignity in a day rich with them.

Kirot heaved a great sigh, stopped, and took a bone pipe from his hat. He tamped tobacco into the bowl, took the stem between his rot-grey teeth, and leaned close to the lantern, sucking at the smoke like a baby at the teat. His face was a labyrinth of ink and age lines. When he looked at Milo, there was a solemnity in his expression that said wherever they had been bound for, they had reached. The old fisherman held out the pipe. Milo considered whether he should pretend to cough on the smoke. Boys weren't allowed tobacco, though most of them found ways to sneak pinches of it from their fathers and older brothers. The bone bowl was warm, and Milo inhaled deeply, the glow of the embers like the bright eye of a Dartinae. It must have been the right thing, because Kirot smiled.

"Listen to me," Kirot said, and hearing a voice that wasn't swimming up from inside his own head startled Milo. "Of all the orders in all the villages of the Haaverkin, only ours knows the great secret of the world. You listening? There are things only we know."

"All right," Milo said.

"Josen, son of Kol. You remember him?"

Milo nodded.

"He wasn't lost in a fouled net," Kirot said. "He spoke of what you are about to learn outside the men's circle. His own father killed him. Yours'll kill you too, if you tell our secrets. What you learn here, no one ever knows, except us. Follow me?"

Milo nodded.

"Speak it," Kirot said. "This isn't time for being unclear."

The warmth of the smoke cleared Milo's head and soothed the aches in his flesh. He took another draw and exhaled through his nostrils. A particularly large wave roared against the stone shore, leaving spears and daggers of ice behind as it drew back into the ink-black sea.

"If I speak of what I learn here tonight, my life will be forfeit."

"And no one will even know why," Kirot said. "Not your mother. Not your wives, if you have any such. To everyone, it will have been sad mischance. Nothing more."

"I understand," Milo said.

Kirot stretched his broad shoulders, the joints of his spine cracking like snapped twigs.

"You know how it is, waking up from a good sleep?" Kirot asked. "You're in some warm little dream about drinking goat's milk with your dead aunt or some such non-sense, and then you come to, and it all fades away. Maybe if you were sick-tired to start or some dog's started yapping in the night and woke you, you're a little here and a little there at the same time. Don't matter, though, because the dream that was all solid and real just ups and slides out of your mind. Then the time comes to haul out for the day, and you can't even say what it was you were dreaming about."

Milo drew on the pipe again. His knees shook less and his back hurt more. A breath later, he noticed Kirot's mildly annoyed gaze on him. Milo shook his head.

"Ask you again, and attend it this time. You know how it is, waking up from a good sleep?"

"I do."

"Good, then. So that dream that fades? That's the whole world. You, me. The sea, the sky. Every retching thing there is. It's all a dream the dragons dream, and if the last dragon ever wakes up, we're fucked. Everything that ever happened comes undone and cooks off into nothing."

He said it in the matter-of-fact voice that belonged to conversations about weather and the odds of a good catch. Milo waited for the rest of the parable. Another wave rattled the stones and ice. In the dim light of the lantern, Kirot looked abashed.

"All right, then," the old man said, turning his back to the sea. "No point waiting here. Come on."

At first, Milo thought they were heading back to the village, and pleasure and disappointment fought for the greater share of his fatigue-drunk mind. Kirot didn't lead him back toward the darkened houses, though. He took him to the cliffside. Centuries of tides had eaten at the hard stone of the land, sucking away soil and leaving the the bones of the world exposed. Caves and tunnels pocked it, pools of darkness within the darkness. Kirot led toward one, the lantern swinging at his side. Milo gave silent thanks that the man hadn't asked for his pipe back.

The cave leaned into the land. Seaweed and driftwood choked the way forward, ready cover for crabs or ice snakes. Brine and rot thickened the chill air. Kirot raised the small lantern, muttered to himself, and waded forward, into the black. Milo followed. The cave sank deeper in, then turned and became a tunnel. The stone changed from pebbled brown and grey and black to an almost luminous green. Milo had seen a knife once made of dragon's jade, unbreakable and permanently keen. This looked the same. A black line marked where the water stopped, even at high tide. Milo wouldn't have thought they'd gone up enough for that, but his mind still wasn't wholly his own. Perhaps he'd lost himself for a time somewhere in the tunnel. Perhaps the tobacco Kirot had given him had a few seeds of some less benign plant.

"Here," Kirot whispered. "Look, but fuck's sake keep *quiet.*"

He held out the lantern. The old man's face looked grim and uncomfortable and as close as Milo had ever seen to fear. Anxiety snaked down past Milo's exhaustion and pain as he reached out for the light. The iron handle scraped against his palm as he gripped it. Kirot nodded him on, then plucked the pipe from between Milo's teeth and squatted down on his wide haunches as if ready to wait there in the darkness forever. Milo walked on.

The tunnel opened out into a larger chamber. Milo had been in any number of salt caves in his life, natural gaps where softer stone or mineral had been eroded away to leave holes in the flesh of the world. Once, he'd even found the remains of a smuggler's camp: rotted steel blades and shattered pottery. The place he stepped into now bore those natural caverns no resemblance. The green walls were plumb and square, black lines carved into them in forms that made Milo's skin crawl to look at. Black streaks bled down from holes where iron sconces had rusted to nothing timeless ages ago. And before him, in the great room's center, a statue of a dragon larger than a house. Its scales were the black of the midnight sea under layers of lichen and moss. The closed eyes were larger than Milo's head, and the wide claws that rested on the ground could have covered his full body and left no sign that he was under them. Great wings lay folded against its sides.

Milo found himself weeping. He had no words to describe the commanding beauty of the thing before him or the ice-in-the-crotch terror that it inspired. He murmured an obscenity under his breath, and the carved dragon before him made it seem like a prayer. His heart fluttering in his breast, he reached out and put his hand against the broad scales.

Stone. Cold, hard, and dead.

He had heard that the great cities had such things. Images of dragons so old they'd been carved from living models, the impressions of massive claws, miraculous bestiaries and towers. He had heard of the great and mysterious ships that fishermen saw in the freezing mist that never came to shore. His world had always been filled with stories of miracles, but never the things themselves. Not until now. He let himself sit, his abused legs folding. The floor of the buried temple was cold and gritty, and the tears dripped down his cheeks, hot and utterly without shame. A warmth seemed to grow in his breast, a heat that came from having a secret. And more than that, from at last being a man. He imagined Kirot decades before, with his hair black and his face smooth, where he now sat. He imagined his father, his older brothers. All of them had carried the secret between them, and no amount of friendship, fondness, or loyalty could bridge that chasm. He had crossed over now. He knew what they knew. He was one of them now, not a child, but a man of Order Murro. And yes, it was a secret he would carry to his grave.

The lantern flame fluttered, and Milo noticed the greasy smell of the oil. He didn't want to be caught in the darkness of the temple, trying to find his way back to old Kirot in the inky black. He rose, but he couldn't bring himself to leave. There needed to be something more. Some gesture that came from him, that made all of this his own.

"I will guard this secret," he said, his thin voice echoing through the chamber. "No man alive will take it from me."

He had a feeling of acceptance, almost of gratitude, radiating from the still stone before him. It was an illusion, of course, no more real than the voice of the water, but its unreality didn't seem to matter. He would carry this moment with him, buried under the world with the sea at his back and the dragon before him, forever.

A sound came like the thunder of a gigantic wave, and Milo fell back. The great statue shifted, ripples passing along the expanse of its side, dust sheeting down. It shifted its foreclaws, raised its head, the vast mouth opening in a massive yawn. Within, the flesh of its mouth was wet and black, and the hot breath stank of oil and bit the air like the fumes from distilled wine. The massive head drooped, took a new position on its folded claws, and went still again. Milo heard something like a small girl's laughter, high and small and paroxysmal, and knew it was him.

A hard-callused hand took him by the hair and pulled him back, another hand clamping down over his mouth and choking off his yelp. Kirot looked peeved; he scooped up the still-burning lantern and pushed Milo back down into the tunnel. Soon the walls around them grew soft and rounded again, and the cracking roar of the waves returned. When they reached the stone beach, Kirot stopped and lifted the lantern.

"I tell you that the world ends if the dragon wakes up,"

the old fisherman said, "and to keep quiet, and what is it you do, boy?"

"Sorry."

Kirot spat in disgust. When he spoke, his voice carried a full hold of contempt.

"Milo son of Gytan of Order Murro, I stand witness that you are now a man. Don't let it go to your fucking head."

Clara Annalise Kalliam, Formerly Baroness of Osterling Fells

Clara woke to the familiar sound of voices raised in the street below her window. The dawn had not yet transformed the darkness of her little room in the boarding house from black to grey, but it soon would. Her window was not glass, but oiled parchment that let in some light and a great deal of cold. She pulled the wool blankets close to her chin, pressed her body into the thin mattress, and listened while the married couple in the street berated one another again, as they did more mornings than not. He was a drunkard and a little boy in a man's broken body. She was a shrew who drank a man's blood and ate his freedom. He was sleeping with whores. She was giving all the coin he earned to her brother. The litany of marital strife was as common and boring as it was sad. And saddest of all, Clara thought, was that the two of them couldn't hear the love on which all their resentments were built. No one shouted and wept in the street over someone they didn't care about. She wondered what they would make of it if she sought them out and told them how very, very lucky they were.

When at last she rose, the light was enough that she could see the winter's cold turning her breath to smoke. She got quickly into her underthings, and then a dress with stays up the side where she could reach them without a servant girl's help. Under other circumstances, she would still have been wearing mourning clothes, but when one's husband is slaughtered by the Lord Regent as a traitor to the throne, the rules of grief are somewhat changed. She made do with a small twist of cloth tied around her wrist and easily covered by her sleeve. She would know it was there. That was enough.

As the light waxed, she washed her face and put up her hair. The sounds in the street changed. The rattle of carts, the shouting of carters. Dogs barked. The sounds of Camnipol in the grip of winter. Dawson had hated being in the capital city during winter. Winter business, he'd called it, and his voice had dripped with contempt. A man of his breeding should spend the winter months on his lands or else with the King's Hunt. Only now, of course, there were no lands. Lord Regent Geder Palliako had taken them back for the crown, to be doled out later as a token to someone whom he wished to reward. And Clara was living on an allowance scraped together by her two younger sons. Her eldest boy, Barriath, was gone God only knew where, and her natural daughter was busy clinging to her husband's name and praying that the court would forget she had ever been called Kalliam.

In the common room, Vincen Coe sat by the fire, waiting for her. He wore his huntsman's leathers, though there was no hunt to call in the city and the master he'd served was dead. The perfectly ridiculous love he professed for Clara shone in his eyes and in the uncertain way he held himself as she walked into the room. It wasn't at all dignified, but it was flattering, and despite herself she found it endearing.

"I've saved you a bowl of the morning oats," he said. "And I'm making fresh tea."

"Thank you," she said, sitting beside the little iron stove.

"May I be permitted to walk with you today, my lady?"

It was a question he asked every day, like a child asking a favor of a beloved tutor.

"I would be quite pleased with some company, thank you," she said, as she often did. Often, but not always. "I have several errands today."

"Yes, ma'am," Vincen said, and did not ask what they were, because he knew.

She was going to overthrow the crown and, if she could, destroy Geder Palliako.

She didn't have a concrete plan yet, but she'd lived her life in court. She had seen any number of quiet campaigns of social sabotage and destruction. The secret was no secret: build friendships and connections, talk about trivialities, and listen closely to what was said. The women who failed were always the impatient, the ones who tried to force others to their own opinion or engineer a false scandal. Making opportunities rarely worked, and watching for them almost always did.

Her first stop, as it had been most days, was a baker's shop near the western edge of the Division. The baker was one of the few Yemmu to make a home in Camnipol, his body wide and thick, the tusks that rose from his lower jaw carved and inlaid with tribal markings of the Keshet. He looked like a curiosity in a show of exotics, but he spoke without an accent.

"Ah! The queen of pigeons! Come in, come in."

Clara smiled, though in truth she thought the man's pet name for her was a bit presumptuous.

"And how are you this morning, Melian? I hope your wife's feeling better."

"Much better, my lady," the baker said, hoisting a cloth bag of stale rolls and yesterday's small loaves from behind the counter. "I'll tell her you asked."

Clara's allowance was generous without being extravagant. It would have kept her in much more comfortable conditions if she'd chosen to spend it differently. The smell of fresh bread was a temptation each day she came, rich and earthy, sweet with molasses and rich with baked walnuts. She pushed two thin coins across the countertop, and the baker brushed them into his wide and waiting palm.

"The pigeons eat well again today," he said, grinning. Apart from his decorated tusks, his teeth were wide and yellowed by time and coffee.

"Perhaps this time they'll be grateful," Clara said with a smile as Vincen took up the bag and held the door open for her.

The streets were white with old ice where they weren't black with mud. Low, bright clouds dropped balls of frozen rain the size of baby's teeth, too compact to be called snowflakes and too soft for hail. The air smelled wet and cold. The great families were gone from the city for the season, but the traffic on the street was hardly less. The year that had passed had left a great deal of work to be done. The short, victorious war against Asterilhold and then the doomed, hellish revolt within the walls of the city. The process of rebuilding was evident in the streets. Carts with great timbers heading toward the north where noblemen's compounds had burned. Great slabs of marble and granite creaking toward the palaces where walls and façades had been broken or scorched past cleaning. And even now, prisoners hauling debris—old barricades or ruined carriages or sometimes still the bodies of the lowborn dead—to the middle of the great bridges and dropping the garbage into the distant chaos at the bottom of the Division. The city as it had been was gone. Busy as a kicked anthill, Camnipol struggled to remake itself. Clara didn't think much of what it was becoming.

The Prisoner's Span was the southernmost of the great bridges that crossed the Division, and the oldest. Its design was plain, and the trunks of the massive trees that had been felled to create it were dark with tar to repel insects and keep the bridge from collapse. The wind bit and made the great structure creak like a ship at sea. The condemned of the city hung in cages below, great iron chains and thick straps of woven leather the only thing between the prisoners and the long fall below them. At the center of the span—as every morning—the prisoners' families and friends gathered, trying to drop enough food and water down through the open air to keep the captives alive until their sentence ended. If a man was condemned without a wife or child who would come each day and lower down water and bread, then even a week's detention was death. The crown felt no obligation to offer care for criminals. Clara had heard stories of brotherhoods of cutthroats and thieves that collected dues like any of the great fraternities, and guaranteed sustenance should their members fall afoul of the magistrate. She'd even seen some men on the span who might have been part of such a group. For the most part, though, it was family. Dirty, small women lowering baskets on twine. Desperate-eyed men dropping bits of cheese down to the opened palms of their wives and lovers. There were tales of someone leaning out too far, and the prisoners watching, trapped, as their saviors fell through the empty air to die far beneath them.

And then there were the others. Boys, mostly, who came to piss off the edge of the span or rain dead animals and rotten fruit on the heads of the prisoners. The city guard did nothing to stop them. Encouraged them, even. There were also tales of one of those boys losing his footing, but those weren't told in the grim tones of tragedy.

Clara went from one end of the span to the other, slowly

emptying her bag. Here was Shuler, the pickpocket's wife, accepting yesterday's roll for her half-frozen husband. Here Cassian the Tralgu, the tips of his doglike, mobile ears almost blue with the cold, come to visit his father in the cages. Here Berrin, whose sister had been caught withholding taxes. Here Taracali, whose son had killed a neighbor's dog. Clara gave food to them all, stopping to talk to each of them, to learn their names and their stories, to touch them on the arm or the shoulder or the hand. She came as an agent of mercy, witnessing without judgment and sympathizing without pity.

And though they did not know it, she gathered them as allies.

When the bag was empty, Vincen folded it into his belt, and they walked together to the eastern end of the bridge, then turned north, toward the Kingspire. The streets widened and the architecture grew more ornate as they went on. Soon, she and Vincen were walking among the houses of the wealthy, and not long after that, the noble. Servants had cleaned the streets here, the black cobbles free of horse shit and old ice. Laborers' carts made way for carriages and palanquins. The houses rose up three and four stories high, and the mansions had gardens and grounds of leaf-bare trees and brown hedge. Clara had spent most of her life in streets like these, riding in carriages and thinking nothing of it. It had only been months since she had been Baroness of Osterling Fells and wife of the Lord Marshal. Already, she felt like she was traveling in a foreign land. She stopped at a café and bought three chicken pies and a skin of watered wine, and the girl behind the counter pretended not to know her.

In the street again, Clara turned east. It would have been faster to go north, but the temple of the spider goddess that Geder Palliako had brought back from the Keshet stood on that street, and Clara didn't want to see its red silk banner and eightfold sigil. It was the new priesthood's influence over the throne that had driven Dawson to act, and his action that had unmade her life.

The first shout could have been anything—outrage, pleasure at seeing an old friend, a teamster scolding a horse. The second was unmistakably pain. She glanced at Vincen and he at her. Without a word, they turned down the narrow side street, moving toward a small crowd that had gathered in a private square. Vincen walked before her, leading with a gentle shoulder that permitted no refusal and gave little offense. She kept close to him, walking with her hand in his to keep the crowd from closing around him. Soon, they reached the front. Too soon.

The Timzinae girl wore the robes of a servant. The dark, chitinous scales that covered her body had been made darker by blood. She crouched on the curb, her head in her hands, and the man with the club standing behind her struck her again. He wore the gold and gilt armor of the Lord Regent's private guard, and beside him, in brown robes, stood one of the priests. Clara looked around her at the faces in the crowd. Some were pale and horrified, but more seemed hungry. Excited.

"We can't help, my lady," Vincen Coe whispered in her ear. "If we tried, it would go worse for her. We should leave."

Answer them, Clara begged the girl silently. *Tell them what they want to know.*

But the guardsman wasn't asking questions, and the priest looked on impassively. Clara turned away, pushing through the crowd without Vincen's help now. Her jaw ached. When they reached the main street again, her legs trembled with each step.

"Is it only me, do you think?" she asked. "Or does it seem this sort of thing is happening more often?"

"It's the Timzinae, my lady. The story is that they were behind the trouble."

"They weren't," Clara said with a mirthless laugh. "Dawson would have taken direction from a foreigner as soon as he answered to his own dogs."

"Yes, ma'am," Vincen said.

"What?"

"Nothing. It's only...you said foreign, my lady. The girl back there was likely a born subject of Antea. There aren't a great many Timzinae in Camnipol, and they keep to themselves, but they're still from here."

"You know what I meant."

"Yes, ma'am."

She had intended to be quiet then, to let her outrage turn inward and turn to something like resolve. She meant to walk down these streets that were no longer hers with head unbowed, and she meant to do it in silence. So when the words forced themselves from her throat, they had a broken sound, soft and low and unpleasant.

"What's happened to us? Simeon gone. Dawson gone. What has happened to my kingdom?"

Vincen made a small sound in the back of his throat. As much as she hadn't planned to speak, she doubly hadn't hoped for him to answer. His voice was gentle and soft, almost mournful.

"Back at the Fells, there was a dog we had. Good hunter. Good nose. When the King's Hunt came, he led the pack. Only, one time, the stag gored him. Took him in the belly and hoisted him in the air. We sewed him closed again, gave him time to heal up. He didn't die, but after that, he ate himself. Started with the paws, just chewing them until they bled. We did everything we could to stop him. Wrapped him in bandages. Put bitter salve on his paws. Kept him in muzzle until his skin could heal. He was still a good hunter, and sweetest dog you could wish for, but he wouldn't stop chewing himself raw. Sometimes shock does that."

"And you think that's what's happening? The empire's been hurt so badly that it's biting itself to death?"

"Yes," the young man said, and his tone made him sound older.

"And does that make me the tooth or the bitter salve?"

"Muzzle's my bet, ma'am," Vincen said. His smile bloomed sly. "Just haven't figured how to strap it on the bastard yet."

They passed by Lord Skestinin's little compound. Its shutters were closed against the winter, and icicles as long as swords hung from the eaves. Jorey and Sabiha—her youngest son and his wife—were following the court for the season, and Skestinin himself spent his time with the fleet in the north. She missed her son, but for the time being it was best that Jorey establish himself without reference to his disgraced parents. She wasn't so naïve as to trust the nobility of their blood to protect Jorey from being beaten in the streets if Geder Palliako's favor should turn. Not in this new Camnipol.

Beyond the houses and compounds, the Kingspire rose. The stone looked dark against the winter sky, and the flock of pigeons that circled it seemed as insubstantial and grey as the snow through which they flew. Clara stood still, letting the traffic of the street pass her by. Her cheeks felt stiff with the chill.

By the time she reached the builder's tents, the pies had cooled, but Clara didn't let it concern her. The ruins had once been a stables and an open market, both burned the night the failed coup began. The charred wooden posts had been cleared away, the ground leveled, and new paving stones and supports were being raised. Piles of white brick stood as thick as two men and tall as three, soft wooden scaffolds clinging to the sides. Men in wool and thick workmen's leather hauled handcarts filled with lime and reinforcing bars from one place to another. Their talk was rough and uneducated and nothing Clara hadn't heard a thousand times in the servants' quarters of her own house. It only took a few moments to find the face she sought.

"Benet! Here you are. I've been looking simply everywhere for you."

"L-Lady Kalliam?" the boy said. Once, he had been a gardener's assistant and plucked weeds from her flowerbeds. Now his hands were callused and his face pale with brick dust and starvation.

"Your aunt mentioned you'd taken work here, but of course the wages don't begin until after you've done the work, do they? I thought I would just bring you a bit of lunch. You don't mind, do you?"

The boy's eyes went as wide as a Southling's when Vincen put the food onto the stack of bricks at his side.

"I...that's to say...Thank you, m'lady. You're too kind."

"Just trying to keep up with the old household," Clara said, smiling. "It wasn't any of your doing that things went the way they did. It seems wrong you should suffer for it. Eat, please. Don't stand on ceremony, we're well past that now. And tell me all about this...well, this whatever it is that you're building."

The tour was short. Benet was most concerned with the pie and not offending his overseer, but Clara took the general shape. Rooms of brick and floors of paving stone. Thin windows and wide corridors. The stables and the market were gone, and they would never return. What little remained of their bones would become the next layer of ruin upon which the city was built, age after age reaching down like rings in a tree. In place, the new barracks. That's what they called it. Clara thought better.

That evening, her feet held up to the little iron stove, Clara ate one of the remaining pies and Vincen the other. Abatha Coe—Vincen's cousin and proprietor of the house—bustled about her chores with a sour expression and the smell of boiled cabbage. The young Firstblood man who'd taken a room on the lower floor near the back came and complained of a leaking window. The Cinnae girl, thin and pale as a sprout, came in from whatever she'd done with her day, took a bowl of the house stew, and retreated to eat in solitude. Clara smoked her little clay pipe and she brooded. Vincen, loyal as a hound, gave her her silence as long as she wanted it, and broke it with her when she was ready.

"That dog," she said. "The one that had the trouble biting himself. Whatever became of him?"

Vincen opened the stove's grate and dropped in a knot of pine. The firelight danced over his face. He looked melancholy and beautiful and young. A wholly inappropriate man.

"Not all dogs can be saved, ma'am," he said.

"No," she said. "I thought not. Those buildings that Benet and others are toiling at. They aren't barracks."

"Looked more like kennels to me," Vincen agreed, but Clara shook her head.

"No, not kennels," she said. And then, "Why, do you suppose, is Geder Palliako building *prisons*?"

Lord Regent Geder Palliako

The stag stood in a clearing, surrounded by the hunting pack. Its eyes were wide with fear, and foam dripped from its lips. The barking and baying almost drowned out the calls of the huntsmen. Beyond the dogs, the men of the hunt sat astride their horses. Snow greyed the leather hunting armor and thick wool cloaks, clinging to the noblest men of Antea like moss on a stone. All eyes were on Geder; he could feel them.

The huntsman who handed him the spear was a Jasuru, bronze scales and sharp black teeth. Geder took the spear in hand, set it. It was heavier than he'd expected it to be. *It's like a joust,* he told himself. *Just a little practice joust with a stag for the target. I can do this.*

He glanced at Aster, and the prince's gaze encouraged him. Geder forced himself to smile, then leaned forward and charged. His horse ran as smooth as a river under him, and it seemed to him that he didn't draw nearer the stag so much as the beast grew larger. The impact jarred his arm and wrenched his shoulder. He felt himself rising up out of the saddle, and for a horrified moment, falling into the chaos of dogs and churned snow and blood seemed inevitable. The stag screamed. The spear's point hadn't pierced him through, but skidded along the flank. A wide fold of skin and flesh hung down, blood pouring from it. The antlers swung toward Geder, preparing for a counterattack, and the huntsman made his call. A dozen arrows flew, striking the stag in its thick neck, its side, the meat of its leg.

The stag stumbled forward, lost its footing, and fell to its knees. Its breath came solid as smoke. Geder looked down at the black eyes, and there seemed to be an intelligence there. And a hatred. Blood gouted from the animal's mouth and it lowered its head to the snowy clearing. The cheer rose from the hunters, and Geder lifted his hand, grinning. It hadn't been an elegant kill, but he hadn't humiliated himself.

"Who takes honors?" Geder asked as the huntsmen came forward to prepare the corpse for its unmaking. "Daskellin? You were up toward the front. Who caught up to the thing first?"

Canl Daskellin, Baron of Watermarch, bowed in his saddle and gestured to his left.

"I believe it was Count Ischian, Lord Regent. I was close behind, but he outran me."

Geder shifted in his saddle. Count Ischian bowed in his saddle. He was an older man, his colors blue and gold, and he was related by blood to half a dozen houses at court. His holdings, however, were in Asterilhold. In the war just past, he had fought on the other side. His loyalty now was unquestionable. He had faced Geder's private tribunal, and the gift of the goddess had certified his honesty. But giving full honors in the King's Hunt to someone who'd been an enemy when last year's hunt had run seemed wrong.

"Even honors to you both, then," Geder said. "And well done. Now let's get back to the holding before we all turn into ice sculptures of ourselves."

Geder had rarely taken part in the hunt before he'd been in the center of it. He had risen from heir to the Viscount of Rivenhalm to Lord Regent of Antea so quickly, there hadn't been time to accustom himself to the circles of power and influence. Even now, as the most powerful man in the empire, he felt a bit outside of things. Many of the men on the hunt had been riding together since they were children younger than Aster, and while Geder might command their loyalty, he couldn't insist on their friendship. Add to that the fact that many of the great houses had risen up against Geder only months before and were now gone forever. Sir Alan Klin, Geder's nemesis, was feeding the worms at the bottom of the Division now. Lord Bannien was rumored to have been richer than the crown itself, and he was imprisoned now, his family broken, his titles stripped from him, and his private treasury funding the reconstruction of Camnipol. Dawson Kalliam, Geder's patron and father of Geder's best friend, had been the Lord Marshal of the war against Asterilhold, and then the soul and center of the uprising. Had things gone differently, it would have been Lord Kalliam who rode down the stag in that clearing, and Geder who lay in a traitor's grave. Jorey Kalliam rode with the hunt, but even after his disavowal he seemed darkened by his father's crimes. And now, with conquered Asterilhold being joined into a greater empire, there came the awkwardness of befriending those who had recently been enemies.

The death of the king, the naming of Lord Regent, a successful war, and a scarring insurrection. Imperial Antea had suffered a terrible year. And the coming spring might be no easier.

Namen Flor's lands sat nestled in a valley in the southeast of the empire, not far from the border with Sarakal. The great city of Kavinpol lay to the west with its river docks and warehouses. In summer, the rich soil of Flor was fed by two rivers, and the grain and fruit that came from that one holding would feed an army for a season. The holding itself rose like a mountain in the plain, granite and basalt hauled overland from the mountains to the south and combined into a building almost as tall as the Kingspire in Camnipol. The dragon's road ran through the heart of the structure, though at the moment ice and snow buried the eternal jade, so that it might have been any road at all until they had passed through the wide gates and under the overhanging shelter.

The cold had set Geder's nose running, and his earlobes hurt like something bitten. He gave his horse to the groom and hurried to the quarters Sir Flor had set aside for his use. And especially the tub. It was beaten copper half as deep as a man standing, and the water that fed into it from the stone dragon's mouth steamed and smelled of sandalwood. And best of all, the room that housed it was small. As Lord Regent, custom had it that his personal guard and body servants would be always in attendance. He hated it, and while he'd won the battle against the body servants, he hadn't quite had it in him yet to keep the guardsmen out when he bathed. After Dawson Kalliam's attempt on his life, Geder actually found the guards reassuring in a way. But here the private bath could be protected from without, and Geder's nakedness wouldn't be on display even to those whose duty it was to defend his life.

While he let the warm water ease the aching muscles in his back and thighs, he watched the lamp flame shift and steady and shift again. He let himself imagine what it would have been like to have a certain part-Cinnae banker woman sitting across from him, her flesh as bare as his own, her pale skin glowing in the light. When his body began to react to the thought, he made himself turn to other matters.

From without, the King's Hunt had always struck Geder as merely a vehicle for court intrigue. King Simeon would travel the realm, gracing his friends and allies with his presence, killing a few animals, and having a lot of feasts. It had looked like one of the sort of parties Geder was bad at, only stretched out over the course of weeks and punctuated by feats of manly athletics, half-drunken poetry contests, and extemporaneous speeches. Only when he'd become Lord Regent and the empire was his to command did he begin to see how the hunt was also a tool of convenience.

Not all men of court came to Camnipol. Not all facts of a landscape could be captured on a map. The hunt might seem to wander through the lands and holdings of the empire, but the path he followed was as set and certain as the dragon's roads themselves. It was not chance that had brought him here, but necessity.

He rose from the water, dried himself, and put on his undergarments before signaling to the body servants that they could enter to finish dressing him. He would have been as happy staying the rest of the day in the warmth and solitude, but the feast was coming, and now that he'd spent some time in the forests near Flor, it was time to attend to the matter that had actually brought him there.

He found Basrahip and Aster sitting together in a withdrawing room. The walls were papered in red velvet and the lamps burned with the rich scent of whale oil. The priest's voice rolled and rumbled like thunder from a distant storm. The young prince in his silk and cloth-of-gold sat looking up into the face of the massive brown-clad priest like an allegory of youth at the feet of wisdom. Geder stopped in the doorway to listen.

"Seeing that the world had fallen from his hands, Morade, in his death, was possessed by the sick pride of his kind. He released a terrible weapon. For three years, the world burned. Every forest fell to ash. Every city crumbled. The thirteen races of humanity took refuge where they could, preserving the animals in pens and the fish in clay pots against the day when they might be freed to fill the world again."

"Three *years*?" Aster said, awe in his voice.

"Yes, young prince. For three years, all was laid waste. And so the freedom of humanity was born in ashes and in starvation. Only the Timzinae, favored of the dragons, kept the old ways alive, sacrificing children of the other races to the memory of the Dragon Empire. All others remade themselves, replanting the forests and rebuilding the cities. And without the guidance of the goddess, all lost their way, as the goddess had known they would. She kept aside the temple in the mountains in the lands of the Sinir that are holy to her, that we could prepare for the day when a great man would come and we would know it was time to reenter the world."

"That was Geder, wasn't it?" Aster said.

"It was," Basrahip said, with a broad, gentle smile.

"Speaking of which," Geder said, stepping into the room. Aster turned to him. He looked stronger, healthier since they'd taken to the hunt. Geder would still see moments of sorrow in the boy, but they were growing fewer and fewer. Whenever Geder worried about it, he reminded himself that Aster had lost his father not a full year ago, and that even the most resilient child would mourn a parent for much longer than that.

"Prince Geder," Basrahip said, levering himself to his feet.

"Lord Regent," Geder said. "Aster's a prince. I'm Lord Regent."

"Of course," Basrahip said, as he always did. The correction would never take.

"Is everything all right?" Aster said.

"Yes, fine," Geder said. "But I need to borrow Basrahip for a time. Before the feast starts."

"Of course, Prince Geder," Basrahip said with a bow. When Geder rolled his eyes, Aster chuckled.

Geder and Basrahip walked together down the long hallways. Here, in the heart of the holdfast, the ceilings rose up higher than four men one atop the other, and a clever series of holes admitted the falling sunlight without letting the warmth of the braziers escape. The color of the light was enough to tell Geder that the winter night would be on them soon. Servants and guards went before and came behind, creating a mobile privacy for him and Basrahip.

"That can't be right, can it?" Geder said.

Basrahip raised querying eyebrows.

"The three-year fire," Geder explained. "A fire that went on that long would have left a layer of ash all over the world. And there are cities that stood where they are now since before the dragons fell."

"If it must be, it must be," Basrahip said. "But the fire years are truth."

"But there are forests in Northcoast that have trees older than that. Not many, maybe, but I read an essay about how you can tell the age of a tree by the number of rings, and it said the largest of the redwoods in Northcoast—"

Basrahip shook his bull-wide head.

"You put too much faith in empty words. No forests live that were not planted after the fire years. All animals that live were sheltered by humanity in the fire years. If you say that the world must be built upon ash, then look for it, and you will find it. Or if you do not, you must find for yourself what became of it. But the fire is true."

"It's just in all the histories I've read—even the ones written within a generation or two of the fall—no one's ever mentioned a catastrophe like that. You'd think they would have. I mean, the utter destruction of everything's not the sort of thing I'd leave out if I were writing a history."

Basrahip waved the words away with a massive palm.

"Words on paper are not even lies. They are empty. The voice that speaks them is your own, and you mean nothing when you say them except that here on this page are these words. It the least important thing that there is. From the time before the dragons, my priesthood have been the keepers of truth. All truth. You know that no one can lie to the goddess."

"Well, yes," Geder said, feeling abashed. "Of course I know that. I mean, you've proved it over and over, haven't you?"

"And you know that her truth cannot be long denied."

"I've seen that too," Geder agreed.

"With every generation, the priests of the goddess have passed on the true tale of the world in voices that cannot be denied to acolytes who would hear any falsehood. What are your books and scroll to this? The living voice has carried what I say across the ages. Your library was all created by a hand, not a voice. Tell me this. Will you say all books are true?"

"Well, no. Of course not. There are some essays I've read that were clearly—"

"And would you say that you can know perfectly which are true and which not?"

"No, but that doesn't mean they're useless. I mean, most of them, you can assume are—"

Basrahip stopped, took Geder by the shoulders, and looked deeply into his eyes.

"I ask you this, Prince Geder. If I gave you a meal that you knew was poisoned in part, and also you knew that you could not know where the poison lay, would it be wisdom to eat?"

"Of course not," Geder said.

"So it is with books," Basrahip said. "Listen to my voice, my friend. The goddess is there, and she will not lead you astray."

Namen Flor looked like a reed. His thin body rose up from his feet to a tall, broad face and hair the color of wheat that he wore close-cropped. He stood as Geder entered the candle-bright private chamber. If he was nervous, his voice did not betray it.

"I was told you wished to speak with me, Lord Regent?"

"Yes, I did. Please, sit. No need to be formal. You know Minister Basrahip, don't you?"

Sir Flor bent his head in a gesture carefully between nod and bow. Physical diplomacy. Geder lowered himself to a divan upholstered in green silk and leaned forward, elbows on his knees. Basrahip took a place on the far wall, smiling absently and looking at at the fire dancing in the grate. Flor turned from one to the other, then sat across from Geder and ignored the priest. Geder glanced at Basrahip, and the priest nodded once. He was ready.

"Are you loyal to me, Sir Flor?"

The reedy man seemed to expect the question, because he answered at once.

"Of course, Lord Palliako."

Basrahip nodded. It was truth, but Geder held up a finger.

"I don't mean to the throne or to Antea in the abstract. Are you loyal to *me*?"

Flor frowned.

"Forgive me, my lord, but I don't see the difference. You are Lord Regent. Being loyal to Antea is being loyal to you."

Another nod. Well, it wasn't as good as raw personal devotion, but it would do.

"I have need of your discretion, Sir Flor. How are your spring crops?"

"Not yet sown. I imagine they will be breaking the ground for the first lettuces in a month or so."

"I would like you to convert your fields to spring wheat. And whichever lands you can spare that are least productive, I will need to borrow from you for the season."

Flor blinked, then shrugged.

"Of course, my lord. May I ask why?"

Geder leaned back. The truth was, he enjoyed this part. Knowing something another man wanted to know was a kind of power. Maybe the best kind.

"Antea is in perilous times," Geder said. "The impression abroad is that the trials of the war and the insurrection have weakened us. That we may be vulnerable. As long as the world thinks we are weak, we will be in danger."

"Yes, I have heard that concern spoken," Flor said. "And I admit I am concerned that it may in part be true. The forces needed to keep Asterilhold from rising—"

"It will not rise," Basrahip said. "There are temples to the goddess in both its great cities. It will follow Prince Geder."

"You have heard that Dawson Kalliam was advised by Timzinae?" Geder said. "That before he began his conspiracy, he met with a dozen Timzinae men?"

"I'd heard rumors."

"It's common knowledge," Geder said with a wave of his hand. "Sarakal and Elassae are the nations under the control of Timzinae leaders. The enemies of the empire expect our attention to be in the north and west. That our border with Sarakal will be lightly defended, and weak. They are mistaken. I require your spare field to build a temporary encampment for an army. And the wheat as bread for men and fodder for horses."

Flor's face went pale, picturing the expense and the burden to his lands a free garrison would bring. To the man's credit, he raised no objection.

"For how long will we be hosting the army?"

"Not long. Two weeks, maybe three. However long the Lord Marshal decides it's needed. Then they'll be off."

"To keep the border?"

"To cross it," Geder said.

Cithrin bel Sarcour, Voice of the Medean Bank in Porte Oliva

Cithrin stood at the boat's prow. The sea stretched out before her in the early morning light, white and pink and blue as if it had been remade from mother-of-pearl. The air was thick with the scent of brine and tar, the creak of wood and rope. She wore a black wool cloak wrapped tight, its hood raised to cover her straw-white hair. She held her chin high, her gaze soft. To the captain or one of the sailors or one of her own guard, she would appear to be a woman at the height of her power, occupied in the privacy of her thoughts. In truth, she'd drunk too much the night before, and her head felt like a sparrow had built a nest in her skull.

On the horizon, the land was little more than a thickening of the water. From the time she had left Birancour, it had remained the same, a darkness to port. Once they had passed into the Inner Sea, it would have been in theory faster to lose sight of the shore, strike out from the straits that divided the Free Cities from Lyoneia, and make a short blue-water transit to Elassae and Suddapal. But speed was not everything, and even on the relatively gentle waters, winter storms could rise, and the option of finding shelter in a cove or harbor was not to be dismissed lightly. There had been troubles along the way: one of the sailors had slipped from the mast and broken his leg so badly that he'd been lost in a fever since; for two long days they had run from dark-sailed pirates before the thieves gave up the chase; and Roach had been nauseated for so long that the dark chitinous plates of his arms had begun to bend and crack as the flesh beneath them thinned away. On some day, indistinguishable from the ones before and behind it, they had sailed past Newport and the ruins of Vanai where her childhood lay in ashes. And the nearer they drew to the five cities of Suddapal, the more the anxious knot in her belly grew, and the harder it became to sleep. The anxiety built day after day, hour upon hour.

Until now.

The calls of the sailors changed. The ship shifted under her feet. Slowly, almost imperceptibly, the dark line of land thickened and took on shape. Hills and valleys, and then the more regular forms of buildings. And then reaching out to her like a thousand fingers, the piers with their forest of masts. Suddapal, the fivefold capital city of Elassae, and home of the farthest-flung branch of the Medean bank.

"We'll have you to land by midday, Magistra," the captain, an old Firstblood man with a patchy white beard, said. "There'll be the matter of the last part of the payment to consider?"

Cithrin smiled.

"As soon as we're in port, Captain," she said.

"Might as well now," he said. "We've time."

"Policy," she said, as if the word explained and excused everything. She turned back toward the growing city and wished she'd had less wine in the night.

Her agreement with Komme Medean had called for a year's apprenticeship, and they had agreed before she left on the long winter journey south from Carse that Suddapal would be the best place. Komme Medean's letters would have reached Magistra Isadau weeks before, but Cithrin had no way to know what the woman would think of the arrangement. Any greeting could be waiting for her on the docks. Or even a refusal.

The sailors scrambled behind her, and the little ship turned its nose to the shore. The noise of the sails as they caught the breeze deafened. A guide boat raced out to meet them, hardly more than a canoe with three Timzinae youths hauling on red-dyed oars. Timzinae had been as common as Firstblood in Vanai, and the young men's dark bodies and shining scales comforted her.

"Magistra," Yardem Hane said from just behind her. She turned, craning her head up toward the Tralgu's broad dog-like face. His expression was impassive, but the tall, mobile ears were canted forward, toward the shore. "We've packed the chest."

"And last payment?"

Yardem patted his hip where his leather wallet hung from his belt, the sound of coins hardly carrying over the din. "I'll take care of it. Enen and Roach will see to the rest."

Cithrin nodded, her eyes following the laughing gestures of the guide boat crew. Their canvas pants and rough shirts seemed too light for the cold of the winter sea, but any discomfort they felt was hidden by their boisterous shouts and friendly profanity. She envied them. She had more money than they would likely see in a decade and had commanded control of a hundred times that, but the ease with which she held her body and the calmness of her affect were all the fruit of study and artifice.

Leaving Porte Oliva had been harder than she'd expected. The white buildings and winter mists, the street dogs and the little café where she had leased the back room, the wide square between the Governor's Palace and the grand temple where the guests of the magistrate's justice served out their punishments. All of it was gone now. Even Pyk Usterhall, officially the notary of the Porte Oliva branch and in truth its voice in all but name, carried a weight of fond nostalgia for Cithrin now, and she disliked Pyk as much as she did anyone breathing air. The only familiar faces were the guards she chose as her companions. Enen because the woman was old, uncompromising, and as hard as last week's bread. Roach because he was the only Timzinae among the bank's guard, and having someone who might pass for a local could only be to her advantage. And Yardem Hane, because he was Yardem and because Captain Wester had quit while she was in Camnipol. He'd vanished into the world without so much as a farewell. He'd given no explanation of his decision to leave, left no note or letter behind for her. She told herself that his departure hadn't stung, but she wasn't quite able to convince.

But even without Marcus, Porte Oliva had been the first home she'd made for herself. She had founded the branch of the Medean bank there without in fact even consulting with the bank's holding company. Her rooms there were familiar and comfortable, the servants at the taphouse down the street knew her and her habits, the queensmen who kept order in the streets touched their brows in respect as she passed by. In Porte Oliva, she had been someone, and more, she understood who and what she was. In Suddapal, she might be anyone. And so she might be nobody.

Her stomach made a little flutter, and she wished that she had a little skin of wine. Preferably distilled.

The piers of Suddapal reached out deep into the waters of the Inner Sea. The planks were black, slippery, and flecked with foam. At the height of a shipping season, Cithrin imagined they would be as full and crowded as the beggar-press walking into Porte Oliva, and she was pleased to have arrived when she could keep herself far away from the churning green of the sea against the pilings. The waves seemed to shift the boards under her feet, the world rolled unsteadily, and she knew it was an illusion of stepping back on land. Any pier that truly swayed so much would come to pieces in a day.

A Timzinae woman stood before a palanquin of red and gold, and two massive Yemmu men with uncut tusks rising from their jaws knelt behind her. Her robes were a vibrant green that would have left Cithrin looking wan and sickly. A necklace of gold splayed itself on her throat. Cithrin put on a smile, tucked her hips the way Master Kit had taught her to make herself seem older, and walked to the woman. The Timzinae smiled, the nictitating membrane sliding over her eyes, blinking and unblinking.

"Magistra bel Sarcour?" the woman asked.

"Magistra Isadau, I presume?" Cithrin said.

"Oh, no. Isadau is my sister. She's folded into some business or other. I am Mykani rol Ennenamet, but please call me Kani."

Behind her, Yardem snapped out a sharp order. Enen replied, her voice respectful and unintimidated. Cithrin found herself on the wrong foot, trying to readjust her expectations of Magistra Isadau and her bank.

"I wasn't aware that the Magistra had family," Cithrin said, and Kani's laughter shimmered.

"There seem like a thousand of us sometimes, but we don't all live in the compound. Just me, Isadau, and our brother Jurin. And the children, of course."

"Magistra Isadau has children?" Cithrin said. She tried to imagine Magister Imaniel with a wife and children of his own. It was as easy to picture a house cat juggling knives.

"Not of her own," Kani said, "but I have my girls, and

Jurin is raising three boys. We have the household to herd them, though. They're all looking forward to meeting you. In fact, I should warn you. Jurin's oldest boy, Salan, just turned twelve. He saw a company perform a play last year about a Cinnae queen who saves Herez from a plague of demons."

"The Ash Burner's Tale," Cithrin said.

"Yes, I think that was the name. Regardless, the woman playing the queen was quite beautiful, and I think he's decided to fall in love with you on that basis. If his mooning around gets bothersome, let one of us know and we'll rein him in somehow. You know how boys that age are with their doomed infatuations."

I haven't got a clue, Cithrin thought, but didn't say. *How are they?*

"We're ready, Magistra," Yardem said. His ear flicked, and the earrings jingled. Kani's attention fastened on them.

"Priest caste?" she said.

"Fallen," Yardem said.

"Oh. Excuse me. I didn't mean to overstep."

"No offense taken," Yardem said. Kani's smile stayed warm, but a reevaluation showed in her eyes.

"You are a fascinating woman, Magistra bel Sarcour. It should be delightful having you in the family," Kani said. The repetition of her formal name and title made Cithrin realize she'd been rude.

"Please, if I'm to call you Kani, you should call me Cithrin."

Kani made a small, playful bow, then scooped Cithrin's arm into her own and led her toward the palanquin. The two Yemmu men coughed to one another and hunkered down, ready to lift Cithrin and her new companion and carry them into the city.

"Cithrin," Kani said. "That's a beautiful name. Was it your mother's?"

The five cities that made up Suddapal stretched along the northern coast of the Inner Sea. Along the eastern side, black cliffs rose. Islands towered a hundred feet above the waves, topped by tiny houses and greenswards where sheep spent their whole lives without ever cropping the mainland's grass. Farther to the west, the docks and piers stretched out to sea, and streets and squares pressed up into the hills. There were no canals as there had been in Vanai. Many of the streets were stone-paved, but in others, a low, tough ground cover grew on the soil, resisting horses' hooves and carts' wheels alike. The puppets and singers that had seemed to spring up on every corner of Porte Oliva were gone. Timzinae children played, running alongside the palanquin, chanting rhymes that Cithrin couldn't quite follow in harmonies that were as complex as the most sophisticated singers she'd heard in the temples. Here and there, she caught glimpses of other races—Yemmu, Tralgu, Firstblood—but for the greatest part, Suddapal was a Timzinae city, and Cithrin realized that her skin, hair, and stature would stand out there like a daisy among roses. Just another thing to consider as she remade herself here. The year ahead seemed to stretch out forever.

Magister Imaniel had always taught her that a bank's public face should be humble. Architecture that boasted was better left for kings and princes and priests. A small house, clean and simply run, told the mechanisms of power that the bank was no threat to them, and since that was not true, the appearance of it was all the more important. In Porte Oliva, Cithrin had taken an old gambler's stall for the home of her branch, and had conducted business in Maestro

Asanpur's café. When the guard grew large enough to require a barracks of their own, she hadn't moved to larger quarters, but taken other places. Other sites. As her power in the city grew, she took pains to appear small even to the people who knew better. Especially to them.

The Medean bank in Suddapal, in contrast, was in a broad, sprawling compound as grand and pleasant as a duke's holding. Halls of polished granite with statues of gods and holy men, monsters and angels in niches at every corner. A massive pasture adjacent with stables enough for a dozen horses. A slave to greet them wearing a decorative silver chain that wasn't even attached to the doorframe. Pillars of carved wood and the scent of pine smoke. If this was how a bank remained unnoticed, humble, and small, then Suddapal had to be the richest city in the world. Cithrin felt certain that it wasn't.

The strangest thing about it all was the openness of the space, the absence of glass or parchment over the windows. The building itself seemed exposed to the air and weather in a way she had never seen before. She wasn't sure it was wise.

Her own room had a black iron stove squatting in the corner with a fire already burning in its belly. Fresh rushes covered the floor. Her bed was square with a soft mattress, a blanket filled with down, and a pillow stuffed with buckwheat hulls. A washing basin of carved stone topped an iron stand at the bedside, and an enameled night pot waited discreetly beside it. The desk was made from carved oak, stained almost black. The window opened onto a courtyard, and the voices of a man and woman carried to her. The hall just outside had a guard's niche where Enen sat. With a Kurtadam's thick pelt, the cool hallway might be almost comfortable.

Cithrin had hardly changed into fresh clothes and washed her face when a gentle tapping came at the door.

"Magistra Isadau's come," Enen said.

Cithrin squared her shoulders, put on her best imitation of an older woman, and opened the door. Magistra Isadau, voice of the Medean bank in Suddapal, was slender with flecks of grey at her temples and the first dusting of frost on the scales of her face and neck. Her gown was simple cotton, embroidered with flowers and vines, and she held a small green pot in her hands with what looked like a wind-blown pine in miniature.

"Magistra Cithrin," the woman said, extending the little tree. "Welcome to my home."

The pot was heavier than it looked. Cithrin put it on the corner of the desk with a distinct clunk. The tiny boughs shivered as if blown by an unseen wind.

"Thank you. Please come. Sit."

Isadau smiled and sat on the corner of the bed, leaving the desk's chair to Cithrin. Her eyes flickered, considering Cithrin without judgment.

"It's a pleasure to meet you at last. I've heard a great deal about you."

"Thank you," Cithrin said, wondering what the head of the Medean bank had said about her, and whether she could find out. "I'm not sure how much Komme Medean said."

"It wasn't only Komme. Mani mentioned you too, one time and another."

It took Cithrin a moment to realize Isadau meant Magister Imaniel. She'd never considered that the two heads of Medean branches so physically near one another must have also known each other, or that Magister Imaniel would have spoken about the girl who was only the ward of his bank.

Her past had always been entirely her own, and her first and unconsidered response to sharing it was resentment.

"I see," Cithrin said. "Well. I hope it was all positive."

"Most was, yes," Isadau said. "Komme wrote that he saw a bit of Mani in you. I can too. You speak the way he did."

"I grew up with him."

"That can't have been easy. Komme also said you had the best mind for banking he's seen in a generation. A wild talent still, but that's nothing to be ashamed of. The phrase was *bold without being reckless and reckless without being stupid*. He can be a bit of a poet when he's in a good mood," Isadau said, then her forehead narrowed. "I have to ask. Did you really boast to the king of Northcoast that you'd bedded the Antean Lord Regent?"

Cithrin felt the blush growing in her neck.

"I wouldn't call it *boasting*. They weren't listening to me," Cithrin said. "Geder Palliako and I were in close quarters for weeks. All they'd ever managed was a few meetings and letters. I wanted them to understand that I knew the man better than they did."

"And that you'd lain him was proof of that?"

"I might have phrased it for effect," Cithrin said.

Magistra Isadau's laughter was warm and delighted, and Cithrin felt the knot in her belly loosen a notch.

"Well, no one can call you timid."

"I don't know I'd say that. I was annoyed with them," Cithrin said. Then, a moment later, "Did Komme say anything else about me?"

"That your heart hadn't died yet," Isadau said, her tone precisely as it had been before, "but that it was in danger of it."

Now Cithrin laughed, but it was a nervous sound even to her. In the courtyard, someone called out, a woman or a child. Magisra Isadau lifted a finger.

"May I ask you a question?"

"Of course," Cithrin said.

Isadau gestured with her chin to the tiny plant on the desk.

"Why did I bring that to you?"

Cithrin considered, chewing the inside of her lip. For a moment, she was a child again, sitting at evening meal with Magister Imaniel and Cam and Besel, answering question after question. It came to her as easily as breath.

"Gifts create a sense of obligation," she said. "Not debt, exactly, because it can't be measured. And because it can't be measured, it can't be definitively repaid. If instead you'd given me the coin you spent to buy that, I'd know what I owed, and I could give it back and be done. By giving me a gift instead, you build the sense of owing without a path to repayment, and so I'm more likely, for example, to grant you a favor or make some concession that I'd never have agreed to if I'd been given an explicit price."

Cithrin spread her hands, as if presenting something. Magistra Isadau nodded, but her smile seemed melancholy.

"Mani taught you well. I can hear him say all of that. Only...there is more than one way of doing what we do. Of being what we are."

Cithrin shrugged, vaguely disappointed not to have been praised.

"All right," she said. "How would you say it?"

"I wanted you to like me, and I was anxious that you might not."

The older woman's frank vulnerability brought a sudden tightness to Cithrin's throat. She didn't know if it was pity or surprise, sorrow or fear, only that she didn't like it and didn't know what more to say. Magistra Isadau nodded more than half to herself and stood.

"We eat our evening meals late, but the kitchens are always open to you. The whole family comes to table, and it isn't formal. Rest if you like, or look around the grounds. If you'd like to go into the city, I have a girl who can guide you. In the morning, I'll show you the office and where the books are kept."

Cithrin tried to speak, coughed, and tried again.

"Thank you, Magistra."

"You're welcome. And truly? I am glad you've come."

For a long time after Isadau had left, Cithrin sat at the desk, her gaze on the little plant as if it might be somehow dangerous.

Captain Marcus Wester

Marcus leaned against the slick, waxy bark of the tree and stared out over the valley. Their recent days in the cloud forest had kept his horizon close. Fifteen feet, twenty at most. The thick-packed trees, stubborn brush, and warm mist had tied a cloth across his eyes until he felt that each day had ended in the same stand of trees by the same brook, lulled to sleep by the same bright-colored birds. When he came to the ridge, it was like the world cracking open. Mountains as steep and sharp as black knives rose toward the white sky. Row after row, each more grey than the one before, until he could imagine them receding forever. The sun, high and to his left, was little more than a brighter stretch of haze.

The steady footfalls of his companion came up from behind him, as familiar as his own breath.

"Isn't..." Marcus said, then coughed and tried again. "Isn't there supposed to be a winter? I remember there being winter."

"I think you'll find we're too far south," Kitap rol Keshmet said, "and that seasons don't behave the same way here that they did north of the Inner Sea."

"No winter, then."

"I'm afraid there's only the wet season and the dry."

"Pity we couldn't have come in the dry season."

"We did."

"Ah." Marcus pushed himself back up to standing. "I'm enjoying all this less than I'd hoped to."

Kit's laughter rolled.

"I'm not joking," Marcus said.

"I know you aren't. The village should be just ahead."

For most of his life, Marcus had thought of Lyoneia as another kingdom, large and divided against itself, but in essence familiar. The great moat of the Inner Sea had kept the threat of war from being a greater concern than the battles and intrigues nearer at hand. There were mercenary companies that wintered in Lyoneian ports or took guard contracts when merchants went overland to the Southling cities for silver and spice. The vastness of the land and its impassibility surprised him, as well as its profound differences from the places he'd known.

The land itself fought against travel: sharp, stony peaks with bogs at their bases; thick, snake-rich forests; wetlands crossed by stone roads long since fallen to rubble. Farmable land was rare and guarded, illness was common and hard to cure, and the villages, towns, and cities distrustful of two Firstblood men traveling alone. When Kit had said that the mules would cause more delay than they were worth, Marcus had disagreed. They'd sold the last of them at a trading post five days before, and Marcus hadn't missed them yet. Marcus found himself longing for the plains and mountains of Birancour and the Free Cities, the Pût and Elassae. Even Northcoast and Imperial Antea, for all their faults, had the dragon's roads, jade green and more permanent than mountains. For the most part, they had set borders too, and the corruption of their politics was a familiar kind.

The Southling guards appeared among the trees. Their massive black eyes and pale skins made them seem young, but they were men full grown. Warriors with bows drawn and swords at the ready. It was easy to underestimate a Southling, but any of the thirteen races could kill. Even the Drowned. Marcus held his arms wide, hands open to show that his blade was sheathed.

"We mean no harm," Kit said. "We are no threat to your people."

Despite all their travels together, despite having seen the spiders that lived in Kit's blood and testing the powers that they gave to the old actor, Marcus couldn't hear anything different when he spoke. The warm tone of voice, the careful diction, the humor and sorrow were all just the same. Only instead of saying, *I believe you will find us harmless*, or *I hope you will forgive our intrusion*—instead of pointing all the meaning back to him and his own fallibility—he made an assertion. The corruption in his blood refused to be doubted.

The Southlings blinked. They didn't lower their weapons, but they held them a fraction less tightly.

"You are what?" one of the bowmen demanded.

"Travelers," Kit said. "Seekers. I am called Kitap rol Keshmet, and this is Marcus Wester. We have come from far to the north to speak with your mother, if she will allow it."

"No blades come to the mother, no."

"You may take our swords," Kit said.

The Southlings turned to one another, speaking in a tongue Marcus had never heard before. His nose itched but he didn't reach in to scratch it. He didn't want the soldiers to think he was reaching for a weapon. Kit's coarse hair and wiry beard framed his calm, smiling face, as if he were an uncle returned from a long journey with salt taffy in his pockets and tall tales to amuse the children.

"If we ever come to a place they can't understand your words," Marcus said, "what happens then?"

"I expect that will be more difficult," Kit said.

The Southlings' gabble reached a climax, and the bowman blinked at them.

"Throw down your blades, you," he said. "We take you motherwards."

Slowly, Marcus unbuckled his belt, pulled it off, and tossed sword and scabbard to the mossy ground. Kit did the same, and added the dagger from his sleeve as well. One of the younger Southlings collected them. The bowman turned and seemed to vanish into the tangle of trees. Marcus and Kit had to struggle to find him again, and then to keep up.

The trail was visible once Marcus saw the Southlings using it, but it would have been easy to overlook. The trees and brush hadn't been hacked back, but shaped. There were no axe-cut branches or roped-back twigs to show that this was the habitation of humanity. The path was obscure. Hidden. Sometimes the way doubled back, often under high trees where archers might perch. There were no great stone walls and no place to build them, but the forest itself was a kind of fortification.

It seemed like half a day before they reached the first unmistakable signs of human habitation. A stone-paved yard with thatched huts all around it seemed to emerge from the trees like someone walking out of a fog. That the stone was only marked by a green patina where moss had been scraped away, that the fissures in the pavement hadn't become home to saplings was evidence enough that the place was maintained. Holding the forest at bay, even for so small a space as this, would have been a lifetime's work. And at the far side of the yard, a massive statue. Perhaps it had once been of a human—Southling or Jasuru or Firstblood. The long ages had eroded it until it was almost shapeless. At its base, a larger hut with a plume of pale smoke rising from the hole at its top.

The bowman turned to them, lifting a hand.

"You will wait here," he said. "I will ask our mother if she will speak to you."

"I am very grateful," Kit said, lowering himself to the stone.

Marcus sat too. The other warriors who had escorted them remained standing and armed, but Marcus felt no sense of threat from them. The way they held themselves was more proprietary, as if they'd brought some bizarre bird back from the hunt. Before long, people began to emerge from the shadows of the huts. Children haunted the doorways, wide eyes so large they seemed about to consume their faces. And then women and older men, yawning and fresh from sleep. Marcus had forgotten more than once that Southlings were more comfortable in the night. The dragons had made them that way. They came out slowly, one at a time, and then in groups, until something between thirty and forty men, women, and children talked and laughed and pointed from the edge of the yard. There were more than could have fit into the little huts, so Marcus assumed that there were structures under the ground—tunnels or old ruins or some such—where the villagers spent their sleeping days.

He wouldn't have been surprised to sit on the smooth stones, legs crossed and aching and the insects making a feast of him, until the middle of the night. Instead, the village mother took pity on them. The sun had sunk behind the forest canopy, the sky turned to rose and gold with only the first hints of twilight's ash, when the bowman returned with an old man who wore a chain of gold around his neck and brightly dyed cloth around his elbows and knees. The cunning man, or anyway a Southling village's version of one. The cunning man walked a slow circle around them, his breath thick and heavy. Marcus felt the air on the back of his neck stirring. Kit watched solemnly as the cunning man finished his course, clapped his hands together, and shouted. A burst of light and sudden, vicious cold, and then the cunning man was walking up to them, grinning. His hand touched Marcus's shoulder, and the two men nodded to one another, smiling. A little show of magic and force to keep them in line, then, followed by welcome. Kit's grin was warm, open, friendly. The wall of guards dissolved, and the villagers came closer, as pleased and curious as if Marcus had been a two-headed puppy. A girl of perhaps six years came up to Marcus, holding out a broad green leaf as a present. When he took it, she giggled and fled.

"The mother rests now, but she will speak to you soon," the cunning man said. "Very soon."

"Give her our thanks," Marcus said.

The haze went grey and then black. No starlight could fight its way through the thick air, and the moon was only a lighter quarter of the sky. Around them, the life of the village bustled. Children carried great buckets of water slung on sticks. A group of old men sat by one of the huts smoking something sweeter than tobacco and weaving long, thin strips of bark into rope. Another group of armed men arrived carrying a dead animal that looked like a long-skulled boar, and for a moment the two strange travelers became only the second most interesting event of the night. Men and women watched as the animal was skinned and butchered. The carcass was being rubbed with a brown savory-smelling paste and prepared for the cookfire when the cunning man appeared again at Marcus's elbow.

"Now," he said. "Come both with me."

The village mother's hut was thick-walled and smaller inside than Marcus had expected. What room there was had been devoted to a single greeting chamber as ornate and impressive in its way as the greatest throne rooms of Northcoast. A dozen silent men knelt against the walls, swords and daggers in their hands. The dim orange light came from a single brazier, and by it the woman in the wooden chair seemed to float in a velvet blackness. Her pale skin caught the light, glowed with it. Her gown was simply cut, but glittering with soft metal thread and gemstones. She could have been a child or a woman Marcus's age. Either way, she was beautiful.

Kit sank to his knees, and Marcus followed his example.

"Most gracious lady," Kit said. "We thank you for speaking with us. We have come very far, and we are in need of your aid."

The village mother smiled. Younger, Marcus thought. She had to be younger than he was.

"It is rare that travelers come so far to ask favors of me. More often, those who ask for my help find themselves where they had not meant to be."

Kit fumbled for a moment in the darkness, then drew a folded parchment from his belt and unfolded it. Marcus couldn't see it, but he didn't need to. He'd studied the curves and angles of that map a thousand times, and in better light. If the village mother kept it or destroyed it, Marcus could draw it again from memory.

"A great evil has woken in the north," Kit said. "A corruption from before the fall of the dragons. Already its chaos is spreading. With time, it will even reach here."

The village mother nodded to the cunning man. He took the parchment from Kit's hand and walked the few steps to her. Her gaze flickered across it, and the faintest scowl touched the corners of her mouth.

"And this?" she asked.

"There are tales of an ancient reliquary. Items of power gathered together by Assian Bey in the days after the fall of the Dragon Empire. Among these, there is said to be a blade envenomed by the art of the greatest of dragons. We have the task of finding this sword, carrying it back to the north, and with it, ending the corruption that threatens us all."

Three of the men against the wall shifted their weight. With the poor light, it was hard to say, but Marcus had the impression that they were less preparing for an attack than seeing how he and Kit would react if they feared one. With as many as there were, he and Kit would be cut down in a breath. He might be able to kill or hurt one of the others. Two if he were lucky. Since there was no way to answer the threat, he ignored it.

"Three generations ago," Kit continued, "a scholar and adventurer led an expedition from Herez. He was a Dartinae who went by the name of Akad Silas. He wrote back to his wife from the field. That which you are holding is said to come from the last reports that came from him. It suggests that he and his men were very near here, and that he believed they had found signs of the reliquary's existence. I have come here to beg of you, gracious lady. If you know anything of this treasure or of the Silas expedition, please tell me. The fate of the world rests upon it."

"And you?" the village mother said. It took a moment before Marcus realized she was speaking to him.

"Following Kit," Marcus said. "Keeping him out of trouble."

Her sniff carried a cartload of contempt. She handed the parchment back to the cunning man, who bowed until his forehead was even with his knees before he turned and put it in Kit's outstretched hand.

"I am sorry, noble wanderer. You have wasted your time," she said. "I know nothing of this adventurer, and I have never heard of any such reliquary."

The soft exhalation, almost a grunt, that came from Kit might have been the blow of bitter disappointment. But Marcus was fairly sure it wasn't.

"The map shows a place not far from here where Silas believed he would gain entrance. There is nothing there?"

"There is not. Nor is there any such place within the range of my people. You have been misled."

Kit ran his hand over his beard to cover a smile.

"I am bitterly sorry to hear this," he said. "But I thank you for your kindness and your hospitality."

"You and your servant are welcome to remain and take your rest." Her voice was gentler now. Marcus imagined that she would be glad to be so easily believed. With a man other than Kit, she might have been.

"You are kind," Kit said. "Please, let me give you this map as a gift. It is a lie set in ink, but it has its beauty. It is of little use to me now, but it does show something of the lands which belong to you and your people."

"I accept your gift. I did not expect northerners to be so thoughtful."

"Northerners are as stones in soft earth," Kit said. "We're all different kinds. And some, perhaps, worth more than others."

The fruit and meat that waited for them when they emerged from the hut would have been the midday meal for any of the other races of humanity. They ate in darkness apart from a small lamp placed near them as a courtesy. Around them, the bustle of village life went on by thin moonlight. The meat from the long-faced boar was sweet and a little gamey, but it was fresh and cooked with onions.

A woman brought clay bowls of fresh, cold water to them. Marcus wouldn't have been more pleased by the finest wine.

On the farther side of the yard, a circle of children sat, whispering into one another's ears and occasionally breaking out in roars of laughter. Kit watched them with a sour expression.

"Problem?" Marcus asked.

Kit nodded toward the children at their game.

"You've played that?" he asked.

"Everyone's played that. Whisper in one ear, then repeat it until something absurd comes out the far end. Harmless enough."

"I dislike it," Kit said. "I'm afraid that all the world's like that. A long chain of men and women speaking what they believe as clearly as they can, and the truth leaking out like they were trying to hold water in their fists. Even without lies, without deceit, that over there is the best we can manage. A crust of misunderstandings. And all of history is made that way."

Marcus nodded. The tone Kit spoke in said more than the actual words. "She was lying, then?"

"She was. Not all of it. When she said the Silas map didn't show where the reliquary was, that was truth. When she said it wasn't in the range of her people . . . that was less than true."

"So it's close, then."

Kit took an onion and bit into it, shrugging.

"Probably. Certainly she believes it is."

"That's good."

"On the other hand, it seems to me she's protective of it. If we press on, the locals may be less friendly than they've been."

The children reached the end of their round, and a great

roar of laughter rose up in the darkness. The sounds of day-
time laid over the shoulders of night left Marcus uneasy.
Now, as guests, it was only a peculiarity of Southling hospitality; the working of a mostly unseen village. When they
pressed on unwelcome, there could be other sounds with
fewer children and less laughter. He remembered someone
telling him that fighting a Southling at night was like fighting with a blindfold. From behind them, a man's voice called
out in the darkness. To their left, another voice answered.
The haze thinned enough that the moon showed through in
a halo of its own light, too dim to cast a shadow. An insect
landed on Marcus's hand and he shooed it away.

"How much do we know about what happened to the
Silas expedition?" Marcus asked.

"Well," Kit said, his voice reflective and philosophical,
"we're fairly certain they didn't come back."

Clara

Once she knew to look, the evidence was everywhere. The snow-paved streets of Camnipol had hardly recovered from the violence of the summer, but the preparations had begun anew. Imri, once the cook's assistant in Clara's kitchens, was seeing a carter's boy who'd been hauling pig iron to the forges since before midwinter. When Clara stopped by the forges on a pretext, all she saw were the long, easily bent spear points Dawson used to deride. They were meant to lodge in a shield and then hang from it, weighting a soldier's arm, slowing him and breaking his formation. She could hear her husband's snort of contempt, could see the dismissive scowl. A weapon for house painters, he'd have called it, and nothing that a nobleman would employ. The men who ran the city granaries smoked in the alley and shook their heads. The orders had come that they should not expect the spring wheat crop to refill the stores. It didn't take Clara a great leap to guess where that food might go. In the temples, the priests intoned psalms about loyalty and the bearing of burdens now for greater glory later, and not of justice or the love of peace. And even in the traditionalist temples, the brown-robes of Geder Palliako's spider goddess sometimes took the pulpit, declaiming in the accents of the Keshet and making cutting remarks about insects and cockroaches that seemed to implicate the Timzinae without ever quite putting a name to them. The magistrates had begun to sentence fewer young men to the cages and more to martial service. The prisons rose brick by pale brick, as much threat as architecture.

The true conversations of power, she no longer had the means to reach. Even those among the noble classes who still took her company were at their holdings or with the hunt. When the first thaw came, it would certainly be different. She would surely be able to discover which direction Palliako meant to send his blades. And also by then, it would all be too far gone to prevent. Walking across the bridges and through the narrow streets, she felt as if she were balancing on a landslide. It was all so much larger than she was that it might as well have been the weather. She had as much ability to stop this as to turn aside a storm.

But Jorey would come back, and Vicarian. Perhaps, one day, Barriath would return from his exile or at least write from it. Her boys. Help from Elisia seemed unlikely, but Clara would send letters to her all the same. The worst her daughter could do was burn them unread. In the meantime, she walked through the city, Vincen Coe at her side, seeking what information she could and putting it together as best she might.

Even when it took her to places that she would have been wiser to avoid.

Stay behind me, my lady," Vincen said.

"M'lady, is it?" the smallest of the three men said, his grin gap-toothed and unpleasant. "'Strue, then, is it? That's Treacher Kalliam's widow."

"What was it like, sleeping with a traitor?" the largest of them asked.

Clara held her chin up. Rage and humiliation fought

against copper-tasting fear, but she didn't let it show. The street was narrow enough that passing Vincen would be difficult without risking the huntsman's blade. She didn't know what would happen if they tried to go on without showing more steel or making their threats explicit.

"You have no business with us," she said. "Let us pass."

The smallest one drew a battered knife and began to clean his thumbnail with it, ignoring her words. "Long way you've come from there to here."

Vincen kept himself between her and the three men. She couldn't imagine Vincen would allow himself to be surrounded, but neither would he wish to make the first blow. It would be a choice of tragedies. Like so many things.

"We don't want trouble," Vincen said.

"Who does?" the largest man said, mock-philosophically, and he strode forward.

Vincen's blade flicked out, cutting the air. The larger man growled and drew a short, curved blade. Its edge shone in the dim light. It was hardly longer than a child's forearm, and well suited for violence in the confines of the narrow way. Vincen stepped back, using the reach of his own blade to keep the man at a distance and set himself for the coming blow.

"We've come to see Ammit No-Thumb," Clara said. "Perhaps you gentlemen could point the way."

The middle one, silent until now, spoke. His voice was slow, but with a depth of intelligence that gave Clara something like hope.

"What business would you have with our Ammit?"

"I met his daughter on the Prisoner's Span last week, and she mentioned that she had had some distress. I have a tea that might be of some use to her, and so I've brought it. Or will, if you'll let us past."

"Ammit's no friend of mine," the smallest said. He had

taken a firmer grip on his blade. The largest took a step forward, and Vincen slid to block his progress.

"What sort of distress?" the middle one asked.

Clara hoisted her eyebrow and didn't speak. In truth, she had nothing more than a few pinches of tobacco and a pocketful of dried apples, but she'd spoken to the girl long enough to know Ammit was a kind soul and that she lived nearby. That she would be known and thought of kindly was a gamble. The silence stretched. The smallest man glanced over his shoulder, then back.

"You're in the wrong street," the middle one said. "Go back to the turning and go three more toward the wall. There's a red house with a half dozen barrels along the side. Turn there."

"My thanks," Clara said with a nod, then turned and walked briskly back along the narrow street. Her throat felt thin as a straw and her heart beat like a sparrow. A moment later, Vincen was behind her.

"Not so quickly," he murmured. "Nothing like running to call the chase."

Clara forced herself to walk more slowly, as if she belonged there. As if she were safe.

"Has it always been like this?" she asked through clenched teeth.

"Ma'am?"

"The knives and the violence. The inability to walk through the city without fear of being bled. Has Camnipol always been like this, and I didn't know it, or is this a change?"

"Change," Vincen said without even a pause for thought. "There's always rough places. A taproom with a bad reputation. A street where men gather when they're unwelcome anyplace else. But since the summer…no, it's worse."

"Well. At least it isn't only that I was too blind to see it."

The pale sky held the red and gold of sunset to the west and the deepening indigo to the east. With every day that passed, the light grew a little longer, the morning a little brighter. First thaw would, she guessed, come early. She hoped it was an omen of a gentler year, but she couldn't bring herself as far as belief. She walked north, Vincen at her side. He didn't take her arm, but stood near enough to her that she could take his if she chose. It seemed the whole of their relationship, writ small. When she passed the turning that would have taken them to the boarding house, he didn't so much as break stride.

Dawson Kalliam, once Baron of Osterling Fells and her husband of decades, had no grave. After his execution, the body had been taken to the Silver Bridge and cast into the Division like common trash. Somewhere, far below, his bones lay amid the water and chaos. Tradition set the penalty for retrieving him for a gentler burial to be death, and Clara felt sure it would be upheld. And so every few days she found herself walking out to the middle of the span to spend a moment with the high and open air that had swallowed the last of her husband.

Below her, the pigeons turned in their flock, gliding on the drafts and perching on the Division's deep sides or the lower, lesser bridges that spanned the gap farther down. She closed her eyes and bowed her head as she'd seen her mother do before her father's ashes. It was what a woman did when she was remembering a man who had been her heart and was gone. It wasn't the first death she'd mourned. She'd lost her own father, her own mother. A brother taken by fever when she'd been hardly more than a girl. She knew what to expect, and how terrible it would be. How terrible it always was. The knowledge took nothing from the pain, or if not nothing, surely not enough.

After a time, she took a kerchief from her sleeve, dabbed away the tears, and walked back to the edge of the span where Vincen was waiting. He knew why she came, and he would not cross with her. Most times, she let the small courtesy pass uncommented. Perhaps it was her growing despair or the aftermath of fear, but today she paused before him, tilted her head, and considered him.

Vincen Coe stood only just taller than she did, his darker eyes cast down only a degree to meet hers. His hair was the light brown of oak leaves in autumn. His jaw was perhaps a little too broad, his nose bent slightly from some long-healed break. This was her self-appointed protector, this huntsman trapped in the treeless paths of the city. He had stolen a kiss from her once, and it had tasted of blood. He'd sworn a kind of love for her, and she had dismissed it because it was ridiculous. And then she had sent him away, because perhaps it was growing less ridiculous.

And that odd, half-acknowledged attachment had saved her life again today.

"Why are you here?" she asked. The question had become something of a ritual between them, and his smile meant that he'd understood her. *Why are you not off chasing some girl your own age? Why do you persist in wasting your own life in service to mine? How can I put so much trust in anything so clearly absurd?*

"My lady," he said, as he often did, "you saved me when I was lost, and I will follow you forever, if you let me."

Clara shook her head impatiently, and Vincen smiled. A dark cart drawn by a black horse clattered by. A crow called out and another answered back, or else its echo. She took his arm, folding her own around it as an aunt might a favorite nephew.

"You are a child."

"I'm older than Jorey."

"Jorey is my son."

"And wed."

"So it's not that you're young, it's that I'm old," Clara said, laughing. "Lovely."

"You're more beautiful than most women half your age."

After her mourning on the bridge, the flirtation was like a drink of sharp wine, cleansing and astringent with a thick aftertaste of guilt. Her husband wasn't a full season dead. Her children were scattered to the winds, and her house was disgraced. Trading honeyed barbs with an infatuated young man, walking with her arm in his, was scandalous, low behavior, and a part of her soul cringed even as she did it. But another part swelled and stretched and unfurled.

Sometimes she felt she was two women at once. The grief-crippled widow who wept every night and forced a smile every morning was one, and she was undeniable in her sorrow. But in the heart of her disgrace and loss, there was another woman. Not a younger one, but one who had caught the scent of a freedom unlike any she'd ever known, and who was dreadfully hungry for it.

From the time she'd been old enough to put on a dress, she had been a woman of the noble class. Her path had been trod by generations, and led more or less to the same grave that held their dry bones. The world was disrupted now, broken, and she was no one. What scandal could touch her that would compare with what she already carried? Even if the highest names in the court saw her now, they would turn away and pretend they hadn't. She had ceased to matter. Her actions and opinions were impotent, and so they could be anything. She was already fallen, and so she'd been freed.

It was an illusion, she knew. All actions carried consequences, even among the disgraced. But it was a convincing illusion, and it gave her hope that the world she had lost was not the only world there was.

"Can I..." Vincen said, his voice breaking into her reverie. She was surprised to see how far they had walked in silence and how close she had been holding his arm. "I'm sorry, m'lady, but can I ask?"

"I reserve the right to lie," she said cheerfully, but the moment of light repartee was gone, and the words sounded hollow.

"Why are *you* here?" he asked. "What is it we're doing?"

"Walking home before sunset for another bowl of your cousin's somewhat purgatorial stew, I believe," Clara said.

"Not that, ma'am. I mean that every day, we speak to people and find out what we can. Put together what's happening in the city and in the empire like we're tracking broken twigs and scat. But... well, but what is it you hope to do after?"

It was a powerful question, and one that Clara knew she'd avoided asking herself. Thus far, truly, she'd done nothing. To wander the city and make what connections she could was a benign occupation for a widow living on her son's limited charity. To conspire against the throne... well, it had an air of danger and romance about it, but what precisely it *meant* was an open question.

In truth, she didn't hate Geder Palliako. She had heard from her son Jorey of the burning of Vanai. She knew of Palliako's thwarted impulse to kill the entire noble class of Asterilhold. She had listened to him slaughter her husband as a traitor, though she hadn't had the strength to watch.

If she had swallowed darkness and sworn revenge, no one could have argued that it hadn't been earned. But she had also seen Palliako frightened and at sea among the young women at her son's wedding. He had been at her side when the treachery of Feldin Maas had been exposed. She felt about him the way she did about fire or flood or a blight that took a season's crop. He was merely a catastrophe. One might fear the flames even as one stood against them, but to hate them was absurd.

But what, then, was to be *done?*

"Tell someone, I suppose," she said with a sigh. "Preferably someone in a position to do something about it. Surely there will be a dissenting group within the court that would—"

"Know and recognize you? Palliako's sent his private guard for you once already."

"He didn't keep me," Clara said, but the point was not lost on her. There had been others to go before Geder's odd religious tribunal who had not been so fortunate. And the next time she might not be either. The winter sun slipped down behind the roofs and walls of Camnipol, the sky fading to a soft grey. The taprooms and coffee houses lit their lanterns, the sounds of music and song curling out to the streets, but even that seemed strained and martial. It would have been pretty to believe that the poison in the blood of Antea was only Geder Palliako, but if she were to be honest, she knew it had already spread. Her kingdom had caught a fever, and it would be years before it was well.

If she hoped to avoid that, she would need to be discreet. Happily, she'd been raised as a woman in the royal court where discretion, subtlety, and the tacit control of information were already something of a blood sport. Clara had never indulged in the destruction of another woman's reputation herself, but she'd seen it done often enough. She had sometimes stepped in to mitigate campaigns waged against her or her friends and allies. This wasn't so different.

When the intention was to undermine without being thought to do so, it was often wise to begin outside one's normal circle and let the gossip travel in, though what that would mean in this case wasn't perfectly clear. And anyone she did turn to would themselves need to be discreet, which was always a problem as so many people who came in possession of a secret seemed incapable of restraining the urge to *brag* about it...

The sound that came from her throat was low and brief, something between a laugh and cough, and it spoke of profound satisfaction.

"My lady?" Vincen Coe said.

"I'll have an errand for you tomorrow. Find a courier headed for Northcoast who can accept an extra letter."

"We have allies in Northcoast?"

She smiled and patted Vincen's arm, but she didn't answer, because there was no advantage in his knowing her intention. Discretion began at home.

Back at the boarding house, she spent a coin for three sheets of rag paper and thimble of ink. Paying for a courier would tax her allowance badly. She would be living on yesterday's bread until the next handful of coin came from Jorey, but it couldn't be avoided. She sat alone by the light of a candle, composing the letter in her mind for fear of wasting the paper.

Sir,

   We have met, but I cannot think you would remember me. For reasons that will become clear, I prefer not to identify myself to you at this time. You have been represented to me as a man of both tact and influence, and for this reason, I wish to share with you some observations I have made concerning affairs in the city of Camnipol and also my concerns for what these observations portend.

To begin, the Lord Regent has, under the pretext of raising barracks for the guard, begun the construction of prisons within the city walls. I have reached that conclusion for the following reasons...

Even with her script tight, small, and as legible as she could achieve, she ran short of paper before things she wished to say. One fact flowed gracefully into another, each observation building on the ones before. She kept the tone calm and conversational, giving room for the reader to draw his own conclusions rather than impressing her own upon him in any but the most unobtrusive way. When she was finished, she sewed the edges herself, fixing the threads in a simple knot. She addressed the outermost face in a single line.

Paerin Clark, Medean Bank, Carse.

Geder

"That they remain unprepared," Lord Ternigan said. "That is our best advantage."

The map of Sarakal lay unfolded on the table, the four men looking down at it as if to divine some secret teaching from the shape of its borders. Geder had chosen Ternigan to be Lord Marshal for the invasion. Lord Skestinin, as always, commanded the navy that was even now leaving the far northern seas for the warmer southern waters. And Lord Daskellin, ambassador to Northcoast, whose duty was to see that the northern border of the empire was protected by a wall of friendship and promises while the blades and bows traveled south. They were the war council. They and, of course, Basrahip.

The hunt had come here last, to the holdings at Watermarch, winter almost at its end. The holdfast was perched on a high granite cliff that looked over the wide sea to the east. The trees in the garden outside the wide window were only sticks, but their brown had the first blush of green. The thaw was coming, and in days. Canl Daskellin, Baron of Watermarch, had set aside a full wing of his home for this meeting, even the most trusted of servants sent away. It was the inner council. The last secret meeting.

"Food's an issue," Daskellin said. He stood between Geder and the wide windows, the light behind him and the darkness of his skin conspiring to make him seem more silhouette than man. "After the struggles in Asterilhold and then the unrest all through the summer, we were looking at a thin spring to begin with. Things are uncertain and unsettled, and people want to feel that the storm's passed."

"There won't be any fighting there," Geder said. "There won't be any fighting anywhere in Antea."

"It's not only this crop I'm thinking of," Daskellin said. "Fielding the army takes food, but it also takes farmers."

"That's what those roaches in Nus are counting on," Ternigan said. "We'll be fine. Once we take their granaries, we'll hardly need support from the Kingspire at all."

"Those granaries are set to feed their cities, not our army," Skestinin said, scratching his beard.

"Being conquered is sometimes uncomfortable," Ternigan said, and the issue was dismissed.

Sarakal was a thin nation, dominated by the port city of Nus in the north and the river city of Inentai in the south. Between them were the flint hills and farmsteads, villages and minor holdings of the traditional families, linked by the pale green thread of the dragon's road like beads on a string. Antea was the center of Firstblood power in the world, and Sarakal was the center of nothing. Its traditional families were mostly Timzinae, though there were some Jasuru and Firstblood, and the cities ruled by a high council drawn by lot every seven years. The influence of Borja and the Keshet showed in its casual attitude toward the nobility of blood and its heaping on of invented titles. A wealthy man of a traditional family might have himself declared prince or regos or exalt without any duties or holdings to come with the name. The council might strip a landholder of his rank without affecting his property or taxes.

But because of the mixture of races, the traditional families had links of kinship to Elassae and Borja, and even to the minor houses of Antea. If Sarakal had as little as half a season to prepare, the Lord Marshal and the armies of the empire might be facing pikemen from Elassae and Borjan cavalry along with the native defenses. Food and soldiers could sail from Hallskar into Nus or ride carts from Elassae or the Keshet into Inentai. To be done right—to be done well—the assault had to go as quickly and as unequivocally here as it had in Asterilhold.

In Asterilhold, where the armies had been led by Dawson Kalliam, Lord Marshal, first hero and then traitor. Even now, months after the fact, Geder saw the old man's face twisted in rage, Basrahip's blood on his blade. It seemed unjust that even after Dawson Kalliam's coup had been defeated and his life ended, Geder still felt haunted by him and his inexplicable betrayal.

"Lord Regent?" Ternigan said. "Do you have an opinion?"

Geder looked at the men around the table, painfully aware of having lost the thread of the conversation. There had been a question, and now he was going to look like a fool for not knowing what it was. He cleared his throat and the beginning of a blush rose in his cheeks.

"Well, yes. Let me see," he said. "Minister Basrahip? Would you care to offer an opinion?"

At his place beside the window, the priest lifted his head and smiled beatifically.

"There shall be no uprising to distract you," he said, his voice rough and melodious. "Prince Geder has lifted up temples to the goddess, and those who hear her voice will remain true."

"All respect, Minister," Canl Daskellin said, "there was a temple in Camnipol last summer, and things didn't go so well there."

"They will now," Basrahip said. Daskellin shuddered and looked away.

"Still," Ternigan said, "I think we won't have the men to control the full nation. Not this season. Nus, without question. We'll have it by autumn, let whoever's escaped to the south sue for peace. Gives us a good thick buffer between Antean land and any of these bastards who think they'd care to make trouble for us again."

"You will have it all," Basrahip said. There was no defiance in his tone. At most, a sense of gentle correction as one might hear a tutor take with a pupil. "As the goddess delivered Asterilhold to you, so she will reclaim the lands stolen by the Timzinae. The false race will be cast out and have no home."

"That's lovely, Minister," Ternigan said. "But these actions carry their own constraints. I have only so many knights. Only so many bows. Only so many blades. Overreaching is worse than failure. A collapse when we've outstripped our own support could push us back past our own borders."

"It will not happen so," Basrahip said.

Ternigan frowned, turning back to the map. His frown wasn't that of an insulted man, though there was perhaps a bit of that, so much as someone reexamining a puzzle, apprehensive that some critical clue had been missed.

"Regardless," Geder said, "the first part of the campaign is in place, yes?"

"The blockade will be there," Lord Skestinin said. "No ships in or out of the port of Nus without our men searching them, and no landings in the coves east or west of the city."

"Good," Geder said. "And the foot troops?"

"Ten thousand sword-and-bows are camped at Flor, waiting for me," Ternigan said. "I have sworn statements from half a dozen barons and counts that they'll raise their levies and ride in once I give the word. I haven't done it yet for fear of raising an alarm, but they should arrive just about when the first force needs relief. We'll be the hammer that breaks the anvil this time, just you watch."

"I'll repair to the west," Daskellin said. "I'll reassure Northcoast and Birancour that we're only looking to secure our borders, and that Asterilhold's done that in the west. They aren't likely to care what we're doing in the east so long as it doesn't affect their taxes and trades."

"And the priests?" Geder asked.

"They will travel with your army," Basrahip said. "Where they go, you shall find always victory."

"Well, that'll be damned pleasant," Ternigan said. "Nothing goes quite as well as constant, unending victory, ah?"

"I'll want reports to me in Camnipol," Geder said. "Daily, if you can."

"We'll wear the courier's hoofs to the quick, Lord Regent," Ternigan said. "You have my word on it."

Geder nodded.

"Well, then. Let's make it official, shall we?"

Without servants to wait on them, Daskellin was the one to clear the table, bring the parchments and the ink. Basrahip shook his head in mock despair and amusement. Making a thing more real by writing it down made as much sense to the priest as cooling something with fire, but Geder shrugged and Basrahip waved him on, as if indulging him.

The pages were short, the wording simple and classic. Geder signed at the end, and then the others each took the pen in turn and stood witness. It took less time from the start to the end than it would to eat a bowl of soup, and after so many weeks of preparation, it felt both exciting and oddly a bit melancholy, as if the pleasant part of the work were over and the tedious stretch about to begin.

"Well, then. That's it," Geder said as Daskellin poured the blotting sand over the ink. "War."

Word spread through the holdfast of Watermarch like it was carried by the wind. The King's Hunt was ending for the year, and those high nobles who had expected to retire to their holdings for the few weeks before the opening of the court season in Camnipol had news to carry back home with them, and tasks that perhaps they hadn't expected. Geder heard the excitement in their voices, even when they spoke of other things—the cut of dresses and cloaks, the marriages and liaisons of the court, the scandalous poets and thinly veiled plays—everything was suddenly really about the war. There was almost a sense of relief that came with it. The victory over Asterilhold should have been a time of celebration, and instead it had become a nightmare. Even when the conspirators had been killed, their lands retaken by the Severed Throne, it had left a sour taste in the mouths of the victors.

And in truth, even the battle with Asterilhold had carried a sense of infighting. The bloodlines of Antea and Asterilhold had crossed and mixed for centuries. The noble banners that faced each other in the fields outside Kaltfel had belonged to cousins, even if often at several removes. While there were some Firstblood relations in the traditional families of Sarakal, they were few, and when the nation's name arose, the image it carried was of a Timzinae or Jasuru, of a chaotic government hardly better than a nomadic tribe with its shoes nailed in one place to keep it from straying. It made the coming slaughter feel cleaner. To see that the enemy came from outside and that they would be brought to their knees by Antean strength was a return to the way things were supposed to be. Even Geder found it relieving.

On those years when the first thaw came after the end of the hunt, tradition called for a final occasion. A ball, a feast, the comparing of honors. Canl Daskellin held the feast in a massive glassed ballroom, braziers burning at the ends of every table keeping the air thick and warm. Outside the massive network of glass, the sea was the color of slate flecked with white, the setting sun a glory of orange and gold. Geder sat at the high table, Prince Aster at one side, Basrahip at the other. It was like something from an old poem, and these men toasting each other and trading barbed rhymes, competing with extemporaneous speeches on patriotism and piety and bragging about how many women they'd bedded in their youth were the dragons of old reborn in human form. It made him wish that his own father attended the hunt, just so that he could be sitting at Geder's side and watching it all.

And yet he was not wholly at peace.

The seating was, as always, arranged by the status within the court. The nearer to the high table, Geder, and Prince Aster, the more honored. Canl Daskellin, as host, shared the high table, as did his wife and his daughter, Sanna. Sanna wore a gown that left Geder feeling something between embarrassed and excited, and kept smiling at him. Then, one table farther, Ternigan and his family along with Lord Skestinin and his son, Bynal. But not his daughter. Geder tried to ignore the absence, but it gnawed at him from the first soup through the pheasant. When the venison came, he excused himself.

The apartments were in the north wing of the holding, positioned well enough for an honored merchant or the lowest of the noble. When Geder's personal guard announced him, no servant came to see him in. Sabiha's hair was the color of wheat, and her cheeks were round and touched with a permanent rose that made her seem younger than she was. The politeness of her expression didn't match the coolness of her eyes. Now that he'd spent some time with Lord Skestinin, he could see something of him in her, but for the most part she only seemed herself.

The sitting room was cooler than the ballroom, though it had no windows. The lamp that burned on the mantel put out a dull, buttery light that almost forgave the worn upholstery of the divan. Geder understood. Like everything in court, the amenities of the hunt meant something. Not so many years ago, he would have been given a room much like this, if he'd bothered coming to the hunt at all. Still, its shabbiness disturbed him.

"Lord Regent," she said with the curtsey that etiquette required of her.

"Sabiha," Geder said. "I was looking for you at the feast. And Jorey. I was looking for both of you."

"My father thought that, given the situation, it would be better that we not appear."

"Yes," Geder said. "Well. I was wondering if I might speak with Jorey for a moment. And . . . and can I have food sent to you? There's a whole feast, and some of it's very good, and just because the politics of the things are what they are, it doesn't mean you shouldn't eat."

He was babbling. He knew it, and he could no more stop it than hold back the springtime. Sabiha's smile was crooked, and he didn't know whether she was amused or annoyed. Not that it mattered. He was Lord Regent of Antea. She would accede to his suggestions, whatever they were. If he'd asked her to throw off her gown and dance naked for him, she would have had to or risk the displeasure of the crown. It was odd how having power over people meant not knowing their true minds. Not without Basrahip there to tell him, anyway.

"It would be kind of you, my lord," Sabiha said.

"Geder. Really, in private, call me Geder."

"It would be kind of you, Geder," she said. "Wait here if you'd like. I'll get Jorey."

"Thank you," Geder said. Sabiha walked into the gloom of the corridor. Geder heard her voice, and then Jorey's, and then hers again. He thought there was a warmth in them, the sound of husband and wife. His own mother had died when he was a child, so he only had the servants and slaves to judge from, but he thought he'd heard the intimate kindness in the servants' quarters in unguarded moments. That, and books he'd read that spoke of the role of men and of women, and the connection between them. His direct experience was somewhat limited.

Jorey emerged into the light. He still wore his hunting leathers and a grey wool cloak. His hair was unruly and his eyes had a darkness under them. Geder popped up to his feet and wiped his hands on his thighs.

"Jorey," he said. "I'm sorry. I wanted to find you and say it. Between us."

Jorey's smile was thin.

"It wasn't your doing, my lord," Jorey said, as if the words pained him. "My father's actions were unconscionable. The death...the death you gave him—"

"Oh, not that," Geder said quickly. He didn't want Jorey to still feel embarrassed about what Dawson had done. "That's in the past. Over with. I meant the war. You did hear, didn't you?"

Jorey sat on the divan, looking up at Geder. It was an utter breach of etiquette, but Jorey didn't seem to notice, and Geder was oddly glad that he hadn't. Geder had Aster and Basrahip, who knew him for who he was instead of the title he answered to. And the part-Cinnae banker, Cithrin, who'd hidden with him during the worst of the troubles. Even with Jorey Kalliam, Geder could still count his friends on one hand and not use his thumb.

"You've decided to invade Sarakal," Jorey said.

"Yes, that," Geder said. "Only I named…I named Ternigan as Lord Marshal, and he picked the men he wanted on campaign with him. And after what happened with your father, and Barriath…"

In truth, Barriath Kalliam had chosen exile rather than give his loyalty to Geder. Nor had he been the only one to do so. Others had tried to lie, to swear that they would never betray Geder as others had, but Basrahip had been there to warn of their duplicity. Those died.

"Don't apologize to me for that," Jorey said. His gaze had wandered to the shadowed corridor. "I've had enough of killing to last a lifetime. I only want to go back to Lord Skestinin's estate and look after my family."

Geder nodded, more to himself than to Jorey. He had never taken the youngest of the Kalliams before his private tribunal, never subjected him to the unyielding certainty of Basrahip and the spider goddess. It would have seemed cruel, and after all, Jorey had renounced his father before the full court. To question his honesty or loyalty after that was like questioning whether the sea tasted of salt.

And there was also some other, deep, wordless reluctance. Geder didn't *want* him in there, and he didn't want to think too closely about why, except that it wasn't a place for his friends. He sat at Jorey's side, not touching, but close. Like two men on campaign sitting on the same log before a cookfire.

"I know how hard this has all been," Geder said. "You don't have to worry, though. I'll be on the throne until Aster's of age, and I'll find a way to bring you back into the good graces of the court. You and Sabiha both."

Jorey laughed bitterly, but didn't speak. Geder felt a twist of anxiety in his belly and plucked at the cloth of his sleeve.

"What...what are you thinking?" he asked.

"I'm thinking about what makes a man good. Or evil. I'm wondering if I'm a good man or an evil one."

"You aren't evil. An evil person does bad things," Geder said. "Even your father wasn't evil. He was...misguided. The Timzinae who poisoned his mind against the throne? They were evil. But he was a brave man, doing what he thought was right, however wrong he was about it. I never thought he was evil."

"Never?"

"Well," Geder said, almost shyly, "almost never. I did lose my temper with him. There at the end. I mean, he did try to kill me."

Jorey's expression was unreadable—amusement, disgust, despair. He could have meant anything.

"I know that you count me as your friend, Geder," he said at last.

The smile began in Geder's chest as a warmth, and it spread out through his body.

"That's all I wanted, Jorey. I just wanted you to remember that no matter what's happened, I am your friend."

Marcus

Good kitty," Marcus said, his sword at the ready, "or... whatever the hell you are."

The beast shifted its head, following the shine of steel with distrust. It stood little higher than Marcus's waist, but nose to tail would easily measure fifteen feet. Its fur was black and mottled as if designed to disappear into the sun-dappled darkness under the jungle canopy. Dagger-long claws cut into the ground as it stepped toward him, and its jaw opened half a handspan as if it were tasting the air.

"I think it's trying to get between us," Kit said.

"Then stay close to me," Marcus replied. "I don't think it has our best interests at heart. Good kitty. Stay back."

The beast opened its mouth with a shriek equal parts windstorm and ripping flesh. Its teeth were broad, low, and hooked. The struggle of prey caught in that jaw would only drive the bite deeper. It took another step closer and lowered its body to the ground, bunching up as if to leap.

They were in what Marcus had come to think of as a clearing. The trees were thinner here, and bits of blue sky showed between the arm-broad fronds twenty feet above him. There was room to move without being caught against tree trunks or thick, leathery scrub. That was likely why the beast had chosen this space to make its advance.

The constant noise of the wilderness—the drip of water

from the trees, the high chirping call of the bright yellow frogs that swarmed over the ground at dawn and dusk, the distant scream of monkeys, the clicking of billions of unseen insects from within the rotting carpet of leaf and mold they walked on—was like an auditory fog, obscuring any sound within it. Sweat sheeted down Marcus's back, and the constant, punishing heat and damp were like a blanket pressed over his face. He was aware of Kit off to his left, but he didn't dare glance over to see what the old actor was doing.

"Why would it want its enemies to flank it? I don't see how it could defend against us both," Kit said.

"Same reason you'd put yourself between sheep," Marcus said. "Lets you put your full attention on the one you're killing. Can we talk about this later?"

"Yes. Sorry."

Marcus shook his sword, and the beast's eyes flickered toward it. Its pupils were cat slits, its nose two flat pits like a viper's. Its chest widened and narrowed as it sucked in air. Smelling them. Gathering information. Making its decision.

Marcus shouted, driving toward the beast with a flurry of stabs. Even in the relative clear, there was little room to swing, and the reach of his blade was the only advantage he had. The beast swiped at the sword, parrying the thrust with a power that almost wrenched the hilt out of his hand. Marcus stepped back, waiting to see if his plan had worked. The beast licked its paw, its tongue the bright red of fresh blood.

"Didn't know it was sharp along the sides too, did you, kitty?" Marcus said. "I've got all kinds of tricks like that. So how about we just call this one a draw and move on, eh?"

The beast screamed, swatting with its wounded paw. Red splattered across Marcus's bare chest, but it was his attacker's blood. Its evil-colored eyes flickered past Marcus's shoulder, weighing the possibility of Kit. Marcus shifted to the side, keeping himself between the animal and the man. The beast hissed annoyance, and for a moment Marcus thought it might turn away, blending back into the shadows of Lyoneia as unnervingly as it had emerged from them. Nothing in its stance warned of what was coming; in one heartbeat it went from half turned away, single petulant eye considering him, to full assault. The rush of flesh and bone, tooth and claw, left no room for mercy. Marcus felt the shout in his own throat, but he couldn't hear it. He pushed forward, into the attack. Retreat even in defense was death now. The shock of impact jarred his arm as the blade struck home, but the animal outweighed him, and no wound however grievous could stop its charge. The smell of the beast filled the air, thick and rank and intimate, and the fur, slick and rough at the same time, pressed against him and bore him down. The filthy litter of the jungle floor pressed against Marcus's back as the beast shifted, struggling to bring its vicious teeth against his head.

Somewhere very far away, Kit was shouting, but Marcus didn't have the attention to spare. He pressed himself in, clasping the beast close, fighting to stay too near to let mouth or paw reach him. With the hand that still held the sword, he pushed and pulled and pushed again, widening whatever wound he had managed. The beast writhed against him, thrusting him away, and whipped its head against his own. Marcus felt the tooth pierce the top of his ear and rip through it. Later, it would hurt. A claw dug at him, trying to find the leverage to cut, and Marcus jumped back. The blood-slicked blade slipped from his fingers.

For a moment, they stood, facing each other. The beast curled against itself like a runner protecting a stitch. Marcus stayed low, feet grounded and knees bent, ready to jump away. Blood poured from the animal's belly. It roared, snapping at the air, but it came no closer. Its eyes fixed on Marcus, then glazed and fixed on him again. Blood poured into Marcus's ear and down his neck. Long ropes of saliva draped down from the animal's panting jaw. Flies were already buzzing around them, drawn by the smells of violence and death.

The beast coughed once, and then a sudden gout of blood shot out from its mouth and nostrils, bright red against the black muzzle. It slipped to the ground, folding its legs underneath it as if merely resting, and its dark eyes closed. Marcus took a long, shuddering breath.

"Well," he gasped. "Hope those don't travel in packs."

Kit stood at the far side of the clearing, his walking stick held above him like a club, his face pale and his hair standing out from his head in all directions. Marcus's legs began to shake, and he sat down. He'd been in the business of violence long enough to know how this would go. A half hour's time and he'd be fine, but until then trying to will himself to normalcy only made it worse. He touched his wounded ear. The rip was rough at the edges and as long as the first joint of his thumb. He was lucky it hadn't gotten more than a single tooth to bear, or the beast might have torn the whole damn thing off. The flies buzzed around him, sliding in to drink up the gore.

"Are you all right?" Kit asked.

"Had better days," Marcus said. "Had worse, for that. If you've still got that salve in your pack, I'd take a couple fingers' worth."

Kit hurried back into the trees and returned with the pale leather pack, one of the few objects that hadn't yet rotted in the jungle. Marcus opened the stone jar and scooped a double finger through the yellow-white salve. It burned like fire when it touched the wound, but it would keep the maggots out.

For weeks, they had battled the land, following animal trails that widened for a hundred feet and then vanished as if they'd never been, avoiding Southling hunters who haunted the nights, and spending as much time scraping for food and water as searching for the reliquary. Kit's face had lost all its cushion, the skin growing gaunt against the bone. Marcus was fairly sure he'd lost a tenth of his own body's weight, and he still had a bit of potbelly. The indignities of not dying young.

"I believe I've heard of these," Kit said, staring at the animal. "Kaskimar, they're called where I came from, but... they were much smaller."

The actor reached out with his walking stick to prod the corpse.

"Don't touch it," Marcus said, a breath too late.

The black eyes clicked open and a paw lashed out. The walking stick flew out of Kit's hand, cracking against a tree trunk. Kit fell back with a curse, and the beast closed its eyes again.

"Sorry," Marcus said. "Should have said before. Did it get you?"

"I'm afraid so," Kit said ruefully. "I may need needle and thread."

"That deep?" Marcus said, levering himself to his feet. "Let me see—"

"No," Kit said sharply. "Stay back. It isn't safe. Just throw me the pack and then get away."

"Get away?"

Kit nodded, licked his lips, and winced. Marcus thought he saw something tiny and black skitter across Kit's arm, and his flesh crawled a little.

"It's the spiders," Kit said. "There's too many of them to keep track of. It won't be safe for you."

Marcus tossed the pack to Kit and made his way to the other side of the dying beast. The shaking was already less. Kit grunted in pain and started pulling their few supplies out and onto the ground before him.

"How bad are the bites from those things?" Marcus asked.

"Hmm? Oh. They raise welts. Itch for a few days."

The beast took a deep, shuddering breath and didn't draw another. In a few minutes, Marcus guessed, it would be safe to retrieve his sword.

"Hardly seems fair that they bite you," Marcus said. "Disloyal, somehow."

"I don't believe they know who I am. What I am, for that. I doubt they have minds themselves, even so much as a normal spider might. They act as the mark of the goddess's authority and the channel for her gifts."

"Which is why we're killing her," Marcus said. "So her power and gifts all go boneless."

"Yes."

"Still seems rude of them to bite you."

"Annoying, yes. But that isn't why they're unsafe. I'm using the last of the salve."

"Use it if you need it. Might as well use nothing as not enough. Why unsafe, then?"

Kit took a sharp breath, his hand pressed to the wound in his leg. His face paled and the red-black blood that ran between his fingers might have been thick with clots or something less pleasant. A yellow frog, long-legged and shining like a river stone, leaped onto the dying beast's head, then off again. The animal didn't stir.

"One might...God, but this does sting, doesn't it? Ah. One might get inside you."

"*Inside* me?"

Kit looked up and managed a smile.

"I wasn't born with them," he said. "If I hadn't been chosen for the temple, I'd be herding goats in the Sinir Kushku today instead of this."

"Better off too," Marcus said. "How do they get inside you?"

Kit fumbled on the ground. The black roll of silk thread had a fine bone needle in it, and Kit held it between his teeth, talking around it as he found the free end of the thread. It slurred his words, but not so badly that Marcus couldn't understand him.

"For me, it was the ritual initiation. I spent five years learning before my mind was ready, or that's what the high priest told me, and I believed him. I suppose I still do, for that. I can't imagine how unpleasant it would be to have the goddess enter you if you were unprepared. It only took one. I cut my skin just inside the elbow, and the high priest cut his thumb and pressed it to my wound. That was all. I felt it come in me, felt it crawling through my veins, and then the next day, there were more. Everywhere, and I knew I was changing. I remember embracing it at the time, but we were always warned that the goddess would break an unready mind. Even as it was, there was a day my brothers had to strap me down to keep me from trying to open my skin and let them out."

"I think I'll stay with the usual empty prayers and overpriced candles," Marcus said. "And that could happen to anyone? And when I say anyone, I mean that could happen to me?"

Kit made a little grunt of satisfaction, holding the needle in one hand and gently rolling the thread through its eye.

The tiny, sharp shard of bone danced between his fingers, seeming to fly in the dimness like a cunning man's conjure. With a sigh, he took it between finger and thumb and turned to the work of sewing his skin closed. Tending your own wounds like that was unpleasant, but sometimes the occasion required it.

"They wouldn't intend to. It isn't as though they seek for it," Kit said. "But if you were unlucky, one might find its way into your blood. A cut would be the simplest, but any path under your skin would do, I think. Eyes. Mouth. Less mentionable paths. I haven't made the experiment, but that's what they told me in the temple, and it seems plausible."

"So it's never happened?"

"Once," Kit said, "when I was very new to the world. It was an accident. I was in Borja, and I was drunk. I got into a fight. Not a serious thing; fists, not knives. But I split his lip, and then later on, he bit me. They decided a demon had possessed him, and they threw him on a bonfire."

"Seems extreme."

"I convinced them it was called for."

Kit said the words lightly, but his closed expression spoke of shame. He drove the bone needle through his skin again, pulling the dark thread until the wound narrowed. Tiny red dots marked his hands and the skin of his leg. Spider bites.

Marcus stepped forward, but not too close. Flies were drinking at the corners of the beast's closed eyes, and he shooed them away. The animal seemed, if anything, heavier in death. Marcus rolled it onto its wide back. His sword stuck out of its chest at an angle, thick with gore and insects. So little time, and the jungle was already hard at work reclaiming the animal, remaking it, folding it into the merciless cycle of eater and eaten. He took hold of the hilt, braced his foot, and heaved. The sword came free on the third try. He squatted on the ground, rubbing the worst of the blood off with moss and old leaves. In a perfect world, he'd have been able to wash it with a real cloth and oil it after. He considered the beast's body, shrugged, and ran the flat of the blade across the slick black fur. There would be some body oils in the pelt. It wasn't the most dignified way to treat a fallen enemy, but it wasn't the worst thing he'd done to the animal that day. He put the sword back into its rotting leather scabbard.

Kit finished his gruesome task and tried standing. It looked awkward and painful. Marcus felt himself making the calculations. If Kit's wound went septic, getting back to friendly territory would be a hard thing. Kit could likely talk any Southlings they came across into giving them aid, providing the man was still coherent and not lost in a fever. If it was all up to Marcus, their chances would be worse.

And even then, there was only so much longer they could go on before the landscape consumed them. They would become another cautionary tale to excite the interest of explorers and idiots. Any man who cared about his own life would turn north now and hope he hit seawater before his strength gave out. Only that wasn't the job.

"We can make camp here," Marcus said.

"And spend all night fighting ants and scavengers?"

"We can make camp a way down from here. Maybe find a little creek."

"I think that sounds wise," Kit said. "Let me get my staff."

While Kit limped into the underbrush to retrieve the fallen stick, Marcus knelt by the dead animal. It was magnificent in its way.

"Your time now, kitty," he said under his breath. "My time later."

He patted the beast's shoulder like it was an opponent
he'd bested in the gymnasium's fighting pit, then started to
stand. He stopped. The ground near the great black claws
had been churned up, black earth and pale roots. Marcus
dug his fingers down, pulling up the fabric of plant and soil.
The stone beneath it was a perfect green. Only it wasn't
stone.

"Kit?"

"Marcus?"

"There's dragon's jade here."

Kit hobbled forward, leaning against his staff. His face
was grimy and streaked with his own blood, but his eyes
were bright.

"Where?"

Marcus stood up and stepped back, pointing to the turned
earth. As Kit knelt down to examine it, Marcus walked
up and down the clearing, squinting in concentration. All
around them, great trees towered up, fighting each other
to reach the sunlight. But here in this strip, the trees were
thinner, shorter, weaker. The roots that fed them, perhaps
shallower. Yes, now that he knew to look for it, it was clear.

"This is a road," he said. "There's a dragon's road running through this valley. North to south, and maybe turning
a little to the east just here."

"Well, now," Kit said. "There's a pleasant surprise."

"Did we expect to find a dragon's road?"

"We did not."

"And if there's a dragon's road, it seems likely that at some
point way back when there were still dragons to make the
jade, it was a road *to* someplace."

"That would seem to follow."

Marcus felt a smile plucking at his lips.

"This is the path to your mysterious reliquary, isn't it?"

Kit hauled himself up.

"I suppose it could be."

For a long moment, the two men stood in the cloud of flies that buzzed around the corpse, grinning at each other like boys.

Cithrin

Magistra Isadau's office was near the center of the compound. It was as understated as Cithrin's back room in the café had been, but like a stone set in tin or else silver, the surroundings changed the nature of the space. Where Cithrin's workplace was clearly built on business, Isadau drew anyone coming on bank business through her house. After meeting with Cithrin in Porte Oliva, a person would step out to see the Grand Market with its queensmen and merchants, traders and cutpurses, shouts and laughter and commerce. Leaving Isadau's meant passing through not only the magistra's home, but her brother's, her sister's, her mother's. Isadau's nieces and nephews wandered the wide hallways with their friends or else their tutors. Mother Kicha had visitors every day, so that even in the afternoons, the broad hall outside the matriarch's bedchamber might be half full of poets or priests or sour-faced Timzinae women embroidering flowers and sunbursts onto dresses and pointedly ignoring Cithrin.

Jurin—the brother—was a farrier, and the stables were his as much as Isadau's. Kani, who had met Cithrin at the docks, did scribe work for the bank and deliveries for Jurin and errands for her mother without drawing any distinction between them. Yardem and Enen and Roach were expected to work with Isadau's own guardsmen, sharing the duties of the watch and escorting payments through the city, and they were also guests welcome at the family dinner table. The kitchens smelled of fennel and cumin and cinnamon, and they fed anyone who came. The cook who oversaw them, an old Yemmu man with a black crack running jaggedly through his left tusk, made a great noise and wailing about being interrupted and then kept whoever had come in conversation harder to escape than a honey trap.

There was no tradition of wayhouses in Suddapal. Travelers negotiated hospitality with whatever family opened their doors to the knock. Coming out of her room in the morning was like stepping into the street had been in Porte Oliva. Anyone might be there on any business. And Magistra Isadau's complex—while larger and better appointed than most—was only one of hundreds that made up the five cities. In the first days, Cithrin could feel her own mind shifting, struggling to put the culture of Elassae into terms of her old experience. The compounds were like villages of a single family, each in competition with the ones around it. Or the compounds were like homes shared through a greater family and in service to all the endeavors the men and women of that family fell into. Or they were like the holdings of the nobility, except without the base of taxation and tribute to hold them up. It was only very slowly and with almost as many steps back as forward that Cithrin came to accept the compound for what it was, and even then it felt profoundly foreign. Nor was its openness the only difference.

"Hold your shoes, ma'am?" Yardem asked.

Tenthday was a moving ceremony, falling on each of the traditional seven weekdays with a mathematical certainty that was like music. Callers marched out from the basilica at dawn, ringing bronze bells and singing the call to prayer. The pious like Mother Kicha and Jurin, and those who wished to be thought well of by the pious, like Isadau and Cithrin, all met the callers barefoot in the streets and joined the procession.

"Thank you," Cithrin said, handing the leather slippers to Yardem. "This will be more pleasant in the summer when the paving feels less like ice."

The Tralgu's wide, canine mouth took on a gentle smile.

"Imagine it will," he said. His own wide leather boots hung in his hand. Roach stood beside him, his race making him seem more a part of the household than of Cithrin's guard. Enen was staying behind; there was a whole genre of jokes about what people found at home after the ceremony. Leaving some family behind was considered an acceptable compromise between the worship of God and the nature of humanity. The callers came, bells breaking like waves against the low bass chanting of voices. Cithrin sighed, stood the way Master Kit and Cary had taught her, and joined the household as they stepped into the street. The steady pace allowed even the oldest among them to keep up, and Cithrin let her mind wander as they passed through the wide streets of Suddapal. The group was mostly Timzinae, but the massive bodies of Yemmu lumbered among them, as well as the tall and tall-eared Tralgu. Cithrin was the only Cinnae or Firstblood; her pale skin and hair stood out like a star in the night sky, and she caught more than a few people craning their necks for a glimpse of the newcomer. She tried not to feel awkward about it.

The city here sloped down to the south. The sea was a greater whiteness behind sun-glowing mist. The sky was pale as opal.

Magistra Isadau appeared at her side, and Cithrin nodded formally. Some swift calculation seemed to pass behind the older woman's eyes before she returned the gesture.

"You're looking well this morning, Cithrin."

"Thank you," Cithrin said over the chant and the bells.

"I saw that you'd begun your review of the books?"

"I have," Cithrin said, then looked around her. They were where the private business of the bank would be overheard if spoken of, and yet the magistra's comment felt like an invitation. Cithrin felt a tightening in her gut, like a rat smelling a dog, but not sure yet which direction held the danger. "I'll want to look over them more this afternoon."

"I suspect we can make time for it," Isadau said. "There are some people I would like you to meet after the ceremony."

Cithrin smiled carefully.

"Whatever you think wise," she said, keeping her tone cheerful.

"Ati Isadau!" a voice called from behind them. A younger Timzinae boy—thirteen summers or possibly a bit less—was pushing his way through the crowd toward them. Men and women made way for him with expressions of annoyance. He reached them winded, one black-scaled hand clutched to his side. "Ati Isadau," he said between gasps. "There's a courier come. Package for you. From the holding company."

Isadau's smile seemed warm enough that she might actually have meant it.

"Thank you, Salan," she said gravely. "I appreciate your letting me know."

Salan, Cithrin thought. It took her a moment to recall where she'd heard the name. This was the nephew, son of Isadau's brother, who'd decided to be infatuated with the exotic girl from Birancour. He looked at Cithrin, then tried to bow and walk forward at the same time. All in all, he managed creditably.

"Yes," Cithrin said. "Thank you."

The boy started to say something, lost the thread of it, and nodded in a sharp, curt way that was certainly intended to be manly. He fell in step between Cithrin and Isadau, escorting them to the temple.

"I'm studying to be a soldier," Salan announced, apropos of nothing.

Yardem, at her other side, coughed once. No one who hadn't traveled with him for years would have recognized the sound as amusement.

"Really?" Cithrin said.

"Entered gymnasium last year," Salan said. "It's a good one. It's run by an old mercenary captain who fought in half the wars in the Keshet."

"What's his name?" Cithrin asked.

"Karol Dannien. Master Karol, we call him."

Cithrin glanced at Yardem. The Tralgu's expression was bland and blank, but his ears were tipped forward, listening. Her heart beat a little faster. His reaction to the words meant more to her than the words themselves.

"Really?" she said.

"I've been there for six months, and I'm already up to third rank," Salan said proudly. "At the end of summer, Master Karol is taking the ten best fighters to Kiaria to try out for garrison duty. It won't be me this year. Next year, probably."

"Garrison duty would be hard work," Cithrin said. Salan's breast seemed to broaden with pride, and his expression took on a seriousness that it would have been unthinkably cruel to laugh at.

"Kiaria's the old-style word for stronghold," he said. "No one's ever fought their way in there. Even during Falin's occupation, Kiaria didn't fall. And that lasted thirty years. Only the best fighters are allowed to work the garrison there. That's what Master Karol said."

"He would know better than I would," Cithrin said. "Is the gymnasium close to the compound?"

"No, Master Karol's down by the piers. He has all sorts of different people come through and help train. A month ago, he had a Haaverkin teach a session. Cep Bailan, his name was, and he taught me the tiger choke. You can knock a man unconscious in three breaths. If you do it right."

The procession turned the last degree in its arc, and the basilica hove into sight. Granite walls rose to twice the height of even so large a man as Yardem, and then three heights more in dark-stained wood. Wide doors of iron-bound oak were open wide, and the chanters stood beside them making graceful figures in the air with wide-spread palms. Isadau put a hand on Salan's head, the unconscious gesture of a woman to a child.

"Go find us a bench, won't you?" she asked, and Salan trotted forward, pleased to have a task. Isadau smiled at Cithrin. "He's terribly proud."

"I could tell," Cithrin said. "It's not a bad thing, having a trade you care about."

"I suppose. Still, I'd hoped he'd take to something less likely to have him killed. For a time, I thought he'd follow Jurin and be a farrier, but—"

"All respect, ma'am," Yardem said. "Farriers die too. I've known several men that caught a hoof. And standing garrison at Kiaria, he's more likely to die of boredom than a blade."

Magistra Isadau set her gaze forward, watching Salan weaving through the crowd as they passed through the wide doors. She rubbed her fingers together, a dry, soft sound like the pages of a codex slipping against each other.

"I suppose that's true," she said. "Still, I could hope for something that reminds me less that he's growing up."

The interior of the basilica arched above them, vast as a mountain. The dark wood benches seemed to catch the light of the thousand candles, drink it in, and return it rich and mysteriously altered. The air was thick with the smell of ambergris, roses, and thick tropical mint, the warmth of bodies and candleflame. At the nave, a Timzinae priest stood beneath a massive rosewood dragon. The spread wooden wings dovetailed into the walls themselves, so that the whole basilica seemed to be within their span. The massive head had been fashioned with an expression that could have been compassion or disdain. Or perhaps Cithrin was only seeing in it what she hoped and feared. Either way, it was nicely done.

They slipped into the outer edge of a bench, Yardem at her side. He handed her back her slippers, and she slid numbed and filthy toes into them, grateful that they could at least begin the journey back toward warmth. His own boots, he laid on the ground. The procession was still making its way in, the murmur of voices still growing within the wide and echoing space. Cithrin put her hand on his.

"Karol Dannien," she said, not whispering—whispering always sounded like whispering, and so it caught attention— but speaking low. "Did you know him?"

"Did," Yardem said. "It was years ago, though."

"Still, he might know. He might have had word of Marcus. Captain Wester, I mean."

"Might," Yardem said, but his ears were pressing back against his skull and his forehead was furrowed.

"Will you ask?"

"I could," Yardem said.

"I'm not angry with him," she said, maybe too quickly. "He was in his rights to leave. His contract allowed it. It's just...I wanted to talk with him. Say goodbye."

Ask him why, she thought, though she would never say it.

Marcus Wester had been the captain of her guard, and before that, the man who'd taken her cause and kept her from being killed. That he'd left while she was gone north to Carse and Camnipol, that he'd stepped away from his work with the bank without so much as a letter to explain his choice, shouldn't have mattered. She didn't answer to him, and he had kept the word of his agreements. But it irritated. Worse, it hurt.

She had her own work to do, her year's apprenticeship under Magistra Isadau, and then her return to Porte Oliva and her own branch of the bank and, God help her, Pyk Usterhall. Whatever Marcus was doing, she wouldn't have been part of it. And still, it would be something to know what had been so much more important than her.

Yardem nodded, and she thought she saw the same distress on his face. He had known Marcus much longer than she had, worked as his second, and even, she thought, taken some responsibility for seeing the captain through his worst times. She felt a passing guilt at reminding him that he had also been left behind. When Yardem spoke, his voice was low and his words as careful as painting eggshells.

"You know that the captain wouldn't have left without... *reason.*"

"Probably," Cithrin said. "And still, I'd like to know what called him away. Wouldn't you?"

Yardem flicked an ear, his earrings jingling against each other.

"I'll speak with Dannien," he said. "See what I can find."

Cithrin squeezed his fingers and took back her own hand. At the nave, the priest raised his hands, and the crowd went silent. The bells had stopped and a deep, throbbing gong sounded three times. The priest closed his hands, opening

them again with a shout. Gouts of flame rose from his fingertips into the wide air, swirling gold and green. Yardem
grunted. Returning Cithrin's glance, he shrugged.

"Cunning men shouldn't be priests," he said so softly that
only she could hear. "Too much temptation to show off."

"Gaudy," Cithrin agreed, as the priest's reedy voice began
to recite from the holy books. She set her expression into an
attentive half-smile and let her mind wander.

The arrival of the courier, she forgot about completely
until Magistra Isadau called for her that night.

Magistra Isadau sat with her legs crossed and her feet resting atop her desk. The night breeze left the lantern flickering. Her full attention was on a letter in the company cipher
that she held in her left hand, so that for a long moment, she
didn't move or acknowledge Cithrin's presence. When she
did, she nodded toward a low upholstered divan. Cithrin sat.
Magistra Isadau tapped the papers against her fingertips. In
the dim light, the darkness of her scales left her expression
unreadable.

"In Carse," she said, "Paerin argued that Antea would
pose little threat for years at the least. You disagreed."

"I did," Cithrin said.

Isadau held out the letter. Cithrin hesitated for a moment,
then took it from her. The handwriting was unquestionably
Paerin Clark's, the cipher as familiar to her eye as normal
script. The words, however, were in a different voice. *We
have met, but I cannot think you would remember me.
For reasons that will become clear, I prefer not to identify
myself to you at this time.* She turned the page over, glancing at the script.

"It appears that someone else has reached your same
conclusions," Magistra Isadau said. "A faceless voice from

the wilds. It happens more often than you'd imagine, and usually it's someone half mad and in need of coin. But this time...Komme and Paerin addressed this to me, but they meant it for you."

Cithrin read the full letter from beginning to end, and she felt some part of herself that she hadn't known was knotted relax. Her mind became stiller than it had been in weeks, clear and cold. For a time, she was in Camnipol, walking the streets that the letter spoke of as best her memory would allow. Detail grew upon detail: prisons, food supplies, the manufacture of weapons, the rising tide of violence against the poor and the powerless, the resentment of the Timzinae conspiracy in which neither she nor the letter's author had the slightest belief. In the end, she folded the letter and looked into the dancing flame of the lantern. She didn't see it. She was elsewhere. She was in the darkness and the dust, hiding with Aster and Geder, working puzzles about the ancient dragons and the wars long past. If the Geder Palliako she'd known was taking these steps, what would he mean by them? For a moment, she saw him again as he had been the last time they'd been together: in the street smelling of vomit and another man's blood, trying awkwardly to invite her to stay for tea.

She shuddered.

"Was there a question Komme wanted to ask me about this?"

"Not specifically. Your impression of the author. Whether your experience matched what he says."

"It does," Cithrin said. "As to the writer...The details are all as I'd expect, or near enough. The conclusions seem sound. I've only been in Camnipol once, and that was under peculiar circumstances, but this description is more plausible for me than the one Paerin gave."

"So you would trust the source?"

"Not without knowing who it is, no," Cithrin said. "But I'd read the next letter carefully and treat it with respect. And I'd prepare for another Antean war, though I couldn't say against whom."

"Sarakal," Isadau said, rising from her chair. "The report came in from friends of Komme in Asinport that Lord Skestinin's fleet had sailed east and south. Komme expects Antea will march early in the spring if they haven't already."

Cithrin felt a deep dread welling up in her breast, but she only nodded.

"What is the bank's position?"

Isadau nodded, her chitinous lips pressing together.

"We've taken contracts on supplies. Food, of course. And we bought out any insurance contracts for caravans heading north and invested in three roundships that will be ready to offer an alternate route."

"And the local coin and spice? Will we be moving it?"

Isadau shook her head.

"Antea can't win against Sarakal," she said. "The traditional families pester each other and play out their vicious little intrigues, but nothing unites them like a common enemy. At the height of its power, the Antean Empire found it easier to respect the border than challenge it, and whether the new Lord Regent recognizes it or not, Antea *is* weakened. There may well be a long and bloody fight. The borders may shift. It's unlikely that Nus will change hands, though I suppose it's possible. There will doubtless be starvation and blood on both sides, but Sarakal won't fall."

"You don't think he'll come here, then?"

"Even the great rulers are constrained by the world," Isadau said. "The empire's ambitions may be vast and ill-considered, but there are still only so many men, so many horses, so many siege engines, and there's a great deal of territory in Sarakal that will resist being passed through. If the armies of Antea come to Suddapal, it will be because the nature of the world has changed in a way that hasn't happened since the dragons fell. So no, they won't come here. Not in my lifetime, and not in yours."

Clara

The end of the winter's hunt had always been a difficult and pleasant time. The long, dark weeks drew near their end, and Dawson returned from whatever corner of the empire his friend and king had taken him. He would come back to the holdfast at Osterling Fells exhausted and moody and spend the better part of a week complaining that the journey back to Camnipol for the opening of the season was coming too soon, that there was too much work to be done on his lands. The progress of every improvement and renovation would be weighed and found wanting, the questions of law that had waited for his word would be answered and justice meted out, and slowly, his shoulders would relax, his smile become easier. He claimed it was the comfort of being at home and with her, but it was also anticipation. She remembered lying in bed with him, their bodies pleasantly spent, and listening to the gossip from the hunt and the dripping of melting ice. Her husband was a prickly man, loyal as a dog and proud as a cat, and he found the guiding star of his life in preserving the world against change. The fears that haunted his worst nights had always been that his children might inherit a kingdom debased from the one he had been given and that his wife might be discontent. When the time came to leave the Fells for their compound in the city, he was champing at the bit to resume the battles and intrigues of court. It was the work he'd been born to.

And so every spring, Dawson would go through the holdings one last time, giving orders and coin, instructions to his vassals that would take them through another summer and guide the lands that he protected safely to autumn. Every spring, husband and wife would travel the dragon's road back to Camnipol, the rhythm of the team's hoofs creating martial music as the couple leaned against one another in the well-cushioned carriage. Every spring, she would take charge of the house and see it washed and cleaned and cared for while he snuck out, sheepish and delighted as a boy, to the Fraternity of the Great Bear to drink and smoke and debate with his friends and his enemies.

Every spring until this one.

Clara had seen the first arrivals. The grand carriage of Lord Flor clattering along the black cobbles inside the southern gate, ribbons trailing from it and a crier on horseback clearing its path. Lady Flor, who had more than once sat in Clara's withdrawing room and shared the intimate details of her husband's infidelities, had been looking out the window. Perhaps she hadn't recognized the grey-cloaked woman walking through the street as her old friend. Perhaps she had. That had been three days ago. Winter's grip loosened, and the court returned to Camnipol.

Clara listened to the familiar knock at her door. Her thin wooden door hardly robust enough to keep the wind out. Not Vincen's tapping, but the proprietary rap of his cousin Abatha.

"M'lady, I know you're in there."

"I am indisposed," Clara said.

"Second day running you said that," Abatha said. "Vincen's worrying you've got lady troubles."

Clara laughed despite herself.

"How delicate of him," she said.

The wooden flooring creaked as the keep shifted her weight.

"I don't like to mention it," Abatha said, and then didn't go on. She didn't need to. The rent was due, and Clara didn't have the coin to pay.

"Yes, thank you," Clara said, still not rising from her bed. "I will see it taken care of."

The creaking footsteps went away toward the kitchen and left Clara alone. Pale, soiled sunlight shouldered its way through the oiled parchment of the window. Clara's body felt heavy and it ached at the joints, but she hauled herself to sitting and rested her head in her hands. Her skin stuck to itself and her hair fell lank at her shoulders. She had to go to Lord Skestinin's little estate and collect her allowance. She couldn't say whether she hoped that Jorey and Sabiha, her natural son and more recent daughter, had come back yet or dreaded it.

Whatever the case, it had to be done.

"Enough," she chided herself. "Just...*enough*."

An hour later, she emerged from the rooms as if stepping into Camnipol fresh from Osterling Fells. A bit of ribbon held her hair in place. Her dress—one of the few to survive the insurrection—was a bit out of fashion, but the cut flattered and the hem was clean. Thankfully, Vincen had gone to the butcher's for his cousin and Clara could make the walk alone without having to argue. Likely she wouldn't have been able to explain why she wanted her two lives kept separate this way, apart from the fact that she did.

That her son had returned became obvious as soon as she approached the mansions. They were modest almost to the point of self-effacement, but fresh banners flew above the door and no moss or lichen marred the stone façade. The windows stood open to the breeze, yellow curtains billowing from one of the second-floor windows where a servant hadn't made them fast. A Yemmu door slave she didn't recognize stood in the entrance, fixed to the wall with a ceremonial silver chain. Black-inlaid designs decorated the tusks that rose from his lower jaw. Clara smiled at him as she approached.

"My lady," the man rumbled. Bowed almost double, he still stood as high as her shoulder. "How may I serve?"

"I've come to see Jorey Kalliam, if he's available," she said.

"Yes, my lady. And who may I say is calling?"

It was an excellent question, and one with several answers.

"His mother," she said.

Sunlight streamed through the sitting room's windows, and a cheerful little fire popped and muttered in the grate. The clean smells of vinegar and soap felt almost like coming home after the months in Abatha's boarding house, and Clara let herself relax for a moment. A Firstblood servant girl brought in a cup of coffee and a crust of sweetbread. Clara nodded her gratitude and tried not to consume it all too quickly.

The person who stepped through the doorway wasn't her son. Sabiha Kalliam, once Skestinin, wore a simple gown of pale yellow that warmed the tone of her skin. Her hair draped about her shoulder, its softness at odds with the thinness of her lips and the solidity of her gaze. Clara stood, uncertain for a moment and afraid, before the girl stepped forward and embraced her. She smelled of mint and chamomile, and the warmth of her flesh felt like walking into summer. Clara felt an anxiety she hadn't known she carried drop away.

"Oh, my dear," she said, and then ran out of words.

The moment passed, and the two women stepped apart and sat. Clara found herself wanting to take Sabiha's hand, to preserve the moment of contact a little longer, but the seating arrangements didn't allow it.

"Jorey will be along soon," Sabiha said. "How have you been?" The hardness in her voice sounded almost like regret. Clara gestured vaguely.

"Some days are better than others. Much as one might expect, I suppose. I have taken the liberty of stopping by and seeing my grandson. They've named him Pindan, which is apparently some sort of family name."

"My uncle that died," Sabiha said. "How is he? My... How is my son?"

"He's a boy," Clara said, chuckling. "He eats his own weight when he isn't fasting, gets everywhere he ought not be, and thinks it hilarious to smear mud on people's legs."

Sabiha's cheeks flushed and she nodded. For a man of the court, an illegitimate child might be an annoyance or even an opportunity to boast. Lords had been known to take their bastards as squires or put them into the more lucrative sorts of trade. It was one of many little asymmetries between the sexes.

"And you?" Clara asked. "I haven't seen you since you left for the season."

Sabiha lifted her eyebrows and looked down.

"Jorey thought it important that we attend the hunt," she said. "My father agreed. It was...I don't know. It was long, tiring, humiliating, and hard. Jorey does what he can to take the worst of it on himself, but it wore on him. He didn't sleep well, and I don't know whether the feasts we weren't welcome to chafed more than the ones he attended."

"Poor boy," Clara said, fitting a river of melancholy into

the two words. Jorey was her youngest son, and in some ways the one of her children the world had been cruelest with. Vicarian was safely in the church. Barriath, before he left, had been in battles, but only at sea and never particularly vicious ones at that. Jorey had helped to slaughter a city, and the ghosts of it walked behind him. The guilt had driven him to marry Sabiha in hopes of cleansing her name, and instead of raising her up, he had made her position in the court less tenable. Clara thought her son's spine was made of pure enough metal to stand the strain. She hoped so.

"Some days were better," Sabiha said.

"And you?" Clara asked, drawing her pipe from her pouch and filling the bowl with a pinch of cheap tobacco. "God alone knows this can't have been easy for you either."

"It wasn't so bad," Sabiha said, her smile thin and oddly cruel. She took a twig from the fire and offered Clara the ember for her pipe. "I'm used to people pointing at me and whispering down their sleeves. I suppose I'm glad it's not my past they're amusing themselves with. It hasn't left me with a deeper love of the court in general, though."

"I imagine not," Clara said, and drew the smoke into her lungs.

The pause was not entirely comfortable. Sabiha moved her head in one direction and then the other, testing out words without speaking them. Clara waited, knowing well how such things took their own time. The young woman's hands relaxed just before she spoke.

"I don't know how to *help* him."

"Mother!" Jorey said, pushing through the door. His smile looked almost genuine. Clara rose into his arms. Regret that he hadn't waited just a few minutes more was washed away by the scent of his hair and the strength in his arms around her. Her little boy had grown to a man, but she would always see him as an infant sitting up by himself for the first time, an expression of wordless triumph on his dough-soft face. Holding him, she was neither the widow of a traitor she had been nor the half-formed woman she was becoming, but only the mother of her child. It was enough.

The moment passed and he pulled away.

"It's good to see you again," he said.

"And also you, dear," Clara said. "Sabiha's been telling me that the hunt was as much a masculine bore as ever, and I was acting as though I missed it."

"I didn't think you ever went," Jorey said, sitting at his wife's side. Clara took her own seat, gesturing with her pipe.

"It seemed polite to pretend," she said. Jorey laughed, and Sabiha looked surprised for a moment before she smiled herself. "I'm sorry to say that I've come begging."

"Of course," Jorey said. "I'm sorry we didn't leave you better provisioned. But—"

"I have been quite content with what I've had," Clara said. And then, with a bit of effort to keep her tone light, "One of your father's huntsmen has taken me a bit under his wing. Vincen Coe."

"Father's private man?" Jorey said. "The one who always went with him when he was intriguing against Feldin Maas?"

"Yes, him," Clara said, silently regretting having mentioned him. Only she didn't want it to seem as if she'd been hiding him if Jorey found out through some other channel, and now that he was back home it was so much more likely that he would, and damn it if she didn't feel the beginning of a blush rising in her cheeks. "His cousin has a boarding house, and she's been kind enough to give me a very pleasant room. Not the best neighborhood, but what is, these days?"

She pretended to catch an ember in her throat, coughing to explain the redness of her face. It wasn't the first time she'd used the subterfuge, though the last time had certainly been a decade or more ago. Jorey called for a servant girl to bring a cup of water, and by the time Clara had drunk it down, she had her composure again.

"I'm sorry," she said, seeming to apologize for the coughing fit but meaning something more diffuse.

"Are you feeling better?" Jorey asked, and she wasn't certain what he meant by the question. She answered the simplest option.

"Yes, dear. Just breathed in something I oughtn't."

"I was hoping to see you," Jorey said. "I'm looking at ways to bring the family back into favor."

"I can't imagine that will be easy."

Jorey held up a hand, asking her to hear him out.

"Geder came to me," he said. "He...apologized to me, in a way. I think despite everything he'd be open to rehabilitating me within the court."

"And would you be open to that?" Clara said, more tartly than she'd intended.

"If he'll have me," Jorey said. Sabiha took his hand as if she were comforting a child, but he took no notice. His voice had the light cadence of conversation, but his gaze grew distant. "Geder is Lord Regent. He's the nearest thing we'll have to a king until Aster comes of age, and that's years from now. We've lost the holding and the mansions. Barriath's gone. I'm living on the sufferance of my wife and her father, and you're in a boarding house, living off the scraps from that. Geder doesn't associate me with what Father did, even if everyone else does. He can put me in position to win a name back."

"So you'd forgive him," Clara said.

"No," Jorey said, "but I don't see that it matters. The world isn't what it was a year ago. I have to take care of you and Sabiha. I want to wake up in a bed I own. I want Sabiha treated with respect. I want you invited to all the occasions that they've excluded you from. If I have to kneel down before a man I hate in order to do that, it's a small price."

He shrugged, and it was the motion he had always had. A gesture she had felt when he'd still been in the womb. Clara smiled and nodded, then turned her eyes to Sabiha. The dread in the girl's expression was like looking into a mirror.

I don't know how to help him either, she thought.

Might be a blessing," Vincen Coe said.

"Odd sort of blessing," she said and sipped at her beer.

The taproom went by the name Yellow House, and it stood at the edge of the Division just by the Silver Bridge. The sun had only just set, and the torches that lit the court-yard radiated heat without going so far as to warm her. But the drink was cheap and the soup wasn't just water and hope, so it would do.

"Puts him in places to hear things," Vincen said. "Even just having him in the Great Bear would be enough to fill one of your letters every day or two. What the debates were, and who was arguing which side. Might even come to a place he'd know orders before they were sent."

"No. I don't want him to be part of this. Not directly, any-way," she said, leaning close to him and speaking softly. "If I find myself invited to tea or a sewing circle because of his place in the court, I won't be so rude as to refuse. But I won't use him without his knowledge, and I won't have him know."

"I can respect that," Vincen said.

"And I'm not going to send the army's orders to the enemy. I'm not a traitor."

"If you say so, m'lady," Vincen said.

At the edge of the yard, a traveling theater company had set up their stage. A round-faced girl and an older man lit a hundred candles in tin reflectors set all along the stage's edge. Beyond them, the deeper dark of the Division, and then the torches and lanterns of the far side, as distant, it seemed, as stars.

She drank the yeasty, thick beer and wondered whether she might be a traitor. Geder Palliako was, after all, the crown. His failure and the failure of the empire were difficult threads to tease apart. She had risked her own life for King Simeon, and without regret. If anything, she felt herself more a patriot now, standing against the crown, than she had standing with it.

But Jorey had been right. The world wasn't what it was a year ago. The Severed Throne as she'd known it was gone. The buildings might be the same, the city, even the people, but the nature of the empire—its soul—had changed. It might be possible to betray this new empire and not what it had been. A loyal traitor, then? It seemed absurd and enticing both. She wondered whether one could be faithful to the past and yet not be bound by its rules. Perhaps it was only the beer, but the question seemed heavy with importance.

"Do you know—" she began, but Vincen shook his head and gestured toward the stage.

"Show," he said.

A dark-haired woman had taken the stage, her smile haughty and wild.

"Come!" she cried, her voice filling the darkness. "Gather near, my friends, or if you are faint of heart, move on. For our tale is one of grand adventure. Love, war, betrayal, and vengeance shall spill out now upon these boards, and I warn you not all that are good end well. Not all that are evil are punished." Clara felt her throat growing thick, her heart beating faster. The words seemed like a threat. Or worse, a promise. "Come close, my friends, and know that in our tale as in the world, *anything* may happen."

Geder

The first battle of the war came at a garrison ten miles from the low hills that marked the border. Ice still clung to the edges of the creek, and snow lurked at the roots of the trees and the northern sides of the walls where the sun could not reach them. Lord Ternigan led the vanguard himself, waiting until midday when the sun offered the enemy no advantage. If the soldiers of the keep had taken the field, it would have been the work of an hour, but instead the iron and oak doors closed, and Ternigan's men withdrew to prepare their brief and bloody siege.

"Why didn't they just go around it?" Aster asked.

Geder tapped his lips with the reports, thinking. In truth, he'd been in the field considerably less than Ternigan had, and though he had read deeply on the theory, practice, and history of war, the analysis of men who'd spent more years conducting it was still sometimes obscure to him. He felt Aster deserved an answer, though, and he did his best.

"If you just go on, then you leave them at your back," he said, fairly certain that was right. "An enemy you haven't destroyed utterly could always regain strength and come at you."

Aster's brow creased as the boy considered this, then he nodded.

"Go on," the boy said. "Keep reading."

The forces of Antea outnumbered the garrison keep by

easily five men for every Timzinae or Jasuru, but the keep walls were well made and maintained. Ternigan began by sending a squad of archers and hawkers to the east to bring down any rider or bird sent to alert the enemy or call for aid. The siege engines were constructed in the dim evening just beyond arrowshot of the keep's walls. In the night, Ternigan patrolled to slaughter the fleeing enemy, and caught and killed nearly a dozen. The priests that had come with the army spoke their sermon by firelight, and their words— that the destiny of Antea to bring peace to the world began here, that the spirits of the dead would ride with them in the morning and make their assault unstoppable, that the rising tide of war would lift them all to glory—so filled the men with lust for battle that Lord Ternigan had to argue against making a night attack.

In the morning, with spring frost still glazing the tents—

"Oh that's nice," Aster said.

"Ternigan's reports do have a certain poetry," Geder agreed. Basrahip, sitting a little apart, coughed out a short laugh.

In the morning, with spring frost still glazing the tents, Ternigan called the attack. The desperation and fear of the defenders came clear at the start. The rain of arrows and stones held no reserve, and a cunning man hidden in the keep's walls threw great gouts of living flame from the keep's single tower. The crew of a battering ram was lost to the flames before a bolt brought the cunning man down. When a second crew began to falter under the defenders' arrows, Ternigan had called the charge, bringing the body of the army up behind them. With their own men blocking the path of retreat, the men's resolve stiffened, and at the last, Ternigan dismounted, putting his own hand to the ram for the final dozen critical blows.

When the keep's doors fell at last, Ternigan led the charge. There were few Timzinae and Jasuru in the keep, but they were wild with despair. Rooting them out took the better part of the day and took its toll in men, including Ternigan's own squire. But the sun set on the banners of Antea flying above the conquered keep, and the first true victory of the war could now be unequivocally announced.

Geder folded the last page and dropped it on his desk. His private rooms in the heart of the Kingspire were grand and beautiful—carved stone and rich tapestry, wide vaulted ceilings. The gentle light of the afternoon sun filtered through the finest glass in the world. The scent of lavender and lamp oil filled the air. They were also home now, the place where Geder could retreat from the demands of the court. Here, he could rest at ease with his velvets undone and scratch himself when he itched. Aster sat at the great table where Daskellin had had a map of Sarakal, Elassae, the Free Cities, and southern Antea built. It wasn't as detailed as the war rooms dedicated to the re-creation of the paths of armies and the death of cities, but it served as a good general reminder of the shape of things. Here was Nus, there the thin green threads of the dragon's roads, at the southern edge the mountains that kept Sarakal from fading into Elassae, and the far city of Inentai that guarded the mountains' end. Each keep and holdfast was marked by a tiny pewter model. Geder leaned forward, plucked the first of these from the dirt of the map, and put it back in place with the red banner of the spider goddess with its eightfold sigil flying from its minute rooftop.

"Do you think it's true?" Aster asked.

"What bit?" Geder asked.

"Do you think it was really like that? With Lord Ternigan

taking the battering ram and the frost on the tents and the cunning man calling up flames?"

"That part, I don't know. The number of lost soldiers is probably accurate or nearly so. I have other men who can confirm all that. And how long it took to win the keep. The things that can be measured and counted, I don't think he'd dare exaggerate. But the rest?"

"You think he lied?"

"I read a fair number of field reports from all through history," Geder said, "and they didn't match my experience."

Aster glanced over at Basrahip, and the massive priest lifted his eyebrows.

Geder hadn't known many children. Growing up, he had been the only child in the manor, and the boys and girls of the village had been only occasional companions. But even then, Geder thought that the patterns of age must be invisible to the people suffering them. Aster was his example. It was almost two years now since King Simeon had come and asked Geder to become protector of the prince. Geder could almost think that the boy he sat with now had been there, but that was an illusion. Aster had grown a bit taller, yes, but more than that, he had grown into himself. The planes of his face were still gentle, but not those of a child. Or at least not as often. He had become stronger too, leaner. There were still years before Aster became a man grown and took his crown, but Geder could see glimpses of that man. That king. It left him proud and melancholy both. If he was going to give Aster a world that was truly at peace for the first time since the dragons fell, he wouldn't be able to rest, and there were days he would have liked nothing better than to sleep late, eat in the library, and nap in the sun. He had known that being Lord Regent would be a sacrifice. Even with all the power and status it gave him, carrying the weight of empire was only supportable because he was doing it for Aster.

That was what he told himself, anyway. He also could admit to himself that there were some parts of wielding power that he would miss, when the time came.

"Lord Palliako?" The old man bowed almost double as he came into the room. Ever since he'd come back after the insurrection with the courage to break from small traditions like letting other people bathe and dress him, Geder had gotten a reputation with the servants of the Kingspire. It made them much more respectful. "The general audience is ready, my lord."

Geder stood, pulling his robes back into their best trim. Basrahip rose from his seat beside the window and stepped toward him, gentle for so large a man.

"All right, then," Geder said. "Let's clean this all up, shall we?"

When he turned toward the door, the servant's face was pale. Geder glanced behind him, half expecting to see an assassin or a bee. Some sort of danger. There was nothing but the room.

"What? What's the matter?"

The servant swallowed and coughed.

"Your crown," Aster said, and Geder's hand rose to his bare brow. "It's back here."

"Thank you," Geder said, taking the metal circlet and putting it on. "How does it look?"

"Regal," Aster said.

Geder struck an exaggerated pose. The boy prince laughed and Geder laughed with him.

The general audience was reputed to be one of the great chores of the regency. Over the long months of the winter, requests for audience had built up like water behind a dam: magistrates who wished to escalate their decisions to the highest possible authority, prisoners of the crown who wished to make a case for clemency, and the assorted small business of sitting the Severed Throne. Geder had never done the thing, never even attended one, and he looked forward to the enterprise.

The hall set aside for the general audience stood a hundred yards or so from the base of the Kingspire, and the massive presence of the building looming above gave the event a sense of grandeur that bordered on the ominous. The seat here was the actual Severed Throne, the ancient metal scarred where Bacian Ocur cut it and Annan the Forge made it whole. Or so tradition had it. The truth behind the legend was anybody's guess.

From his seat, Geder looked out over a sea of faces. Gold and gems glittered from the arms and breasts of the nobles. The merchants wore furs and fine wool. And behind them, kneeling, what serfs, peasants, and prisoners had managed to convince the bureaucrats of the court that their issues merited the Lord Regent's attention. His personal guard stood at his back, and palace guards lined the processional that led to him. Geder couldn't help grinning, at least at first. The empire had brought its knottiest puzzles to him for judgment—the terms of land rights, the disposition of slaves, the judgment of crime, and the assessment of punishment. All manner of questions of justice waited for his mind to untangle, and whatever he decided right would become right by the mere act of his decision. In all, it seemed the best entertainment possible.

Only, of course, without Basrahip at his side, it would have been awful.

"Are you ready?" Geder asked.

"Yes, Prince Geder," replied the priest, bowing. He lumbered down to his place in the closest row of observers, standing to the side, where Geder could see him. Geder felt a moment's anxiety, worried that Basrahip might move out of earshot or be blocked by someone in the court. And then by the sense of being exposed. He had the sudden, powerful image of hidden archers loosing arrows at him where he sat. He never used to have worries like that. Another legacy of Dawson Kalliam. Eyeing the crowd with a wariness they didn't deserve, he raised his hand, and the general audience began.

The issues came before him in order of precedence: the nobles first by rank, then the untitled of noble blood, ambassadors and foreign nobles with Antean family, then those without, then the merchant houses with letters of association, then those without, with mere people filling whatever time was left before king or regent grew too weary and postponed the rest until next year. Two illegitimate sons of a minor lord each claimed to have been promised the same dyeyard from their father's estate. Geder had them both recount their versions of the tale, and then watched for Basrahip's gentle nod or slight shake of the head. A Jasuru woman presented a contract that bound a local merchant to sell to her at a price lower than the market would otherwise provide him. The merchant swore the document was forged. Basrahip's tiny movements assured him that the document was genuine, but Geder made a show of asking probing questions and examining the document before he ruled, and for the crime of lying to the Lord Regent, he had the merchant taken to the new gaol for a month and his left earlobe cut off. With each issue put before him, Geder became more comfortable in his role as the dispenser of justice and wisdom. By the time they had reached the last of the merchant houses, he hardly needed Basrahip's advice any longer. For hours, the assembly had watched him cut through lies and misrepresentations, finding the truth with the unerring skill of a hunting dog. He saw fear in the faces of the liars and respect in those whose fortunes he made whole. Really, there was nothing better.

There were some issues that didn't hinge on deceit, in which the facts were established and uncontested, and only the interpretation of them was in question. He didn't like those as much, but he gave them his best guess or else put off the decision until he could look into some fine point of history and common practice in more detail. He could see the disappointment in the faces when he said that, but no one objected. He was Lord Regent Geder Palliako. He was the man who had revealed the treachery of Feldin Maas and Asterilhold, waged a war of reunification and defeated a coup in a single year, and saved the empire twice over. He was a hero. Anything he did was right by definition.

The only unexpected event came nearly at the day's end. The Dartinae man came to the foot of the throne, kneeling in a bow so deep he pressed his knuckles to the floor. He was strong for one of his race, his skin dark from the sun, and his eyes glowed as bright as torches. His tunic was well-worn leather with the sigil of a dragon inked on the chest like a poor man's coat of arms.

"Dar Cinlama?" Geder said, reading the name from the petition.

"Lord Regent. Thank you for hearing me out. I was afraid your other business might eat the day," the man said. There was an amusement in his voice and a sureness of purpose. Even though his words were appropriate and acceptable, they gave the sense that they were equals, two men speaking as men instead of a dusty petitioner before the guiding hand of the Antean Empire. Geder envied him his certainty and disliked him.

"You want me to fund a mission to ... where?"

Cinlama smiled.

"If I was sure of that, it would already be too late. Someone would already have found it."

"It?"

"What there is to be found. The Temple of the Sun. The Salt Scrolls. The lost books of Erindau."

"Those were forgeries," Geder said, pouncing too quickly. Cinlama smiled.

"The ones presented so far have been. The true ones are still out there. That's the thought, isn't it? My father and his spent their lives in the lost places where the dragon's roads don't go. I've climbed caverns mankind hadn't touched in centuries and found carved stone at the bottom. There's mysteries out there still. Treasures going back all the way to the Dragon Empire. Gems and jewels. Books of knowledge and magic. Devices from the war we don't even remember except in stories we tell the kids to get them to sleep."

"And you know how to find these marvels." Geder loaded the words with skepticism.

"I know how to look. Finding's a gamble, but if it pays out, there's no higher prize."

No was already on his lips when Geder glanced over at Basrahip. The minister's eyes were wide, his brows lifted. The pretense of prayer and contemplation were gone, and in their place something that could have been alarm or delight. Geder swallowed his refusal and waited, but Basrahip neither nodded nor shook his head.

"Um," Geder said. "I will have to consider my answer."

"My thanks for that, Lord Regent," Cinlama said, smiling.

Geder leaned toward his guard captain. "See him somewhere safe. And don't let him leave."

The captain nodded, but there was a hesitation in it.

"You mean the gaol, my lord?"

"No. A guesthouse. Or put him in one of the gardens.
Just...just don't let him leave."

After that, Geder heard a shepherd asking recompense for
his flock, slaughtered by a drunken priest, but by then the
joy had gone out of it. He called the halt and withdrew, his
guard walking ahead and behind. He stopped at a dry fountain, a copper dragon almost lost to verdigris throwing itself
toward the sky, the bodies of the thirteen races of humanity
drawn along behind it. Or, looked at differently, pulling it
down. Basrahip came shortly thereafter, his face pinched in
thought.

"You heard something?" Geder said. "The adventurer.
You...I mean, do you think he means what he says?"

"He does," the priest said. "He did not mislead you,
Prince Geder. He seeks what he claims to seek. I would
speak with him, if I might."

Geder pulled his hands into his sleeves, warming his fingers with the ends like mittens.

"I thought as much. I had the guard take him somewhere
comfortable and hold him."

"You are good to us," Basrahip said, but he seemed distracted. "This man's errand may be of importance. For time
beyond time, the dragons have envied and hated the goddess. If buried shells survived the fire years, we must know.
His coming may be the hand of the goddess in the world."

"Oh," Geder said. "Then you think I should accept his
petition?"

Basrahip put a thick hand on Geder's shoulder.

"I will speak with him and know more. The goddess's web is wide as the world and deeper than oceans. Nothing escapes her notice. If he is indeed sent by her, we must honor him."

"I suppose we will, then," Geder said. "If the conversation goes the way you hope."

"My thanks, Prince Geder."

"I'm chosen by the goddess to bring peace to the world. Really, whatever she says needs to be done, we should do it," he said.

For the most part, he meant it. The little tug of reluctance was only caution and a rational skepticism. They were in the early stages of a war, after all. They might need to buy food or mercenaries, and if the coin was already spent, that would mean levying taxes or borrowing. So it was best to be certain. He was Lord Regent of Antea. He was the most powerful man in the world. This Dar Cinlama was a wanderer and a beggar, and if Basrahip was enthusiastic about him, it was only because the Dartinae man might be an apt tool for Geder's projects. That was all. Of all people in the world, Geder told himself, surely he had the least reason to be jealous.

Marcus

No one knew how long the dragons had ruled the world, only that they had. The greatest empire that could be imagined had spanned the seas and lands of mankind and for all anyone knew more besides. The skill and rigor of the dragons had bent the nature of the world to their desires. The thirteen races of humanity and the dragon's roads were two of their great works that had survived, but many others had passed away. Great cities had floated in the distant air, competing with the clouds for space in the sky. Poems and chants had been composed by inhuman minds with such complexity and beauty that a lifetime's study still might not do them justice. Devices had been built that set the stars themselves in order and laid plain the books of fate.

Or perhaps they hadn't. A lot of history could be lost in a generation. One of Marcus's grandfathers had been a minor noble of Northcoast who'd kept his grandmother as mistress. The other had been a sailor who'd made his money fishing cod and avoiding port taxes. All he knew of them was a dozen or so stories he'd heard as a boy and likely misremembered.

The ages since the fall of the Dragon Empire had swallowed that a thousand thousand times over and left only legends and stories, roads and ruins.

What little there was, though, still had the power to awe.

Larger than the palaces of Northcoast or Birancour, the vast stronghold spread out before them, sinking down into the flesh of the earth level upon terraced level. Ivy clung to the spiral towers and magnificent stone arches. A few brave trees had forced their way through seams in the great blocks of dragon's jade, their bark bellying over the pavement and their roots spidering out in the vain search for deeper soil. Black water pooled in the low places, thick with slime. Bright-plumed parrots fluttered and complained from the trees and the towers, and tiny scarlet frogs leapt from leaf to broad leaf with a ticking sound like dry twigs breaking. Stepping out from the jungle canopy for the first time in days, Marcus stared up at an open sky the color of sapphires.

"My *God*," Kit said.

"Wouldn't think it'd be so easy to hide something that big," Marcus said. "Any thoughts as to what we do from here?"

"I expect that the reliquary itself will be in the deepest part of the ruins, guarded and barred."

"The intent being to keep out people like us."

"Yes."

"Wish I'd brought a pry bar," Marcus said. "We should find shelter for the night. This isn't our territory, and those very hospitable Southlings who told us none of this existed won't be pleased we proved them wrong."

"Can you imagine it, Captain?" Master Kit asked. "This was a citadel of the dragons. These walls have stood here since before the war. Humanity might well have been feral when these stones were set."

"Or they might have caught us all as slaves to set them. Careful. Snake."

"What?" Kit said. Then, "Oh." He moved to the side,

and the black-and-silver serpent slid away down the steps toward the dark pools below.

By the time they found a chamber that met Marcus's approval, the sapphire sky had darkened to indigo, the parrots had all vanished, and the evening's swarm of midges filled the air. An early bat, its wings fluttering wildly, spun through the air above the ruins, eating its fill of the insects. The smells of decay and still water filled the air. Marcus sat with his back against a cool stone wall while Kit measured out the evening meal of nuts and the last strips of dried meat from a foxlike animal Marcus had trapped three days before. His clothes were little more than rags, and he'd had to put another hole in his belt to keep it from slipping off his hips.

The journey had thinned Kit as well. The actor's handsome face was craggy now, and his beard looked brittle and dull. Marcus took the food with a nod of thanks and Kit lowered himself to sit across the narrow chamber. Likely it had been storage, back when it had been anything. The door had stood a bit ajar for centuries before Marcus was born, its hinges rusted away to black streaks. The ceiling was low enough that any attackers would have to come in hunched and vulnerable, and whatever animal had left its spoor in the corners hadn't been back recently. It was as good as home.

"Start searching at first light?" Kit asked.

"That suits. And we'll need to find something to eat. Freshwater. Ancient hoard of the dragons won't do us much good if we starve to death."

"I suppose not," Kit said.

"I'll take first watch."

Kit nodded in the growing gloom. Even if they'd found something dry enough to burn, they couldn't afford the luxury of a fire. Any Southling patrol would see the light of it from seven miles off, jungle or no. Kit yawned and settled down against the far wall. Marcus took his sword in its rotting sheath and laid it across his knees, preparing for the long hours of darkness. Outside their little shelter, something ticked, ticked again, and began a whirring insectile song. Another joined in, and soon the ruins were alive with the sound of inhuman life. The walls and terraces that the dragons had designed were a vast city for beetles and midges, frogs and snakes. And two men whose minds and comprehension of the world was likely nearer to the midges than the dragons. Marcus let himself wonder what the builders of his little shelter would have thought if they'd known, however many centuries ago, that in the vast span of time their work would fall this far. Despair, maybe, that all their efforts were doomed. Or pride that what they did would leave a mark on the world that, though it might change its shape and meaning, would not be erased.

And nothing could ever really boast permanence. Every castle fell in time. Every empire. Every man. Even these walls would eventually be buried by the jungle, though the slow accretion of fallen leaves and grit might take ten times longer than had already passed. There was a kind of consolation in the thought that nothing lasts forever.

"Do you think they're all right?" Kit asked. His voice was gentle, already half asleep. "Cary and Sandr and the rest?"

"Probably," he said, and Kit chuckled.

"I keep thinking of things I want to say to them. Two days ago, I thought of a simple, clear explanation for Charlit Soon about why the king's role in The Song of Love and Salt has to be played as a Haaverkin or Jasuru. When I realized I couldn't tell her, it was disappointing."

Marcus grunted.

"And Cithrin. I assume your own thoughts are with her."

"And Yardem," Marcus said.

"What are you going to do, when it's over? Will you go back to them?"

The last time he'd seen Cithrin bel Sarcour, she'd been leaving for Carse with two of his guardsmen and not him. The last word he'd had of her, she'd been lost in the chaos of a political coup in Camnipol. He knew all too well what happened to rich, unarmed women during political uprisings. He tapped a thumb on the body of his blade.

"Once we're done, I'll find them," Marcus said, "and if Cithrin's hurt or dead and I could have stopped it, I'll kill Yardem."

Kit shifted in the gloom.

"You would do that?" he asked, though he already knew the answer.

"Well, I might. Yardem's good, though, and he's got reach on me, but one of us will be leaving on a plank."

"And if Cithrin's well?"

"Likely the same."

The chirring song of insect wings was the only sound for a moment. When Kit spoke again, he sounded more awake.

"You're not having the nightmares any longer, are you? About your wife and daughter. What happened before doesn't seem to be troubling you."

"They'll come back," he said, meaning the dreams of burning. "They always do. Right now, I've got more than enough nightmare just getting up in the morning."

"I think Yardem was right about you and the shape of your soul."

"Then he knew the consequences of locking me in that

dovecote," Marcus said. "You should sleep, Kit. We have a lot of ground to cover and no particular idea what we're looking for. Tomorrow is going to be long."

For five days, they searched the ruins, waking with the first light and stopping when the darkness forced them to. Even in the torrential rains that came with midday, Marcus pressed on, pulling back growth of vines and scraping through layers of moss and lichen that had grown hard and thick as armor. Twice they found nests of broad gold-and-red beetles that defended against his intrusion by rising in the air, thick as smoke, forcing their bodies into their noses and mouths as if to choke them. Once, something paced them for a long hour, though Marcus never saw more of it than a massive shadow, low against the ground.

The ruins were vast and complex, not a palace buried in green. Halls led into the body of the earth. Doorways lurked, hidden by the growth of the jungle. Towers stood, their windows empty and open as the eye sockets of sun-bleached skulls.

They knew they were coming close when they found the bodies.

The first bones had been a massive beast once, its jaw as long as Marcus's arm. Three rows of teeth, serrated edges still as sharp as knives, littered the paving stones, a scattering of pale bone on lichen black. Marcus knelt. Thin bits of gristle still clung in the depths of the joints, but the time that had cleaned away the flesh had replaced it with moss. He brushed it off with his fingers.

"What was it, do you think?" Kit asked.

"Big. You see the notches in the bone here and right there? That's where spears took it."

"A guardian, perhaps," Kit said. "A sentry set to watch over the reliquary for the ages."

Marcus rubbed the back of his hand against his chin.

"Would have been on the old side," he said.

"Assian Bey was said to be an engineer for the dragon Asteril," Kit said. "There are tales of the dragons setting guards who could sleep away years until they were disturbed."

"A trap with teeth, then," Marcus said. "Well, the good news is that someone's killed it for us."

"And the bad?"

Marcus didn't answer.

The chambers beneath the ruins were dim as night, and the improvised torches of tree branch and moss smoked badly. They walked carefully through a hall larger than the grandest ballroom in Northcoast. The walls were complex with carved designs, and high above them, almost obscured by the shadows, the ceiling seemed to have claws and teeth. It might have been carved stone or stalactites built from the soft fungus of the invading jungle, but it gave Marcus the sense of stepping into the maw of a vast animal. He walked slowly, watching for traps and dangers, and so it was almost an hour before they found the next bones.

The ten men had died quickly and lay where they had fallen. If there had been survivors, they hadn't buried their dead or raised cairns. A vast bronze door stood before them, its seals broken. Marcus and Kit stepped carefully among the dead.

"Dartinae," Marcus said. "One over here that might have been a Cinnae or a very young Firstblood, but most of these were Dartinae."

"I suspect we've found where Akad Silas died. I think I would feel better if I knew what had killed him."

"Poison's my bet," Marcus said, poking his head through the opening of the great bronze door and peering into the inky darkness beyond. "Fill the chamber here with bad air, and when someone opens it, all the swordsmanship in the world won't help you."

"I am beginning to think Assian Bey might perhaps have been a bit overfond of his own cleverness," Kit said sourly.

"It is a vice. Come on. This is as far as they got. Whatever comes next is our problem."

Despite everything they had seen, despite the warnings of bone and flesh, Marcus very nearly didn't see the third guardian of the reliquary before it was too late.

The corridor had narrowed, the ceiling dropping down so low that Marcus could touch it with his fingertips. The statues of dragons clung to the walls, shifting evilly in the dim torchlight. Kit walked beside him, humming tunelessly under his breath. Ahead of them, something glittered in the darkness. And then it moved. Marcus froze, and half a heartbeat later, Kit did as well. Something like massive eyes blinked in the gloom ahead and a low, reedy sound like the breath of a vast animal filled the narrow space. Another beast, Marcus thought, only that seemed wrong. Repeating the same sort of trap didn't seem the thing an overly clever engineer in the last days of the Dragon Empire would do. And anyone who'd come this far would be expecting another trap, would be watching for it. Marcus's blood went cold.

It was a distraction.

He whirled, drawing his sword by instinct, as the massive toothed blade descended from above. He pushed Kit forward and down with the back of his arm, and swung in a desperate parry. The ancient steel met the new and snapped. The evil blades drove in toward Marcus's belly, rusted spikes scraping his sides. The impact knocked the breath out of him but the mechanism would not let him fall. For a moment, Marcus stood in the darkness, uncertain whether he'd just been impaled, waiting for the shock to fade and the pain to come in. He looked down at his belly.

The spike that would have ended him, weakened by centuries of rust, had been broken by his parry. The stump had cut into his skin, but not badly. If he hadn't seen it, if he hadn't turned in the breath that he had, the rusted teeth would have punched into the small of his back deep enough to kill.

"Are you all right?" Kit asked. He sounded awed.

Marcus considered his answers and settled on, "Yeah." He pulled himself out from between the spikes and walked toward the false beast with a confidence born of relief and fear. The eyes were half spheres of gold, the reedy breath a vast bellows.

Beyond it, a long hallway stretched, thick with webs and the scent of rot. They moved through it slowly, alert for the next trap. At the end stood two vast bronze doors with a massive complex of locks, fitted with dozens of crystal vials that still had thick, noxious-looking fluids in them. Turn the wrong wheel, it seemed to say, and release the poison. It took several hours to see that it was a trick, and that the doors could be opened by lifting the bar.

And beyond them, like the boasting display of a king, lay the treasures of the Dragon Empire. A huge tome with letters in worked bronze on its side that Marcus couldn't read. A silver case, the metal tarnished to black, filled with stoppered vials fashioned from dragon's jade. A roll of copper hung like a tapestry with fine lines etched into it showing what appeared to be a massive ship floating in the sky and doing battle with a vast dragon. An urn of orange-and-gold enamel with the image of a weeping Jasuru woman painted in its side. There was no gold, no gems or jewelry, but it hardly mattered. Anything there would have called forth wealth enough that Marcus need never work again for any king of any nation. If they didn't just kill him and take it.

Marcus walked slowly through the reliquary's deepest chamber, his torch held high above him. A mirror in the back caught the light, but its reflection was some other room in a sunlit tower. A wide throne of black wood and yellow silk sat in a corner, and Marcus's skin crawled just being near it.

"Here," Kit said. "It's here."

Kit stood before a simple wooden stand that held a single blade. It was longer than Marcus preferred, designed perhaps for a Tralgu or Yemmu. It would have been unworkable for a Cinnae. The scabbard was green, but deeper and more complex than enameling would explain, like the emerald carapace of a vast beetle.

"Strike a man with it, and he will die," Kit said. "Strike a man like me with it, and all the spiders within him will die as well. We had blades like it at the temple to purify the unclean."

"Meaning kill people like you."

"Meaning that, yes."

"And stick it in a goddess's belly, and we save the world," Marcus said, reaching for it.

Kit stopped him, the old actor's hand on his wrist.

"What's the matter?"

"This is an evil thing. An evil object."

"Come a long way for second thoughts now," Marcus said.

"I know that. I agree with you. But I brought you here, and I feel wrong letting you take this without being certain that you know what you are sacrificing. What I am asking of you...I think I am asking a great deal of you, Marcus. And I consider you my friend."

Marcus tilted his head. Kit's face was somber. The grit and dirt of weeks had ground itself into the man's pores and the greasy wires of his beard and hair. Kit swallowed.

"This weapon is poison," Kit said. "I believe that the cause we carry it in is just, but that will not protect you. It is not only death to those whose skin it cuts; it holds a deeper violence within it. If you carry it—just that, carry it and nothing more—the poison will still affect you. In time, you will grow ill from it, and eventually, *inevitably*, it will kill you."

"It's a sword, Kit," Marcus said, lifting the green scabbard from its place. "They're all like that."

Cithrin

The market houses of Suddapal sat at the edges of the wide, grassy commons. Pillars of black wood carved with delicate whorls and spirals marked the corners of every room, and wall hangings of rich green felt hung where Cithrin would have expected tapestries to be. Where the Grand Market of Porte Oliva assigned stalls to merchants and let the buyers move between them, everything here was in flux. Halfway through a negotiation, some third party might intrude with a better price or an accusation of poor quality, and this was true whether the issue hinged on the price of a single apple or a shipping contract worth half the value of the city. Nor was that the only aspect of the market that left Cithrin feeling at sea.

Her youth had been spent in the Free Cities where Firstblood and Timzinae had lived and worked in very nearly equal proportion. If asked, she would have said that she was perfectly comfortable with the race, with any of the thirteen races of humanity. The market houses of Suddapal showed her that that was not perfectly true. Walking through rooms and corridors filled almost exclusively with the dark-scaled bodies and twice-lidded eyes, she felt conspicuous. She was aware of her slight frame and unscaled, pale skin in a way she had never been before, and she disliked the feeling. And while no one was cruel to her, she could not help noticing that she was watched, considered, and commented upon. By stepping on a boat in Porte Oliva and stepping out in Suddapal she had become an oddity, and she didn't know how to play the role.

Adding to that was the depth of family connection and history that seemed to inform every negotiation. In her first hour, Cithrin heard reference made to the marriages of cousins three generations dead, to favors done by one man's uncle for another's niece, to shelter given by one family to another during the flood of a river whose course had shifted twice in the century since the kindness was offered. The same care and analysis that concerned the noble houses of Birancour or Herez applied to everyone here, and Cithrin despaired of ever mastering it.

Though Cithrin didn't complain, Magistra Isadau seemed to recognize her discomfort. The older woman introduced Cithrin as the voice of the Medean bank in Porte Oliva, gave Cithrin what context she expected her to need before they entered a negotiation, and explained any obscurities that came in once the discussions were over. Isadau never spoke harshly, never condescended, never reminded Cithrin through word or act that one of them was the master here and the other an apprentice in all but name. She didn't need to. The resentment that Cithrin felt came from being aware of her failings already.

"Oh no," Magistra Isadau said, smiling as if she were sad and shaking her head. "We can't accept last year's terms again."

The man across the table from them chuckled. Even seated, he was half a head taller than Isadau. The chitinous scales on his neck and face had begun to grey and crack with age. Cithrin sipped at her tea and smiled politely.

"You don't do yourself any favors gouging us when we're low, Isadau," he said.

"You aren't low. You're at war."

The man's name was Kilik rol Keston, and Cithrin knew from her review of the books that he traded spice and olives from Elassae north to Borja, returning with worked leather and medicines. The bank had insured his caravans every year for the past decade and paid out the contract only once. It was the sort of information she would have used to make her determination in Porte Oliva or that Magister Imaniel would have considered in Vanai. It appeared to be only a part of Magistra Isadau's calculations.

"This isn't a war," Kilik said, "it's the world teaching Antea a lesson about the price of overreach. If anything, it makes my work safer. The traditional families aren't going to be arguing over who gets to levy taxes every half mile of the eastern passage."

"You're hauling food and medicine past refugees," Isadau said. "Next you'll be storing your seed corn in a sparrow's nest."

A thick man passing by their table clapped a wide hand on Kilik's shoulder.

"Why do you even talk to this woman?" the new man asked. "She's only going to rob you."

"Misplaced loyalty," Kilik said sourly.

"Oh, did you want the contract, Samish?" Isadau asked, smiling brightly. Then to Kilik, "You know Samish has been offering very good terms on his insurance contracts."

"Better than yours, that's truth," Samish said, sitting down at Kilik's side. Cithrin felt her gut go tight. Anywhere she had ever been, the intrusion would have been unforgivable. Here, it meant nothing. "What's this hag offering?"

"Half recompense for six on the hundred," Kilik said, and Samish's eyebrows rose like birds taking wing.

"You're joking," he said, and Cithrin thought he sounded genuinely surprised.

"Half recompense on expected sale," Isadau said, "not on cost."

Samish's expression changed to a sly smile and he wagged a scolding finger at Kilik. "You're being tricky with me, brother. But because our fathers fought together, I'll give you five and a half on the hundred."

Kilik looked at Isadau and pointed toward Samish as if to say, *You see how much better I can do?* Cithrin felt a rush of anger, but Isadau laughed.

"My terms don't change," she said, rising from the table. Cithrin sipped down the last of her tea too quickly and got a mouthful of soaked leaf for her trouble. When she stood Isadau took her elbow like they were close confidants and steered her back through the overwhelming din and chatter of the trading house. As they reached the door to the yard, she squeezed Cithrin's arm once and tilted her head in query. Cithrin shrugged.

"I wish we could make our negotiations at the house," Cithrin said. "I hate losing a contract because we were where we could be overheard."

"We didn't lose the contract. Kilik's an old hand at this. He'll spend the rest of the day wandering about talking, and he'll find that Samish is overcommitted. The caravan will take insurance with us because he wants to be the gambler and have the insurance be his safety. He won't risk his trade on someone who might be destitute when the time arrived to make a claim. Not for one-half on the hundred," Isadau said, then paused. When she spoke again, her voice was softer. Her easy joy was gone from it. "I do worry about this war, though."

In the yard, Enen and Yardem Hane leaned against a low stone wall, talking with a Timzinae girl old enough to have a woman's figure but still with the light brown scales of youth. Yardem's ears shifted toward them as they approached and Enen lifted her soft-pelted chin. The girl turned, caught sight of Isadau, and trotted up to meet them.

"Magistra," the girl said.

"I'm afraid you'll have to be more specific, dear," Isadau said. "Maha, this is Magistra Cithrin bel Sarcour from the new Porte Oliva branch. Cithrin, this is my cousin Merid's daughter Maha."

Cithrin nodded her head and the girl matched her before turning back to Isadau.

"Papa said you should come when you can," she said, then leaned closer and shifted to a whisper. "He's got information about the lemon crop."

Isadau nodded and let Cithrin's arm go free.

"I'm afraid I'll have to meet you back at the house," she said.

"That's fine," Cithrin said. The girl took Magistra Isadau's hand, and the pair of them walked briskly off through the gate and out to the uncurbed stone-paved road. Yardem and Enen came forward.

"Is all well, ma'am?" Yardem asked in his soft low voice.

"Apparently," Cithrin said. "But I couldn't start to tell you why."

Enen scratched her collarbone, setting the beads woven into her pelt clicking. "I had that experience of them too. Timzinae are the worst. Haaverkin or Jasuru—even Tralgu, if you don't mind my saying it, Yardem—you deal with them and you at least know you're in for something odd. Timzinae seem just like anyone right up until they don't, and then who the hell knows what they're thinking?"

The city was low all around them, the wide streets with stretches of grass and low scrub between them and the houses making it seem less a city than a village grown vast. Horses and mules drew large carts, men small ones. The air smelled of the sea but also of turned earth and damp. Above them, the sky was a blue so intense it was hard to look at and the sun glowed like a great burning coin. Cithrin crossed her arms as she walked, realizing only after she'd done it that she missed Magistra Isadau's touch and was trying to make up for its loss. She dropped her arms to her sides.

"Where's Roach?" she asked. "Wasn't he on duty today?"

"Took his shift for him, gave him a day's liberty," Yardem said. "He has a nephew getting wed."

"Really?" Cithrin said. "I didn't know he had family in Suddapal."

"Some," Yardem said.

"He never mentioned them to me."

"Don't know that he felt it was his place to, ma'am," Yardem said. Enen cleared her throat in a way that sounded more for preparation than for comfort. Cithrin turned to look at her. The Kurtadam woman's face was masked by the oily seal-like fur of her pelt, but the discomfort showed through in her eyes.

"I was just thinking, Magistra," Enen said. "You might not want to call him that while we're here."

"Who? Roach?" Cithrin said. "Isn't that his name?"

"His name's Halvill," Yardem said. "Halvill rol Kausol. Roach was just what people called him in Porte Oliva. Sort of the way people might call a Southling 'Eyehole' or a Kurtadam 'Clicker.'"

"Oh," Cithrin said. "I didn't know it bothered him."

Yardem shrugged. "He's never said it does. He's not the sort that makes trouble."

"Only if other people hear you saying it, they might take it wrong is all," Enen said.

"I understand," Cithrin said, trying to recall how many times she'd called the little Timzinae guard by name and who had been present when she had. "Thank you."

Cithrin had spent most of her life being alone. As a girl, she had been the odd one of her cohort, fitting as poorly with the children of nobility as the urchins who ran in the streets. When she left Vanai, she had adopted false identities, from boy carter to agent of the Medean bank, which had required a certain distance from the world to remain plausible. The work of banking itself was isolated. Simply being known as the woman who could lift a poor man to wealth so long as he was wise, prudent, and lucky—or destroy the highborn if they were prodigal and weak—made her a race of one. She was a banker, and so of course she was alone.

Still, the isolation she felt in the compound at Suddapal was unlike the cultivated distances she'd experienced before. Here, she could retreat to her room, close the door behind her, and feel like a prisoner waiting for the magistrate's justice, or else she could go out into the compound and be greeted and welcomed to half a dozen conversations and endeavors from quilting to shoeing horses to sitting with the children of the family and improvising poetry, and never once feel she was truly at home. Being alone in her room, trapped by the walls, was unpleasant. Being alone in the midst of a group that seemed to go out of its way to make her welcome was worse. The only solace she could take was the branch's books and kitchen's wine cellar, and so over weeks, she had become a citizen of both.

The evening meals came late, the wide hall with Magistra Isadau and her siblings and their families and friends often making room for twenty people. Afterward, the diners would withdraw to the yard or to private rooms. The sound of lutes and drums and living voices lifted in harmony were as much a part of the after-meal as sweet wines and cups of chocolate. Cithrin, though, excused herself from the merriment, took a bottle or two of the rich red wine the house imported from Pût and some ledger or company book from Magistra Isadau's office to her room to read like a girl lulling herself to sleep with a volume of poetry. The wine calmed the tightness in her body, the play of numbers and agreements occupied her mind until the music of the house didn't bother her and the cold of the night drove her under her blankets and, at last, to sleep.

Except that some nights, sleep would not come. On those, she would rise, dress in her dark wools, and walk the halls of the compound. There were always a few men and women still awake or else woken early for the next day. The capacity of the Timzinae to go without sleep was remarkable to her. On one such night, she found Yardem sitting at the watch fire alone, staring at the stars scattered above them and listening to the first crickets of spring.

She looked up, tracing the few constellations she knew. Stars were not her passion.

"Evening, ma'am," he said. "You're up late."

"I suppose," she said, her words careful and deliberately unslurred. "You are too."

"Am," Yardem said and flicked one jingling ear. It might have been only her imagination, but the Tralgu's wide, canine face seemed wistful. "Seems we're settling in well."

"Yes," Cithrin said. "Magistra Isadau is a very intelligent woman. From everything I saw at the market house, I'd have thought the bank would be barely turning a profit, but she manages to do quite well."

"I was thinking more of the household," Yardem said.

"They're very kind," Cithrin said. "I've never been around a real family before. To see the way they treat each other... the way they treat us, for that. They're all so open and loving and accepting. It's like we've always belonged here and just never knew it."

In the trees at the compound's edge, an owl launched itself up against the stars, a shadow moving on darkness. Yardem traced its arc with eyes and ears, and Cithrin followed it by following him. The silence between them was calm, companionable. Cithrin put her small hand over the back of his.

"I hate it here," she said. "I have never hated anyplace as much as here."

"I know."

"It is obvious? I try not to let it show."

"I've known you a while," Yardem said.

"They're all so kind, and all I can feel is how little I belong with them. Magistra Isadau? She's like a good witch from a children's story. She's sweet and she's wise and she wants the best from me, and it makes my skin crawl. I keep thinking that I wouldn't know it if she hated me. God knows she'd treat me just as well."

A falling star streaked overhead, there and then gone.

"I knew a man once," Yardem said. "Good fighter, pleasant to keep watch with. The sort of man who'd have done well in a company. Might have gotten as far as running one if he'd kept at it. Only he'd spent his whole youth as a slave. He'd do well enough when we were on campaign, but when we were done and he had time and money of his own and no one telling him what to do? He didn't know how to act."

"How did he deal with it?"

"At first, the captain tried keeping him back, giving him duties even while the other men went out and drank themselves poor. Treated the boy like he was still enslaved. That worked for a time, but in the end it wasn't enough. It took the boy a season to manage it, but the magistrates stripped his freedom and sold him to a farmer."

"That's sad."

"Is it?"

An insect landed on Cithrin, its legs struggling against the fine, pale hair of her forearm. She flicked it away.

"We say our souls want joy, but they don't," she said. "They want what they already know, joyful or not."

Yardem grunted as if he'd taken a blow to the gut and pulled his hand away from her to scratch an itch she doubted was really there.

"What about you?" she asked. "Shouldn't you be asleep?"

"Should."

"But you can't."

"Apparently not."

"What are you thinking about?" she asked.

"The war, partly. The word in the trade has it that Antea is stretched tight as a drumskin. Wore themselves thin last year, and on the edge of falling apart. Except there's other stories too."

"You can't say that and not tell," Cithrin said. "I'd fire you."

"They're saying that the spirits of the dead march with the Antean army. And that the birds and dogs all start running away before their army comes the way they do from a fire. Makes it sound as if there's something uncanny about the Lord Regent, like he's some sort of cunning man."

"Geder's not a cunning man," Cithrin said. "He's...he's just a man of too little wisdom and too much power."

"You sound sad for him."

"No," she said. "He burned my city. Killed the people who raised and looked after me. I lived with him for weeks.

Took comfort in him. I don't think there's a word for what he and I are to each other."

"Do you love him?"

"Are you *drunk*?"

"You took comfort in him," Yardem said. "For some people—"

"He got anxious, I didn't say no. What's love got to do with that?"

"Nothing," Yardem agreed. "Only there are people who don't see it that way."

"They're fools," Cithrin said, without rancor. And then, "You said partly. What's the other part?"

"I don't know where the captain is. What he's doing. There's no word of him anywhere. It...bothers me."

"I wish he was still here too."

"Not sure I said that, ma'am," Yardem said ruefully. "I'd hoped to know where he went and what he did. The captain and I didn't part on the best terms. People who betray him don't tend to end well, and there's a good chance he feels I betrayed him."

"Then he's a fool too," Cithrin said.

Yardem didn't answer.

Geder

W ell, you know how it is," Geder's father said, scratching at his belly. "Rivenhalm in winter. Spent a fair part of the season listening to the ice crack. Not a great deal more going on. Though this might amuse you, hey? You remember old Jeyup the weirkeeper? The one with the crooked nose?"

"Yes, of course," Geder said, though the truth of it was that he had only a vague impression of a tall man with dark hair and an unfortunate voice. The room in which they sat now was less than halfway up the Kingspire, and still higher than any other tower in Camnipol. He'd thought that the view might impress his father, and perhaps it had. It was hard to tell.

"Well, just before thaw, he was out cutting ice away from the weir. Making repairs. Only he'd misjudged the ice. Fell right through, half died from the cold of it."

"I'm sorry to hear that," Geder said, and glanced at the great spiral stair of rosewood dressed in gold that led to the floor above. The floor where Basrahip and his pet adventurer Dar Cinlama were meeting even now. He hoped to catch sight of the great priest as he descended, but the only form on the stairway was a servant in ceremonial robes trotting off on some errand or another. Geder leaned back in his seat.

"Don't be," his father said, "because that's just the thing. Good came of it after all. The cunning man was away in the east seeing to a man who'd had a tree fall on him, so until he got back old Jeyup had Arrien, the butcher's widow, coming to nurse him along. And they married at first thaw, if you can picture that!"

Geder's father slapped his knee in merriment that invited Geder to join in. Geder did smile, pretending pleasure he didn't actually feel. Rivenhalm had been his home for the whole length of his childhood and the early part of his time as a man, but the fine points of it seemed as vague as someone else's memories. He remembered the weir and its keeper, the long path behind the manor house that led to the cave where he'd hide in the summer, the smell of the library, the small niche his father kept always lit by a single candle in memory of Geder's mother, and those tiny fragments would be rich and full of meaning. But they had no context.

"So," Geder's father said, "tell me. What translations are you working on these days?"

"I'm not really," Geder said. "You know. Being Lord Regent. Running the empire. The war makes it hard to have the time, really."

Lehrer's face fell a bit, and Geder felt he'd said the wrong thing.

"Of course," his father said. "It's just that it was so important to you when you were a boy. I hoped you'd be able... Well, that's the world, isn't it? We do what we have to do."

A long, low, rolling laughter echoed in the distance. Basrahip. The urge to leap up from his seat and go up the stairs, the desire to know what had happened in the meeting was like an itch, but he also didn't want to seem anxious. It would have been beneath his dignity, and he didn't want Basrahip to laugh at him. He hated it when people did that.

"I've, ah, I've kept you too long," his father said. "I'm sorry."

"No," Geder said. "I'm always happy to see you. As long as I'm Lord Regent, you should come by the Kingspire any-time you like. I could get you rooms here."

"My own rooms are fine," Lehrer said. "They suit me."

He levered himself to his feet and Geder rose with him. The older man looked frailer than Geder remembered, his hair thinner, his skin more ashen. It was just the winter, Geder told himself. With the summer sun and the court season to keep him busy, his father would get his color back. They stood for a moment, both of them unsure what eti-quette demanded. At last, Lehrer made a little bow appro-priate for the Viscount of Rivenhalm to the Lord Regent, but with an ironic smile meant for the father and son. Geder followed his example, and then watched as his father turned and walked away. He felt a lingering sense of having failed somehow. Of having disappointed. He shouldn't have been thinking so much about Basrahip.

Basrahip. He glanced at the stairway, licked his lips, and started walking toward it, forcing his demeanor to be casual.

Basrahip and Dar Cinlama stood together under an arch-way of pale stone. The priest was speaking too quietly for Geder to make out the words, but his huge hands were ges-turing, massaging the air. Cinlama nodded his understand-ing and agreement, the light from his eyes casting shadows across his cheekbones. The vastly large Firstblood man and the thin, muscular Dartinae looked like a woodcut, an alle-gory for something more than what they actually were.

"Well, then," Geder said, walking up to them. "All the plans are made, then, yes?"

"Lord Regent," Dar Cinlama said as he bowed. The

amusement in the man's voice was probably only Geder's imagination.

"Yes, Prince Geder," Basrahip said, putting his hand on the Dartinae man's shoulder. "My friend Dar and I are quite pleased. Your generosity and wisdom will bring you great rewards from the goddess."

Geder felt his smile curdle.

"That's good," he said. "I'm pleased to hear it."

Cinlama made another little bow, but Basrahip frowned and Geder bit his lip. He shouldn't have said anything. The falseness of the words would be clear as daylight to Basrahip. But then, Geder considered, that might have been why he'd said them.

"Forgive me, friend Dar," Basrahip said. "I must speak with Prince Geder now."

"No problem with that," Dar Cinlama said, grinning happily. "I think the list of things I'll need to prepare should keep me busy for days."

He bowed to Geder a third time and then trotted away, self-congratulation radiating from him like heat from a fire. Basrahip's wide face was a mask of concern. Geder crossed his arms.

"What troubles you, Prince Geder?" Basrahip asked, gesturing that they should step into the meeting room that priest and explorer had just abandoned.

"All sorts of things," Geder said. "The grain stores we're capturing in Sarakal aren't as rich as we'd expected. Ternigan's saying the siege at Nus may take longer than he'd thought it would. I've got half a dozen decisions from the grand audience that I still need to do something about, and they're just gnawing at me. It's all just…"

Geder held his hand out, trying to express his frustration and the sense of loss that words could not quite encompass.

It had all come so suddenly. The sense of being the most important man in the world had been wonderful, and it had been transitory. Geder couldn't explain it precisely. It was as if everything had been fine before Dar Cinlama had made his petition, and then tasted of ashes afterward. He could no more justify it than deny it away.

He walked to the balcony and looked out over the massive city below him. It was his, for the time being at least. Camnipol was his, and Antea, and so, in a sense, was everything. It stretched out before him like a map of itself—the Division, the wide manors and compounds of the noble classes, the maze of narrow streets in the south. Even the sun high in its blue arch of sky seemed part of Geder's domain. The air smelled of smoke from a thousand forges, bakeries, and hearths. Tiny shapes moved on the ground far below, distance reducing them all to less than ants. It should have been enough.

Basrahip's footsteps approached from behind him. Like a boy poking his tongue at a sore tooth, he remembered again the pleasure and interest on the priest's face when Dar Cinlama had made his proposal.

"I was thinking," Geder said, "we should move your temple. The highest floors of the Kingspire aren't being used for anything in particular, and there's a beautiful theater space you could use for sermons. It looks out like you're a bird. And then if something else like Dawson Kalliam happens, you'll be safe. No one can take the Kingspire."

Basrahip was silent for a long moment. His nod was hardly visible in the corner of Geder's eye. The disappointment and shame he felt could have been the echo of speaking with his father. It could have been something else.

"The meeting with the adventurer," Geder said. "It went well, then? We're going to do what he said."

"I have asked that he give over all the information he has about places where the bones of the world may lie near its skin," Basrahip said. "He has agreed. The man himself will lead one group, but there will be others to go where he feels it wise to send them. With your permission, Prince Geder."

"Of course you have my permission. Why would you not? Here's my permission. Take it."

Beyond the southern wall of the city, the land fell away into a deep plain. From where he stood, it was almost as if Camnipol stood at the edge of the world. A flock of pigeons rose in the air below them, grey wings glittering white in the sunlight. Basrahip's sigh carried the weight of years.

"What is troubling you, Prince Geder?"

"Nothing."

"That is not true, my friend," Basrahip said, his voice gentle. "Try again."

Geder crossed his arms. Without meaning to, he picked out the tiny blot of color that was Yellow House. He wondered if Cary and Smit and the other players who'd hidden him and Aster were still there. He wondered if they had heard from Cithrin. He started to speak, stopped himself, and then tried again.

"This man Cinlama. He's going to go off into the world and find things, isn't he? He's going to follow these tiny traces of history, these clues and rumors and half-remembered stories, and try to dig up wonders. I used to be the one who did that. I'm the one who left Antea and went looking for the Sinir Kushku and found the temple. I was the one who brought you and the goddess back out into the world. And now..."

"Do you fear that this man would take your glory? Your place in the goddess's favor?"

Geder shook his head. "I could have Cinlama killed for

any reason. For no reason other than that I said so. It's that I see him and I think of the ways I used to be him. Or the way I used to be my father's son, and I'm not anymore. Or the way I used to be Dawson Kalliam's client before he turned on me. I used to be the one who led you into the world and showed you all the things that had changed since your people went into seclusion. And I'm not any of those people anymore."

"Would you wish to be?" the priest asked. "Lord Prince, what do you want?"

The question seemed to float in the air like a feather. Geder tried to imagine himself strapping a leather sack of books to the side of a horse, taking a handful of servants, and pressing out into the forgotten corners of the world. In truth, he hadn't particularly enjoyed the journey when he had gone, and the prospect of sleeping in a tent and worrying about where the next freshwater would be had more charm in theory than in practice. It wasn't what Dar Cinlama was doing that Geder envied, it was what he signified. For a moment, Geder was suffering the summer just gone by, hiding in a hole under a collapsed building, spending days and nights in darkness with Aster and Cithrin bel Sarcour. He heard her laugh again and the slight bitterness that seemed to flavor everything she said.

"I want to *matter*," Geder said.

"Ah," Basrahip said, as if he understood.

There were, Geder supposed, things in the world that deserved his hatred more than ancient precedents of grazing rights. The worse sorts of stinging flies, for example. Or the way a man's bowels turned to water if he ate bad meat. Those were worse, if only slightly.

"You see, my lord," the scholarly man said, "the question

you ask hinges on whether the men in question are grazing animals that come from the same stock. If, for example, they are sheep who descended from the same ram three generations previous, then they are by imperial standards within the same greater flock. In that case—"

"The old Miniean precedents apply, and this Sebinin fellow doesn't owe the other one a single coin."

"Exactly," the scholar said, "but if there was another ram—"

"He owes a tenth of a sheep for every day he grazed on the land without permission."

"Precisely. If you don't mind my saying it, your lordship is very quick to understand the intricacies of these questions."

Geder nodded and leaned forward, elbows on the table like a schoolboy before his tutor. It was another of the unresolved issues of the general audience taken care of, or if not taken care of, at least moved to the next stage. He'd send a messenger to the people in question and find out the lineages of their sheep. He had never in all his life imagined that the role of governing an empire would cook down to such a thin broth as this, but he understood now why the general audience came only once a year and usually ended well before the last of the petitioners came before the throne. If he'd chosen to stop an hour or two earlier, he wouldn't be sitting here now. Nor would Dar Cinlama and his team be preparing to depart. Around him, the small library held the least command of his attention that any collection of books had ever managed. Volume after volume, codex after codex, trailing back through centuries to the founding of Antea, and many older even than that, without a single one being particularly interesting. He wondered whether Basrahip's disdain for the written word was beginning to seep into him, or if this was genuinely the least interesting subject known to humanity.

"All right," Geder said and consulted the page of notes he had sketched for himself, his heart sluggish and grey. "Let's see what's next. How much do you know about the legal differences between spring lettuce and autumn?"

The scholar's eyebrows rose as Geder's heart sank.

"Well, my lord, that is a fascinating question."

It isn't, Geder thought. *No, it really, truly isn't...*

"Lord Regent?" a familiar voice said from the doorway. Canl Daskellin stood uncertainly, hesitating to step in or to leave. Geder sprang to his feet.

"Lord Daskellin! Come in, please," he said, and then turned to the scholar. "I'm afraid the rest will have to wait. War and all. I'll send someone for you when there's time."

The scholar bowed his way out and Geder led Daskellin to a chair, only realizing when he got there that he'd been pulling at the older man's sleeve like a puppy worrying a dog's ear. Daskellin smiled as he sat, but his expression seemed abstracted. It was as if he were still making some internal argument and had not come to a conclusion that entirely satisfied him. The dusting of white at the man's temples stood out against the darkness of his skin, making him seem older than he was.

"I've been...speaking with Minister Basrahip," Daskellin said at last.

"Yes," Geder said. "Did he tell you I've decided to move his temple into the Kingspire? There are all of those levels at the very top that no one ever seems to use, and since the old one was damaged last summer...along with everything else, I suppose. But that way, he'll have a place that's protected."

"He'd mentioned it, yes," Daskellin said, tapping his fingertips idly against the spine of a book on taxation precedent. "It wasn't the meat of our meal, though. It's the Lord Marshal."

"Ternigan?"

"Not Ternigan, no. Not precisely," Daskellin said. "More the role of the Lord Marshal in the larger sense. As an extension of the power of the throne."

Geder tilted his head. Daskellin licked his lips, his gaze on the farther wall.

"The king, or in your case the man taking the king's role, isn't a leader in the field," Daskellin said. "His place is to coordinate among his subjects, see to it that the nobility are unified and direct his will through them. Through us."

"Of course," Geder said.

"But," Daskellin said, sitting forward, "the minister had a point about the present situation. About Nus, in particular. You've read Ternigan's reports, I assume?"

"Of course."

"Minister Basrahip suggested that if you were to join the Lord Marshal in the field—if you were to be physically present—it might rally the troops and end the siege sooner. And the sooner Nus falls, the more likely we are to recover food and supplies that... Well, we're going to need them to make it through next winter, aren't we?"

"You mean," Geder said, his heart suddenly leaping within his chest, "you think I should go to the war? To Nus?"

Daskellin shook his head ruefully.

"I didn't," he said. "Not at first, but the minister kept repeating his arguments, and by the fourth or fifth time he'd said it all, it seemed to have some heft to it. It is critical that things go well in Sarakal, and Ternigan is a fine strategist. Only he isn't... he isn't a man who inspires the men around him. He isn't a hero."

"A hero?" Geder echoed, and he felt the smile not as an expression, but only a pressure at the back of his jaw. A bud that was growing into a bloom.

Thank you, Basrahip, he thought. *This is what I wanted.*

Clara

Disruption was, in its way, a constant. No season passed without its share of scandal. In a court the size and complexity of the one that attended the Severed Throne, someone was certainly being sexually unfaithful on a near-daily basis. Someone's health was failing. Someone had delivered a deathly insult to someone. Really, if nothing else, someone would wear a jacket with an unfortunate cut or rouge their cheeks too much or else too little. Falling from grace, like anything else, had its protocol and its expectations. And, provided one didn't fall too far, so did returning to court.

Allies would announce themselves by their invitations. The staunchest might invite the unfortunate soul in need of rescue to a dinner party or hold a luncheon in their name, but that was boldness that bordered on the rash. The more cautious might include the recently fallen into a sewing circle or private tea casual enough that the guests sat wherever they pleased. Even a nod or a smile in the street could be noticed by others and commented upon.

Clara's misfortune, she knew, would be difficult to parse. Her husband, whom all in court knew she'd loved deeply and sincerely, had led the rebellion against the Lord Regent and been slaughtered. Attempted regicide should have been too dark a stain to recover from, but there were Jorey and

Vicarian. Even, in her grudging way, Elisia. Each of them had some distance from the tragedy, and Geder Palliako had even kept Jorey in the court. Clara's position, then, became something of a cipher. She was without precedent, and even the most experienced etiquette master might be permitted to confess puzzlement at how best to approach her.

The common sentiment appeared to be that sending a servant to her boarding house was a bit too sordid, and so slowly, as the groaning mechanisms of social play took their positions, notes began to arrive at Lord Skestinin's small manor. Not invitations, because that would be almost a statement of allegiance, but mentions of small gatherings. Most were ostensibly for Sabiha with the understanding that she might choose to bring a guest. But there were a few addressed to Clara herself.

Lady Tilliaken's gardens spilled out from her family's manor house in an artful display of carelessness. To an untrained eye, the ivies and spoke-roses that curled around the stone walkways might have looked wild, but it was a tended wildness. The bright green runners never found their way into any inconvenient place. The buds of the flowers all came, as if by chance, into positions that would show their petals to the best effect. The finches and butterflies that found their way there hadn't been drawn by any obvious caches of seed or sweet water. The style was called Hallskari, though Clara's understanding was that real gardens in Hallskar were much more spare and put greater importance on the bitter herbs that Haaverkin seemed to prefer. The servant girl, a young Cinnae with hair as pale as daylight and eyes the color of ice, led Clara directly to the garden tables without bringing her through the house. The other women were already there, and it took Clara less than five long breaths together to assess the situation.

Lady Enga Tilliaken, at the head of the table, rose to greet Clara with kisses on both cheeks, which taken with the invitation put her as Clara's ally. Merian Caot, second daughter of the Baron of Dannick, looked pleased and amused in equal measure much the way Clara's own daughter might have done when she was young and going to inappropriate garden parties in order to play at rebellion. Lady Nikayla Essian, seeing Clara, gave a little coo of concern and rose to her feet, her eyes the perfect image of sympathy. She had come to gloat.

"Don't get up on my account," Clara said with a smile. "I don't intend to stand for long. I'm too old for it."

"You will take some tea, though, won't you?" Lady Tilliaken said. "I've discovered this fascinating blend from that merchant from the Free Cities. What was his name?"

"Not the Timzinae!" Essian said.

"Of course not. The Jasuru woman."

"Nufuz, you mean?" Clara said, and Tilliaken clapped her hands together.

"Yes, her."

"If she recommended it, I can hardly refuse," Clara said, taking a seat at the little stone table. A wasp hissed by her ear, gold and green as a gem in the sunlight. "I haven't seen her in an age."

"Of course, you wouldn't have," Essian said, touching Clara's wrist. It promised to be a long and unpleasant afternoon.

It was necessary, of course. And more than that, it was expected. Dawson had thrown everything about her into question. The role she had played at court her whole life had been made uncertain, and now those who were willing to accept her company would be watching, testing, to see who and what she was. Did she show remorse, and if she did was it for her husband's death or his actions? Did she speak harshly, or was she kind? In a hundred small ways, the Clara Kalliam they had all known was dead, and this new woman with her face and voice had stepped in. If she were ever to be reintegrated at court, they would need to know who this new woman was.

And, for that matter, so would she.

The tea was lovely—smoky and rich with a brightness that came from adding rose hips—and the cakes seemed to be made entirely of butter and honey with only enough flour to give them shape. The smell of turned earth from where Tilliaken's servants were preparing the beds floated through the air like perfume, and the soft warmth of the spring sun slowly undid the stays at the necks of their dresses. Clara listened and spoke, doing the best imitation she could of the woman she had been only a year before, except she didn't smoke. She'd run out of money for tobacco, and she would not allow herself to ask for it.

"Oh, did I tell you about my son's new commission?" Essian said. "It's very exciting. His first command."

"Command?" Clara said. "Is he joining the forces in Sarakal?"

Essian's cheeks pinked slightly, and not, Clara thought, from pride. That was interesting.

"No, it's a smaller force. Bound for Lyoneia. Fifty men, he said."

Clara felt something deep within her wake, tilt its ears forward, narrow its eyes. *Why is he going there? What is he doing?* Had Palliako given the order, or had someone else, and if someone else, who? She wanted to interrogate Essian the way Palliako had once questioned her. Instead she sipped her tea and nodded.

"It's a great honor," Essian said, almost petulantly.

"Command is always an important thing," Caot said with a thin smile. Why was it that the young were so adept at being cruel? "It's only a pity he's being sent so far south when Sarakal's to the east. He must be disappointed."

"I don't see why he would be," Clara said. "If the Lord Regent's sending him so far, it does imply a certain trust, wouldn't you say?"

"Yes, trust," Essian said, leaping at the word. "The Lord Regent trusts him."

"Sending him as far as Lyoneia," Clara said. "And I have to assume that it's a matter of some importance. Surely we wouldn't be sending men away in wartime unless the matter were critical."

Essian sipped her tea, but didn't answer. Either it was something trivial or else she didn't know what the errand was. Clara wished she could think of some way to draw the woman out. Better to be patient and not be seen to ask. Better to seem to be what they thought she was. Clara suppressed a small and frustrated growl.

"So," she said, "since I have been somewhat away from the center of things, you must tell me about the dresses at the opening of the season. Did Ana Pyrellin wear that impressive fur of hers again?"

"The one with the heads still on?" the young Caot girl said, laughing. "She did, and worse. You won't believe it."

Clara let the conversation drift into safer waters. The afternoon was brief enough. Had she remained until twilight, it would have been taken quite differently in court. Small steps would get her where she wanted to be more swiftly than great strides. They spoke of Geder Palliako's decision to inspect the troops in Sarakal, of the rise in status of Fallon Broot, of the great debate about whether to replace the chairs in the Fraternity of the Great Bear. Clara listened and offered perhaps a bit less comment than she would have before. She felt the two different versions of herself sitting together, one hurt and shamed and cast out from her home, the other listening carefully for scraps of information that might give her advantage. When the time arrived, Caot and Essian left together, but Lady Tilliaken kept Clara back, inviting her to a small niche for a moment. She was still not welcome in the house even so far as a withdrawing room, but that Tilliaken wished a moment alone was interesting. Clara sat on the wooden bench while the lady of the house disappeared for a moment. She reached for her pipe before remembering that she couldn't make use of it.

"Clara," Lady Tilliaken said, stepping into the niche. She carried a folded cloth of yellow cream. "I wanted to ask if you had any need of this. It's perfectly serviceable, but I'm afraid it doesn't fit me any longer."

The dress spilled forth from her hands, flowing like water. Clara felt herself go cold. It was a pretty enough piece of sewing, strong at the seams and the lacework well crafted. That wasn't at issue. It was the offer itself. The fact—for it was now a fact—that the Baroness of Osterling Fells had become the sort of woman one offered secondhand clothes to. She wished now that she'd asked for the tobacco. If she had descended to charity, there seemed no reason to step away. She forced a smile.

"It's lovely, Enga," Clara said, taking the silk between her fingers. "And I have the perfect use for it."

No, ma'am, I can't," the woman said. Her name was Aly Koutunin, and Clara had met her on the Prisoner's Span the month before when Clara had gone to pass out free bread. She was younger than Clara by almost a decade, but the years had worn harder on her, and they might almost have been sisters.

"Your daughter's getting married, isn't she?" Clara asked. "She's almost the right size. Even if she doesn't choose it for the ceremony—"

"Not that. It's just so *rich*."

"If you don't take it, it will be on the ragman's cart by morning."

"No!"

"I swear it," Clara said, and her sincerity left no more room for dissent. Aly folded the cloth carefully, reverently, and pressed it into her sack. They stood at the edge of the Prisoner's Span, looking out across the southernmost reach of the Division. In the west, massive clouds were building, high and white at the top, grey as slate at the bottom. Late spring storms often washed the lands near Camnipol this time of year, but just as often they missed, clinging to the horizon like a shy boy at his first ball. On the bridge itself, a Firstblood man was leaning over the railing, shouting down to a woman in one of the hanging cages. From what little Clara could see, the prisoner's expression was empty, her arms and legs poking out between the bars and over the abyss. The man shouted something about being a bad mother to her children and spat down toward her.

"True love, eh?" Aly said, following Clara's gaze. "They've been like that most of the day."

"And how is your Mihal faring?" Clara asked.

"He'll come back up in three days, unless the magistrate's too drunk to come," Aly said. Mihal, her son, had been caught stealing coins from a merchant's stall and had hung over the open air for two weeks now. It wasn't his first time in the cages, and the magistrate had made unpleasant jokes about sending him over without one next time. Aly pretended to treat it lightly, but Clara saw the fear at the corners of her eyes.

The previous year's battles had wounded the city, there was no question. Blades in the street and fires in the noblest quarters. Nothing like that could happen without leaving a mark. Only in the gardens and mansions at the northern end of the city did Clara see how it could be possible to view the worst as passed, the wounds as healing. Walk south and west far enough to reach the Prisoner's Span, and the infection showed. It wasn't only that there were more beggars, though certainly there were. It wasn't only the merchants' stalls closed and abandoned.

Palliako's war against Asterilhold had taken the able-bodied men from the farms in planting, and the insurrection against him had distracted the noblemen from the business of managing their holdings. Now the armies fought in Sarakal, and another spring planting had almost passed with fewer hands than it needed. There was still bread at the bakers, meat at the butchers, beets and carrots at the carts along the streets, but there was also the growing sense that all the reserves had been spent. It felt like desperation, and it showed the most in the city's desperate places—the Prisoner's Span, the vagrant encampments that clung to the sides of the Division, Palliako's new prisons. The places that had been beneath her notice and were no longer.

To her left, Vincen was talking to a thin older man. He glanced toward her then away, reassuring himself that she was still there, still well, in a way that could only remind her of a hunting dog checking on its pack.

"What's happened to Oldug?" she asked, taking her pipe out from her pocket.

"Hauled him up early," Aly said, bitterness in her voice.

"Hardly seems fair, does it? My boy in for taking a few bits of copper and staying his full time. Oldug was running his ship from Hallskar and back for five years before they put hands on him. Must have cost a hundred times what my boy did."

"Is odd, isn't it? What's become of him since?"

"Not around here. Likely took his good fortune back to sea with him."

"Or got pressed into service for the war," Clara said.

"Or that."

Clara took her tobacco pouch out before she remembered again that it was empty. She pressed it back, but Aly plucked the clay pipe out of her hand and started filling it from her own supply. Clara began to protest, but then stopped. It was rude to ask, but it was worse to refuse. A young man of status given a small command to Lyoneia. A smuggler shown leniency. The feeling it called forth in her was little more than a slight discomfort, an itch, but Clara sat with it patiently, and it grew into something larger and more complex. Suspicion, perhaps. Aly lit the pipe from her own match, drawing on it until blue smoke billowed from her lips, then passed it back to Clara. The leaf was old and stale-tasting, but after a few days of nothing it might as well have been ambrosia and incense. Clara puffed out a careful ring of smoke and watched it spin and diffuse while she thought.

"If you hear what happened to him, I would be interested," she said. "Anyone else who's been let out early and then gone too."

"I'll ask around if you'd like," Aly said, leaning against the great stone abutment that gave the bridge its strength. "Anything else you'd want to know?"

Of course there was. She'd already gathered so much from so many places—the knights in the field from an old porter who had taken a position at the Fraternity of the Great Bear; the grain and fodder being diverted to the army from a disgruntled baker arguing with the miller who usually supplied him flour; the movements of the army from a dozen friends, lovers, and relatives of the soldiers. It was all there, floating through the city waiting only for a careful listener. But like drinking saltwater and growing thirsty, every question answered left her curious. What kinds of supplies were going south to Lyoneia with Nikayla Essian's son. What other commands were being scattered to the odd places of the world and who was leading them. Whose sons they were taking with them, how many horses, and how much food. Her curiosity was piqued, and it would be days or weeks finding what she wanted to know, all of which might amount to nothing. She smiled at Aly and drew another sip from her pipe. Was there anything else she'd want to know? Only everything.

"No, dear," she said. "Just an old woman feeding her idle fancies."

"Not so old as that," Aly said and cast a leering glance at Vincen Coe. Clara felt a moment's stab of embarrassment, and then laughed. Across the little square, Vincen turned to look over his shoulder at them, checking in with his pack.

"He is pretty to look at," Clara said.

They stayed there for the better part of an hour, Clara visiting and trading gossip with men and women she had come to know over the last months and Vincen following her lead. At last, the sun began to reach down toward the western wall of the city, and Vincen came to take her arm and lead her home to the boarding house.

"We should talk," he said as they stepped into the shadowed alleyway. "I'm starting to get worried about staying in the city. I'd like to speak to my uncle about going out there for the summer."

"That's sweet," Clara said. "No."

"I'm afraid there's going to be more trouble. Not right away, but soon."

"All the more reason I should stay," Clara said.

"It would be safer if—"

"I'm sure the letters I wrote from your uncle's farmstead would be fascinating," Clara said. " 'There may be more piglets this year than expected.' No, if I'm going to do this, I have to do it from here."

"Then perhaps you shouldn't do it," Vincen said. His voice was so gentle she almost laughed.

"Of course I'm going to continue with it. It's what I have left."

"You have me."

This time she did laugh, and the flicker of hurt on his face was terrible and hilarious both. She leaned up and kissed him on the corner of his mouth. The taste of his sweat was surprising and immediate, and Clara wondered whether she'd just crossed some unspoken boundary. And if she had, whether the boundary was his or her own. Vincen's light brown eyes were fixed on hers, his cheeks flushed. She didn't realize they'd stopped walking until someone passed them.

"My work's here," she said. "But I hope you'll stay with me."

"To avenge your husband," Vincen said, and she could hear the complexity of sentiment in his words.

She shook her head and pressed two fingers to the huntsman's lips. "To redeem my country," she said. And then, a moment later, "By betraying it."

Marcus

Looking back at it afterward, the journey from the heart of the Lyoneian rainforest to the rocks and crags of the northern coast took on the feeling of a dream. Marcus remembered bits and pieces—the bone-deep exhaustion, the day an annoying welt on his leg had opened and spilled out live maggots, the tension between taking time to search for food and pressing on to reach the end of the forest—but they formed no single coherent string. They had walked and hidden and been bitten and starved and tried to find water that wouldn't fill their guts with worms when they drank it. When Marcus thought back to the morning he had stepped out from the trees and onto a paved road, his ribs showing through his skin and half naked where his clothes had rotted away, he saw the scene as if he had witnessed it, as if he had been outside of his own body watching it happen to someone else.

It was only on the ship back north that his mind returned to him enough that he understood. After months lost in the interior, he'd been starving and fevered and prey to insects that had been feasting on the blood of humanity since before the dragons. He told himself that the sword and its venomous magic likely didn't have much to do with it. As weak as he'd been, he would likely have fallen just as ill, been just as confused. Still, as their little ship bobbed on the summer waves, Marcus left the green scabbard in with his things.

He had no need of it on board, and less time carrying now meant more time later.

The only disturbing thing was coming back to his cabin to find a circle of tiny dark-carapaced bodies around his bags where the fleas and insects had come out to die. It wasn't that Marcus had doubted Kit about the sword's nature, but seeing it confirmed was unsettling.

Kit was looking skeletally thin as well. But as the days passed and the pair ate the sailor's diet of fresh fish and old limes, salt pork and twice-baked bread, the flesh of the actor's cheeks began to fill in, and Marcus felt his own strength returning. By the time the expanse of the Inner Sea began to break into islands and reefs, Marcus was near enough himself that he could keep pace with the sailors. Or at least with ones his own age.

Kort was an island city, and ancient. In the story it told of itself, Kort was the site of the last battle, where Drakkis Stormcrow arranged the death of Morade, the mad Dragon Emperor. Its bay, wide and shallow and protected by a massive chain of dragon's jade, went by the name Firstwater on the strength of being the first saltwater claimed by humanity for humanity. The high, narrow houses that rose up the steep rise from the shore were, it was said, the first built by free men, or at least they stood where those houses had. It was not the largest of cities. Carse in Northcoast could have swallowed six like it. It didn't claim the imperial beauty of Camnipol or the wealth of Stollbourne. Its streets were narrow, its trade restrained by the constant wars and turmoil of Pût and the Keshet, its people a rough-spirited crew. But even if the flowers of Kort bloomed tough and simple, their roots grew the deepest. Marcus might even have found himself moved by it, if he hadn't known three other places that made the same claims.

They pulled into port near evening, the summer sun fling-
ing gold and crimson across the clouds. At the chain towers
great fires burned, a guide to ships at sea and a warning. The
air smelled of brine and smoke and the subtle homecoming
scent of land and stone. Marcus found himself standing at
the bow and watching the city as it fell into twilight. Windows flickered with candlelight all up the side of the mountain like an army of fireflies.

"I don't believe I've seen you look so content in weeks,"
Kit said.

"I'm home," Marcus said.

"I didn't know you came from Kort."

"Never been here before," Marcus said. "But after *that*,
it's home."

The inn sat at one end of a public square so small that only
the thin cistern distinguished it from a widening of the road.
Seven lanterns hung around the door, the ochre wall seeming to eat as much light as it reflected. The keeper was a
Yemmu man with yellowed tusks and a friendly demeanor.
Marcus stood in the street, letting Kit make the negotiations. The moon above was the blue white of snow. It was
summer now, and Marcus had gone a full winter without
seeing snow or feeling cold. It made time seem odd. He
wouldn't have thought that a rhythm so slow and deliber-
ate would affect him from day to day, but looking up at the
moon, he felt how much he missed cold.

The room was hardly wide enough for the straw ticking, and it had sawdust on the floor instead of rushes, but
Marcus couldn't help grinning as he lay down. Kit poured a
cup of water from the earthenware jug and drank it, leaning
against the wall.

"I'm not going to ask how we're paying for this," Marcus

said, throwing an arm over his eyes. "I'm just going to be here enjoying it."

Kit chuckled.

"I've proposed to the keeper that I perform in the common room. Songs. Stories. Nothing fancy, of course, since I don't have props and the others aren't here. But I would be surprised if I couldn't raise enough to pay for the room and make good inroads toward a ship to the mainland."

"Malarska?"

Kit made a disapproving sound in the back of his throat. "It's farther south than I would like. I believe there are some fishing villages on the border of the Keshet that would serve better."

"Borders of the Keshet," Marcus said. "Didn't know they had borders there."

"I find the term has a more diffuse sense than they use in Northcoast," Kit said, chuckling. "If you'd care to come down, it might not be a bad thing to have an ally in the crowd. Laugh in the right places. Quietly threaten the hecklers."

"I'm in a real bed. I may never move again." After a moment's silence, Marcus moved his arm and squinted up. "No choice, then?"

"No choice," Kit agreed.

After the cramped feeling that the rest of the city gave, the common room was a pleasant surprise. The wide wooden tables had benches enough for two dozen people, and a firepit—empty now except for a few blackened ends of logs—had enough for seven more. Kit sat by the empty fire, smiling and at ease as if he'd been there a thousand times before. Marcus took a place nearer the door, watching with admiration as Kit began speaking. There were sixteen people in the common room, men and women both,

Firstblood and Tralgu for the most part, with two Timzi-nae huddling together in one corner. Their annoyance at the interruption lasted less than a dozen heartbeats, then, one by one, they turned, leaned elbows against the tables, and fell under Kit's spell. The story was one Marcus had heard before about how Haris Clubhand had tamed the Haaver-kin tribes and become the first Hallskari king. Kit's retell-ing had more humor than most, and Marcus found himself enjoying the story for its own sake and joining in with the laughter more than leading it. There were no hecklers, and the keep dropped a plate of chicken legs and a mug of beer in front of him with a wink.

Marcus wondered, though, how much of Kit's skill came from the taint in the man's blood. When the actor lifted his hands, describing how Haris Clubhand walked up the mountain at Zanisstun with a mug full of Astin Look's blood in his good hand and an axe strapped to his bad wrist, Marcus half believed it had happened. He knew he would shrug the feeling away once the tale was told, but in the moment it was hard to remember that it was only a story, and that sounded too much like the power the spiders held. Even after the performance ended, his rumination was so deep that he didn't notice, when the door to the street swung open and four men in light armor stepped in, that he knew one.

"Well, Marcus Wester. As I live and breathe."

The Jasuru man's face had the lines of a map too detailed for its own legibility, the bronze scales falling into the folds of underlying skin. A white scruff of hair clung to the back of the man's skull like frost hidden from the sun, and a black tongue lolled behind vicious pointed teeth. Scars from a life of violence seared the man's thick arms and neck.

Marcus grinned.

"Merrisen Koke," he said, standing and embracing the old mercenary captain. "God, but you're looking old."

"What I get for being the best," Koke said. "No matter what contracts I take, I keep not dying, yeah? These are my boys. Terrin, Saut. That one's Davian. You'll have met him before at Orsen."

"I remember," Marcus said, taking the lieutenant's hand in his own. "Good to see you again."

"An honor, sir," the young man said.

Kit stepped over from across the room, curiosity in his gaze. Marcus waved an open hand toward him.

"This is Kitap rol Keshmet. We're traveling together."

"A job?" Koke asked.

"Small size, high stakes," Marcus said.

"Pay?"

"Miserable."

"And that," Koke said, slapping Marcus on the shoulder, "is the man I knew. You're eating. You mind if we come join?"

"As long as I'm not paying for you."

Between them, they took up the better part of one table. The keep's initial surprise at his two actors falling in with fighting men washed away quickly as Koke and his men paid for sea bass in black sauce and good ale. For the better part of an hour, Koke retold the things that had happened since he and Marcus had last seen each other. Marcus traded stories of his own, many of them changed to omit details. The food was all eaten and the dishes cleared away when Koke leaned forward, his scaled fingers laced together.

"So Marcus, old friend," he said, the softness of his tone meaning that the business discussions had now begun. Marcus felt a chill run down his back.

"Was too much to hope this was only a social call."

"I've got a fair number of hired eyes in this town and one of them told me Marcus Wester had come ashore."

"You were watching for me?"

"I was. Seems there's people looking for you. Offering a bit of coin for information about where you are and what you've been up to."

Kit's gaze sharpened, his attention sudden and focused. The two Timzinae at the far table broke out into peals of laughter that no one at the table took up.

"Admirers or enemies?" Marcus said.

"You tell me," Koke said. "It's Yardem Hane."

"Really? Imagine that," Marcus said. He idly cracked a knuckle. "And what's old Yardem doing these days that he wants to know about me?"

Koke's eyes narrowed, and his gaze jumped across Marcus like he was a puzzle he couldn't quite figure out.

"Don't know what he wants with you. We'd all assumed he was still padding around in your footsteps trying to get square with you saving his life. Now the story is he's hooked up with a bank in Suddapal," Koke said.

"Porte Oliva," Marcus said. "The bank's in Porte Oliva."

"Not this one. Karol Dannien's set up a gymnasium in Suddapal. Yardem found him there and offered a fair trade for anything anyone heard of you. Said it was an open offer, and Karol spread the word. The place to send to's Komme Medean's branch in Suddapal."

Marcus drank a sip of his beer to hide the sudden stab of dread. He'd imagined Yardem back in Porte Oliva with Cithrin, but that was as much hopeful fantasy as anything. The last he'd heard of Cithrin, she'd been caught in a civil war in Antea. If she'd escaped it, surely she would have gone back to her branch in Birancour. That Yardem was still with the bank but in Elassae raised a thousand questions, and Marcus's neck prickled with the fear of the answers. If Cithrin had died in Camnipol because he hadn't been there to protect her...

He put down the beer and belched.

"So," he said through his smile. "Dannien's remade himself as a teacher, has he? God, we are getting old, aren't we?"

"Not a permanent thing, I don't think. A few of us found something else to be doing when Antea lost its mind. Until that war's over and we see what shape the world's taken, it's hard to know what's a safe contract."

Until that war's over. All the time he'd been gone, the Antean civil war had been burning. Every night he'd spent digging through the vines and trees was another one where Cithrin might have been captured or killed. Every day was one she'd been in dangerous territory.

"Camnipol's still burning, is it?" he said, forcing his tone to be casual. From Koke's reaction, he saw he'd failed.

"God damn, man. Where *have* you been? I'd thought this spending coin to track down Marcus Wester was a joke, but you've been outside the whole damned world, haven't you? Camnipol's fine. Palliako's invaded Sarakal."

Most men wouldn't have noticed the change in Kit's expression, but it was plain as daylight to Marcus. Not surprise. Maybe despair.

"How's that going for him?"

"Better than it has a right to," Koke said. "And you're looking to change the subject."

"Am I?"

The old Jasuru sighed and leaned forward. The first time Marcus had met him, his scales had been bright and burnished, his hair dark and pulled back in an oiled braid. Now he looked spent. Still the same man, but worn down by the years and the battles and unable to break free of the patterns and demands of a life spent fighting for pay.

"I can clear three hundred in Birancour silver for writing a letter about you, old friend," Koke said. "And the truth is my company can use whatever falls off the trees. But I don't have to if I don't have to."

The other fighters looked down, pretending not to be there. Kit turned toward the door as if he were expecting someone to barge through it at any moment. No one did.

"You're asking if I want to better the price to keep you silent?" Marcus said.

"If it's worth that to you," Koke said. "Seeing how we've worked together, I wouldn't ask more than matching. I'm not greedy."

Marcus pretended a yawn and stretched his arms. His body felt as tight as a bowstring and his mind was cold and sharp.

"I appreciate the thought, but if I were you, I'd take all the coin Yardem's got to hand out. In fact, if you're sending to him, give him a message from me. Let him know as soon as I'm free, I'll come see him."

Koke chuckled, low and mirthless.

"More than one way to hear those words," he said.

"Don't jump at shadows," Marcus said. "I'm guessing our mutual friend has a contract he'd throw my way or something of the sort. Nothing sinister in that."

"For three hundred silver?"

"Maybe he needs my help badly," Marcus said. "I am awfully damned good at what I do."

"Which is what, in this instance?"

"Same as always. Whatever needs doing," Marcus said, and rose to his feet. "Good seeing you again, Koke."

"You're going to bed already?" Koke said. "Night's only just starting."

"Not for me, it's not. Kit, you're on your own. But this

bastard's clever, and if he tries to get you drunk, he wants something."

"My boyish affections, perhaps," Kit said with a perfect timing that set Koke and his men laughing.

Koke stood and embraced Marcus again. "Take care of yourself, old friend. We're in odd times."

"Always have been," Marcus said, then retreated to his room.

The bed that had been so comfortable not hours before seemed lumpy and awkward now. The rest his body had ached for couldn't be coaxed back. Marcus lay in the darkness, hands behind his head, and listened to the murmur of distant voices like the rushing of a river. Yardem's name had ripped off a scab he'd forgotten was there, and now he felt exposed and stung and less than halfway healed. He wanted to know why Yardem was in Suddapal, and what he meant by paying for information about Marcus. And he needed to know whether Cithrin was all right and what had happened to her in Camnipol, whether she'd lived, and if she had, at what price. The dread was like a weight on his breastbone. His mind flitted to all the sacked cities he'd been through, all the innocent victims of war he'd seen, and his imagination put Cithrin in their places.

The nightmares would come back tonight. The old ones of Alys and Merian. Women he'd failed to protect. If Cithrin was dead or hurt, someone would die for it. Yardem first, and then whoever had done it. Marcus knew from experience that the effort wouldn't redeem anything, and that he would do it anyway.

He hadn't fallen asleep when the door opened and Kit stepped in. At some point in the evening, something had spilled on him, and he smelled beery. The actor sat on the end of the bed and began unstrapping his boots.

"Asterilhold and Antea last year," Marcus said. "Now Sarakal."

"Apparently so," Kit said. The first boot thumped against the floorboards.

"Your spider goddess eating the world. This is the beginning of that, isn't it?"

The other boot thumped and Kit turned to lean his back against the wall. The light spilling in under the door flickered, barely more than darkness.

"I think this began long ago. Perhaps very long ago. But yes, this is what I feared would come. This and worse," Kit said. And then, "I hear there is a ship leaving in five days for Suddapal."

"Suddapal's farther from the temple than Malarska."

"It is. But if your unfinished business with Yardem Hane—"

"After," Marcus said. "Job is we kill a goddess and save the world. Let's not complicate it."

Geder

You're most kind, Lord Regent," Ternigan said. "Your visit is an honor I hadn't looked for."

Geder smiled and shifted his weight, stretching his legs under the camp table. The tent was thick leather stretched on iron frames, almost as solid as a true building, but movable provided the work of enough servants. Lord Ternigan's bed stood against one wall with a real mattress and wool blankets. An unlit brazier squatted in the room's center, tinder and sticks already laid out in case the Lord Marshal should want to warm himself later. A decanter of cut crystal held wine, and Geder couldn't help wondering whether it always did or if this was something special put together to impress him.

"I thought it was important to see the men in the field," he said. "Raise their spirits. Let them know that the strength of the empire is with them."

"Yes," Ternigan said. "They were quite excited when they heard. I hope the journey wasn't unpleasant?"

"Much more pleasant than the first time we were in the field together," Geder said, and Lord Ternigan laughed. Geder's first campaign—his only one, really—he had been under the command of Alan Klin, Klin under the direction of Lord Marshal Ternigan. Then, Geder had ridden with a single squire and a tired horse from Camnipol to Vanai.

Now he rode in a wheelhouse almost wider than the road, slept when he wished to, ate where he chose. He lifted his eyebrows and glanced toward the decanter. Ternigan rose from his chair and poured a glass for him. Outside, the army of Antea waited in their own less elegant tents. The smoke from their cookfires tainted the air, reminding Geder of another night, another city, another fire.

The wine was decent, but a little acid. Too much, Geder suspected, would upset his stomach, but a glass wouldn't do any harm.

"What is the situation?" he asked, and Ternigan sat back down, spreading his hands like a merchant in a stall.

"We knew this would be a siege," Ternigan said. "They call Nus the Iron City for good reason. But we've cut off all approaches from land and Skestinin's done a fair job keeping relief from coming by sea. No food is going in, and they have only the water they can draw from their wells inside the walls, much of which is brackish."

"Why haven't they surrendered, then?" Geder asked. "If they don't have good water, they have to know they're going to lose."

"They don't have good water, but they aren't dying from thirst either, and we"—Ternigan paused to sigh—"don't have a great deal of food. When the farmers retreated, they burned their crops and collapsed their wells. They took to the countryside. If we send out parties to forage, they're harassed by the locals. There's no one to buy food from, and if there were, there's reason to expect it would be poisoned. It will take time and fortitude. The traditional families are wagering that we don't have those. We will have Nus, my lord. Don't mistake me, the city will fall. And when it does, we'll be able to make whatever terms we want in the peace."

"I don't want Nus," Geder said. "I want Sarakal. Nus and

Inentai and every garrison and farm in between. It doesn't do me any good to come here and *half* win."

Ternigan's face pinched in, and he pressed the backs of his fingers to his chin. When he spoke, his voice was measured and careful.

"There are constraints, my lord, that are outside our control. However much I want to break the city today, the enemy is in a strong position. Even the most noble causes sometimes have to compromise."

"How long?" Geder asked.

"How long for what, precisely?"

"How long before Nus falls?"

"It will be ours by winter," Ternigan said without hesitation.

Geder sat, letting the silence stretch. Over the course of a minute, Ternigan's expression went from uncomfortable to embarrassed to angry to a kind of petulant confusion. Geder smiled without meaning it.

"You'll tour the city's fortifications with me and Minister Basrahip in the morning," he said.

"If you like, Lord Regent."

"Good to see you again, my lord," Geder said, standing. "I think it's good that I've come."

The walls of Nus stood grey and seamless on three sides of the city. The iron gates that gave the city its name rose to the height of ten men one atop the other, and great bands of the metal reinforced the stone so that the whole city had the sense of being a single great mechanism devised by a huge, inhuman mind. Which might, after all, have been true. The dragon's road came to the sea here, and had since before the dragons fell. There had likely been a city in this place since before history itself began.

Though, as Basrahip pointed out, not before the goddess.

They rode in a company of twenty. Geder wore his black leather cloak against the morning chill, but pulled it off almost at once when the sunlight warmed them. Ternigan wore bright steel armor like a boast, Basrahip and his two fellow priests the brown robes that they always did. And Geder's personal guard. If there were assassins in the brush, they didn't trouble the group. All around the city, Ternigan explained the difficulties of an attack. The long wings of the wall hung over the water and forced any approach from the sea to suffer under the defenders' bolts long before they could come to shore. Here, the walls were topped with spouts to pour down stones or flaming oil. Here, the shape of the land itself forbade the siege ladders. There, a team of engineers might be able to tunnel under the fortifications and collapse them, and Ternigan had in fact begun the project, but it would take time. Weeks at least, months more like. The seawall couldn't be surveyed, but Ternigan brought diagrams and maps with him to fill any time that wasn't already rich with discouragement.

As the hours passed, Ternigan's tone shifted from defensive to conciliatory as Geder began to understand the scope of the problem. Geder had helped to take and even briefly ruled the Free City of Vanai, and he realized now that the experience had set his expectations poorly. When he thought of taking a city, he imagined Vanai. Nus was no Vanai. It was one of the great cities of humanity.

When near midday they returned to the army's main camp, the arrayed forces of Antea that had seemed vast as an ocean only hours before had shrunk in his view. They were the same men, the same horses, the same engines of war. What they weren't was plausible.

"You see my situation," Ternigan said as they dismounted. Geder's thighs and back ached, and a sense of growing embarrassment sat in his gut as uneasy as the first pangs of illness. He nodded to Ternigan as he passed his reins to the groom, but didn't say anything.

If Ternigan's tent was near to a house, Geder's was like a movable palace. It was still the same framed leather walls, but arranged into half a dozen different rooms, including a separate latrine for his own private use and a copper bath-tub that they'd apparently hauled all the way from Cam-nipol in the event he might feel dusty. Rosemary and lilac had been scattered on the ground so that every footstep belched forth perfume. A plate of dried apples and flatbread waited for him, and he sucked at the fruit disconsolately. Ternigan was right, damn the man. Nus would have to be starved out or its walls undermined. It would take months. It would take longer than he could afford. This was his war, and he'd managed to lose it already. His ears were already burning with the whispers at court, the jokes told where he couldn't hear them. He could already see the brave loyalty on Aster's face as the boy tried to lift his spirits. He could see the pity in Cithrin bel Sarcour's eyes, should he ever be lucky enough to see them again.

By the time Basrahip joined him, he had worked himself into a bleak and self-pitying despair. The priest stood across the desk, his expression a question.

"What?" Geder snapped.

"You seem troubled, Prince Geder," Basrahip said.

"Of course I'm troubled. You saw it all just as well as I did. Those walls?"

"I saw walls," Basrahip said.

"We can't beat that."

Basrahip grunted deep in his throat, his eyes narrowing as if in deep consideration. He turned, stepped to the leather wall. When he struck it, it sounded like a massive drum.

"What are you doing?" Geder demanded.

"I am trying to think why you would beat a wall."

The rush of anger in Geder's throat felt like a dam ready to burst.

"Are you laughing at me?"

"A wall is a thing, Prince Geder. A gate is a thing. A well, a granary, a ship. Things. You don't defeat things. You defeat people, yes? So we see all these beautiful, strong things and think that the ones behind them must be beautiful, strong people. But they are Timzinae and the puppets of Timzinae. They are the slaves of dead masters. There is nothing in this place to stop us."

"They could be toys made of sticks and tree sap, but we still can't get to them," Geder said, but he felt the darkness and anger slipping in him. Losing its hold. Basrahip sat at the desk. In his fingers, the apple seemed tiny. When he bit it, the white of the flesh seemed vaguely obscene.

"Have faith in the goddess," Basrahip said. "You have kept your promise to her. She will keep faith with you. These walls will bow to you, if you wish them to."

"How?"

Basrahip smiled.

"Speak to the enemy. Do this."

"Call the parley, you mean?"

"This," Basrahip said. "Let us hear our enemy's voice."

It took the better part of three days, but on the fourth, a lesser gate swung open and a small group came out carrying the banners of parley. The man who led them was old, his broad scales greying and cracked, but he held himself with a haughtiness and pride so profound they radiated. Mesach Sau, patriarch of his family and war leader of Nus, sat across the table from Geder and folded his arms. The nictitating membranes under his eyelids slid slowly closed and open again, blinking without breaking off his stare.

"You wanted to talk," Sau said.

"Open the gates of the city," Geder said.

"Kiss my ass."

Geder looked over. Ternigan and Basrahip both sat on camp stools like matched statues, Ternigan the image of dour seriousness, Basrahip serene and smiling. Geder cleared his throat, and Basrahip's smile grew a degree wider.

"You cannot win," the priest said. "Everything you care for is already lost."

"He can kiss my ass too," Sau said.

"You should listen to him," Geder replied.

"You have no hope but surrender. The armies of Antea are powerful beyond measure. Their mercy is your only hope."

"Is that what I've come here for?" the old Timzinae asked, then turned his head and spat on the grass. "We have the food and water to sit on our thumbs and grin until this time next year. Your boys will be starving in a month. We know all about your engineers and their mining, and that's not going to do you any damned good either."

"Listen to my voice," Basrahip said, and it seemed as though his words took on a wild music. Geder felt himself almost lifted by them. "Prince Geder cannot be defeated. He cannot be stopped. It is not in your power to defeat him. If you stand against him, your children will die before your eyes. And their children as well. It is inevitable."

"This is shit," Sau said, standing. Geder lifted his hand and ten men approached, bare blades in their hands. Sau turned, his mouth a gape of rage. "We're under parley! You kill me and you'll never get another chance, boy."

"Don't call me boy," Geder said. "I'm trying to save your life."

"You cannot win," Basrahip said again, as old Sau retook his seat, his hands in fists at his sides. "The dead will rise and march with the soldiers. Any you cut down will stand again, stronger and without fear. You cannot win against the power facing you. Everything you love is already lost."

The hours of the parley passed slowly, but with every one, Geder felt his fear lose hold. Nothing had changed. The walls of Nus were just as tall, the defenses just as vicious, but what had seemed doomed before began to take on the mantle of possibility, and then credibility, and before sunset, it was certain. Old Sau sat just as proudly in his seat, his head just as high, but tears leaked out of his eyes, the scales of his cheeks black and bright as a fountain.

"I won't do it," Sau said, but his voice broke when he said it. "I'll die before I'll do it."

"Another will come," Basrahip said. His voice had taken on a dry rasp from the hours he'd spent talking. "If you will not, the next one will, and then his family will be the one to take Prince Geder's mercy and your grandchildren will die bleeding in your streets."

"I won't do it. Won't do it. Better we die than give in to bastards like you." Sau broke off, sobbing. Geder didn't clap his hands in delight—it would have been rude—but the impulse was there.

"Go," Geder said. "We can continue the negotiation tomorrow."

Sau stood up and turned without a word. He stumbled as he left the camp. The red of the setting sun made the walls of Nus glow like iron in a forge. Geder watched the old man make his journey back to the city, watched him disappear within it.

"I'm damned," Ternigan said, and his voice was soft with

wonder. "He's going to, isn't he? We're going to take this bastard of a city after all."

"It may take time," Basrahip said. "Perhaps as long as two full weeks together. But yes, Prince Ternigan. The gates will open to you. The city will fall. Your victory is certain."

Ternigan shook his head again, pressing a palm to his temple.

"I don't understand all that I saw here today, my lord," he said. "But..."

"You don't have to understand," Geder said. "Just have faith in it."

They walked back toward camp slowly. In the broad arch of sky, a handful of stars appeared. Then a scattering. Then countless millions.

"We will have to make arrangements for a protectorate," Ternigan said. "That may be a trick. I thought I'd have much more time. Did you have someone in mind to take control?"

Jorey Kalliam, Geder almost said, but stopped himself. Now that it was asked, he realized it was a question he should have been considering from before he'd left Camnipol. Jorey was still reestablishing himself in court, and while having a few visible honors like the protection of a conquered city would help in that, it would also mean being away from Camnipol. He wished he'd thought to ask. But there would be other cities. Other chances.

That night, they all dined on fresh chicken and a sweet mash made from sugar beets and rice. Ternigan had the captains he commanded compete in extemporaneous poetry praising Antea, the Severed Throne, Geder, and Prince Aster. The night was like something from the histories Geder had read of the great generations of the empire, a bit of the past with new life breathed into its nostrils. It was as if he'd taken all the romances of campaign life and made them real. The comradery, the joy, the bluff masculine competition. All of the things he'd hoped for and never found were his now. All evening, Basrahip and the other priests walked through the camps, speaking with the soldiers, laughing with them, cheering them, and near midnight the whole camp broke into song at once, literally singing Geder's praises.

He went to bed drunk as much on the affection and loyalty of his men as on any sort of wine, and lay in the darkness grinning and satisfied. He let his mind wander, remembering the darkness of his mood the day he'd seen the city's defenses. The thought was almost pleasant now, and he turned it in his mind like a glass marble held to the sun, watching it glitter and flash. He'd been so sure that he'd have to return humiliated. He imagined Aster looked up at him again, solid and encouraging even in defeat, and Geder was filled with a kind of love. Aster was such a good child. Geder felt the depth of his own good fortune in getting to deliver the prince a vastly expanded empire when the time finally came for his coronation. A world at peace. It would be a beautiful thing.

And then, after. When Geder was only the Baron of Ebbingbaugh again, he could return to his own life. His books, his holding. Perhaps a wife, or since Cithrin bel Sarcour wasn't of noble blood, at least a consort. If she'd have him. Or he could travel. Aster could name him as a special ambassador to Birancour, and he'd have reason to visit her in Porte Oliva. He closed his eyes and conjured up the feeling of her body against him, the sound of her breath. He didn't know he was falling asleep until a servant's apologetic voice woke him.

Mesach Sau hadn't slept. Fatigue showed in his clouded eyes and the droop of his shoulders. He hadn't bothered with the formalities of parley, but walked directly to the camp, to the sentry. It was as if the old man didn't particularly care whether he was brought before Geder or killed on the spot. As Geder arrived, Ternigan came trotting from his tent as well. Basrahip, serene and pleasant, was already there.

"I'll do it," Sau said, his voice breaking on the words. "Swear that you'll spare my family, and I'll open the fucking gates for you."

Geder turned to Ternigan and swept a hand to indicate the weeping man, defeated even before the sack began.

"And that, Lord Marshal, is how it's done," Geder said. "Now. Bring me Inentai."

Cithrin

Living in the midst of a family changed many of the small details of life. Privacy was often a matter of politeness and etiquette in a way that it wasn't when she'd had rooms of her own. Bits and pieces of other lives seemed scattered through the halls like fresh rushes, and had Magistra Isadau and Maha, her cousin's daughter, been speaking of matters of family or politics, even questions of finance and the running of the bank, Cithrin would not, she told herself, have eavesdropped. But instead, she walked down the wide polished granite hall bright with the light of morning, heard the voices of the older Timzinae woman and the girl, and picked out the words *love* and *sex*. Her journey to the kitchens suddenly became less immediate. Curiosity sharpened her ears and softened her footsteps and she edged closer to the office chambers.

"That too," the magistra said. "But not *only* that."

"But if you really love him, doesn't that make it all right? Even if there is a baby from it?"

Maha's voice was strong, but not confrontational. This wasn't an argument, but a deposition. A discovery of the facts. Magistra Isadau's laughter was low and rueful.

"I have loved many, many people," she said, "and I've never meant the same thing by the word twice. Love is wonderful, but it doesn't justify anything or make a bad choice wise. Everyone loves. Idiots love. Murderers love. Pick any atrocity you want, and someone will be able to justify it out of something they call love. Anything can wear love like a cloak."

There was a pause, and then the girl's voice again.

"I don't understand. What does that mean?" Maha said. Cithrin felt a warm glow of gratitude for the child and the question. She didn't understand it either.

"Love isn't a word that means one thing," the magistra said. Her voice was gentle. Almost coaxing. It was the voice of a woman trying to gentle an animal or call it out from under a table. "You love your father, but not the way you love this hypothetical boy. You love your brothers. You love that girl you spend all your nights with. Mian? You love Mian. Don't you?"

"I do," the girl said as if she were conceding a point to a magistrate.

"Someone may love their country or their gods. An idea or a vision of the world. Or because it can mean so many things, it's possible to call something love that's nothing to do with it. If the edict comes to march north into Sarakal, chances are it will say it is for the love of our brothers and cousins in the north. But it will really be fear. Fear that the war will come here otherwise. Does that make sense?"

"Yes."

"Love is noble," the magistra said. "And so we wrap it around all the things we think perhaps aren't so noble in hopes no one will see what they really are. Fear. Anger. Shame."

"I'm not ashamed," the girl said.

"You want this hypothetical boy. Don't. Lie to your mother about it if you'd like, but not to me. He opens your body in ways you can't control. He fills your mind in ways that disturb you and wash your best self away. You're drunk with him. And so you want it to be love, just the way the generals want their fear of Antea to be love."

"But..."

"I'm not telling you what decision you should make. God knows you have enough people to do that for you. But I am reminding you that you love a great many people you don't want to take your dress off for. Longing isn't love. Not any more than fear is."

A discreet scratch interrupted, and then the sound of the office door sliding open.

"Courier come for you, Magistra," a man's voice said.

"Bring the reports here, then."

"Can't, ma'am. Courier says he can't give 'em to anyone besides you or Miss Cithrin."

In an instant, Cithrin was powerfully aware that she was standing in the bright corridor, bent like a child trying to overhear her parents. She turned, back the way she'd come, took a half dozen near-silent steps, and then turned again, collecting herself as if she were only now beginning her interrupted errand.

Maha came into the corridor. The brown, insectile scales that covered her face and neck, her hands and arms, were darker than Cithrin remembered. Perhaps it was how Timzinae blushed. She didn't know.

Cithrin smiled, and the girl nodded back but didn't speak. Cithrin strolled down the corridor, wondering what to do. On the one hand, she wanted to go back and see what the courier had brought; on the other, doing so without it being mentioned to her might lead the magistra to suspect she'd been spying. With a sigh, she went on to the kitchens as if she didn't know anything that she wasn't expected to.

In truth, Maha wasn't much younger than Cithrin herself.

She wondered what it would have been like to be first coming into herself with older women there to speak with. Her own mother was little more than a few fleeting impressions and entries in an old, yellowing ledger, but had she lived, she might have given Cithrin advice on questions of love and sex, men and hearts. In the kitchen, Cithrin exchanged banter with the cooking servants as they made her a bowl of stewed barley with butter and honey, but her mind was elsewhere. Even the rich sweetness of the first bite hardly registered.

Whom did she love? Did she love anyone? Did anyone love her? Now that she asked the questions straight on, she realized she'd been thinking at the edges of them for some time.

Since, in fact, the day she'd heard that Captain Wester had gone. Now *that* was interesting.

She considered whether she loved Wester the way she might have a proposal of business. Dispassionately, and from a careful distance. Yes, she thought, maybe she did. She didn't feel any particular desire toward him, but that was the point Magistra Isadau had been making. Desire and love weren't the same thing.

Cithrin sat at one of the low stone tables, looking south over the wide sprawl of Suddapal's third city. Where the land ended in a spray of small islands, she could just see the traffic of tiny boats, black against the throbbing morning blue. Desire wasn't the same as love. Love, she decided, was when something went away and left you emptier. By that definition, certainly—

"Magistra?"

Cithrin looked up. Yardem Hane towered in the doorway. He looked older than she imagined him, but perhaps it was only the light.

"Yes?"

"A report's come. Magistra Isadau wanted to consult with you on it."

"Something from Porte Oliva?"

"Carse," Yardem said. "I think it's about the war."

The pages themselves were fine linen, made without a watermark. Paerin Clark's hand was, as always, neat and precise.

"More information from the mysterious source?" Cithrin said.

"Or a forgery," Magistra Isadau said. The cheerfulness in her voice was as false as paint. "Komme wanted you to look it over. See whether you had any insights to add."

The information was clear and succinct. The first section was a rough accounting of the armies in the field. How many sword-and-bows, how many mounted knights. The supplies of food and fodder. Cithrin found a map of Sarakal and plotted each of the groups against the small nation on the desk before her. With each new mark, her belly grew heavier. Nus, the Iron City, had capitulated, but the garrisons on the path to Inentai hadn't fallen. Not yet.

"I thought Antea was losing," Cithrin said.

"They were. They should be," Magistra Isadau said. Her expression was unreadable. "They go into battle with fewer men and barely enough to supply them. And then they win. They reach a town that should be ready to hold back a siege for months, and it falls in weeks." The older woman spread her hands.

"They can't come as far as Elassae, though," Cithrin said. "They don't have the men or food. And we're seeing the refugees from Inentai starting to come through."

"They don't have the men or food to take Sarakal either," the Timzinae woman said. "But they're doing it."

Cithrin turned back to the report. The unknown writer

went on to list a half dozen other forces outside of the churn of war and violence in Sarakal. These were smaller groups with less than a dozen soldiers, but better supplied. The names of individual captains leading these smaller forces were listed with them. Emmun Siu and fifteen men, the report said, moving into the northern reaches of Borja. Dar Cinlama and twelve men traveling over water to Hallskar. Two groups totaling fifty men answering to Korl Essian bound for Lyoneia. Another group, the smallest, with only seven people, two horses, and a cart, led by someone named Bulger Shoal requesting diplomatic passage into Herez.

"What are these?" Cithrin asked. "Scouting missions for new invasions?"

"We don't know," Magistra Isadau said. "I think Komme was hoping you might have some insight."

Cithrin cast her mind back through the long months into the darkness under Camnipol. Hallskar, Borja, Lyoneia, and Herez. She tried to recall whether in the long hours of darkness, Geder or Aster had said anything to connect those places. The office with its gentle arches and brilliant sunlight seemed to defy the memories of darkness and dust.

Magistra Isadau's nictitating membranes clicked closed and open. Cithrin felt the pressure of the older woman's attention and frowned, willing herself to think of something—anything—that would justify it.

Nothing came.

"There's no hurry," Magistra Isadau said, folding the papers and putting them back into her private strongbox. "I don't need to send a reply for a day or two. If anything does come to you, I can add it."

"How old is the information?" Cithrin asked.

"Weeks, at the least. But Inentai isn't under siege yet. So perhaps it still counts for something."

The Timzinae woman shrugged and smiled. Cithrin thought that she saw unease in her dark eyes and the angle of her mouth. It was hard to be sure.

"Do you still think that the war won't come here?" Cithrin asked, and the physical memory of making the same query assailed her. She'd said almost identical words once to a man now dead, in a city now ashes.

Magistra Isadau lifted her hands in a gesture of confusion and despair.

"I don't know any longer. The truth now is that your opinion carries more weight than my own," she said. "All I have is the numbers and reports. You know the people."

"The person," Cithrin said.

"The person. So. Knowing what you do of Geder Palliako, will the war come here?"

Cithrin sat forward, her hands clasped. Memories of the Lord Regent of Antea rose before her mind like fumes from a fire. His laughter. The roundness that fear gave his eyes. The rage as he slaughtered the traitor from within his own court. The taste of his mouth and the feel of his body. A cold shudder passed through her. Magistra Isadau made a small clicking sound at the back of her throat and nodded as if Cithrin had answered.

Perhaps she had.

A thin fog rose just after nightfall, the first Cithrin had seen in weeks. The summer in Suddapal rarely grew cool enough to allow it, but now wisps and patches littered the streets as if a cloud had shattered and fallen to earth. Cithrin sat in an open garden with a lantern behind her, sluggish moths beating at the glass with thick, furry bodies. She had contracts and ledgers spread before her in the buttery light. The wide carved timbers above her gathered the shadows in close, cradling them. The history of the Medean bank in Suddapal seemed less important now than its future.

The trade of Elassae relied on the traffic of metalwork from the north, textiles and cloth from the Free Cities, and spice and gold from Lyoneia. The mines and forges of Sarakal might fall under the control of the Severed Throne, but the trade would remain. Or she thought it would.

Or the armies of Antea might burn them all, as they had Vanai. Surely Magistra Isadau was selling letters of credit to the nervous and wealthy, transferring the gold and jewels of Elassae into paper that could go west, to the safer ports, father from Antean blades. There would be a way to move that wealth away from Suddapal before the end came. Before the armies. Before it burned.

She shook herself, turned back to her books, and found she'd lost the thread of them. Her fingers were on a payment entry, and she could no more say what deposit it came from than she could will the sun to dance on the seashore. She said something vulgar and closed the books. She could sit here enjoying the moment of cool in the midsummer's heat with her mind scattered and lost or go back to her rooms and stare sleepless at the walls. The knot in her belly didn't permit anything else.

She snuffed out the lanterns and stacked the wax trays with her notes in a corner with a strip of red cloth that would tell the servants to leave them undisturbed. The sensual music of reed flute and sanded drum that made their hymns murmured even in the darkness of midnight. More than any other race she knew, the old men and women of the Timzinae turned away from sleep. The compound— indeed the five cities of Suddapal—only rested. They never slept. She found herself drawn toward the music and the promise of company and warmth, but it was an illusion. She didn't know the songs. The snapping of her pale, soft fingers wouldn't give the sharp percussion of Timzinae hands.

She wondered if Yardem was on guard duty. Or any of her little retinue from Porte Oliva. She wondered where Cary and Sandr and Hornet were tonight. She wondered what Captain Wester was doing and what would make him think that Yardem Hane would ever betray him. She wondered where Geder Palliako slept that night and if he ever thought of her. She hoped he didn't.

In her own room, the servants had left a lamp burning low. Her window let in a spray of moonlight, the cool blue mixing with the gold of the flame. She changed into her night clothes and slipped her legs beneath the thin summer sheets, sitting with her back against the wall.

Sleep wouldn't come. She already knew it. She could lie in the darkness and stew in her own thoughts or turn up the lamp and read through the essays and histories Magistra Isadau had assigned her along with the books of the bank. Both options sounded equally unpleasant. For an hour she only sat, listening to the fire mutter in its stove, the distant whisper of drums.

She rose sometime in the darkness well after midnight, turning up the lamp's wick more for variety's sake than from any real desire. The floor cooled her feet. The papers waited on her bedside table, held down against the breeze by the old dragon's tooth. Cithrin lifted it now, running her finger idly along its serrated edge, as she considered the writing beneath without really caring what it said.

The war was coming. It was all happening again, just the way it had in Vanai. She could feel it like a storm. The blades of Antea wouldn't be stopped. As much as she wished otherwise, she knew the violence would spill past Sarakal. Perhaps to Elassae. Or into Borja. Or turn west toward

Northcoast and Birancour. It was like a fire. She might not know where the flames would jump, but wherever it landed it would burn. And Magistra Isadau knew it too, as much as she pretended doubt. Cithrin understood the impulse to wish the danger away. She'd done it herself in Vanai, and she'd had so much less to lose. Isadau had family—sister, brother, nieces, nephews, cousins. Cithrin had only had Magister Imaniel, Besel, Cam. Or perhaps it was the same. Losing everything was still losing everything, however little someone began with.

But Herez? Hallskar? Lyoneia? None of them shared a border with Imperial Antea. Perhaps Geder and his counselors were looking farther ahead, to a wider, greater conquest. She tapped the dragon's tooth against her palm. The thought didn't sit comfortably. There was something else. Something about the dragon's roads and the places they didn't pass through.

Understanding came to her with an almost audible click. She stood up, her heart racing and a grin pressing her lips. She didn't even pause to throw a cloak over the night clothes. The dragon's tooth firmly in her hand, she strode out into corridors darker than mere night. Her footsteps didn't falter. She knew the path.

Magistra Isadau was in her office chamber, reclined on a divan with a book open on her knees. She looked up without any sense of surprise as Cithrin entered the room.

"May I see the new report again?" Cithrin asked.

The Timzinae woman marked her place and closed her book. Opening the strongbox was the work of a minute. Cithrin took up the pages, turning them silently until she found the passages she sought.

A small group to Borja, led by someone named Emmun

Siu. Two groups to Lyoneia under Korl Essian. And one to Hallskar, led by Dar Cinlama.

Dar Cinlama, the Dartinae adventurer who had once given her a dragon's tooth. Cithrin tapped the page.

"Something?" Magistra Isadau asked.

"These aren't scouting groups for the armies," Cithrin said. "They're looking for something."

Clara

Someone in the house was screaming. Clara found herself out of her bed before she had wholly woken, wrapping the thin summer blanket around her waist, alarm running through her blood. The sound was constant, barely pausing to draw breath. A woman, she thought, or a child. Her first thought was that one of the new maids had encountered Dawson's hunting dogs again. Except that was wrong, because Dawson was dead, and the dogs sent back to Osterling Fells or set loose in the streets. Somewhere nearby, a door slammed open or perhaps closed. Footsteps pounded down the hall. Clara dropped her blanket and snatched up the pewter candlestick from beside her bed, holding it in a clenched fist like a tiny club. She willed away the last confusion of sleep and prepared herself for the onslaught, whatever it was.

A man's voice came from just outside the door of her rooms. Vincen Coe.

"My lady?"

"Vincen? What's happening?"

"Stay where you are. Bar the door. I will return for you."

"Who's hurt? What's going on?"

The man didn't answer. His footsteps went away down the corridor, then to the rough stair at its end before being lost under the shrieking. Clara hesitated in the darkness.

Only the faintest moonlight shouldered its way through her window, and the room hadn't lost the stale heat of the day. The air felt close as a coffin. She put down her candlestick and walked to the door. The rude plank that assured her privacy was already in its brackets, but she put her hands to it all the same, as if touching the wood might assure her safety. The screaming paused, and masculine shouts took their place. She winced at each new sound, then strained at the silences. Footsteps pounded across the floor below her, and a man shouted once, wordlessly, but in triumph. It wasn't a voice she knew.

Her rage surprised her. The sane thing, the right and expected one, would be to stay where she was, cowering in the heat and gloom and hoping to be overlooked by violence. For most of her life, it was what she would have done. With both hands, she heaved the plank up, then dropped it to the floor, and then stepped back for her candlestick, making a short internal note to herself that provided she lived to see morning, she would want a weapon of some sort in her bedroom in the future. A cudgel, perhaps.

The woman's voice was screaming again, but there were words in it now. Vulgarities and threats. Clara made her way down the hall, her chin forward and her head high. The sharp sound of metal against metal announced swordplay, but she didn't pause. As she marched down the stairs, the screaming resolved itself. Abatha Coe, the keeper of the boarding house. Her voice came from the kitchen. Clara pushed her way in.

The ruddy light of the open stove showed two Firstblood men, young and thin, their ragged beards hardly enough to cover their naked throats, holding Abatha on her knees while she screamed. An older Kurtadam man, broad across the shoulders, his pelt shining red in the firelight, was load-

ing haunches of meat into a rough canvas bag. Vincen lay on
the floor, a fourth man—also a Firstblood—kneeling on his
shoulder blades, pinning him in place. Vincen's sword was
in the kneeling man's hands.

"What," Clara said in the stentorian voice she kept for
intimidating servants, "is the *meaning* of this?"

As if for punctuation, she swung the candlestick against
the kneeling man's head, just above the ear with as much
power as the close quarters allowed. The pewter candlestick
jarred her fingers, the kneeling man yelped and put a hand
to his ear, and chaos erupted. One of the men restraining
Abatha let go and turned toward Clara, drawing a cruelly curved dagger. Vincen surged forward, reaching for
his sword, the kneeling man struggling to get back atop
him before he could. Abatha screamed, wrenching herself
around, trying to free her one trapped arm.

The young man with the dagger slid forward, knife at the
fore, and Clara threw the candlestick at his head. It bounced
off his temple without any clear effect, and Clara's righteous
anger drained from her in an instant. She stepped back into
the corridor, her hands held before her. *Because better he
cut off my fingers before I die*, she thought, ridiculously.
The man feinted to the right, then the left. In the dim light,
she could see his teeth as he grinned.

"Ossit! Behind you!" the Kurtadam man called, and the
knifeman turned in time for Abatha Coe to come boiling out
of the kitchen, her face a mask of supernatural rage. Clara
reached forward and grabbed the knifeman's wrist, pulling
it toward her so that the blade might not find its home in
Abatha's belly. The man was stronger than he looked. Clara
pulled at his wrist, drawing the blade closer to herself as
Abatha shrieked and cursed and flailed at him.

Someone barreled into her side, breaking her grip and

pushing her into the wall. She stumbled, and the bite of the knife caught her arm, the pain bright and intimate. She grabbed at her wound with the opposite hand and felt the slickness of blood. Men were surging around her, and she braced herself for the next blow. But it never came.

They ran past her, the Kurtadam man at the lead, his canvas bag hanging heavy against his back. The three First-blood toughs followed him with blades drawn. Clara saw joy in their faces. Abatha, crouched on all fours in the frame of the kitchen door, called out threats and epithets, her voice raw and ragged. The door to the street flew open and then closed again behind them. One of them whooped in victory when he reached the street. One of the Firstbloods. One of the men of her own race. Her kind.

"The food," Abatha said bitterly. "They took the food. That was everything for the next week. How'm I going to feed everybody now?"

"Are you hurt?" Clara asked, clasping at her arm. As long as she kept her palm pressed against the blood, she didn't have to see how deep the cut had gone. Better to tend to Abatha before that.

"Hurt?" Abatha said, as if the word were one she'd heard before but never used. "They took the food."

"Vincen?" Clara called. "Are you all right?"

There was no answer. Clara felt her heart go tight. The pain of her arm faded to nothing as she rose to her feet, floating, it seemed into the ruined kitchen. The bench by the little table lay on its side. The pale bodies of dried beans were scattered across the dark planks of the floor. Vincen sat with his back against a cabinet, his sword in his hand. As Clara watched, he heaved a breath, and then another. His gaze struggled its way into focus, and he frowned.

"You're hurt," he said.

"Vincen?" Clara said, kneeling at his side. Behind her, Abatha stood in the doorway. "Are you well? Can you walk?"

He lifted his left hand as if he meant to scratch his nose. The fingers were black with blood and gore. Clara heard herself gasp.

"Don't believe so, m'lady," he said, and then, more softly, "Oh dear."

Abatha's hand tugged at her shoulder, pulled Clara back and up. Vincen couldn't die. It was unthinkable. He was young and healthy and he had no enemies. And he was in love with her, and she, God help her, was in love with him, and he couldn't—could *not*—die stupidly in a fight over ham. Clara's breath came in sips and gasps. The world seemed to narrow. Abatha was saying something, and shaking her while she spoke. Clara tried to bring her mind back, but it was slow, difficult work.

"It's three streets to the east, two to the north," Abatha said. It wasn't the first time she'd said it.

"Three east," Clara said. "Two north."

"It's a low house. Green with a red roof."

"Three east, two north. Green with a red roof."

"The cunning man's named Hoban."

Clara nodded. Of course. A cunning man. They needed a cunning man. She would go and get one.

"Three east, two north. Green with red. Ossit."

"Not Ossit. Hoban."

"Hoban," Clara said. "I'll be back. Don't let him die while I'm gone."

"Wait!" Abatha said, shrugging out of her house robe and holding it out. "Take this. Y'ain't decent."

Clara looked down at herself. The simple sleeping shift was torn and soaked down one side in blood. What a sight that would be. Lady Kalliam half naked and bloody running through the streets before dawn. She would have done it without a second thought.

The air in the streets felt cool against her skin, the rough cobbles scraped at her bare feet. The half moon dodged between rooftops, here and gone and back again, as she ran. Three streets to the east, then turning left into a thin passage hardly more than an alley that stank of shit and piss and old blood gone to rot. She'd feared that in the dim light she might not be able to make out the colors, but the green was the green of new grass and the red almost crimson. Even by moonlight, there could be no mistake. Clara hopped up the single step and hammered on the door until a huge First-blood man with a greying beard to his navel and strange tattoos up both of his arms answered her. His accent spoke of Stollbourne and perhaps cities even farther to the west. She had to assure him twice that she wasn't the one in need of help, but once he understood, he came quickly.

Abatha had laid Vincen out on the kitchen table like a body being prepared for his funeral. His skin looked like wax, and webs of dark blood marred him. His eyes were closed and his mouth drawn back in a grimace of pain and determination. The greatest wound was in his side, just below his lowest rib, and the skin there hung loose and open. The cunning man crouched, placing his palm over the injury, closing his eyes and murmuring prayers and invocations that seemed to echo in a space larger than the kitchen.

With the violence done, other occupants of the boarding house began to creep out. The Southling girl who always ate by herself. Two Firstblood workmen who'd just come to Camnipol from the north and taken a room together. They haunted the shadows, drawn to the blood like flies. Abatha's cold gaze kept them at bay, and Clara ignored them. The cut on her own arm had begun to hurt again, but she paid it little attention.

Without warning, Vincen howled. Light poured from his mouth and nose, from the cuts in his skin. His back arched until only his toes and the top of his head were touching the table. Clara cried out in alarm, but as quickly as it had come, it was over. The cunning man sat heavily on the bench. The terrible wound in Vincen's side was still there, but instead of blood, a thin, milky fluid ran from it. The kitchen filled with the smell of onions.

"He will live," the cunning man said. "He will be weak for a time, but this is not the wound that kills him."

"Thank you," Clara said. Her vision went wet and blurry. "Thank you so much."

"Now. Will you let me see to that arm?"

Clara looked down. Fresh blood was still sheeting down to her wrist. When she moved, the living muscle shifted and twitched. She felt dizzy.

"If you would," she said. "That would be very kind."

The first light of dawn pressed at the windows as Abatha counted coins into the cunning man's hand. The boarders who hadn't made their way out already began to appear, and Abatha enlisted three of the strongest to carry Vincen to his room while she put together something edible from the ruins of her kitchen. Clara went with Vincen, and when the others left, she remained with him, watching him sleep. The reassuring rise and fall of his breast. The calm in his face. Her own skin itched where the cunning man's words and herbs had knit it closed, and she scratched at it idly.

He was so young, and yet older than her youngest son. Older than she had been when she'd married Dawson and become the Baroness of Osterling Fells. There were scars on his body, testaments to the life of a huntsman. And new ones now. She remembered the half-kiss she'd given him, the roughness of his stubble against her lips. The softness of his mouth. She let herself weep quietly without any particular sense of grief. Exhaustion and the aftermath of violence were surely enough to justify a few tears.

She heard Abatha's steps long before the woman appeared. She'd put on clothes and carried a carved wooden bowl of wheat mash that she held out to Clara. It tasted sweet and rich and comforting.

"How is he?" Abatha asked, nodding to her cousin unconscious on his bed.

"Well, I believe," Clara said. "I don't know."

Abatha nodded and looked down at her feet. Her lips moved, practicing some words or thoughts. When she looked up again, her expression was hard.

"This is your fault, you know."

Clara wouldn't have been more surprised if the woman had spat out a snake.

"Excuse me?" she said. "If I'd stayed in my room, you would both have—"

"I told him we had to leave," Abatha said. "I told him that food was coming short, and people were going to get desperate. Get mean. Get out of the city, I told him. Close up the house and good riddance to it. There'll be more than enough work needs doing on the farm. And he'd have gone too, if it weren't for you and your letters, whatever they are."

Clara's lips pressed thin. The sudden mixture of guilt for keeping Vincen in harm's way, annoyance that he had spoken to Abatha about her work, and outrage that she should be asked to carry the responsibility for the actions of thugs she didn't even know confused her into silence.

Abatha waited for a moment, then shrugged.

"He's a man grown, and he makes his choices," she said.

"I do too. He's family, and I'll stand by him as long as he needs me. But the day he dies, you're sleeping on the street, m'lady, because I am done with this shithole of a city."

At the end, the woman's voice wavered. Of course it did. The woman had been attacked in her own home by men with knives. She'd been held helpless while her food was stolen. She'd seen her own family nearly killed before her. This anguish grew from seeds that Geder Palliako had planted. This was what Clara had chosen, in her way, to stand against. It was uncharitable to forget that, and so she wouldn't.

"I understand," she said.

"I don't know what the hell you think you're doing here anyway."

"I understand," Clara said again. "Thank you."

That afternoon, the sun shone warm as a fire. Clara wore a grey dress with strong lines. It wasn't her most attractive, but it gave a sense of authority without being overbearing, and even if no one agreed with her opinion of it, it helped her play the part she had chosen for the day. Vincen was still asleep when she stepped out into the street, and the smell of cooking lentils followed her. All the meat for seasoning it was gone, and meals were going to be a bit bland around the place for a time. Small price.

Clara walked to the south with a pleasant smile and a nod for every familiar face. She forced herself to own the road without commanding it. To take it for granted, and by doing so, make the city itself wonder if perhaps it was hers. She had four people to call upon, and no assurance that any would be able to help her. There was no option but to try.

She found the third house she'd sought in a cul-de-sac near the western wall. A dozen children raced through the dim, grimy space playing as children did everywhere. Even in the shadow of evil. *I don't know what the hell you think you're doing here anyway*, Abatha said again in her memory.

Clara stepped up to the door. It was thin wood held by a leather hinge well on its way to rot. She rapped on it smartly with her knuckles and set her shoulders. Inside, someone stirred, grunted. A bar was pulled away and the door swung open. The man standing in the shadows blinked at her, as astounded by her presence as he would have been at a gryphon or a dragon. Baronesses were clearly well outside his experience. Even fallen ones.

"Good afternoon. I'm Clara. You must be Mihal," Clara said.

"Yes," he said, then bowed as if only then remembering to do so.

"I'm a friend of your mother's," Clara said. "I don't think we've met formally."

"She...ah...talks of you. On occasion. Ma'am."

Clara smiled, nodding. It was always so difficult to put young men at ease. They all seemed to look at her as something out of a myth. All except Vincen.

"Your sister's wedding. It went well, I hope?"

"Quite, ma'am," Mihal said, scratching himself sincerely and indelicately. "It was a nice dress you gave her."

"I'm glad it suited. May I come in?"

Mihal's expression went uncomfortable and he glanced back over his shoulder in concern.

"I have three boys of my own," Clara said. "I've seen worse."

"Well, then. Certainly?"

The rooms were tiny, squalid, close, and repellent. Clara sat on a stool and crossed her ankles as if this were the finest drawing room in the Kingspire.

"I was wondering, Mihal, if I might put upon you for a favor."

"Ah. Sure, I suppose," he said as she drew out her pipe and packed it with tobacco. She lifted her eyebrows, and he brought her a burning candle to light it from. The smoke tasted wonderful and smelled much better than the room. Clara took the bowl in one hand, tapping her teeth with the stem.

"I am looking for a young man. A Firstblood. He probably thinks of himself as a tough, and he associates with a Kurtadam man of middle years," she said, "and his friends call him Ossit."

Marcus

After his season in Lyoneia, the plains of the Keshet in summer felt as strange and exotic to Marcus as walking into a dream. The wide horizons under the uncompromising bowl of sky felt too large, and the desert air strangely cool now that it wasn't too humid for his sweat to dry. A few distant clouds scudded overhead with the dim quarter moon showing pale in the blue among them. The caravanserai, as near a thing to a permanent city in this part of the Keshet, centered on a stand of massive obelisks that rose in a circle toward the sky. The stones curved like the claws of some massive beast that could hold a hundred wagons and their teams in its palm, and in the center a spring of clear water trickled from a broken stone into a wide and shallow pool. Half of the travelers in the little oasis were Tralgu, the other half Yemmu, and so two Firstblood men on foot and without so much as their own tent stood out like blood on a wedding dress. Everything smelled of dust and horse shit, and the suspicious looks from the caravan guards promised violence if Marcus or Kit spoke the wrong words or laughed at the wrong jokes. Marcus suspected that it said something unpleasant about his choices in life that he felt so comfortable there.

He sat beside the water, his little pack at his side. He'd wrapped the sword in cloth and bound it with leather straps.

No particular use if he wanted to draw the thing, but there was less chance he'd need its use if it wasn't obvious he was hauling magical treasures from the Dragon Empire about with him. His own blade still hung from his hip, though in a new scabbard. The old one had rotted through with his clothes. The sand-colored cotton robes they'd bought on the Lyoneian coast weren't so different a cut from the local. Kit made his way through the camps, listening and talking, being charming and using the power of the spider goddess to ingratiate himself to the carters and guards and nomadic hunters. Marcus only saw him when he came back with money or a bowl of boiled millet and roasted goat.

"What're we looking at?" Marcus asked, biting into the meat.

"I think it could be worse," Kit said softly enough that his words didn't carry. "I haven't found anyone heading in our direction, but I have been promised a mule for a reasonable price."

"That's the good news?"

"That and no one seems to have decided to kill us and take our things."

"Counts as a good day, then," Marcus said. "Let's go meet our new mule."

It was a good mule, as mules go, sturdy across the shoulder and placid-eyed. Marcus and Kit had little to carry besides sleeping rolls, food, and waterskins. The Yemmu man who'd agreed to sell it lumbered along behind Marcus as he looked the animal over, his expression vaguely disgruntled as if he might be regretting the agreement.

"He limps sometimes," the Yemmu said. "Have to rest him for a day or two so he don't go lame."

"I'm sure that won't be a problem," Kit said in a pleasant voice that meant the man was lying. The more Marcus saw the spider goddess's power in action, the more useful it seemed to be. Not much in a battle, maybe, but in everything that came before and after. And in his experience, before and after were what determined who bled in the field.

"Marcus?" Kit said.

"She'll do," Marcus said, putting his hand on the beast's shoulder. The mule didn't respond even to look at him. "Get us where we're headed, anyway."

The Yemmu sighed and accepted a pouch of coins from Kit. They stood together as the huge man counted through the silver and copper, nodded to himself, and waved at the beast.

"She's yours now," he said. "Too damn small to be any use to me anyway. Where you poor bastards going anyhow?"

"Borja," Marcus said.

"Trying to keep clear of the war, then," the Yemmu said. "That's wise. Uglier than a camel's asshole, that is."

"There's a charming image," Marcus said.

"Have you had word from the west, then?" Kit said before the Yemmu could reply. "I have friends in Sarakal, and I'd be glad of any news."

The man's shrug was massive.

"Had word. Don't know how much of it's true. Say Nus fell and the fucking empire stripped the damn place to the walls. Put half the city in chains for their crimes."

Marcus lifted an eyebrow. A black fly as thick as his finger settled on the mule's ear, and the mule twitched it away.

"That's a fair load of crimes, if you're depriving half a city of their freedom over it," Marcus said.

"Timzinae were behind the coup last year," the Yemmu man explained. "New Lord Regent took it personal. He's a strange one. Stories are he's some kind of cunning man, only more powerful than I've ever heard. Talks with the spirits of the dead's what they say. Dead march with him. It's why he can keep going. No one thought he'd win as far as he has. No one's sure when he'll stop."

No one's sure if he will hung in the air, unspoken.

"Inentai's a hard city to take," Marcus said. "Anteans will be getting harassed by the locals and river raiders from Borja. Supply lines'll be vulnerable."

"Oh, and you know all about war, do you?"

"Some," Marcus said.

"Well. Probably you're right. Can't see it going over the winter. So long as the bugs can hold out until then, the empire'll go home by first frost." The Yemmu man nodded, agreeing with himself. Talking himself into believing what he only hoped was true.

The Keshet spread out before them, dry and vast. The shallow hills rose and fell, their sides green and grey from the thick-stemmed, tough brush. In the mornings, Marcus woke before dawn to the sound of birds. They made some simple meal, packed what there was on the mule's back, and headed for the next oasis or creek. Twice they saw the great dust plume of a princely caravan, the moving cities of Jasuru and Tralgu who dominated the plains but didn't settle them. Both times, the larger groups passed without bothering them. Two men and a mule were probably too small a group to care about, and Marcus was fine with that. As long as there were rabbits and lizards enough to eat, creeks and wells enough for water, and fodder for the mule, he'd walk from one end of the Keshet to the other without seeing an unfamiliar face, apart from the occasional stop at a caravanserai for food, and count himself pleased to do it. The days grew subtly longer, the midday sun more intense, but the nights were still bitterly cold.

Kit didn't complain. Marcus assumed that his years wandering with his acting troupe had left him accustomed to long journeys in the empty places of the world. The old actor's face was thinner, his body narrowed by months of living without steady food and too much work, but it didn't make him look worn. If anything, he seemed younger, fuller, more vital. Even at the end of a punishing day's walk, on rationed water because they hadn't found fresh, Kit's step seemed to bounce. Marcus tried to imagine what it would be like for him. They were walking back across decades toward the place where Kit had been a boy. He imagined the years and losses and adventures peeling away from Kit and being left behind on the open plain. The fear was there—Marcus could see it by the light of the fire at night, could hear it in the man's voice when he spoke—but there was a joy that came with it.

The circle, Marcus thought, closing. Something was ending for Kit, and the sense of impending completion was pulling the man across the Keshet like the north calling a lodestone. Marcus didn't have that, but he kept pace. One leg in front of the other, eyes sharp for snakes, mouth too dry for comfort. He wore the poisoned sword across his back; the mule had refused to carry it after the third day. So far as he could tell, he hadn't suffered any particular bad effects except that his dreams seemed more vivid and confused than usual and his food all tasted bad.

Then one day, the horizon thickened. Dark hills marked the edge of the world, and beyond them, mountains. Marcus sat by the low, smoking fire as the setting sun turned the world the color of fire. His shadow stretched toward the hills, toward the temple and its goddess. Beside him, the mule sighed and closed its black eyes.

"How far do you think they've gotten?" Marcus asked.

Kit lay back on his bedroll, his hands behind his head and staring up at the stars.

"You mean the Anteans?"

"Them and the ones we're here to stop. You think they've gotten to Inentai yet?"

"Probably," Kit said. "But perhaps not. There might have been illness in the ranks. Or they might have run short of food or water. I've found armies to be large, unwieldy things, haven't you? It seems they're always finding some new way to break."

"Nothing I'd care to bet on," he said.

"Me either," Kit said. "Still, I can hope."

"You know they shouldn't be winning."

Kit's sigh was hardly more than a breath and degree more hunch in his shoulders. Marcus sat forward, his palms toward the low flames. When the darkness came, the fire-light would ruin his night vision, but for now he could still see his companion's expression.

"What else can your goddess do?" Marcus said. "Raise the dead? Can you do that?"

"I don't believe anyone can bring back what's gone," Kit said. "But I imagine there are other ways to win battles. Inter-rogate prisoners when they cannot lie, and how can they keep their secrets from you? Or frighten the enemy with stories of grand magics against which they couldn't possibly stand. Or tell them that they have already lost until they think it true. I believe that the priests are making these victories possible."

"Inentai?"

"I expect it will fall. If they are taking slaves, I expect they will do so there as well. And build a new temple. And begin taking converts to school in the holy secrets of the goddess. All of it. In the end, it won't matter if Antea out-strips its own abilities. It won't matter if the empire falls.

The goddess will be back in the world, and men who can do what I do will be everywhere. Men with blood like mine. That is all she will need."

"To do what? What is it she wants?"

Kit's smile surprised him.

"Peace."

"Peace?"

"On her terms. The death of those that oppose her. The creation of a narrow world that holds her word to be unquestioned and unquestionable. Only the world she believes and the world that I've experienced aren't the same place, and so for there to be peace, the world as it is must die and be reformed into the one she dictates. They cannot both be, and so... and so she will eat the world."

"This hairwash about the Timzinae plotting against Antea," Marcus said.

"There were levels of initiation into the secrets of the temple," Kit said. "Not all servants of the Righteous Servant were equal. I didn't learn everything there was to know before I left. But the Timzinae... the story is that they aren't entirely human. That the twelve true races are all related, and that they all rebelled against the dragons, but the Timzinae were fused with dragonets hatched early from their eggs and fashioned to resemble humanity. They were the one race that remained loyal to the dragons."

"But that isn't true."

"I don't believe it is, no," Kit said. "But when I came out from the temple, I brought the stories with me. Timzinae sacrificing the young of other races to their ancestor dragons and so on. It was why I chose to travel to Suddapal. To live among them and see if what I had been told was... true's a strong word. If it was plausible. It wasn't."

The massive disk of the sun dropped lower, touching the

horizon like it was setting fire to the world. Kit glanced over at Marcus, his expression reluctant. Almost shy.

"I don't believe this is a war, Marcus."

"A culling, then?"

"A purification. The slaughter of a race because..." Kit shook his head, coughed, and tried again. "Because the men I used to know and love and to whom I dedicated my life for a time have a wrong idea."

"Well, I don't see talking sense to them about it and hoping for the best," Marcus said.

"I can't permit this destruction. Whatever the price, I can't permit it."

"Destruction's inevitable," Marcus said, and spat. "You do know we're about to destroy Antea? If you're right and their success is all based on your incarnated goddess, when we take her away, we'll take their successes away with them, and they're in the middle of a fight. Soldiers of Antea are just men. Some of them are bastards and some aren't. Some have children and wives. It's not their fault that your old pals came and made their homeland into a tool for a spider, but they'll die because of it."

"Or, I suppose, kill for it if we don't."

The angry disk of the sun slid away out of sight. For a moment no longer than two breaths together, the plain was in shadow and the mountains to the east still burned, and then the darkness took them too. The world faded to the grey of twilight and ashes.

"I don't see there's any choice, though," Kit said.

"Isn't. And since I've got business in Suddapal, I'd rather the place was still standing when I got there. Just didn't want you to get your hopes up about this being clean."

"I appreciate that. Should we keep watch tonight?"

"Always. I'll take first, if you're tired."

Kit settled into his bedroll, the meat of his bent arm for his pillow. A breath of wind moved across the plain. Made visible by the shifting of the low scrub, it reminded Marcus of a vast banner. In the high darkness, stars were spilling out from behind the twilight. Already, the temperature was beginning to drop. There wouldn't be frost by morning, but it would be cold enough that he'd be damned glad to see that same sun coming up over the mountains.

"Whatever the price, you said. You'll lose the spiders too."

"I expect to," Kit agreed.

"Any idea what that will be like?"

Kit shifted to look up at the stars.

"I feel I have been astoundingly lucky," he said. "Imagine living a life of constant eavesdropping. Of wherever you go, knowing more than the people around you intended you to. I have heard a million lies from a million lips, and I feel it's taught me all I know of what it means to be a living part of humanity. It taught me to love."

"Lies taught you to love?"

Kit lifted a hand, motioning Marcus to silence.

"There was a woman I saw once in a market of Sara-sur-Mar. Young Firstblood girl with a child in her arms. The child was asleep. I don't know how they came to be there or why the child was sleeping in the marketplace. But this woman—this girl—was stroking the child's back and saying over and over, *I love you. Your mother loves you.*"

"Only it was a lie, wasn't it?" Marcus said. "She didn't love the kid."

"It seems she didn't."

"And that's what made you love humanity? Because I don't think I'd have taken that lesson."

"You can't choose who you love," Kit said. "Or at least I've never been able to. A mother is supposed to love her child, but when that doesn't come, what? That girl knew that something beautiful and profound and important had abandoned her, and so did what she could do. She lied. She told her sleeping babe that it was loved and cared for not because it was, but because she wanted it to be. Not because she cared, but because she wanted to care. And if I hadn't carried the spiders in me, I would never have seen that. Almost every day, it seems, I've come across something like that. Some moment in a stranger's life that's unfolded before me, shown me what I wasn't meant to see. And Marcus, there is a great nobility in ordinary people. The world disappoints us all, and the ways we change our own stories to survive that disappointment are beautiful and tragic and hilarious. On balance, I find much more to admire about humanity than to despise."

"And if we win, you're going to lose all that."

"If we win, I'll become human," Kit allowed. "I think it isn't so terrible a price to pay."

They were silent for a moment. Marcus leaned forward and put a fresh twig on the fire. There weren't enough trees in the Keshet to gather real wood, so the night was going to be spent feeding in small twigs and bits of scrub every few minutes. Kit laughed.

"And," he said, "I'll finally get to find out whether I'm any good as an actor."

"Well, even if you're terrible, I'll tell you that you did well."

Kit's grin was brilliant in the gloom.

"Thank you. I would very much appreciate that."

"Least I can do. Sleep now. We've got a long way still, and I want to be in those hills before nightfall tomorrow."

Geder

I wish I could have gone too," Aster said, pitching a stone into one of the garden pools. It struck with a dull plop and set ripples opening out across the water.

It was striking how changed the prince looked. Geder had been gone for only a few weeks on his trip to Nus and then back, but Aster seemed almost a different person—taller, thinner, more awkward in his movement. It wasn't magic, just the normal progression of child to youth to man, but Geder had never had the chance to see that happen to someone else. And maybe there was a little magic in it, even if it was only the ordinary kind.

"I couldn't take the crown prince into a war," Geder said from his bench. "The Timzinae had raiders and assassins. Anything could have happened."

"You went."

"I'm just the Lord Regent," Geder said. "If someone stuck an arrow in my neck, they could get you another protector. You're the prince. You aren't replaceable."

Aster sat on the grass, disappointed and petulant.

"They'd find some cousin or other," he said. "They always do. I just wanted to see a war. By the time I'm old enough to go, there won't be any left."

Geder had stayed in Sarakal to watch Nus fall and to witness the sack of the city. He'd even gotten up before dawn to walk down the line of troops, Basrahip at his side, and encourage the men. Then, as the still-unrisen sun lit the horizon, the army moved into position. If he thought about it, he could still feel the cool of dew soaking his boots and weighing down his cloak. He hadn't been able to keep Vanai entirely out of his thoughts, even though he knew this was different. And then the great iron doors gave out a massive boom and cracked open a fraction.

The foothold was all his army needed. They roared like a single being with ten thousand throats and charged. Geder was almost sorry he wasn't riding with them. In the moment, he'd wanted nothing more than to grab a horse and a sword and spill into the city streets.

By afternoon, the siege was over and the matched banners of Antea and the spider goddess hung from the walls as an announcement and a boast. Any lingering resentment he'd felt over Dar Cinlama and the other expeditions was gone. The Lord Regent had gone to Nus, and the city had fallen. Geder left the next day, but ten of Basrahip's priests remained with Ternigan. Sarakal would fall before autumn, and the rest of the empire had gone without his attention for long enough.

Aster threw another stone into the pond as the ripples of the first reached the edge and either echoed back faintly or died.

"Lord Regent?"

Geder turned to look over his shoulder. The servant at the edge of the garden bowed until he was bent almost double.

"Yes?"

"Your advisors await you, my lord."

Geder rose, but Aster only scowled at the surface of the pond.

"Are you . . . would you like to sit in?" Geder asked, then

when Aster didn't answer, "All this is going to be yours. Probably best that you see how it all works."

"Not today," Aster said, and threw another stone. This one skipped twice before it sank.

"Is something wrong?"

The prince didn't respond, and Geder, for want of a better idea of what to do, let the servant lead him away. As they walked along the paths of crushed marble, he brooded. He'd been selfish, perhaps, to go to Sarakal and leave Aster behind. The prince was usually so mature and well contained, it was easy to forget he was still a child, and more than that, a child who'd lost his father. Who'd been the target of assassination. Geder was his protector, and he'd gone off to the war. And now he was making jokes about his own death and his replaceability. He reimagined the conversation that he'd just had, but from Aster's point of view, and he cringed. He'd only meant to make Aster see that being prince made him special and important, and instead he'd brought up the idea of yet another person Aster relied on dying. Little wonder the boy hadn't taken comfort in it.

"Stupid," Geder muttered to himself. "Stupid, stupid, *stupid*."

"My lord?" the servant asked.

"Nothing. Keep going."

The official meeting room was halfway up the vast Kingspire, so it wasn't used except for great ceremonial occasions. The more common business of the empire took place at ground level. Today, the men Geder had set to help him manage the kingdom were seated at a low stone table not far from the dueling grounds. The Kingspire rose up to Geder's left, the vast chasm of the Division away to his right, and the gorgeous sprawl of Camnipol before him.

Canl Daskellin sat to his right with Cyr Emming, Baron

of Suderland Fells, at his side. Across from them were Noyel Flor, Earl of Greenhaven and Protector of Sevenpol and cousin to Namen Flor, and Sir Ernst Mecilli. Had Lord Ternigan and Lord Skestinin been in the city, they would have sat at a larger table. As Geder sat, it occurred to him that a year ago this same group would have included Lord Bannien and Dawson Kalliam, both of them dead now as traitors. And the year before that, King Simeon would have been in his own seat. Of them all, only Canl Daskellin and Noyel Flor had served as steadying hands on the rudder of state for more than three years. It was sobering to realize that so much had changed in so short a time.

"Well," Geder said, "thank you, gentlemen, for keeping the city out of the flames while I went to help Lord Ternigan. And now that that's done, where exactly do we stand?"

Noyel Flor stroked his beard and made a sound like a cough but with greater intent behind it. Mecilli nodded, took a breath, held it, and then spoke.

"The food, Lord Regent, that we had hoped to gain by attacking Sarakal is not in as great a quantity as we had expected. In specific, the grains we've recovered are half what we'd projected, and the livestock hardly better than a third."

"On the one hand," Daskellin said, "Ternigan's not moving as quickly as we'd hoped, so more of it's being eaten by the locals. And on the other, they've been slaughtering their own stock and leaving the grains to rot rather than let us put hands on it. We're looking at a thin year. But I've been talking with my friends in Northcoast, and if we're willing to pay a small premium, I think we can import enough of their wheat to see us through."

"I don't like it," Lord Emming growled. Between his tone of voice and the bulldog flatness of his face, he seemed almost a caricature of himself. "We should be sustaining our own, not buying from Northcoast like we were servants at market."

"It's one season, Cyr," Daskellin said. "Be reasonable. There's more than enough precedent for—"

"Is it one season?" Emming snapped. "Is Ternigan going to get the job done and get our men back here in time to prepare the farms this autumn? Because my people have had the most productive fields in Antea for three generations, and I'll tell you sooner than anyone that what you do before first frost tells whether the spring's hungry or full."

"With the money we'll have from Nus, we could import food for at least three years," Daskellin said. "And as long as we're buying from Northcoast, they aren't likely to get nervous about us or start talking to dissident factions in Asterilhold about whether they should throw off the yoke of Antean rule."

"They wouldn't dare," Emming said.

"Actually," Geder said, "I think if we can make it through one year, the problem will go away. I have a plan that will give us full production from the farms and let us keep a standing army." Noyel Flor coughed again, and this time it sounded almost like laughter. Geder waited for the cutting remark. Something like, *And will it make all the cows shit gold too?* But the men stayed silent, waiting. Geder felt a stab of nervousness, but he kept it hidden. "You've all seen the prisons I've built over the winter? Well, the time's come to use them. I'm having all the children of Sarakal sent here to live as hostages. We can distribute the adults as workers on the farms to replace the men we've put in the army. If the farms produce as they were doing before the war, then the children are kept safe. If there's trouble, we have a census of which slaves are at which places, and all their children will stand as communal hostage. So even if there's one trouble-maker in the group, all the other Timzinae will put them down to protect their own children."

"And so if there's a problem, you kill all the children?" Daskellin asked.

"All the ones that belong to the people on that farm. Or in that group. Yes," Geder said. "I haven't worked out all the details yet. I was basing it on an essay I read about how Varel Caot enforced peace after the Interregnum."

The four men at the table were silent. Geder felt a flush of annoyance and embarrassment that he couldn't entirely account for.

"It might be difficult to ... maintain enthusiasm when the time comes to kill these children," Mecilli asked.

"Enthusiasm or loyalty?" Geder asked.

"You could spell them the same," Mecilli said.

"The point is we won't have to," Emming said. "I think the Lord Regent's right. The threat alone will keep the roaches in line."

"*Thank* you," Geder said, and leaned back, his arms crossed before him. "It's not like I want to kill children. I'm not a monster. But we have to get the farms producing again. And anyway, I've already had the census made and the children are being marched here now."

"Well, then there's nothing we need to argue about," Daskellin said. "Let's move on, shall we?"

The meeting continued for the better part of the morning, but Geder felt distracted. There were questions upon questions upon questions. The remaining high families of Asterilhold—the ones who had survived the purge that came after the death of King Lechan—were eager to cement relations with Antea, resulting in a swarm of proposals of marriage between the young men and women of the two courts.

There were even suggestions that Aster and Geder make alliances with several young women, none of whom Geder recognized by name. Once that was all disposed of, they moved on to whether the spoils of Sarakal would support Ternigan's army or if a tax should be called, and if it were whether to accept payment exclusively in coin, or if food and horses would suffice. Through it all Sir Ernst Mecilli's expression was sour and he didn't meet Geder's eyes.

They ended before the midday meal, and Geder excused himself to his private rooms, feeling out of sorts and not at all in the mood to be fawned over by courtiers. He would much rather eat a simple meal of bread, cheese, apples, and chocolate by himself where no one else's needs or judgments could intrude. When Basrahip lumbered into the room, Geder only nodded at him. For the briefest moment, he imagined dressing down the guard for letting him be disturbed, but the thought was gone as soon as it came. Of course the rules that bound the rest of the palace didn't apply to Basrahip. Everyone knew that.

"How is the rededication going?" Geder asked.

"It will be time soon, Prince Geder. You are very kind to offer your servants such beautiful rooms in your home."

Geder shrugged as Basrahip settled himself on a chair. The priest looked worried, which was a rare sight. Geder popped a sliver of tart apple into his mouth and spoke around it.

"Is there a problem?"

"You have taken a new city," Basrahip said.

"And I'll have at least one more by winter," Geder said. "And the goddess is going to have a temple in both of them. At least one. More if you want."

"She sees your generosity, Prince Geder. I know this to be true."

"You're not going to ask if you can bring more priests here, are you? You know you can. Just tell me how many we need to accommodate and I'll make the room. It's the least I can do."

"It is not that," Basrahip said. "You have always been kind to me. I have seen the truth of your heart, and you are the great man that was foretold. Your greatness has exceeded my small powers."

"I don't understand."

"Your new cities in the west. Now more to the east. The priests of the goddess march at your army's side and stand in your court. We walk through the streets of your cities and hold the people's will to the will of the goddess. But we are only a single temple. To do these new temples justice, they must have the faithful and the holy, and I have few more that I can bring forth."

"Oh," Geder said. It was an odd thought. Now that it was said aloud, of course there were only so many men at the temple in the Sinir mountains east of the Keshet. Somehow he'd always assumed there would be more if they were needed, as if they sprang full-grown from the earth out there. "Well. Can you initiate new priests? I mean, you must be able to . . . make more?"

"It will be necessary," Basrahip said. "But the rites of the goddess are not simple things."

"All right. I can write to the seminaries. We have temples and priests of our own, and with half the court coming to your sermons as it is, I'm sure there are plenty who'd be interested in learning from you. And really, the rededication's a perfect time for it."

Basrahip smiled and lowered his head to Geder in a half bow. "My thanks."

"Basrahip? Can I ask you a question? Have you spoken

with Aster at all lately? I just notice that he seems... unhappy. And I wondered whether you might have some idea why?"

"I do not," Basrahip said. "But if you would like—"

"No. No, that's all right. I was just wondering."

"Have you asked him?"

Geder broke off a bit of cheese and chuckled ruefully.

"I suppose that would be the most direct way, wouldn't it?" he said. "It's just hard. I don't want to make him feel like he's on trial."

"Ask gently, perhaps," the priest said.

It was almost twilight when Geder found Aster again. The boy was at the dueling ground alone, walking the dry strip where questions of honor found their answers. He held his wooden practice sword carelessly, swinging it through the air more for the sensation of movement than against an imagined foe. The shadows of the coming night cut across the ground, leaving part of it bright as midday and the rest almost blue with darkness. Geder motioned his personal guard back and took another practice blade from the rack. When he stepped out, Aster took a guard position, but even then, it wasn't serious. Geder lifted his own blade.

"How was the council?" Aster said, circling to Geder's right.

"Frustrating," Geder said. He feinted and pulled back. "Mecilli seems to dislike everything I do. I'm starting to wonder about him."

"Take him before your private court?"

"Probably," Geder said. Aster stepped in, swinging his blade low. Geder blocked it. "It may just be he had some bad fish and it made him disagreeable. But we can't have another Dawson Kalliam."

"Can't we? Some days I think it'd be nice."

Geder thrust, and Aster trapped the blade, the report of wood against wood resounding from the buildings.

"Why would you want that?" Geder asked, pressing in.

"I don't know," Aster said as made his release. He let the wooden blade's tip sink until it was almost on the ground. "It's just...I keep having this dream where we're back in that hole with Cithrin's actor friends sneaking us food and the cats that wouldn't come close to us. I dream that I'm asleep, and that when I wake up, I'll be there. Only I'm not. I'm here. And it's always disappointing."

Geder's own blade sank. Across the wide gap of the Division, a flock of pigeons wheeled in the air, grey bodies catching the light of the falling sun. It was coming close to high summer, and the nights were short. Geder felt the weariness in his body that came from having been awake since first light. Kalliam's insurrection had been terrible, violent, and uncertain. For weeks, Camnipol had been a battleground, and the scars were still there. Burned-out compounds that hadn't yet been rebuilt or razed. Street barricades pulled aside or into alleys, but not dismantled. And it wasn't only the city. Geder felt it in himself too, as much as he tried to deny it or find some joy. Dawson's betrayal had changed him too.

But in those days and nights squatting in the darkness, hoarding the candles and eating whatever the actors had snuck to them, there had been a kind of distance from the world, a sense of time standing still. He'd spent more time talking to Aster in those few weeks than he had in the whole year since. No council meetings, no servants plucking at him, no duties or expectations or demands. It might have been terrible at the time, but looking back, it seemed benign. A kind of golden moment, barely recognized when it happened.

"It is disappointing, isn't it?" he said. Aster sighed and looked up at the massive expanse of the Kingspire looming above them.

"I miss Cithrin."

"I know," Geder said, swinging his sword through the empty air just the way Aster had been doing not minutes before. "I do too."

Cithrin

The stream of refugees from Inentai began with a handful that arrived after the fall of Nus. At first they were the sort of people who moved easily through the world—people without work or with the sorts of trade that called for travel, with family in Suddapal to support them or without family anywhere. They came to Suddapal to find new places for themselves, and some petitioned the Medean bank for the coin that would help them begin again. Cithrin sat with Magistra Isadau and listened to the requests, discussed which to accept and which to reject. The woman who needed a loan to join the tanner's guild had years of experience in Inentai and would be nearly certain to find the work to repay them. The three young men looking to buy a boat had lived all their lives in a landlocked city, and by giving them the money the bank would also be providing them the means to flee the debt should it go bad. Cithrin learned the etiquette of the market houses: when she could step into another conversation and when it would be rude, how to bid up a competitor's contract to lower their profit and how to build temporary partnerships with them to increase them again. The deep structure of the city slowly became clear to her, like a musician learning a song composed in a foreign style.

But the stream did not stop. More people in larger groups,

and of a different nature. As the summer ran its course, whole families came together, carts laden with the possessions of lifetimes. Almost weekly, Magistra Isadau offered the hospitality of the compound to groups too large to find shelter in smaller households. The stories weren't unexpected. The war in Sarakal was too dangerous, and they had a child or a mother or a cousin in health too fragile to withstand a siege. Often the men of fighting age stayed behind to defend city and country, but not always. Magistra Isadau and her siblings fed their guests and welcomed them to their table. And as if following their example, the five-fold city of Suddapal opened wide its arms and gathered the fugitives of Sarakal into its vast bosom. Even as she watched it, Cithrin understood that the generosity was a symptom of something rotten.

History was clear: refugees of war were seldom if ever welcomed in the cities to which they fled unless they brought with them something of value. And yet all, or nearly all, of the citizens of Inentai were welcomed. And so they all, even the poorest, had something of value. The explanation was simple: by their presence, they carried the story that Suddapal was safe. That image of the city was powerfully reassuring, almost intoxicating, to its citizens, because they knew it wasn't true.

It was a matter of time before the grand and glorious fabrication collapsed. It would begin with one or two pessimists and dissenters, then a handful more, and then everyone. And when it came, it would come as letters of credit. The carefully coded instruments could be purchased with anything—coin, cloth, spice, steel—and presented at any of the Medean bank's branches for nine-tenths of the value they'd been bought at. Lightweight, portable, and valueless to anyone besides the one named on them, the papers were perfect for anyone who had come to the conclusion that Suddapal had become a place to flee from rather than to. And they were not greatly in demand. Not yet.

After the day's work at the trading house was finished, Cithrin followed Magistra Isadau on her walks through the city. They would stroll through the wide commons where the tents and carts of the refugees had become almost a township in themselves, or down to the massive piers where ships from across the Inner Sea came and went. Isadau had introduced Cithrin to many of the secret wonders of the city: an herb market in the third city where three full streets were lined with tables filled with living plants and the scent of soil; an ancient Tralgu cunning man whose talents let him turn berries and water into a sweet, icy slush; the hidden cove at the city's edge where the Drowned had been bringing the wreckage of old ships and constructing some vast and arcane sculpture just below the waves. Often they would talk about the day's trades as they walked, or the history of the bank, or more general topics: family, childhood, food, coffee, the hungers of men and of women, the pleasures of books. Cithrin tried to push past her reticence, sensing that Isadau was offering something that she deeply wanted. A better idea, perhaps, of how to become the woman she pretended to be. And Isadau listened carefully and deeply, and tried to make herself clear in reply.

Still, Cithrin felt that half the time they spoke past each other. Isadau was a Timzinae who had lived her whole life among not only her people, but her family. Cithrin was an orphan half-breed who'd never had a close friend among the Cinnae, much less a mother or sister. But she tried, and usually Isadau tried too. So when one day they left the trading house early and walked directly back toward the compound, Cithrin knew something was amiss. And what it was.

"Sold more letters of credit than usual today," she said.

"I suppose we did," Isadau said.

"May be there's a market growing for them."

"Oh, I think it's early to say that."

Cithrin scowled. Isadau's stride was brisk and wide, and Cithrin had to scurry a little to keep up. They crossed a wide and grassy square, where a spire of black stone in the center was dedicated to the memory of someone or something. Cithrin fought the urge to pluck at Isadau's sleeve like a child asking for attention.

"This isn't the usual pattern for the season," she said. "I've been looking through the books. You've sold most of them in the autumn or early spring, and even then, not more than ten or fifteen in a season. We took five *today*."

"We did," Isadau said as they turned the corner. The familiar lines of the compound hove into view and Isadau's pace seemed to increase. Far ahead of them, Jurin and Salan—Isadau's brother and nephew—were shoeing a horse. They were too far away to hear even the sound of their voices, but the positions of their bodies were eloquent. Jurin with his head turned slightly away from the beast as he spoke to his son. Salan upright and serious. Father and son as they had been since the beginning of time, it seemed. Isadau's steps faltered, and Cithrin managed to reach her side. The older woman wasn't even breathing hard. Her gaze was fixed on the men, her smile serene and content. Cithrin felt a moment's frustration until she saw the tear that streaked down Magistra Isadau's cheek and was quickly wiped away.

"Tell me, Cithrin," she said. "Do you think the Porte Oliva branch might be able to make use of our extra capital?"

"I think they'll need it if they're to make good on the credit we're selling," Cithrin said.

Isadau turned her smile on Cithrin and nodded once. "We should arrange that, don't you think?"

Cithrin had been in Vanai when the Antean army came in conquest. This was the same, and it also wasn't.

She remembered being the only one among many who had feared the coming battle in Vanai. The others had seen it as an evil and an inconvenience and prepared themselves for Antean rule with an air of resignation and the sense that whether it was the prince in the city or the king in Camnipol, taxes would be taxes and beer would be beer and not much call to worry about it. Even Magister Imaniel had been more concerned with keeping the wealth of the bank away from the prince than with fleeing the city himself. He was dead now. They were all dead now, burned with their city.

Suddapal, on the other hand, knew its danger. The fear bloomed in the market houses and the streets, on the piers and in the coffee houses. The whole city waited with bated breath for runners from Inentai with news of the siege, perched to fall on any scrap of information like carrion crows. Every rumor spread through its citizens, ripples in a pond. The debates in the taprooms changed from whether Sarakal would fall utterly to when, from why Antea wouldn't march on Elassae to whether. The very rich who could afford it and the very poor who were no worse off anywhere left first, some by ship, others on foot. The governor and the council repaired to their estates, pretending to be in conference, though no one expected them to return. The stores of silver and gold, tobacco and spice, silk and gems and rare books filled the storerooms of the compound, and letters of credit left Isadau's private study, written in cipher and sewn with knots as individual as a written chop.

Cithrin watched it all with dread, but also a strange sense

of relief. At least this time, she wasn't the only one worried. At least Suddapal understood.

The work of the bank also quietly shifted. Depositors came to withdraw their wealth, often arriving at the compound late in the evening rather than coming to the market houses. Even these were often taken as letters of credit rather than the actual coinage, but some coin did spill out. Isadau, on the other hand, began buying debts. If a taproom owed its brewers three months' payments for their beer, Isadau paid the brewers half the full price today. If the taproom made its payments, the bank's profit would be massive. If it burned, its owners and workers dead under Antean blades, the money would be lost utterly. Once, Cithrin had chafed under the timid strategies of her notary, Pyk Usterhall. Now she watched Magistra Isadau buy as much as she could of a city doomed to be conquered, and the risk of it took her breath away and left her giddy. It was optimism forged out of silver coins and paper contracts. A statement that Suddapal might change, but it would not be destroyed, that business done now, in the face of disaster, had meaning. It was banking as patriotism, and something more. Faith, perhaps.

But along with it, Cithrin noticed new entries in the books. Payments and expenditures marked with Isadau's personal chop. Money given quietly without expectation of return to men and women whose names were not recorded. Subsidies paid to the weak and vulnerable to help them escape before the storm. The beginnings of a network of ships, farms, businesses, warehouses that might also last beyond the arrival of the Antean army and give those many, many people who didn't or couldn't leave some hope of escape. The city, and with it the bank, had become a thing of hope and desperation and calculated risk.

It was late at night, and Cithrin was in her room tracing

through the connections that Magistra Isadau was building when the scratch came at her door. The sound was so soft, so tentative, that at first she thought she'd only imagined it. Turning the page of her ledger was louder. But it came again.

"Come in?" she said, still half expecting no one to be there. But the latch lifted and the door swung open. Roach stood framed in the doorway, his leather cap in his hand. His scales, light brown when he'd first come to work for the bank, had darkened with age and the summer sun. He looked older and slimmer. He nodded.

"Magistra," he said. "I was wondering...That is, I was hoping for a moment of your time."

Cithrin closed the ledger's cover, but kept her thumb between the gently pinching pages to mark her place. Roach stepped in and closed the door behind him. His nictitating membranes opened and shut rapidly as a bird's wing and he held his hands at his side in fists. Cithrin wanted to call him by his name as a way to reassure him, but she couldn't remember it. Harver or Hamil. When she saw him, all she could think of was Roach.

"What seems to be the trouble?" she asked, trying to put the comfort into her voice the way Magistra Isadau did.

"I was hoping, Magistra, that you might be able to help arrange a meeting with Merid Addanos. For me. With me."

Anxiety radiated from him while Cithrin racked her brain. The name was familiar, but she couldn't recall where she'd read it. Or no. Not read. Heard. Not one of the depositors, she didn't think. Roach cleared his throat.

"Magistra Isadau's cousin," he said. "Merid. Maha's mother."

"Oh," Cithrin said, and then a moment later. "*Oh*."

"I can resign if you like."

Cithrin withdrew her thumb. The pages of the ledger closed over the gap like water. She put her palm to her forehead, pressing gently while she gathered her thoughts. Roach wasn't one of the few who knew Cithrin's past and secrets. He thought she was considerably older than she actually was, and likely assumed she had more experience than he did. That was a mistake on his part.

"How...ah...how serious is the situation."

"It'll need a priest," Roach said. "And a wedding cup."

"Oh. Well then."

"I'm very, very sorry, Magistra Cithrin." Roach's voice was shaking. "I know that becoming involved with a member of the household was a betrayal of your trust in me and a failure of my duty. And I can just hope that you...that you can..."

"Oh stop. Let me think."

She would have to speak with Isadau first. And Yardem. She wished she knew how the pair of them would take the news. Certainly it wasn't the first time in history that a young woman and a professional soldier had found themselves possessed of an unexpected third party. Cithrin thought for a moment about the pregnancies she'd been lucky enough to avoid and shuddered.

"Give me a day or two to lay the groundwork," she said. "I will do what I can."

"Thank you," Roach said, and turned to go.

"Wait, Ro— Wait. A moment." He paused. Cithrin gathered herself. "Isadau and I may be shifting some of the capital from Suddapal to Porte Oliva. The ship will be heavily guarded, of course, and I'll want someone from my branch there to oversee it. Make sure nothing goes missing between here and home."

"Ma'am?"

"It will get you and Maha out of the city." She could see the struggle in his expression; leaping hope fought with shame. She thought she understood. "I would have needed to send you or Enen regardless. All you've done is make the choice of which a bit simpler."

"Yes, Magistra."

After he left, the door closing quietly behind him, Cithrin let her forehead sink to the table. Her personal guard was getting the magistra's family pregnant. How lovely. And, in the shadow that was falling over them all, how obvious. Cithrin put on her cloak and walked out through the corridors. The compound was emptier than she was used to. There was music, but it came from a long way off, and it wasn't the bright, lively sound of dancing. She felt a knot tying itself in her gut and knew that her choices were to drink herself to the edge of sleep or stay awake until morning. Neither appealed, but they were all she had.

She found Yardem at the watch fire alone. The flames lit the back of his head and glittered off the rings in his tall ears. He never sat facing the fire. She sat next to him, her hands between her knees.

"Ma'am."

"Yardem," she said.

Across the road, someone struck up a mournful tune on a violin. The eerie reeds of a bellows organ rose with it. Yardem held up a wineskin, and Cithrin took it, wiping its mouth on her sleeve after she drank. It was a bright taste, and it warmed her throat, but it didn't have enough bite to it to affect her thinking. She looked out at the night, trying to see the buildings and streets, lanterns and alleys of Suddapal the way she imagined Yardem did. No walls to speak of. Streets too wide to block. Commons big enough to field an army. History had made Suddapal a wide sprawl of a city. Rich with the trade from the Inner Sea, safer than the Keshet, and natural partner to the Free Cities and Pût. Indefensible. Even if the Imperial Army arrived exhausted and half dead from thirst, Suddapal would fall.

There was nothing she could do to stop it. No hope she could offer up. She wondered whether Magistra Isadau would leave when the time came, or go down with her city like the captain of a sinking ship. She wondered how long she would stay and watch before going back to Porte Oliva. It was the time for asking questions like that.

"Looking bleak, ma'am."

"The situation or me?"

"Meant the situation, but either works. Talked to Karol Dannien this morning. He says the defenses are going up at Kiaria. It's the traditional stronghold. Thick walls, deep tunnels."

"And are they going to fit everyone in Suddapal into it?"

"No."

"Half?"

"No."

"One in three?"

"Two in ten."

"So the city falls with most of the population still in it."

"Yes."

"Isadau's putting together a group to smuggle people out afterwards. She hasn't told me, but it's what she's doing."

"Brave."

"Doomed."

"That too," Yardem agreed. "But it's her people. Her family. Likely a third of the people in Suddapal are related to her if you squint hard enough. People do that sort of thing for their families."

"I wouldn't know."

"There's more than one kind of family," Yardem said. "It's the kind of thing the captain would have done for you."

"If you say so."

Yardem sighed and drank more of the wine. Cithrin closed her eyes.

"Yardem?"

"Ma'am?"

"What's Roach's real name again?"

"Halvill."

"Halvill's gotten the magistra's cousin's daughter pregnant."

"That's a problem," Yardem said. A moment later, he chuckled. Cithrin found herself smiling too.

For a while, they laughed.

Marcus

The mountains changed when they got close. The air still tasted of dust and the sun still pressed down on them like it bore a grudge, but before, the rise and fall of the land had been rough and stony. Here, it became knifelike. They skirted the village, but the spoor of goats and men in the few, weedy meadows made Marcus nervous. They were in the enemy's land. Every turn meant the risk of another chance encounter. Kit promised that the path they were taking was the least traveled, only of course he didn't say it that way. He said, *I believe it is the least traveled*, and *I expect there will be fewer people here*, constantly reminding Marcus that his guide was decades out of date. In truth, almost anything could have changed in that time, and something almost certainly would have. The only question was what.

And still, Kit knew the landscape well enough to be a guide. Without him, the long dry paths would have taken months to pass through instead of weeks. And all along the way, they talked of what still lay ahead.

"The great temple has a statue of the goddess," Kit said as they walked through a defile so narrow Marcus could touch both sides with his outstretched fingers. "The *hral kaska* is through there, and down."

"*Hral kaska?*"

"In the old tongue, it means something like 'private chamber.'"

"Past massive golden statue, into bedroom of incarnate goddess. All right," Marcus said. "Do you have any idea how big she is? Physically, do goddesses run the size of horses or houses?"

"I was never allowed past the outer chamber. I never saw more than a glimpse of her. But I have heard her breath."

"So at a guess?"

Kit frowned.

"Houses."

"Lovely."

"From what I was told in the temple and the stories I've gathered in my travels, I believe that you need only cut her. The poison of the blade will end her."

The gorge tightened and began to slant upward. Marcus let Kit go ahead, then followed, the mule's woven leather lead in his hand. The mule snorted but made no other comment.

"Any thoughts how quickly this ending would happen?" he asked. "A long, lingering death that gives her time to slaughter me doesn't do as much good as a sudden collapse."

"I don't know," Kit said.

A long shelf stood at the top of the rise, the stone marked by shallow indentations where rain had eaten away at the softer stone. Far below them, a great wall stood, massive sentinel statues along its top. Thirteen figures eroded to facelessness by water and wind and time, with the spread wings of a vast dragon above them all. Banners flew by each of the statues, all in different colors, and all marked in the center by the same sigil: a pale circle divided in eight sections. The sign of the spider goddess. From above, the great iron gate looked like the mouth of a gaol. The ironwork above the gate seemed to form letters, but Marcus couldn't read the script. Behind the wall, the living face of the stone was marked by caves and paths.

"That's the temple?"

"The home and seat of the spider goddess over whom deceit has no power."

Marcus squatted, looking over the edge. Practiced eyes took in the details of the hundreds of openings. The paved space at the wall's base. What might have been a simple well, with a man in a brown robe kneeling beside it.

"It looks...empty. How many men are in this."

"When I was there, we were almost five hundred," Kit said, his voice bitter and gentle at the same time. "The best and strongest children of the villages, chosen by fate and skill for service."

"Did you sleep in shifts?"

"Hmm? Oh. No, we slept at night and kept the temple during the day."

"So this is the busy time."

Kit nodded. Marcus adjusted the sword against his back.

"Not many people at home. All off bringing truth to the unwashed, I suppose. Better for us. This back way you were talking about. Where down there would it put us?"

Kit described the rest of their path, as best he recalled it. Marcus listened, considered. What he wanted more than anything was to draw the blade, charge in swinging, and God help any man who stepped in his path. He wouldn't, though. They'd come too far and through too much to fail now. The wise thing was to wait for night and make it as far as stealth could take them. Then, if he had to, he would fight his way through the last of it, and try to sink one good stroke on the body of the monster before the priests took them down.

He felt tired, but also alive in a way that reminded him of who he'd been as a younger man. He'd plotted the death of King Springmere for months, putting each piece in position until the man who'd ordered his wife and daughter burned lay dead at his feet. Then, he had been fueled by anger and the lust for revenge. Now, he mostly felt weary. It took the better part of the afternoon, sitting in the shade of a great stone, before he figured out why. Both plans ran to a point and then stopped. If he died when the job was done, then he died. If he didn't, he'd have to come up with something else.

The night was dark, the moon low. Marcus tied the mule to a gnarled pine that had found purchase in the stones. If he and Kit died, the priests would find it, maybe give it a nice life hauling water while humanity descended into chaos and war. The path wound through the rocks, higher into the mountain, through a short tunnel as black as closing his eyes, and into the halls of the temple. Kit lit a thin stub of candle and led the way. The passages were high-ceilinged and round. They reminded Marcus of the holes that worms ate in rotten wood. Doors loomed in the shadows and passed away behind them. Kit moved quickly and silently, with a sense of certainty. The passage opened into a larger chamber. A slight breeze made the candleflame gutter, and Kit cupped it with his hand. The air was hot as breath.

"Any idea where we are?" Marcus whispered.

"I believe so," Kit replied. "The great chamber should be through the next hall, and then—"

"Who's there?" a rough voice asked. "Atlach? Is that you?"

Marcus reached out and tapped Kit's candle out with his palm. A soft and flickering light remained, dim shadows dancing on the vast stone wall. An old man stepped around a corner, a brass lamp held above his head. His white hair looked only a lighter shade of grey in the darkness. Marcus stepped away to the side and eased the blade out of its scabbard. Kit, understanding his part, lowered his head and stepped forward. The old man came closer.

"Atlach?"

"No, I'm afraid I am not."

The old man raised the lantern higher.

"Who—" he began and then stopped. Marcus saw his eyes go wide. "*Kitap?*"

"Ashri, isn't it?" Master Kit said. "You were younger when I saw you last."

Marcus waited. The old man took a step back. In the dirty light, his face had become a mask of revulsion and horror. His chest swelled as he drew breath to scream the alarm, and Marcus slipped the sword between the bones of his spine just where his neck widened into shoulders.

The old man fell, his lantern clattering to the stone. Oil spilled, and the flame grew bright. Marcus dropped the blade and hurried to right the lamp before the fire grew worse. As the flames spread and smoked, the light in the chamber grew brighter. Benches lined the walls, and a dais stood in the room's center, but nothing made from wood was near enough the oil to catch fire. Ancient markings in white and red filled the walls.

"Sorry about that," Marcus said, lifting the lamp away from the flame.

"About what?"

"Killing your old friend," Marcus said.

Kit nodded, then shook his head.

"We weren't close. I think he'd have been just as pleased to kill us. And look."

Marcus turned to the body. At first he didn't see anything, just an old man in a pool of blood that seemed to echo the burning oil. Then, as the flame brightened for a moment, the tiny spiders that boiled up out of the old man's wound were visible. Tiny black bodies whirling in mad distress, pulling hair-thin legs tight to pinpoint bodies. Dying. Marcus handed the still-lit lamp to Kit, took the sword by its hilt, and pulled it free. The blade glittered green and red and a black as dark as a starless sky.

"Good to know it works," Marcus said. "We should hurry."

The temple reached deeper into the mountain than Marcus had imagined. The great carved arches drank in the light from their little lantern and spat it back in the browns of sand. Marcus followed along after Kit, his blade ready. The old actor's steps rarely faltered, and when they did, only briefly. Once, they heard distant voices lifted in song, the echoes making any sense of direction impossible. But the voices faded, and Kit motioned him forward.

There was something else, something eerie, about the place that for a time Marcus couldn't quite put his hand to. At first he thought that there was something off about the angles of the spaces, as if the stones were set in some subtly wrong way. But in truth it was only that he had never seen anything so ancient that had no dragon's jade to it at all.

The great chamber was a vast darkness that swallowed the light. Marcus could only judge by the hushed echoes of their footsteps that the space was vast. As they moved quickly, almost silently, between two huge pillars of beaten gold, Marcus looked up to see the vast, shining body of a spider above him, the pillars its legs.

"Come along," Kit hissed, and Marcus realized he'd stopped in his tracks, overwhelmed by the size of the thing above him. As he followed Kit's silhouette down the dark passages, the fear grew in his belly and thickened his throat. He didn't let himself think, only willed the numbing terror to be exhilaration instead. This was no different than charging into battle or holding a wall against a hundred siege ladders. At worst, it was death.

Kit stopped at a wide black door. The black wood shone in the madly flickering light. A wide bar in iron brackets as thick as Marcus's leg kept it closed.

"Here," Kit said, and the dread in his voice was unmistakable. And behind that, a deeper sound like a vast, rolling exhalation. The breath of the goddess. Marcus smiled.

"Well then," he said. "Help me with this bar."

It took both of them to lift it, and Marcus was sure that the noise would bring the priesthood running in alarm or startle the beast on the far side of the door. But no one came, and the vast sound of the goddess didn't alter. Marcus steadied himself. The blade was longer than he usually liked, but nicely balanced. He didn't have any armor, not even a thick jacket. Speed and surprise were his only hope. And the poison of the blade.

He closed his eyes. He knew any number of men who made peace with their God before they went on the field. He thought of his family. Merian and Alys were waiting there, cut into his memory like scars. He felt the old love and the old pain again, the way he always did. *Maybe this time*, he thought. *Maybe this time it'll be the last*. For a moment, Cithrin was there too. Cithrin who might be alive or dead. Cithrin, who wasn't his daughter, but could have been. He opened his eyes. Master Kit was looking at him nervously.

"It's been good working with you, Kit. I've enjoyed your company."

"I've also enjoyed traveling with you. I think you are a genuinely good man."

"You think a lot of strange things. Open the door."

Kit pulled on the bracket. The door inched open, a ruddy

light spilled out, and the sound grew louder. Marcus steeled himself, then ran through, knees bent and body low. The chamber had high stone walls with a dozen braziers of low, smoky flame. The beast stood perfectly still in the center of the room, a massive spider twice the height of a man. A low stone altar squatted before it. The light glittered from eight massive eyes and mandibles long as a man's forearm.

Marcus leaped forward, vaulting over the altar, and swung the blade at the closest leg. The impact numbed his finger, and he let the force of his charge carry him forward, under the massive body. Both hands on the hilt, he thrust up into the vast belly. The blade rang with the force of the blow and skittered off the spider's carapace. With a cry of despair, Marcus pulled back for another strike, ready to feel the hooked claws grabbing at him, the knives of its mouth ripping his flesh.

The spider goddess hadn't moved. Marcus swung again twice, before the oddness of it sank through, and he stopped. Tentatively, he reached out the sword, poking at the joint of the nearest leg. The clack was of metal against stone. He lowered the blade. The rushing of air filled the room, but the beast's abdomen didn't shift. Carefully, sword at the ready, Marcus stepped to the great, many-eyed head. The fire of the braziers reflected in each eye.

"Kit?" Marcus called.

For a long moment, there was no answer.

"Marcus?"

"This isn't going quite as I'd pictured it."

Kit stepped through the door, his eyes wide and filled with barely controlled terror. Marcus pointed to the spider's great leg and hit it with the flat of the blade.

"This is a statue."

"Be on your guard," Kit said. "It may come to life."

"It also may not," Marcus said, but a twinge of anxiety passed through him all the same. He moved away from the vicious mouth. Kit stepped closer. He was trembling so badly Marcus could see it.

"She's petrified? Turned to stone?"

"I don't think so. Look here, where the feet meet the floor. You can see the chisel marks."

"Where...where is the goddess? There must be a deeper chamber. A secret path. She must be close. Her breath—"

"That's not breath, Kit. That's air moving. There's been wind running through these caves since we got here, or all the fires would have suffocated all these priests years ago and saved us the trouble. No offense."

"None taken," Kit said by reflex. He put his hand on the spider's leg where Marcus's first strike had chipped it. The fresh stone was white and grey. The actor licked his lips, his gaze flickering over the massive beast as if searching for some hidden meaning. When he spoke, his voice was weaker. "They may have taken her. Moved her to some—"

"Kit, has it occurred to you that this goddess might not be real?"

"But her gifts, the power she gives. You've seen it."

"Have. And those little bastards in your blood too. Those I won't deny. But that's all I've seen. I don't know what's giving it power."

"There must be a central force. A *will* to direct it. There *has* to be—"

"Why? Why does there have to be?"

Kit sat on the empty altar, staring up at the many-eyed face. Tears welled up in his eyes, streaked down his cheek to disappear into the thick grey brush of his beard. He coughed out a single, painful laugh. Marcus sheathed the blade and sat at his side. The statue looked down on them, motionless and blind.

"There is no goddess, is there?"

"Might be, but no. Probably not."

"It seems I'm an idiot," Kit said. "I thought I had overcome her madness. I thought I had questioned *everything*, but..."

"Well, there may have been madness to overcome. Just maybe it wasn't a goddess. Plenty of crazy to go around if all you have are priests."

The fires in the braziers fluttered in the breeze. Marcus thought he saw, high up along the walls, where the air shafts were hidden by curves in the stone. Whoever had built the chamber, however many centuries ago, they'd been brilliant. Controlling the air flow alone would have been impressive.

"It's what I feared, isn't it?" Kit said. "All of it. All the tales and histories. All the sermons. I think they were all just children whispering to each other down through generations, each believing and repeating what the one before had said, all the misunderstandings building on each other, until anything became plausible. Not a mad goddess, but human dreams and fears given the reins."

"We should probably have this conversation someplace else, Kit. If your old friends come and find us here, they're not likely to thank us for pointing all this out."

"Why?" Kit said, and Marcus recognized the despair in his voice.

"Why won't they thank us, or why should we leave?"

"We came to kill a goddess and break her power, but there's nothing here to break. Nothing here to die. She can't be stopped if she doesn't exist. What's happening out there is only men lost in a terrible sort of dream. I don't know how to stop that. What sword kills a bad idea, Marcus? How can we win against a mistaken belief?"

"I don't know," Marcus said. He rubbed his hands together, the soft hissing of his palms a counterpoint to the deep rumble of the false breath. "But someone did."

"What do you mean?"

Marcus spoke slowly, the thoughts forming as he spoke them.

"This temple is a hiding place. The men like you have been out of the world for centuries at least. Maybe all of history. Something put you in here. Something scared your however-many-generations-back predecessors so badly that they crawled off to the ass end of nowhere and pulled the desert up over their heads. Something *drove* them here."

"Can you think what?"

"No. And I can't think how we'd find out. And if we did, I don't have any reason to think it's the sort of thing we could manage. I'm only saying it's been done before, so it can be done. And we should find out how."

Kit pushed his fingers back through his wiry hair. His tears had dried, but the salt tracks still marked his cheeks.

"Where do we start?" he asked.

Marcus rose to his feet and put a hand on the spider goddess. The stone was warm and hard and dead. There was a vast world outside. Nations and races tearing themselves apart, blood and war and tragedy. He didn't have any idea where to start looking for the way to stop it. And then he did.

"Suddapal," he said.

Clara

Flor and Daskellin, I understand, but I can't imagine him getting on with Mecilli at all. And of course Emming will fit right in," Clara said. "The man is full of argument and bluster, but only so no one will notice he never has an opinion of his own. Could you pass the butter, dear?"

Sabiha handed across the jar. The butter was white and fresh, without the waxy cap or echo of the rancid that Abatha Coe's had. The bread was soft and pale, the eggs and pickles served in a fashion that reminded her of mornings in her own solarium, back in some previous lifetime. At these occasional and treasured breakfasts with her family, her first impulse was to wolf everything down and eat enough that she wouldn't have to put another bite past her lips for a day. Her second was to pull back, to take only what she would have taken and leave what she would have left. The first would have been rude to Jorey, and the second would have been untrue to herself, so she usually managed a middle path.

"Well, the line to the Lord Regent's council chamber got a bit shorter after last year. It would have been Father and Lord Bannien at the table," Jorey said, and then, changing the subject, "I heard from Vicarian. I have a letter for you from him as well."

"Oh good. How is he, poor thing?"

"There was a call for men to study under Minister Basrahip," Jorey said, his voice intentionally casual the way it always was when he was trying not to have an opinion. "He's thinking of volunteering."

"I'm surprised," Clara said.

"He thought it might help show that his allegiance is to the throne," Jorey said. "And it would bring him back to the city. They're rededicating Minister Basrahip's temple. They're actually going to put it inside the Kingspire. He'd be able to come for lunch whenever he had an open day."

"Besides," Sabiha said, "it's Palliako's pet cult, and anything to do with the Lord Regent is astoundingly fashionable."

"Even that dreadful leather cloak of his," Clara said, hoisting an eyebrow. "I've seen it everywhere, and really, it doesn't suit anyone well. Jorey, dear. I was meaning to ask. Whatever became of Alston?"

"The guardsman? He's here. Lord Skestinin took him on when the household..."

"I thought I remembered that," Clara said, smiling to herself. "I must look in on him and pay my respects. It takes so little, you know, to maintain those relationships, and good servants are so rare. Now, Sabiha, dear, tell me all about that dinner at Lady Ternigan's. I haven't seen any of the new dresses, so you must describe everything."

The danger for her was that it was so easy here. So comfortable and calm and welcoming. Some of that drew, she was certain, from Jorey and Sabiha's guilt at turning her out. Some was the decades of practice she'd put into being Lady Kalliam, Baroness of Osterling Fells. But some was deeper. There was a genuine love between her son and his wife, and unaffected kindness was a pleasure to be near, even if only for a moment. Clara wanted to gossip and laugh and tell stories from when Jorey had still been in his small pants and watch Sabiha's delight and Jorey's blush. She wanted to be that woman still.

But already they had said things that she knew, despite her best intentions, would be in the next letter to Carse, and she didn't want that. Jorey might say something that only he knew, and then if the letter was intercepted, suspicion would fall on him. The fact restrained her, but it didn't stop her.

And after breakfast, and after Jorey had discreetly given her a week's allowance and kissed her cheek, she stopped at the servants' quarters, found a private corner, and had a serious conversation with Alston the guardsman.

Four days later, she woke early, left her rooms, and met her old servants. Rain soaked the predawn streets, and the birds sang the songs that came before the light. The tiny, cool drops tapped against Clara's cheeks and ran in an invisible runnel down past her collar and into the space between her breasts. Alston walked behind her, a looming darkness inside the darkness. His cloak was oilskin the deep brown of freshly turned soil. The other men with him were likewise dressed. The proper clothes, she thought, for the proper occasion. It was good to know the basic rules applied everywhere.

The taproom near the Silver Bridge hardly deserved the name. It wasn't a business so much as an excuse for one— beer went in and piss came out—but it was also the sort of place where men with no name slept during the daylight and stolen coins and food appeared without questions. The lantern by its door was filled with oil and lit only because Clara had snuck it away and put it back herself. And that only because she needed to see the faces of the men who stepped out to the street. Clara had been waiting for less than an hour when the rude little door swung open and four men tumbled out, their arms around each other's shoulders. The only good thing she'd discovered about Ossit and his friends was the regularity of their habit. Three Firstblood men and a Kurtadam. The middle of the three Firstbloods was unmistakably Ossit, the man with the knife who would, she was certain, have split her from heel to throat if Abatha Coe hadn't distracted him.

Alston must have seen the reaction in her stance, because he didn't ask whether these were the men they were waiting for. He stepped forward, and the two men with him followed. Clara came behind. After all the time she'd spent and work she'd done to arrange this, it wasn't something she could look away from.

By the way their conversation stopped and they closed ranks, it was clear that Ossit and his toughs sensed the danger even before the first of her old guardsmen stepped out of the shadows. Three of her men loomed up in the street before Ossit. Clara, Alston, and two more took station behind the enemy, blocking their retreat. The bared blades on both sides caught the light like tiny flecks of lightning.

The Kurtadam was the first to stop. His grin was wide enough to show teeth. The blade in his hand was long for a knife, short for a sword. Ossit, to his left, had the same curved blade he'd brandished at her in the boarding house. The other two had clubs of wood with their ends dipped in lead.

"Looking for trouble, are you, then?" the Kurtadam growled.

"Only delivering what was ordered," Clara said, and the men started at her voice.

"Who in fuck are you?" the Kurtadam asked.

"Put down your weapons and come to the magistrates," Clara said. "I'll see you're not hurt."

"We've got numbers and experience on you," Alston said. "No reason to do something you'd regret."

"Well, then," the Kurtadam said. "I guess there's nothing to be done, then." The words were calm, but the tone still spoke of violence.

"Put the weapons down," Clara said again. The Kurtadam glanced at the three men around him and shrugged. With a shout, the four of them dashed toward the three men farthest from Clara, knives and clubs swinging. Alston said something obscene under his breath, and he and the other two dashed after them. She hesitated, and then followed. She had heard swordplay before. She knew the sound of blades. There was none of that here, only the thick masculine grunting, dull sounds of impact, and a cry of pain. She couldn't tell whose voice it had been. Street fighting was mean and it was ruthless. Honor had no place here. One of Alston's men—her men—lay in the gutter, his fingers holding in a long loop of intestine. The Kurtadam put his back to the wall, his long knife dancing in the pale and growing light. With a shout, one of the bandits leaped past Alton's wide form and came pelting toward her, his club gripped hard in his fist.

"Lady!" Alston shouted, but too late. The attacker was too close for Clara to flee from, too close for anyone to intervene. Clara tasted the coppery flush of fear, but held her ground. She had never trained to fight—it wasn't something ladies did—but Dawson had spoken to her many times on the strategies and tactics of a duel. The first rule was not to do what the enemy expected. A young man with a lead-tipped cudgel running at an unarmed woman in her middle years. He'd assume she would shy away, turn from the blow. Clara's eyes narrowed.

The club rose in the air, ready to splatter her brain on the cobbles. Clara stepped in toward the man and brought the point of her toe up into his sex with a force she hadn't used since she'd been a girl with rough cousins. The man's yelp was as much surprise as pain, and he hunched forward, barreling into her. His shoulder struck her just under her ribs, and she felt the breath blow out of her. His club fell to the ground, bounced along the cobbles, then rolled. She sat down hard on the pavement, her hands to her belly, fighting the urge to vomit. The man scrambled to his knees, tried to stand, but Alston was on him.

"Are you well, my lady?"

"Fine, thank you," Clara said, hauling herself to her feet.

The men had been subdued. One of her guards had Ossit's face pressed in the gutter and his arm bent cruelly back. The clubman who hadn't assaulted her lay on the walk, his hands held to his face and black with blood. Only the Kurtadam remained on his feet, his hands lifted in a surrender that managed to speak defiance.

"Well done," Clara said. "We'll take him to the magistrates."

"You," the Kurtadam said. "I remember you now. You're the high-class bitch from Coe's rooming house. I knew I'd heard your voice before."

"I am," she said. "And you made a mistake when you chose to steal from my household."

"You made a mistake when you stepped in the street," the Kurtadam man said and spat. "Go ahead, then. Take me to the magistrate. Hang me in a cage. It won't be the first week I've spent pissing down the Division. But ask yourself what you'll do when they pull me back up, eh? So how about instead you let my boys go and we call it truce. You made your point. I got it. The house is yours, we won't be back that way again."

Alston knelt beside his fallen man. The guard's face was pale and the bright pink loops between his fingers meant he needed a cunning man quickly or a grave digger slow. Dawson would have tied them all to the wall outside the compound and whipped them until the bones showed. But that had been when he was a baron and meting out justice was his right. If he had been here now, if he had seen her with the muck of the street on her skirts and the thugs threatening her in the still-falling rain, he would have been outraged. She thought of Vincen lying in his own blood. Of Dawson, slaughtered before the full court. Outrage was yet another luxury she could not afford.

"I don't think I can trust you," Clara said, surprised by the coolness of her voice. The resolve in it.

"Madam, I need to get Steen to help," Alston said. "He's falling into shock."

"I understand."

"Well," the Kurtadam said, "what's it to be, then? March us off to the magistrate and have an enemy for life, or you go your way, take care of your boy with the open gut, and I'll go mine."

"Will you give me your word of honor that you will exact no revenge?" Clara asked.

"You have my word," the Kurtadam purred.

Clara hesitated for a moment, caught between two versions of herself, and unsure which was the true one. Her inclination was to let the man go, and farther down the road have him appear in the night with his knives and laughter again. She knew in her bones that was how the story would go, and still the power of compromise was so ingrained in her soul that it was hard to turn away from. For so many years, the rules of court and etiquette said that a man was to be taken at his word, and if he should break it, the humiliation was his. Old rules for old times. Ruthlessness was called for now. And so, ruthless she would be.

"Your word," she said, "isn't worth shit. Alston?"

"Ma'am?"

"Will you please kill these men and throw the bodies in the Division?"

The Kurtadam's eyes went wide as Alston sank his blade in the man's belly. Ossit cried out in despair, but it cut off quickly. Clara watched them die, and a part of her died with them. She had seen pigs at the slaughter. She had seen bodies hanging from the gallows. The two together gave the proceedings some context, but they did not make them easy.

I'm sorry, she thought.

The morning traffic across the Silver Bridge took no particular notice of her or of the grime on her hems. The blood on them. Mules and carts moved behind her, crossing from one side of the city to the other while she stood in the center with the memory of her husband. *I'm sorry,* she thought, and then knew the word was wrong. Not sorrow. She was horrified, of course, but that wasn't what had brought her here either. Regret had and the sense of something ending, but nothing so apologetic as sorrow.

Dawson, my love, she thought, speaking each word without giving them voice. *I would have stayed the same for you if I could. I loved being the woman you loved. I miss her. I miss you. Perhaps I should have been more careful of myself. Not done things that would change me.*

Behind her, a man cursed and a horse snorted. Before her, crows spiraled down into the depths of the earth. The depths of the city. The rainclouds had cleared, and the morning sun drew steam from the streets. It poured over the sides of the Division like fog settling. She looked to her left. Vincen Coe stood at the edge. His face was pale, but his spine straight. He didn't look at her. Hadn't asked where she'd been or what she'd been doing. She knew already that she wouldn't tell him and that this new woman she'd become was the kind who could keep secrets. Secrets made anything possible. They made her free, but alone. The price was small.

The Kingspire seemed almost to glow in the morning light. The vast new banner—the red of blood, the eightfold sigil—hung from its heights, marking the newly founded temple. On the far side of the Division, a troop of men herded another group of Timzinae children toward the prisons. The small, brown-scaled bodies moved slowly. Clara had seen the way exhausted children moved, the slackness of their joints and the dullness in their eyes, the same for every race. Even from halfway across the Division, she recognized it. These were the prisoners Geder had prepared for. She closed her eyes for a moment.

There was so much to mourn. And so much that could still be lost. One of the guards shouted out abuse. Another laughed. Servants of the Severed Throne every one of them.

She wanted to say it was Palliako who'd done it all. That Geder's sins had infected the city, the kingdom, and the world. In a sense, she even believed it was true. Except that none of those men driving children from their homes and families had a knife to his throat. None of the women at court were forced into the black leather cloaks. They did it, all of them, because it was easier for them not to weigh their loyalty against their conscience. Palliako might be the occasion of it, but she herself was evidence that the choice belonged to each of them. She wondered how many other loyal traitors there might be out there, thinking private thoughts much like her own. She wondered how she might find them without too terrible a risk. She noticed that she wasn't thinking about Dawson.

Clara gathered herself together, put a pleasant smile on her lips, and turned away from the bridge. It was the nearest thing she had to a tomb for her husband, and it left her heart feeling empty to know she wouldn't feel the need to come back to it.

Vincen smiled and nodded when she stepped back onto the solid ground of the street. Apart from a paleness to his skin that the days hadn't quite erased, the only sign he had been near death was a scar of living silver where the cunning man had called on angels or spirits or dragon's art to fuse flesh that wouldn't have mended. She had seen it when she sat by his side, nursing him back to strength. With his shirt on, it wasn't visible. She took his arm and wrapped it around her own. It felt different than it had the times before. Likely it was only that he held himself more carefully, but she liked to imagine it was also that she had changed as well.

"Are you well, my lady?" he asked. The formality in his voice told her that he knew the answer, and that it was *no*.

"I have been thinking, Vincen," she said.

"Yes?"

"Writing letters has been very useful in gathering my thoughts," she said, "but I feel the time has come for something more."

Cithrin

The trick to moving the wealth of the bank was not being seen to do so. If word went around that the Medean bank was leaving Suddapal, it would cause any number of problems. The people still under contract with the bank would stop paying their loans, because why give money to someone who wouldn't be present to take the complaint to the magistrate? The scent of coin and cloth would call pirates and bandits, making it less likely that the goods would survive the trek to Porte Oliva. Tax assessors and agents of the city's governor, seeing the wealth trickling away, would want to eke out as much as they could quickly, before the chance disappeared. Or the high council might send guards to take command of the gold and use it to hire mercenaries, if any mercenaries would accept the work.

So Cithrin and Isadau carved the wealth of the bank into smaller pieces. A private crate sent in a caravan through the Free Cities that purported to hold bolts of cotton actually contained silks. A message box sealed with lead and wax sent by courier carried gems and jewelry. An earthenware statue sent as a gift to Pyk Usterhall, notary of the Medean bank in Porte Oliva, was hollow and filled with coin. Technically, it was smuggling, since they only paid the tax on what the goods appeared to be and not what they were. Cithrin's conscience didn't bother her on the point. If the governors of the five cities couldn't assure the safety of her bank, they had already broken their end of the contract. Besides which, every other business and family with ties outside Elassae was doing the same.

Roach—Halvill, dammit—and Maha married in the private chapel at the compound amid great revelry. The priest was the same she had seen on her very first Tenthday, and he used his skills as a cunning man to make his voice sound grand and resonant. She caught Yardem rolling his eyes and shared his amusement. But when the guard and the pregnant girl sipped from the wide silver wedding cup and swore to make the journey of this life in company, Cithrin found herself inexplicably weeping.

They were slated to leave the next day on a ship bound for Cabral with enough of the bank's capital that, if they stole it and ran, they'd be able to set up a very pleasant life together in Far Syramys. But they wouldn't. Halvill would put it on a cart and trek back to Porte Oliva, just the way he'd promised. Halvill and Maha had forged a new family, it was true, but they both had other ties. Halvill to the bank, Maha to her family and, because of that, the bank.

Before that, Isadau had arranged a party that would fill the compound for a day and a night. It was a bit more extravagant a celebration than the union of a minor bank guard to a girl with an occupied belly warranted, but Suddapal was in need of reasons to celebrate. And so was Isadau.

Cithrin wore a dress of pale blue with highlights of cream and a ribbon in her hair. The colors went well with the paleness of her skin and hair inherited from her mother. For jewelry, she chose a thin silver chain necklace. More would have been ostentatious. She knew, looking into her mirror, that she looked too young. Magistra Cithrin bel Sarcour was supposed to be almost a decade older than she actually

was, and she knew what Master Kit and Cary would have
said. Darken the lines under her eyes, deepen the folds that
ran between nose and cheek. Stand with her weight lower
in her hips. Tonight, though, she decided to let herself be
younger. They all knew her already. Opinions were set. And
it was a relief to step out of herself, if only for a moment.

It was also uncommon for the employees of the bank
to take part in the celebrations as if they were equals, but
Halvill's family had insisted that Yardem and Enen sit
among them, and so when Cithrin stepped out of her room,
Yardem stood before her in the long formal robe of a Tralgu
priest. Red tiles as big as her thumbnail marked the collar
and ran down the left side. If he had still been an acting
priest, they would have been on the right. She only knew
that because he'd told her. The air was warm with high summer and the smell of fresh bread and basil mixed with the
strumming of guitars. Cithrin doubted there would be much
sleep in Isadau's compound that night.

"You look handsome, Yardem," she said. "You can cut
quite a figure when you put your mind to it."

"Thank you, ma'am," Yardem said. "Wanted to speak
with you before the revels began, though."

Cithrin glanced back toward her room in query. *Is this a
private conversation?* Yardem nodded, and they went back
inside. Yardem sat on the end of her bed, his elbows resting
on his knees. She leaned against the door. She could have
taken the chair, but she didn't want to disarrange the drape
of her dress.

"All respect, ma'am, but I think it's time we considered
leaving Suddapal."

"Is there word from Inentai? Did the Anteans break the
siege?"

"Not so far as I know," Yardem said. "But there's other

news. Karol Dannien's taken contract to man the walls at Kiaria. They'll be boarding up his school at the week's end and going north. I don't think there's any question that the war's coming here, and if he's going, it means it's likely to be here soon."

"And better if we weren't here to greet it," Cithrin said.

"Hear it's lovely in Porte Oliva this time of year," Yardem said grimly.

Outside her window, glass shattered and someone laughed. She crossed her arms.

"You know I can't go," she said. "Komme Medean was clear about the terms. A year's what he called for. It hasn't been half that. If I walk away now, I'll have broken my contract with him."

"All respect, but he didn't know he was sending you into the wrong side of a sack."

"No," Cithrin said, "he knew he was sending me to a bank. Navigating wars is part of what we do. Or floods. Or plagues. It's not as if the business only runs on sunny days. If I leave now, Komme will be right to wonder what I'd do if something happened in Porte Oliva. I wouldn't leave there, and I won't here."

Yardem's ears turned back, but he didn't say more.

The yard of the compound was bright with fireflies, and the first of the torches were being lit. The men and women who came for the party weren't the highest in the five cities. The affair might have been held by the Medean bank and Magistra Isadau, but it was still the wedding of a minor guard. Instead, there were carpenters and brewers, dyers and shipwrights. The artisans and small merchants of Suddapal come to glory together. The women wore flowing dresses or fashioned metal corsets or the stained trousers and blouses they'd left work in. The men wore formal robes

of silk brocade or rough-cut canvas belted with lengths of
rope. No one was overdressed for the occasion, and no one
too casual. It wasn't possible to be.

The compound's servants carried out a wide wooden
table, then hurried back to fill it with plates of glazed ham
and fresh shrimp and roast lamb. Bottles of wine were
opened and tuns of beer tapped. And instead of retreating
back to their quarters, the servants stayed in the yard. They
didn't mix with the higher orders of guests, but neither did
they avoid them. The music rose with the darkness, bright
strings strumming against each other, mixing melody and
percussion until the stars themselves seemed to throb with
it. Cithrin ate a little, drank a lot. The constant knot in her
belly, so familiar that she hardly noticed it anymore, loosened a notch, and she felt the blood warm in her cheeks.
She heard a woman whooping at the edge of the yard, and a
moment later saw a band of ten men leading a cow straddled
by Isadau's sister, Kani. She was listing wildly, and the cow
looked, to Cithrin's admittedly tipsy eyes, long-suffering
and patient. A young Timzinae man she didn't recognize
asked Cithrin to dance with him, and she found that she
was, in fact, drunk enough to do so.

It wasn't about Halvill or Maha. It wasn't about Isadau or
paying respects to the bank. It was about fear, and the joy
that comes in the shadow of fear. It was about celebrating a
night when Suddapal was free, and the clear knowledge that
such nights might be countably few. It was as intoxicating as
the wine.

When she paused to find some water and meat and give
her head a moment to clear, she saw Yardem standing at the
entrance to the compound, his ears canted forward. Magistra Isadau stood before him, looking up, her arms folded.
She didn't need to hear the words to know what they were

saying. She was gathering herself up, ready to go explain her decision to stay and dress Yardem down for interfering, when a voice speaking her name interrupted her.

Salan, Jurin's son, stood before her. In the light from the torches, he looked older than he was. He held himself upright, his bearing almost military, and his clothes had the look of a uniform without actually being one.

"Magistra Cithrin," he said again. His breath smelled of wine, and he spoke with the careful diction that came of consciously not slurring his words. "I hoped I might have a word with you."

Oh, this can't be good, Cithrin thought. But she only said, "Of course, Salan. How can I help you?"

The boy frowned. Cithrin felt her heart squeeze a little tighter with dread. It was such a pleasant evening, and a young man humiliating himself wasn't going to improve it. If she had excused herself, maybe she could have avoided this for them both, but now it was too late.

"I know that I am a child to you. My..." He looked down, searching for a word. The nictitating membranes slid closed and open again. "My affection toward you isn't something to be taken seriously. I understand that."

"Salan—"

"I have volunteered to go with Karol Dannien and his company to Kiaria. I leave within the week. And I didn't want to leave with you thinking of me as the idiot boy with the hopeless puppy love. It's not how I want to be remembered. If I could choose to feel differently about you, I would. If I could choose not to embarrass you and myself, I would. I don't mean to be laughable."

"I haven't laughed," Cithrin said. "Credit me that much."

"I...of course. I'm sorry. I didn't mean to accuse. I only wanted..." He shook his head, then held out his clenched fist, knuckles up. It took Cithrin a moment to realize he was giving her something. She put out her hand, and he released his grip. A thin strand of silver snaked onto her palm, a tiny worked figure. She held the necklace up. The figure was a thin silver bird, its wings outstretched. Cithrin shook her head, about to refuse the gift, when the boy spoke again. "Captain Dannien says we aren't to bring personal items with us. I was hoping you could hold this safe for me. Until the war's over."

Until the war's over.

The Antean armies hadn't crossed into Elassae. Inentai, at last word, hadn't fallen. And still, it was a given that the war would come. And its end was so uncertain that *until the war's over* could sound like *forever*. Salan's black eyes met hers. If she laughed now, he would hate her. He would be right to.

"Of course," she said. "I'll be pleased to."

"Thank you, Magistra," he said, with a small bow, then hesitated, turned, and walked stiffly away. Cithrin fastened the necklace, letting the small silver bird rest just below her collarbone. It was so light and fine, she could almost forget it was there. Almost.

The music and dancing went on, the wine and the beer. The night grew a few degrees cooler. Cithrin willed herself to enjoy it, to throw herself into the revelry and celebrate Halvill and Maha being young and stupid and making decisions that would shape the rest of their lives without so much as a moment's consideration. Then she remembered a time not so many years ago when she'd lain down beside an ice-bound pond with an actor. If God hadn't sent Marcus Wester at the right moment, she might have Sandr's son on her hip right now, so perhaps she wasn't in a position to pass judgment.

The revel ran on, and Cithrin drank and danced, but some

of the joy had gone out of it. Given the Timzinae's small need for sleep, it was quite possible that the music would go on until dawn drowned the torches, but it would have to do so without her. She sought out Halvill and Maha, gave them small presents of her own because custom required it, and then retreated to her rooms. The sound of guitars and the smell of torch smoke wafted in through the open window, but more softly. She undid her dress stays, changed into the sleeping gown, but she didn't take to bed. Not yet. The alcohol in her blood was fading, and with it the chance of sleep. She sat, looking into the candleflame. When the scratch came at her door, she realized she'd been waiting for it.

Isadau looked lovely. The silver of her dress set off the darkness of her scales. Her smile carried a gentleness that Cithrin had come to expect.

"Good evening," she said.

"Magistra," Cithrin replied. "I saw Yardem talking to you. I assume you've come to make the case that I should leave."

"Less case and more plan," Isadau said, sitting where Yardem had sat. "I'm not going to ask you to leave."

"You're going to tell me to?"

Isadau's eyes went merry. "Do you think that would work? All I've seen of you suggests otherwise."

"I don't have a brilliant record for following the dictates of authority," Cithrin said, laughing despite herself.

"Well, then. You came to me to learn how to build up a bank, and I'm not certain how much longer I will be doing that work."

"I don't understand."

"I've protected Komme's interests as best I can. I have funneled what capital I could out of harm's way. And as we move forward, I will follow the contracts and honor the deposits that I can. But this is not the holding company.

This is my bank, and the power of money is not only that it makes more money."

"I wouldn't tell that to the holding company," Cithrin said, but the joke fell flat.

"Money is the physical form of power. And the time is coming for that power to be expended," Isadau said. "Coins are only objects until they're used. Then they become something else. Food for the hungry. Passage for the desperate. It's the magic that we do. We take a bit of metal and use it to remake the world in the shape we want."

"To stop a war?"

"To avoid its worst excesses, yes," Isadau said. "I have spent my life tending this bank. Building it up like a fortune. And now the time is coming for me to spend it. No one thinks that Antea will stop with Sarakal. Kiaria may stand, but Suddapal will fall. And I will bankrupt this branch saving as many people as I can from it. I will bribe whoever I can. I will suborn and corrupt and trade. I will take risks that have no rationale in the world of finance. Moral risks. They won't save my city, but they will preserve some part of it. In the end, I doubt the branch will survive."

"Or you."

"In the end, I doubt I will survive," Isadau said. "I won't be a good teacher for you anymore. It will be time for you to go."

Cithrin rose from her seat, looked out the window. The flaring torches were hardly brighter than the star-strewn sky.

"I thought you were saving my heart," she said. "The part that hadn't died yet, but was in danger. Isn't that what Komme said?"

Isadau hesitated. Cithrin turned to look at her.

"It is."

"You're choosing to use your power for something besides

profit," Cithrin said. "I understand that there are things of value that aren't priced. Or...no. I *know* that, but I don't understand it. This project you're taking on is what Komme sent me here to learn."

"And so you won't leave. Even if your life is in threat."

"I'm not bent on dying. I'd prefer not to. But I won't leave you here," Cithrin said. And then, "It's your own fault, you know. You gave me a plant."

Isadau's laughter was delight and despair mixed. She rose, taking Cithrin's hands, and for a moment they embraced. The older woman smelled of cinnamon and smoke. Cithrin rested her cheek on Isadau's shoulder. She could feel the woman weeping.

"I will tell Yardem I failed," Isadau said. "Once he hears why, I think he'll be pleased that I did."

"It won't make his work easier."

"He's flexible enough, I think. You are doing something dangerous and unnecessary and wild. I don't know whether to thank you or dress you down."

"Neither one will alter my position on it," Cithrin said.

"I believe you."

After Isadau left, Cithrin felt the first tendrils of sleep. It was as if she'd been waiting to say those words, and now that she had, her day could end. She curled under the blanket, one arm raised up as a pillow, and let her mind drift. Coins as bits of metal with the power to make the world the way you wanted it to be. Coins that become food for the hungry or robes for the powerful, but rarely both. It struck her that blades were also metal, also used to remake the world. In the murk of her sleep-soaked mind, something stirred. The half-formed thought that her coins could, perhaps, cut deeper if she could only find *how*.

A week later, the news came that Inentai had fallen.

Geder

If the siegecraft of Baltan Sorris is to be understood, it must be in the context of Drakkis Stormcrow, for General Sorris was a student of the ancient classic texts. The more common, and in my view mistaken, interpretation is that the early kings of Northcoast had catapults and siege engines capable of lofting stones or burning pitch so high into the air that all parts of a besieged city were under threat from them. What I have shown is that, instead, the instructions Sorris gave were an unconsidered artifact of more ancient wars in which the field of battle was not restricted to the plane of the earth, but included dragons, wyverns, and gryphons capable of attacking from the sky. While this image of Sorris as a hidebound follower of outdated precepts contradicts the traditional account of his military brilliance, I will, in the next section, make the case that it better explains his decisions in the latter half of his career, especially in the Third Siege of Porte Silena and the infamous Four Kings War.

Geder closed the book and sighed. It happened every few weeks. He would find some spare hour that could be carved away from the needs and responsibilities of the kingdom and retreat to his library. He remembered spending hours—days—lost in his books. There had been a time when exploring the speculative essays of history had been like the adventurer Dar Cinlama walking in the forgotten places of the world, discovering forgotten eras and stumbling upon insights that changed his understanding of history. It had brought him to the Righteous Servant, the Sinir Kushku, and the place of highest power in the world. But the price, apparently, was the joy he used to have and couldn't find any longer. Basrahip derided all printed words as dead, and Geder found the position more and more persuasive. In all his books, there had been only a few mentions of the spider goddess. None at all of the fire years. Or of the oppression of the goddess and her followers by the dragons. Or their flight from the ancient lands that had become Birancour. The true history of the world was preserved in the temple at the edge of the Keshet, and so far as Geder could see, nowhere else. What evidence was there, after all, that Baltan Sorris had studied Drakkis Stormcrow? Or that Sorris had even existed, for that matter? The battles and struggles and intrigues of history might be nothing more than make-believe given dignity by print.

In that light, Geder's personal library seemed empty. Not a field rich with truths to be uncovered, but a desert where if there were any truths, they were indistinguishable from lies. It was a conclusion he reached over and over again, forgetting every time, then going back and disappointing himself again. Perhaps it was time to find some other pursuit to distract him from the burdens of rulership.

Perhaps he could learn to play music.

"Lord Regent?"

"Yes, I know," Geder said. "I'm coming."

The chamber had been a ballroom once, before Geder had appropriated it. The tiers of benches that rose up on three walls had once been intended for men and women of nobility to take their rest while still seeing and being seen. Now Geder's personal guard stood there, swords and bows at the ready. Where the wooden parquet that had supported some forgotten generation of dancers had splintered and warped, Geder had had black stone put in. The graceful lamps and candleholders he'd replaced with dark iron sconces and pitch-stinking torches. His own seat rose high above the floor, like a magistrate's counter, only higher, wider, and grander. Basrahip's station was across the way, where Geder could glance up from the prisoner and have the priest tell him whether the statements were lies or truth. He'd used it first to assure himself of the loyalty of his guards, and then of his subjects. The noble classes of Asterilhold were still being brought, one by one, through the chamber, and while the constant repetition of questions—*Are you loyal to me? Are you plotting against the throne?*—sometimes became tedious, the pleasure of catching out a liar never lost its charm.

Abden Shadra had been head of one of the most powerful of the traditional families. His sons and daughters, nephews and nieces and cousins had controlled almost a third of the nation that had once been Sarakal. He knelt on the black floor without even the strength left to rise. His hair was white against his dark scales, his lip swollen. Bruises didn't look like bruises on Timzinae. The blood pooling under their skin shoved the scales up and stretched them. Abden Shadra's left arm looked almost like a sausage because of it. The rags that hung from his shoulders might have been fine robes once. They were certainly humbled now.

Geder leaned forward on his elbows, looking down at the man.

"You know who I am?" Geder asked.

The Timzinae's gaze swam up and up until it found him. Even then, it seemed that he lost his train of thought, forgot the question and then remembered it. He licked his lips.

"Palliako," he said.

"Yes, good," Geder said. "Tell me about your part in the plot against my life."

Abden Shadra swallowed, worked his mouth like he was trying to expel some foul taste from it. Even from where he sat, Geder could hear the dry clicking of tongue against teeth. The man's eyes shifted to the left and then the right and then back again. Geder felt the stirrings of hope, of excitement.

"You started the war," Abden Shadra said. "We didn't attack you."

"No. Before that," Geder said. "Did you meet with Dawson Kalliam?"

"Never met him."

Geder glanced up, and Basrahip nodded. It was true.

"Did you meet with his agents?"

"No." True.

"Did you conspire to have me or Prince Aster killed?"

"No."

"Do you know who did?"

"A great lot of your own people." Geder didn't bother looking at Basrahip for that one.

"Who in Sarakal? Who among the Timzinae?"

"I don't know of anyone," the man said. "You could talk to Silan Junnit. He had a reputation for caring about you people." Geder glanced up. True. And interesting. He added a name to the list he had built. Silan Junnit. He'd have to see if that was one of the prisoners he'd taken. He'd had a few suggestions like this before, but more often than not, the person named was already dead. It was frustrating. The conspiracy always seemed on the edge of exposure, and then it would dance just out of reach. It never seemed to be the person he'd captured, but one they knew of or had heard about.

It frustrated him. And it frightened him more than a little.

"Will you swear to take no action against Antea, the Severed Throne, me, or Aster?"

"I will. If that's what you want from me, I'll do it." Basrahip hesitated, shrugged, nodded. It was true. Geder's eyes narrowed. This was always the hardest part, but he felt he was genuinely getting better at it.

"Would you *mean* it?"

"Yes." Basrahip shook his head. No. He wouldn't, and he knew he wouldn't, and now Geder knew it too. It was as predictable as it was disappointing.

"Take him back to his cell," Geder said. "Bring in the next one."

Two guards stepped forward and hoisted Abden Shadra by his shoulders.

"No!" the Timzinae said. "I'll swear whatever you want! I'll do what you say, just don't send me back there."

Geder leaned forward.

"You," he said coldly, "don't get to lie to me. Take him back."

The man's cries echoed as they hauled him back. The great doors opened and then closed again. Two new guards hauled a woman's form into the light. She was younger, her scales a glossy black. Her dress was rough canvas, and likely given to her in the prison. When they let her go, she sank to her knees, wrapping her arms around her chest. Geder checked his list.

"Sohen?" he asked. "Sohen Bais?"

The woman nodded, but the only sounds she made were

sobs. Geder looked at Basrahip, but the priest neither nod-ded nor shook his head. In the absence of the living voice, there was nothing. A gesture was only a gesture, whatever the intent behind it.

"You have to answer," Geder said. "You have to actually talk. Do you understand?"

The woman wailed. Geder felt a pang of guilt followed instantly by resentment at having been made to feel guilty. He pressed his thumb against his nose and considered call-ing the proceedings to an end for the day. He didn't want to be here anymore. But once he started slacking off his duties, it would only get harder to pick them back up.

"Sohen," he said, speaking as gently as he could manage. "Sohen. Listen to me. Listen to my voice. It's going to be all right. It is. No one here wants to hurt you."

She looked up. Tears ran from her eyes and mucus from her nose. Her mouth was set in a gape. Geder tried a smile, nodding encouragement. She closed her mouth and nodded back. He let his smile widen and felt a little better about himself.

"Good. You're doing fine. No one here wants to hurt you. You just need to tell me the truth. Your name is Sohen Bais?"

Her voice was a creak. "It is." Behind her, Basrahip nodded.

"See?" Geder said. "Just like that. You're doing fine. Now. Do you know who I am?"

There was a feast that night, just like every other damn night of the season. One of Canl Daskellin's daughters—Alisa—was to marry a young baron from Asterilhold. On the one hand, since he'd conquered Asterilhold, it would be better if the noble classes there were fully engaged with ingratiating themselves to Antea. On the other, it was exactly this sort of political marriage a few generations back that had given rise to the mixed bloodlines that had allowed Feldin Maas to conspire against King Simeon. It was strange how long ago that seemed. Geder sat at the high table with Aster and Lord Daskellin and his family looking out upon the assembled courtiers. The trees in the gardens had been draped with bright cloth. Lanterns of colored glass glowed all around them and scented the air with sweet oil and smoke. The slightest breeze set the trees to nodding to one another like old magistrates impressed with their own wisdom, while the men and women of the court gabbled to each other below them. Geder tapped his knife against his plate, not because he wanted anything. He only felt restless, and it made a pleasing sort of clink.

Sanna Daskellin sat across from her father, near enough that Geder could easily catch her eye, and she his. There had been an incident not long after he'd become Baron of Ebbingbaugh and before he'd been named Lord Regent when he'd been fairly sure that Sanna had been, if not wooing him, at least making it very plain that she was open to being wooed. Tonight, though, her face was a mask of politeness and decorum. Geder couldn't tell if it was because her father was present or if her opinion of him had changed. She leaned forward a degree, her eyebrow rising in query, and Geder realized he'd been staring at her a bit. He shook his head and waved his hand.

"Nothing," he said. "Just lost in the haze of it all. Running the empire does tend to consume all one's spare thoughts."

"And yet you manage it wonderfully," Sanna said with a smile, so perhaps her view of him hadn't entirely shifted. Canl Daskellin shifted nearer as the servants refilled his wineglass.

"The fighting season is nearly at an end," he said. "Summer's high now, but autumn's coming. All these leaves will be losing their green before you know it."

"I suppose that's so," Geder said.

"Still," Daskellin said, "we've done better than anyone expected. All of Asterilhold conquered one year, all of Sarakal the next? I don't think anyone will dare cross the Severed Throne now. You've done a brilliant job of it. Brilliant."

Geder smiled, but he didn't particularly mean it. He heard the unspoken argument. Autumn would come. The army would have to be brought home and the disband called. The veterans would have to return to their lands and work. The war would have to end. Mecilli had been making the same argument in less oblique terms, and Geder didn't find Daskellin's softer approach any more endearing.

"The work's not done," Geder said. "Whichever group is behind all this, they've evaded me so far, but they can't hide forever."

A young man in the colors of House Daskellin fluttered by and Geder's plate seemed to sprout a pink ham steak, two large bites already taken out where his official taster had already sampled it. There had been a time when Geder had been able to eat his own food without someone hovering over it. Maybe there would be again, someday. He cut a bite free and popped it into his mouth. At least it tasted good.

"Have you considered, my lord," Daskellin said, his words careful as a cat walking along the top of a wall, "that there might not be a Timzinae conspiracy?"

Geder put down his knife.

"Have you forgotten how I came to be here? One of our own joined with King Lechan of Asterilhold to kill Aster and his father and take the throne. A year after that, my own patron tried to open my side with a knife. He actually cut Basrahip. This court has been so rotten with schemes and lies and covert plans, it's amazing we didn't all slaughter each other and hand the throne to the first idiot to wander across the border."

"Of course no one disputes—"

"Everybody knows Dawson Kalliam was suborned by Timzinae," Geder said, "and I am close to finding them. Very close. Almost every third person I've questioned from the traditional families knows someone who they say might have been involved. Our mistake was thinking we could catch them easily. The ones who escaped when Sarakal fell were the ones who knew the war was coming. The ones who knew there was a reason for it."

Daskellin's smile had wilted a bit, but it hadn't vanished. He lifted a single finger, his skin smooth but as dark as a Timzinae's.

"I'd thought the reason we'd crossed into Sarakal was to prove the empire wasn't weak, despite all we'd been through. I would have thought we'd made that clear."

"By letting our enemies escape?" Geder asked.

"Would my lord care for some of these greens?" Sanna asked, leaning in toward them. Her smile had a nervous edge. "The cooks used garlic and oil and salt, and the flavor is amazing."

"You'll have to send them to my taster," Geder said. "My point—" The servant placed a cup of cool water beside his plate. "My point is that if we stop now, call Ternigan back, give him a triumph, and call the disband, the men who started this will still be out there. And everyone who knows of them will see that. Yes, I've heard Mecilli's arguments, and yes, it will mean some sacrifice. But consider what happens if we're too timid. We'll see all the chaos and war we've suffered a hundred times over."

"A hundred more years like these, and we'll have conquered the stars," Daskellin said, but Geder didn't find the joke funny or the flattery convincing.

"We have to press on," Geder said. "I know winter campaigns aren't well thought of, but Elassae's fairly warm, and if Ternigan does as well between now and next spring as he's done so far, the whole problem will be solved by first thaw."

"I understand," Daskellin said. "My only concern is that the roaches may—"

Aster made a false cough that meant he wanted to speak. The boy was so quiet that it was easy to forget that he was there with them. Geder turned to him, even though it meant putting his back to Daskellin.

"If Elassae wants to avoid war, they can," the boy said sweetly. "All they'd need to do is hand over the conspirators. And if they won't do that, then we can't really pretend they haven't chosen sides."

Geder felt objections boiling up, but he closed his lips against them. Talking to Aster wasn't like sitting with Emming or Daskellin. Or even Jorey Kalliam. Aster would be king when he was old enough. The Severed Throne was his, and Geder was only protecting it for him. And Aster watched Geder as he'd watched King Simeon. He studied with his tutors and with Minister Basrahip, and his young mind, while not yet fully formed, was engaged and lively. Already, the shape of his face had changed from the roundness it had had. The first planes and angles were in his cheeks, showing what he would be when he'd grown to manhood. The same was true of his words. Letting him have his voice in the decisions of the crown wasn't handing him live steel. Geder would still sign the commands. Hearing the boy out was the least he could do.

"So you think we shouldn't press on?" he said.

"I think giving them the chance to avoid war would be the kind and honorable thing."

"I agree with the prince," Daskellin said. "If there is a way to end this gracefully and turn back to the business of rebuilding the kingdom, we should."

Geder folded his hands together. "I will put together a proclamation for Ternigan to deliver before he comes to any more battles. If they turn over the conspirators—*all* the conspirators—we'll show mercy. Agreed?"

"I do," Aster said. "Though honestly, I can't think they'll take it. They're Timzinae. It's not as if they were people."

Marcus

The dream came again. After so many months away, it was like encountering an old enemy. Marcus knew, even as it began, as the normal meaningless patterns of his sleeping mind began to change to the terrible and familiar, that it wasn't real. Perhaps it should have helped.

Alys and Merian were there, with him. He couldn't see their faces anymore. They had been lost from memory years ago, but the sense of their physical presence was unmistakable. His wife. Their daughter. The flood of love and joy filled him against his will. He didn't want it, but it came. The sense of relief was like an assault, because he knew what would follow it.

The crackling of fire. Merian was screaming. Marcus ran, his legs refusing him. Tree branches held him back, or men's arms, or the thickened air itself. He panted and gasped, he willed himself forward even as he knew that he was already years too late. The green scabbard bounced against his back, the poison of the blade making him stumble. Merian's shrieks were like a cat being strangled. Even though he couldn't reach her, he could feel her breath against his ear.

He was in the fire, cradling her. She was still in his arms, and he thought—as he always did in this part—that she was safe. That he'd saved her. This time, he'd saved her, and when he woke, she would be alive because of it. And then he understood. The grief was wider than oceans. He screamed out for a vengeance that he'd taken almost a decade before.

The burned child in his arms was Merian, but it was also Cithrin. He didn't put her down, but in the logic of dreams he was also drawing the venomed blade. He felt himself running, and this time the speed was like falling. He would take his revenge.

He woke up trying to bring the blade down.

The stars of the Keshet glowed above him, a vast and milky horde. He muttered an obscenity and rolled to his side. His body ached like someone had beaten him, but at least he wasn't dreaming anymore. Long experience had taught him that he could. If he closed his eyes again now, it would all begin again from the start. He'd known men with fevers that let them be for months or even years at a time, and then descended again, pulling them into delirium and illness for weeks. This wasn't so different. Except that it was his, so he had to suffer it.

He sat up, yawned. The sky was clear, but the air smelled like rain. There would be a storm by midday. They'd stop and try to gather some drinking water from it. Not that they needed it. The dragon's road they were following would meet another in a day or so, and there'd be a few semi-permanent buildings there. A trader, a well, a place to sleep with a roof. The height of civilization.

"You're awake," Kit said. He was sitting by the dim embers of the last night's cookfire, the blanket from his bedroll over his shoulders. His expression in the starlight seemed distant. Maybe sad.

"I guess that makes it my watch," Marcus said.

"If you'd like," the old actor said, shrugging.

"Doesn't make sense both of us staying awake."

"I find myself needing less sleep," Kit said.

"You find yourself sleeping less than you need to," Marcus said. "Not the same."

"I suppose that's true. Good night, then."

Kit shifted from sitting down to a curled heap on the ground without actually seeming to move very much. Marcus stood, stretched, tried to decide whether he needed to piss. The mule woke enough to flick a wide ear, then went back to ignoring the men. Near the southern horizon, a plume of smoke stood dark against the dark sky, so dim and subtle that Marcus could only see it in the corner of his eye. A caravan or one of the nomadic cities. They'd have news, perhaps. They'd have something more convincing to eat than the two-days-dead rabbit that was his planned breakfast. Under other circumstances, he'd have discussed the possibility with Kit, come to an agreement. But he didn't want to spend the time, and Kit didn't care.

Kit didn't care about much of anything, it seemed.

"You're not sleeping," Marcus said.

"I'm not."

"Any particular reason for that?"

"Not that I'm aware of. Only I close my eyes, and then they seem to open again."

"Well, a fine pair we are."

Kit rose, taking his old position as if he'd never lain down. Marcus scratched at his shoulder. The place where the sword rode against him had a strange burned feel, and every few days a layer of grey skin would flake off. In truth, they were making good progress. They were two men accustomed to travel, carrying only what they needed and perhaps a bit less. If one of them grew sick or stepped on a snake, it would be a bad day, but they were going quickly. They'd be out of the Keshet and into Elassae well before the season turned. He was looking forward to it, and he wasn't.

"I was a fool," Kit said. "I feel I've wasted my life."

"If you feel like that, you probably are a fool," Marcus said.

"I thought of myself as wise," Kit said. "I carried the secrets of the world with me like a bag of pretty stones. I knew of the goddess, which was a secret held by only a few. And I knew her madness. Her weakness. Her confusion of certainty and truth. And for that I was singular. The only man in the world who saw it all for what it was. I am astounded I could carry that arrogance so long and not notice the burden."

"Arrogance doesn't weigh much," Marcus said. "No heft to it."

Kit chuckled. "I suppose not. Still, I am ashamed."

"You should get over that," Marcus said.

"I appreciate that," Kit said, "but I think you don't understand."

"Might. You thought you were some kind of God-touched cunning man because you had your spider tricks, only it turned out you were more like the rest of us than not. I was the greatest general in an age, determining who sat what throne and shaping the world with my will and a few thousand sharp blades. Only it turned out we were both men, and we both made mistakes. Yours set us off through some of the least pleasant terrain I've ever had the poor fortune to walk through and ended with me trying to hack a hunk of stone to death with a magic sword. Mine ended with a couple graves and a lot of bad dreams."

Kit was silent for a moment. Something scuttled through the grass off to his right, but it didn't sound big enough that Marcus cared.

"I believe I see your point, and I apologize. I didn't intend to make light of your loss."

"You don't see my point, then. My loss doesn't matter. Alys. Merian. They don't care that I failed them. They haven't cared for a long time now. I care, but I can't do anything. I carry it because it's mine. You lived your life either in service to or revolt against something that turns out not to be real. I can see that's embarrassing."

"It's more than that," Kit said. "It leaves me unsure whether my life has had any meaning at all."

"While you figure that out, you'll need to get some rest. And start eating enough. And stop trying to take half of my watch along with yours. We have a job to do, and you need to be in a condition to do it."

"I'm the one that brought you the job," Kit said. "You recall, don't you? You were the chosen one because I chose you. And if I was wrong…"

"It doesn't matter where the job came from," Marcus said. "It doesn't matter if it's something we can do. It's the job. And you only get to pity yourself and sulk when it doesn't get in the way of it."

"And you feel it's begun to?"

"Yes," Marcus said. And then, "This is why you picked me, you know. Apart from needing someone to haul this damned uncomfortable hunk of metal, you knew at some point you might fall down and not want to get back up. I'm here to kick your ass."

"Your job."

"Part of it."

"I suppose that's true," Kit said. "Thank you, Marcus."

"Anytime, Kit. I'm pleased I can help. Now, honestly? Go the hell to sleep."

The Keshet in the falling days of summer had a severe kind of beauty. The white morning sky carried shades of yellow

and pink. The blue of midday served as backdrop for tow-
ering clouds that reached up a hundred times higher than
mountains, white as sunlight at the top and angry grey blue
at the base. At the day's end, the slow sun would seem to
linger on the horizon, red and swollen. The moon waxed
and then waned. Before it waxed full again, they would be
in Elassae. In Suddapal.

By choice, they met few other travelers. Sometimes Kit
would spend the day singing, and his years on the boards
gave his voice a range from barrel-deep to sweetly high,
depending upon the song. Marcus didn't object. Sometimes
he even joined his voice with Kit's. But beneath that, he felt
himself growing narrow. Sharp. Focused. The anticipation
was like being on a hunt, but it lasted for weeks. He was
preparing himself. It was a sensation he'd had before, once,
and it brought the nightmares.

There was no single moment when the western edge of the
Keshet became the eastern reaches of Suddapal. No garrison
marked the border, no tax man squatted by the side of the
road. The oases and crossroads only became a little larger,
a little more permanent, until at last they were villages. The
dragon's road became better traveled, and then thick. The
flood of war refugees was mostly Timzinae, but Jasuru and
Tralgu and Firstblood families were among them in numbers enough that Marcus and Kit could fold themselves in
among them unremarked.

They approached the fivefold city from the east, passing
through farmlands and pastures Marcus had never seen. The
commons were so thick with tents that it was as if new towns
were forming within the city, and men stood in lines at the
larger houses, negotiating hospitality from the locals or else
begging it. Everywhere, the word was that Antea's army was
on the march, that they would be in Suddapal very, very soon.

Displacement was a part of war, and Marcus had lived his life around it. It was a tissue of misery, fear, and uncertainty. Children would be sleeping hungry and in the streets tonight and tomorrow and likely for months if not years to come, provided nothing worse happened.

"We can go to Ela and Epetchi," Kit said. It took Marcus a moment to place the names as belonging to the café owners they'd stayed with before leaving for Lyoneia. "They'll take us in if they can."

"You should stay with them for a few days," Marcus agreed.

Kit shot a glance at him, and Marcus shrugged. There wasn't anything more to say. They both understood why he'd chosen Suddapal. When they reached the café, it was already full to the top with refugees, but they found room for Kitap. And they knew the way to the branch of the Medean bank. It was in the western end of the cities, and a way inland. Marcus thanked them, bought a bowl of charred mutton with a few coins Kit gave him, and walked out into the city.

For months, he'd traveled with Kit. In the unfamiliar jungles of deep Lyoneia and the unforgiving mountains and planes of the Keshet, over the Inner Sea and back. The sense of being alone again, even on the busy streets and crowded commons of the city, surprised him and left him comforted. He wondered how much he'd been worried about carrying Kit and keeping him from despair. He wouldn't have said he was much concerned, except that now he felt relieved in his isolation. Or maybe it was only that he now didn't have to pretend he wasn't hunting.

Yardem Hane was one of the best fighters Marcus had ever known, and the acuity of the Tralgu's great, mobile ears had saved them from ambush more than once. Marcus's advantage was that he knew his old companion as well as he was known by him, and Yardem didn't know he'd come. He would only have one opportunity.

The compound of the Medean bank in Suddapal was a wide, low group of buildings around a vast yard. It looked more like a small, self-contained village than a bank. The streets were wide, which was good in that he could get a clear line of sight without coming too near the place, and bad in that there wasn't cover enough to safely move in close. He found a place in the shadows of an alley and sat patiently, his face hidden and his shoulders sloped in dejection. Another doomed wanderer in a city sick with them. He waited. He watched. He noted the rhythms of the compound and its people. For a large place, it was well watched. He needed to wait until Yardem stepped out.

Or until everyone else did.

Three days later was Tenthday. The population of the city shed their shoes and marched together through the streets to the temples. Marcus watched them come out. Among the Timzinae guardsmen, Enen the Kurtadam stood out. But not so much as Cithrin. Marcus felt the sight of her like a blow. She looked taller. No, that wasn't right. Not taller, but older. Her pale hair was pulled back and her green velvet gown was well cut without being boastful. She was walking arm in arm with an older Timzinae woman, her expression sharp with concentration. Seeing her from the distance of the alley was dreamlike and strange. The last time he'd been this near to her, she'd been leaving for Carse and telling him that taking him to Northcoast would be a mistake. If he'd fought against that, insisted that he stay with her, how different the world might be. He forced himself to look down for fear his gaze would draw hers. But she was here. She was well enough, it seemed. That was as it should be. But it didn't change what he needed to do.

Yardem wasn't among the temple-bound throng. He'd stayed back, then, to guard the compound. Marcus forced himself to wait, but the tension growing in his back and legs made it difficult. The time had come. When the last of the household had turned the farthest corner, Marcus counted his breaths to a hundred, then did it again, then stood. The sword hung heavy across his back. He crossed the wide road to the compound's gate, then walked down the wall until he found a place low enough to vault it.

He found Yardem Hane on a low porch, a book in his massive hands and his ears canted forward. Marcus pulled the blade clear of its scabbard, keeping a finger against the steel so that it would not ring. The angle of his approach kept the Tralgu's wide back toward him. He reached the edge of the porch in silence. A fast lunge would be all it took. Even a shallow cut, and the sword's venom would do the rest.

Marcus put the sole of his foot against the bare dirt and twisted. Yardem's ears swiveled back at the sound, but he didn't look up.

"Sir," he said.

"You know why I'm here."

"Yes, sir."

"You betrayed my trust."

Slowly, carefully, being certain no movement could be mistaken for an attack, Yardem placed a twig between the book's pages and let them close.

"I did."

"How long were you planning to let me rot in that little prison?"

Yardem put a hand to either side and slowly lifted himself up to standing. He was tall, even for a Tralgu. He had the old sword at his side, but his fingers didn't touch its hilt. His earrings jingled.

"Until Cithrin came back, sir."

"And if she hadn't?"

"I'd have given myself a fair head start," Yardem said. "All respect, sir. You were going to loot her bank and hire a company to march into the middle of someone else's civil war."

"What of it?"

"It was a bad idea."

Marcus tightened his grip on the blade, his mouth bending into a scowl. For three long breaths together, they stood motionless. He felt the rage in his breast reach its high-water mark and then recede.

He pressed his lips together, and then lowered the blade.

"Fair point," he said. "So. Where do we stand?"

"Pyk Usterhall's running the Porte Oliva branch. Cithrin's agreed with Komme Medean to a year's apprenticeship with Magistra Isadau, and then a year back in Porte Oliva. Only it's not certain we'll make the full year here. Antea's expected to invade at any moment. They've sent runners to say if we hand over the people responsible for the coup in Camnipol last year, they'll leave, but no one seems to know who that would be. We've sent most of the bank's capital out of the city, but the local magistra's dedicated to staying and helping people get out of harm's way for as long as she can. Cithrin's apparently decided to do the same. And Roach just got married, only we're calling him Halvill now."

"Halvill?"

"His name."

"Ah."

"You, sir?"

"Well, the war's actually being driven by a set of mad priests who have power over truth and lies. The plan was to kill the spider goddess they worship and take away their power, only it turns out she's a figment of their collective imagination. Kit used to be one of them, but he turned apostate. He's at a café down by the port having what's left of his faith collapse around him."

"I see."

"Oh," Marcus said, holding up the blade. "Magic sword."

"Full year."

"Has been," Marcus said. Then, "It's good to be back, though."

"Happy to have you, sir."

Cithrin

T here are two books on my bedside table," Isadau said. Months of close contact let Cithrin see her anxiety. The others—even Yardem—almost certainly didn't.

"Probably," Kit said. "Certainly you believe there are."

"I also have a lamp there."

"No, Magistra," the old actor said. "You do not."

Isadau sat back in her chair. Her smile might almost have been amused, but her inner eyelids were fluttering madly.

It was profoundly strange. Cithrin had walked out on the Tenthday routine, her mind occupied with thoughts of the bank and the war, Isadau's network for refugees of the old conflict and the coming one, and her own growing sense of dread. When she came back, Captain Wester was sitting in the courtyard and Master Kit was walking in from the street. She'd heard of people who'd gotten fevers and lost their minds in them. She had to think it felt similar. Isadau didn't seem to be put off her stride, but for her these were two men loosely associated with the bank who'd arrived much as a courier might. For Cithrin, they were two people she'd trusted and relied on who had left her without a word and arrived without a warning. She wanted to run to them both and hug them and yell at them and make sure they would never go away again, and so instead she fell into a politeness and distance that she hated even as she employed it.

They gathered in a private courtyard with a small fountain and ivy growing up three of the four walls. It was cool
and beautiful, and the tiny clapping hands of the ivy's leaves
meshed with the muttering of water to make eavesdropping
almost impossible. Marcus and Yardem shared a bench, while
Master Kit perched on the fountain's edge. Cithrin sat in a
chair beside Isadau. A servant brought a small wooden table
and filled it with cups of cool water and bowls of cut apples.
To anyone in the household, it would have seemed nothing
more than another meeting among hundreds where the two
magistras spoke about the private doings of the bank.

Captain Wester's absence hadn't been kind to him. He was
thinner than she'd ever seen him, his cheeks gaunt and his
neck so ropy that she could trace the individual muscles and
tendons. Master Kit also looked worn down by the road, but
with him it almost seemed like a shedding of old clothes. His
eyes were brighter, his smile just as open and pleasant, and
the darkness of his skin a testament to weeks out of doors.
He had none of the greyness that dulled Marcus's skin, and
his eyes hadn't taken the same slight tint of yellow.

And then, just as Cithrin began to feel she had her balance back, Master Kit had pricked his thumb with Yardem's
dagger and tiny black spiders had come out.

"And if you were to speak to me," Isadau said.

"I would be very difficult to disbelieve," Master Kit said.
"Even those things which you had evidence against, you
would eventually find some way to justify."

"Even if it was absurd?"

Master Kit's smile was melancholic.

"I have tried to dedicate my life to the discovery of the
world as it truly is," he said, "and even knowing what I
knew, it seems I have been unable to avoid believing absur-
dities. I believe I could convince you of anything."

Yardem made a low sound in his throat, part growl and part chuckle. Master Kit's glance was a question.

"Just recalling all our philosophical debates," Yardem said. "You could have won all of them if you'd cared to."

"I hope I chose my words carefully enough to respect the beliefs I did not share."

"All the same," Isadau said, "you are an abomination."

Cithrin scowled and began to object, but Kit beat her to it.

"Certainly I agree that I have a potential for evil that those unlike me do not. And I am afraid that this present violence is the fruit that grew from that bloom."

"What is it they want?" Yardem asked, his voice a low rumble. "The other ones."

"I believe they want to bring the world together under the banners of the goddess," Kit said. "To place everything within her and make it part of her flesh. Before I fell from grace, I was told that we were waiting for a sign, and when that sign came we would return to the nations of humanity, stand against the forces of the dragon, and free the world at last from lies and deception."

"By spreading their story," Marcus said.

"Until there are no other stories," Kit finished. "By ignoring or destroying anything that failed to match with the certainties of the goddess who is immune from lies."

Magistra Isadau sat forward, her head sinking into her hands.

"Geder was that sign," Cithrin said.

"In a sense, yes," Master Kit said. "Though if it had not been him now, I suspect it would have been another at another time. I suspect signs are fairly easy to see for one dedicated to seeing them. And if a high priest believed that he had seen the hand of the goddess at work in the world, he would only need to say it, and it would become as true as anything else. As certain, at least. I don't know the man who has taken the high priest's place."

"Basrahip," Cithrin said. "His name's Basrahip."

"I assume he was initiated after I left," Kit said. "But what he believes, he believes sincerely. And all the other priests will also believe. And then anyone who listens to their voices. And then...everyone."

"Explains some things," Yardem said.

Marcus turned to the Tralgu. "Explains what, for instance?"

"Why the Anteans haven't been sent back with their tails between their legs," Yardem said. "They're overreaching badly, except that they keep winning. They've found a way to use this on the field. Give false reports to the enemy or some such."

"Not to mention all the rumors about Geder's strange powers," Cithrin said. "All that about how he speaks with the dead and the fallen warriors rise up to fight alongside him. It's not the man I met. Easier to think that's one of those tales the priests convince everyone of than that it's actually true."

"And right now," Magistra Isadau said through her fingers, "at this moment, the only people in the world who understand what this war is and what it means are sitting in this garden."

"Yes," Marcus said.

"You," Isadau said, turning to Master Kit. "How do we stop this?"

"I don't know," Kit said.

Isadau nodded. The nictitating membranes closed over her eyes.

"Komme has to be told," she said. "Oh, God. I have a very long letter to write, don't I?"

For the rest of the day, Cithrin tried to go about her usual routine, but it all seemed false as rehearsing a play. There were contracts to review, but the armies of Antea were on the roads already, carrying the false goddess's banners. The histories of the bank hadn't quite all been read through, but Marcus and Master Kit had come and neither were quite the men she'd thought they were. Though that was more the case with Kit than Captain Wester. She tried sleeping, but the late summer sun defied her. She tried working, but her mind escaped its leash. She wanted to be back in Porte Oliva or Carse, someplace where she understood the system of the world. Suddapal, with its echoes of Vanai and Camnipol, was too complicated. Or if it wasn't the city, she had become too complicated for it.

Master Kit and Captain Wester joined the family at dinner, and anything else would have seemed strange. Kit regaled the table with stories from his years on the road, and Cithrin watched as people fell under the benign and compassionate spell of his voice. It was that same magic that had brought Sarakal into ruins. And Vanai. Only no, Vanai had burned before Geder's discovery of the temple. That atrocity, at least, hadn't been driven by the things in Master Kit's blood.

She'd hoped to find Marcus alone after the meal, to sit with him. Breathe the same air. She felt that she had a thousand questions for him, only she didn't know what any of them were. In any case, Marcus went to his room claiming exhaustion almost before the last plate of beef found its way to the table. Cithrin sat alone in the crowd as eating gave way to music and talk. The only one who seemed equally distracted was Isadau. When Master Kit withdrew from the hall, Isadau didn't follow him. So Cithrin did.

The old actor was sitting alone in one of the smaller

rooms, a wool blanket draped over his shoulders, when Cithrin came in.

"Kit," she said.

"Ah, Magistra Cithrin," Kit said, shifting on his bench to make room for her. "Have I mentioned how pleased I am to find you doing so well? It's a long way from the last caravan out of Vanai."

"I don't know," she said, sitting. "Seems like the same place to me, almost."

"Yes, I suppose I see that," he said.

"Are you...are you really you?" she asked. "I mean...I don't know what I mean."

"I think I do," he said. "I carried a secret with me for many years, and now it's uncovered. It must change how you see me, but I feel like the same man I always have been. My affection for you is what it was. My fears for the future haven't changed. I feel more threatened, I suppose. But that may only be truth. When your friend Isadau said I was an abomination—"

"She didn't mean it," Cithrin said.

"She did, Cithrin. She very much did. And I think I understand why."

A cricket took up its song, and then another. The chirping was thinner than it had been at midsummer. Fewer insects and a slower song.

"Marcus left when I was gone away to Camnipol."

"Yes," Kit said. "That must have been hard for you, his disappearing that way."

"I was fine," Cithrin said. Then, "God, you know that was a lie, don't you?"

"Yes," Kit said. "But it's one that speaks well of you both."

"Having him back...just back. It's like Magister Imaniel

popping up out of the grave and coming to the dinner table. Magister Imaniel or else..."

"Or else your father?"

"I didn't know my father," Cithrin said.

"Ah yes. I remember that," Kit said. They were silent for a time.

"Can I ask you something?"

"Of course," Kit said.

"Basrahip. The priests. If they were looking for something, what would it be?"

"What do you mean, looking for?"

"Sending out hunting parties. Looking in the empty places in the world."

"Well," Kit said, then took a long, deep breath, giving himself time to think. "I think we have established that I may not have perfect insight into the workings of the priesthood. But I would think they were looking for other remnants of the dragons' power. Something like the Timzinae or the sword that Marcus and I recovered. Are they? Looking, I mean."

"I think so," Cithrin said. "We've been getting reports from someone in Camnipol. We aren't sure who. But one of the things he said was that there were expeditions going out. And one of them is being led by a Dartinae man I almost worked with in Porte Oliva. He gave me a dragon's tooth."

"Did he really?" Master Kit asked.

"I think he did," Cithrin said. "I suppose it could be a fake."

"I wonder..." Kit said.

"I could show it to you."

"What? Oh, thank you, but no. I was remembering something Marcus said about men like me being driven into hiding once. A very long time ago. If my former companions are searching for something, I imagine it's because they want to possess it or destroy it. Either way...What do we know about this man in Camnipol?"

"Almost nothing," Cithrin said. "If Isadau doesn't object, I can show you the reports."

"I would very much like that."

Cithrin felt a thickness in her throat, a sudden welling up of sorrow. Master Kit's brows furrowed and he took her hand. Cithrin shook her head until she could find her voice. When she did speak, the words were thick.

"Now that he's started this, he's not going to stay," she said. "Is he?"

Comprehension washed over Master Kit's face. He looked down.

"I expect Captain Wester will remain here to protect the compound as best he can until the city's fallen. Beyond that, I don't know," he said, and then chuckled ruefully. "In truth, Cithrin, these days I feel I don't know anything."

The armies of Antea arrived in the morning unopposed. It was understood that the fighting would be in Kiaria, where the soldiers had gone. Even a token resistance to the invaders in Suddapal would have meant a few dozen corpses and nothing more. They didn't even try. The morning sun slanted down over the roofs and tent-thick commons. The Antean carts rolled through the streets, and soldiers marched behind them. Timzinae refugees who had left their homes behind to escape this same army sat quietly at the sides of the roads. Cithrin stood by the compound's wall and watched. After so long, the mass of Firstblood faces seemed wrong. Out of place.

"Don't stare, ma'am," Yardem said. "Someone might take offense."

"And what if they do?"

Marcus answered. His voice was tired.

"There's still going to be a sack. If we're lucky, it'll be a short one, and centered someplace else."

"What?" Cithrin said. "The soldiers just loot the place? Go through like bandits and take what they want?"

"If we're lucky," Marcus said again.

"We'll stand against them," Cithrin said.

"We'll take everything of value in the compound," Marcus said, "put it in the yard here, bar the doors, guard the windows, and hope for the best. This is going to be a bad night."

He was right. It was. Through all the long hours of the night, Cithrin sat with Isadau in the relative safety of her office, reading by a small brass lamp, and remembering none of the words. The guards—Yardem, Enen, Marcus, and even Master Kit included—kept watch. Once, near midnight, voices came from the streets, a mad whooping followed by screams and then the sounds of something large and possibly wooden being broken. Then near dawn, the unmistakable sound of blades. Cithrin felt fear and fatigue grinding in her belly. She wanted badly to be drunk. Even if the worst came, at least she'd be insensible.

The morning air stank of smoke. Plumes of it rose from near the water, and Master Kit watched them with an expression so closed it frightened her. She remembered hearing that he had friends in the city. Their houses might be fueling those fires. Or their bodies.

Isadau stepped into her compound to survey the damage. Half of what they'd left out had been taken, and the other half destroyed. She lifted the remains of a lacquered box, and then let the pieces fall from her hands. Tears streamed down her cheeks, but otherwise her expression could have been carved from stone. This was more than her bank. It was her family's home. It was her city. That she'd known this would come didn't seem to pull the blow. She found Marcus and Yardem speaking with Jurin. Marcus nodded in salute. The gesture was familiar, and Cithrin felt herself clinging to it.

"Could have been much worse," he said. "It was a near thing, but we didn't lose anyone. And the Anteans are all falling back. Worst may be over." Cithrin coughed out a mirthless laugh and Marcus nodded as if agreeing with her. In the street, someone was wailing. "Likely, they'll send an order. The bank's powerful enough they'll want someone at the naming of the new protector."

"Isadau?" Cithrin asked.

"It's who I'd choose," Marcus said.

"I'll go with her."

Marcus frowned and Yardem's ears went forward, but neither of them made an objection.

"Come back when it's done," was all that Marcus said.

Cithrin went back to her rooms and changed into a formal dress and put up her hair. The city might be conquered, but the Medean bank was more than a city; it was the world. She would not pretend to be humbled. When she was done, she touched her lips and cheeks with rouge, vomited into the chamberpot, and applied the rouge again. The cut of the collar didn't call for a necklace, but she put one on anyway: the silver bird in flight that Salan had given her. No one else might know the defiance it signified, but she would. When the order came, carried by a sneering Firstblood in Antean uniform, she accepted it on Isadau's behalf. It was, after all, addressed to the magistra of the branch, and technically she fit the description. They were to come to the central square of the third city at noon. Lord Marshal Ternigan would accept their formal surrender of the city and introduce the new protector of Suddapal. Also every household was to surrender any weaned children younger than five against the good conduct of the city. There would be no exceptions made. Any children not turned over to the protector's men would be killed without question.

Half an hour before the time came, Isadau let Cithrin guide her out to the street. The magistra wore ragged grey mourning robes and her eyes seemed empty. Shocked. When they passed the temple, a vast banner the red of blood hung from its roof. The eightfold sigil of the goddess looked out from its center like an unblinking eye, the symbol of nothingness. And below it, the body of the cunning man and priest that Cithrin and Yardem had snickered at from the pews. Terrible things had been done to him.

"She doesn't even exist," Isadau said, her voice quiet and brittle.

"She doesn't need to," Cithrin said.

Clara

When Clara's only work had been the running of her household, it had still been enough to fill most days and even bring some occasional worries to bed. When things were well—and they were well more often than not—Dawson and the children were utterly unaware of the mechanisms and habits that kept the shoes cleaned and the food brought from the kitchen. If she asked Dawson to please keep his hunting dogs out of the servants' quarters, he saw only her somewhat trivial focus. She didn't tell him that one of the maids had been mauled as a girl and broke into sweats whenever the animals trotted through. Dawson would have told her to get a different maid, but this one had been the best at polishing the silver, and accommodations had to be made whether Dawson knew of them or not.

Her plan of battle was simple enough. Find competent, trustworthy servants, treat them with respect, and let them do their work. Listen when spoken to. Remember everybody's name and something about the peculiarities of their lives. Forgive any mistake once, and none twice.

In the long, subterranean struggles between the women of the court, she held her own. Someone else might have a more fashionable tailor or hairdresser in any given season, lured away by promises and bribes, but Clara's was always perfectly respectable, and they didn't leave her in times of difficulty. As compared with some who thought training servants meant alternating between throwing fits and showering them with praise. She couldn't count the number of ladies of the court who, one time and another, had managed to throw their own houses and lives into chaos by losing the service of their more competent staff.

And running a household, she supposed, was not so unlike running an empire.

As the long days of summer began to grow short again, she found herself invited to more informal gatherings. Women who had pretended not to know her began smiling or nodding to her when she walked through the more affluent streets of the city. Few went so far as to speak, but some did. The gossip around her shifted from the balls and feasts at the season's opening, and turned toward the preparations for its end. Clara smiled and laughed and wished people the best in ways that made it clear she didn't care for them. She fell into the patterns of the woman she'd been for most of her life, and it felt like wearing a mask at a street carnival.

Behind it, she was cataloging everything she heard. Of Geder Palliako's inner court, Daskellin was far and away the best political mind. His daughter, who had been putting herself in compromising situations with Palliako before he'd been named Lord Regent, had fallen back into propriety. So perhaps Daskellin had gained a better insight into the kind of man Palliako was. Emming was a blowhard who played the gadfly on trivial matters and followed anyone more powerful than he was when the issue had weight. Mecilli was an honest man with a reputation for caution and tradition that most reminded Clara of Dawson. The two would have been friends, except that Mecilli had spoken out against dueling and Dawson had decided the man was a coward. Noyel Flor wasn't dim, but he was the third generation of his family to be Protector of Sevenpol, and in everything he considered what was best for his city first and the empire as a whole after. Lord Skestinin commanded the fleet, which made him valuable to Geder, but he was also family, now that Jorey and Sabiha were married.

And, of course, there was Ternigan.

The Lord Marshal was an excellent strategist and had more experience commanding in the field than anyone else at court, and perhaps because of his habit of strategic thought, he'd placed himself on the winning side of almost every conflict in a generation. By being the man of talent, he made himself someone to be won over. Someone to be wooed.

And so he also made himself vulnerable.

For Geder to fall from power, he had to be alienated from the best minds in the empire and surrounded instead with charming idiots and the pleasantly incompetent. Knowing what she did of Geder's temper and distrust, she thought the exercise might not be that difficult. At least not with low-hanging fruit like Bassim Ternigan.

The temptation was to rush. To hurry. To create some crisis out of whole cloth. The wiser choice was to wait and listen until the world in all its incomprehensible complexity presented her an opportunity, and then to be ready for it. She stayed at court as much as she could, maintained what friendships she had, and tried to keep her private role gathering information as loyal traitor separate from being her sons' mother.

It was not always possible.

"Having a permanent port on the Inner Sea will change everything," Vicarian said around a mouthful of roast pork. "There's rumor that Palliako's going to send Lord Skestinin there."

"Well, Father hasn't mentioned anything to me," Sabiha

said. She was looking better, Clara thought. Brighter about the eyes, easier with her smile. She wasn't a pretty girl exactly, and all the more interesting for that. "All he's said is that wintering in Nus will be much more pleasant than Estinport."

"May just be a rumor," Jorey said.

"Likely that," Vicarian agreed. "Honestly, I thought the court was the breeding ground for unfounded guesses spoken as fact, but it's nothing compared to the seminary. I think it's because we're supposed to spend so much time praying that we all get bored."

"Don't be impious, dear," Clara said without any real heat in her voice. "And don't speak with your mouth full."

"Yes, Mother," Vicarian said. With his mouth full.

Though she had known that he might arrive at some point, her middle son's arrival in Camnipol had been a pleasant surprise. It had occasioned dinners at Lord Skestinin's manor three nights in a row with the family and a few close friends. Elisia had even come with her child, Corl, but without her husband. Seeing her daughter and grandson had been joyful in a way that Clara hadn't expected, but even as she cooed over the boy, her other self was noting that dining with Jorey and Sabiha wasn't too shameful for Elisia's delicate social sensibilities any longer. It would be interesting to see if the effect outlasted Vicarian's visit. If so, it would hardly have been a year before Dawson's treason was being forgotten. Only, no. Not forgotten. Ascribed to someone else. The attempt on Geder's life and the plot against Simeon and Aster were both hidden assaults by a vast and shadowed Timzinae conspiracy now, and in the process, the truth of the matter was forgotten. It was eerie to watch it happen, but it was also to Jorey's benefit, so while she could see the rank injustice of it, she couldn't think it entirely evil.

"I'm not sure you can accuse him of impiety, Mother," Elisia said. "It's his newfound piety that brought him, after all."

"My piety's not newfound," Vicarian said. "It's my appreciation for what it's going to take to get a placement worth having. Everyone with any power at all is tripping over their toes to study under Minister Basrahip."

"Is his cult that important?" Clara said. "Why, it seems only yesterday everyone was laughing down their sleeves at it."

"It's nearly the only important sect in the kingdom now," Vicarian said. "Temples are going up in Kaltfel, Asinport, Nus. Now Inentai and Suddapal. And everyone's assuming Kiaria, once Ternigan's burned it clean enough for civilized habitation. All of them are dedicated to the spider goddess. Anyone who's keeping strictly to the old rites won't be placed there. And there's talk of converting the temple in Kavinpol. This is the first time Minister Basrahip has taken on initiates from outside wherever he was out in the Keshet. Everyone put in for it."

"But you got lucky," Jorey said.

Vicarian grinned, and Clara could see for a moment the boy he'd been at six years old. "May have called in a couple favors for it."

It was what she had hoped for, of course. After Dawson's death, she had done everything she could to see that her children were safe, that they had the chance to reinvent themselves in Palliako's court. She had only lost Barriath, and that to exile rather than death. And yet she sat in the dining hall with the richest dinner she'd enjoyed in months, the windows all opened, and the evening breeze setting the candles to flutter and snap, and her pleasure was tainted by doubt. She felt she was helping her boys scramble up a tree as she cut it down. But that was simplistic. If Palliako fell and a new Lord Regent took his place, the court would still be made from the same people. Rearranged by the rupture, perhaps, as they had been before and would be again.

Still, she could wish that Vicarian had saved his favors for a better occasion.

After the last of the meal was finished, Elisia made her farewells and went off, Corl and his nurse trailing along behind with her guardsmen. Clara wasn't sure when walking with guards had become normal for members of court, but it was now. Then they sat together in Lord Skestinin's narrow drawing room. The taste of Jorey's tobacco reminded her what real leaf was like. She was in real danger of becoming used to the cheap-ground that sold in the alley mouths near the Prisoner's Span. They joked and played at tiles and cards. Except that Dawson and Barriath weren't there, it was a perfect evening, and it passed too quickly into night.

When, at last, Clara prepared to make her own farewells, Jorey took her discreetly aside.

"I haven't been keeping you up with everything," he said. "I didn't want to raise hopes if I wasn't sure. But from the last letters I've had, I think Lord Skestinin is going to back me at court. Between his word and Geder still seeming to like me, I think I'll be able to take on the management of some of his lands while he's with the navy."

"That's lovely, dear," Clara said, tears jumping to her eyes. "I'm so glad for you. And Sabiha too. She's…I'm so glad you married her. She seems simply perfect. And by that I mean strong, because strong is so important in a woman's life, even if no one particularly says it." She was babbling, words flowing without her knowing what they would be or if she meant them.

Jorey took her hand and pressed something into it. A

small cloth purse of the sort she usually took her allowance from him in.

"It comes with a slightly better income," he said. "Sabiha and I talked about it, and we wanted you to have part too."

"Oh, I can't," Clara said, her fingers curling around the coins. Clutching them. "Really, you mustn't."

"I must, Mother. And I will."

It didn't help stop the tears. She kissed Jorey's cheek and wiped her eyes on her sleeve.

"You are very good to me," she murmured. "You have been very, very good."

"I turned you out," he said.

"Of course you did, dear," she said, and for a moment, her new self spoke. The woman she was still becoming. "I will always be complicit in what your father did. It's part of who I am now. Your distance from me was necessary, and it still is. You did right."

"Still—"

"No, dear. No *still*. No *if only*. What your father did and what I do can't be part of what you are. Not any longer. Don't be ashamed of that. If I'd had more strength and wisdom, I'd have gone on my own."

Jorey looked at his hands.

"I don't believe that for a moment," he said. "But thank you for saying it."

Vincen Coe waited at the door to the street, chatting with the door slave and looking in the torchlight like a servant waiting for his master. That gave Clara pause. Treating Vincen as if he were only what he had been before seemed somehow monstrous. And yet what option did she have? She could no more invite a lesser huntsman formerly in her husband's service to sit at the table with Jorey and Vicarian than she could call Dawson back from the dead. She tried to imagine

Vincen sitting in the drawing room with Jorey. Or worse, with Elisia. The familiarity with someone so clearly of a lower class would make her daughter's eyes explode. She really was more Dawson's child than her own. Nor would it be a kindness to Vincen to place him in a context in which the gulf between their stations was made obvious.

Sabiha was the one to see her safely to the door, to Vincen's arm, as was appropriate after all for the lady of the household. She'd done the same a thousand times while Dawson sat in the drawing room with his dogs. Vincen stepped forward, bowing the way he would had he been only what he seemed. Clara had the sudden and powerful impulse to put the young man's arm around her waist. Sabiha would certainly have been shocked, but she had also stepped outside what women were permitted, and shocked wasn't the same as scandalized.

"Clara?" Sabiha said. "Are you all right?"

"Yes. Yes, dear, I am. Just lost in my own mind for a moment."

Sabiha took her hands and smiled into her eyes. Clara smiled back from across a gulf as wide as the Division that only she knew was there. Then the moment passed, and Clara marched off resolutely into the dark streets of Camnipol, Vincen walking a pace behind and to the left, as a good servant would until they crossed the bridge and Clara brought him to her side. Even with his injuries and the time spent recuperating, Vincen's arm was solid. Clara tried to remember when Dawson's had been the same, but in truth, it hadn't. Strong, yes. But Vincen was a degree shorter than Dawson had been, and the proportion of his arm different. Their two bodies couldn't be mistaken. Vincen was unavoidably and utterly Vincen, and Dawson was gone past all recall. She had mourned him for a year, as best she could

when she was mourning everything else and rejoicing in
between.

It had been a year, and imperfect as it was, she had done
the best she could. Her children were reestablishing themselves in the lives they'd chosen or forged or found.

All around them, the city was preparing for a bad winter. The men and women of noble blood knew that the food
would be thin this season the way they knew a particular
march, recognizing it by the first notes. The men and women
in the streets of Camnipol would be the ones playing the
instruments and singing the melodies. For Jorey and Sabiha
and even Vicarian, it would be the difference between eating meat every day or only once a week. For Abatha and
Vincen, for Aly and Mihal, it would be the difference
between eating every day or every other. And as hard as
winter would be, spring before the first crops came would
be worse. It expressed itself in small ways: the timbre of the
voices of begging children, the weariness and resignation in
the shoulders of carters, the growing competition for day-
old bread. Things she might have lived and died and never
have known had only a very few things gone differently.

And instead, here she was, walking through the darkness with this peculiar, unlikely masculine animal at her
side. They reached the far side of the Division, passed by the
great yellow taproom with the same band of players she'd
seen there before in the yard, declaiming to perhaps a dozen
people.

"You know that I am entirely too old for you," she said.

"You've said so, m'lady," Vincen replied as he had before.

"You should find a woman your own age."

"None of them are as lovely as you."

She coughed out a laugh. "And I'll wager you played with
fire when you were a boy."

"M'lady?"

At the mouth of an alleyway she paused, and he paused with her as she had known he would. She put her hand on his shoulder and, before he could grasp what was happening, shoved him into the wall. She felt the impact in the palms of her hands. She only had to bend her neck up a little to reach his lips, and she kept the pressure constant, pinning him in place like a flower pressed in a book. Her mouth opened his, and she bruised him. For a moment, he was too shocked, and then he wasn't. When she stepped back, he staggered.

Her breath was fast, her heart racing. The warmth in her body was strange and wild and familiar as an old coat, long forgotten and rediscovered. When she laughed, it came from low in her throat. It came from the girl she had been at eighteen.

"My lady," Vincen said unsteadily.

"Clara, Vincen," she said. "My name is Clara. Now take me home with you."

Marcus

The first days of an occupation said a lot about the war that brought it about. In the best case, the new protector would reach out to the older, established powers in the city and find ways to make the habits and expectations of the citizens work gracefully under the new regime. The worst was slaughtering everyone and burning the place to the foundations. Suddapal fell in between. There were few fires, and what there were got doused quickly. Three ships sank during the sack, and given the number of vessels at the docks, Marcus suspected they'd been scuttled by captains who for whatever reason couldn't put out to sea. The physical city itself was treated, for the greatest part, with respect. But it was the respect of an owner for their property. It didn't bode well for the citizens.

And neither did the march of children.

Suddapal had three gaols, a legacy of the different cities it had been before they grew together. One stood safely inland with great stone walls around lines of iron cages. The second was at the top of a cliff near the shore with cells that lay open to the weather, foul or fair. The third was an island with only a single bay and currents cruel enough to defeat even the most experienced swimmers. All three had been emptied of their prisoners and refilled with the young. From his first glance at the children packed twenty in a cage meant for six, Marcus understood what he was seeing. Not a city folded into the empire. Not a people made subjects. Slaves, then, at best. And more likely, the culling that Kit had feared. The man did pick the worst times to be right.

The new protector—an improbably mustached Firstblood named Fallon Broot—had set a curfew for all Timzinae in the city. No one on the streets from dusk to dawn. Marcus had seen a fisherman at the piers shouting that the catch would be gone before he was on the water. The new Antean portmaster had him whipped in the street until there were bright tracks of raw meat along the chitined back. A dozen soldiers watched, laughing.

All of it put Marcus in an odd place. Like the Anteans, he was Firstblood. Like them, he was an unfamiliar face in the city. He could walk the darkened streets that the citizens no longer could. And more than that, he could pass unremarked by the new masters of Suddapal because he looked like them. Even Enen and Yardem, not technically bound by the curfew, would be noticed for their race. Marcus looked like what he was, a Firstblood soldier out of uniform and a little long in the tooth. He looked like nobody. He could ferry messages between the elements of Magistra Isadau's shadow company with less danger than anyone else in the branch.

Or at least less danger from the invaders.

"Isadau sent me," Marcus said, his hands at his shoulders, palms out. The blade pressed against his throat.

"The hell she did," the Timzinae man holding it said.

"My name is Marcus Wester. I'm guard captain for the Porte Oliva branch." It might not be true, but going into the complexities of his employment seemed like a poor decision. "I came here with Magistra bel Sarcour."

"Prove it."

"You have seven children hidden in the attic right now.

You sent the message this afternoon as a letter asking about a loan for a new millstone."

The blade came tighter, drawing a trickle of blood. The compound around him was less than a fifth of the bank's size. Hardly bigger than a Northcoast farmhouse. They were in the dining room, the remnants of the night's meal still on wooden plates. In addition to the man presently in position to open his throat, there were four by the benches with knives. This, Marcus thought, would be a profoundly stupid way to die.

"System could have broken," the man behind him hissed. "Been intercepted. How do I know you're not one of them?"

"Because I don't have fifty Antean soldiers outside throwing lit torches through the windows and putting arrows in anyone who runs out," Marcus said. "Why would they bother trying to trick you?"

There was a long pause. The blade went away, and Marcus put his hand to his neck. The cut wasn't much worse than he'd do to himself shaving, but it was embarrassing to have been overcome. His reflexes were getting slower. He wondered if it was another effect of the poisoned sword he'd left with Yardem and Kit or just the creeping in of age.

"Sorry," the man said, wiping his blade clean of Marcus's blood. "Can't be too careful."

"I'll keep that in mind," Marcus said. "I have a message from the magistra. There's a ship going out to Pût tomorrow just before noon. Captain's name is Brust. His ship's got a double hull."

"A fucking smuggler, then," one of the men at the table said and spat. "I hate smugglers."

"What exactly do you think it is we're *doing*?" Marcus said crossly, and a pounding came at the street door. The Timzinae froze.

"In the name of the Protector, open the door!" a voice called. The accent was Antean. The man who'd been ready to kill Marcus moments before pushed him back into a pantry closet.

"Stay here," he said. "Don't make a damned sound or you'll get us all killed."

Marcus nodded and pulled the door almost shut. Through the slit he left himself, he could hear the doors open and the Anteans pushing in. The voices were harsh, pressing in over each other. Marcus wondered if the children hiding above him could hear it all too.

"We had a report. Someone came here in violation of the curfew," a new voice said, and Marcus felt his blood go cold. He peeked out. The man wore no armor, but brown robes. His wiry hair was pulled back and his long face could have been Kit's twenty years ago. One of the priests. The man with the blade drew in his breath to lie and doom them all and Marcus stepped out of the closet.

"That was likely me," he said.

"And who are you?" the priest said. There were four more Antean blades behind him, and God knew how many waiting in the street.

"Marcus Wester. I work for the Medean bank."

The priest's eyes narrowed as he consulted the spiders in his blood. Marcus's flesh crawled a little, just thinking about it. Behind him two of the Firstblood men exchanged a glance. Nice to have the name recognized.

"What are you doing?" the blade man said.

"Telling the truth," Marcus said, and stopped himself before he went on with, *We have nothing to hide.* Because of course they did.

"Why are you here?" the priest asked.

"Business. The magistra had a note this afternoon about

a loan for a new millstone. She wanted me to follow up on it since she can't. Curfew and all."

"A millstone? Was there nothing else?"

No would be a lie. Marcus smiled and shrugged, his brain casting about wildly.

"I can get you the note, if you'd like," he said. And then, "You won't find anything else in it."

"And yet when you heard us, you hid in a closet? Why was that?"

"I've been in occupied cities before, and they can be intimidating. I got scared, and I didn't think it through."

The priest cocked his head, nodded. "Thank you. It seems there's no violation here."

"You shouldn't be doing business with bugs," one of the swordsmen said. "What kind of merchant works with these?"

"Bankers can be surprisingly flexible where there's money involved," Marcus said. "But I'll tell them what you said."

It was over, but there was still a chance it could go the other way. If the Anteans still thought of themselves as coming to enforce the curfew, they'd go now. If not, there was still plenty of chance for a bloodbath. But with him and the five Timzinae, the odds were good that at least one of the Anteans wouldn't walk out. Apparently the swordsmen came to the same conclusion.

"Next time, you open the door faster," he said, pointing his blade at one of the Timzinae who hadn't actually opened the door at all, "or there'll be trouble. You understand me?"

"I do," the Timzinae man said, and the Anteans withdrew, scowling as they went.

When the door was shut, Marcus sagged down onto a bench. The sense of narrowly avoiding death left him slightly nauseated. There was a time when things like that had felt exciting, but he'd been a younger man.

"You all right?" the blademan said.

"I am," Marcus said. "Or anyway I will be. Listen, those priests? You can't ever lie to them. Or listen to them if you can help it. They've got spiders in their blood that give them power over truth and lies."

The blade man's nictitating membranes closed, and he nodded slowly.

"All right," he said. "You say so."

Marcus chuckled mirthlessly. "Well, I have a friend. If *he* told you, you'd think it was true."

This, Marcus thought, *isn't going to work.*

They're good people," Magistra Isadau said. "Reliable. They won't say what they know."

"And in another situation, that would matter," Marcus said. "But you built all this thinking you'd have to deal with swords and magistrates. Cunning men, maybe. Torturers. But this? These things change everything. The network you built didn't take the spiders into account."

The Timzinae woman gazed out the window, her face hard as stone. The meeting room looked out over the street, the city. The wind was coming in from the north, pulling low clouds with it. It wouldn't rain, or not much; the mountains north of Kiaria would have wrung the clouds dry. All of Suddapal's rain came from the south. What these brought was the first bite of the coming winter. Marcus looked at Cithrin. She had the distant, calm look that came when she was thinking. That was good. One of the magistras of the Medean bank needed to be able to look at things coldly, and Isadau's grief was going to make that hard.

"What would you recommend?" Cithrin asked.

"First off, tell everyone what we're working against. The biggest advantage they have is that people don't know what they are. But be quiet about it. It's a hard thing to believe unless you've seen it, and if they start marching the priests through the streets with speaking trumpets talking about how they can't tell when you're lying, people will believe them and we'll be right back where we are now."

Cithrin nodded. "And we can't work together. Not safely. It has to be individual, uncoordinated efforts. We'll need a way to support them without anybody knowing who's giving the support or who's receiving it."

"Don't see how that's practical," Marcus said.

"Really?" Cithrin said. She seemed genuinely surprised. "It isn't difficult. We put a bounty on safe children. Anyone who brings a child from Elassae to Carse or Porte Oliva is paid out of a fund that's administered by...oh, I don't know. A mysterious figure in black, only of course it's really the bank. Anyone who cares to add to the fund can send gold to some particular address and we won't know who they are. Anyone who arrives with a child gets the payment without questions being asked. How they get there is their own problem. They solve it however they solve it, and they can't be betrayed, because we won't know."

"They'll send assassins," Isadau said. "The Anteans will send men to kill whoever does it. They'll send their filthy priests."

"So we have guards and make them cut thumbs, just like on any contract," Cithrin said. Then, to Marcus, "I can draw up a full plan in a day or so. If Komme approves it, we can have it in place before the first frost."

"And how would we tell people?" Isadau snapped.

"Piece of chalk, and a dark night, and as many walls as you can reach," Marcus said. "Best not to get caught, but that's going to be true of any of this."

"And it doesn't have to be only the children," Cithrin

said, her voice a mix of contemplation and pleasure. "We can put bounties on anything we want done. Bring proof that you've killed an Antean soldier or stolen their food or interfered with the flow of orders. The same coins can pay for any number of things. That's what makes them dangerous. Of course, it'll be messy. We'll have to expect a certain amount of fraud. Unless...If we had Master Kit—"

"It's a good thought," Marcus said, "but we've only got one of him, and I'll need him worse."

Cithrin's expression fell. He'd guessed it might. He tried to ignore the knot of guilt under his ribs. He ran his fingertips against the grain of the tabletop and waited for her to speak.

"Need him," Cithrin said, trying to keep her tone light. Merely curious. "What for?"

"Job hasn't changed," Marcus said. "We have to kill the goddess. I'm taking Kit to Camnipol. We'll see if we can't find that mysterious source of yours and learn what we can about the expeditions they sent out. What they're looking for. Whether they've found anything."

Isadau's voice was harsh. "You'd take the one man we have who can match their power and run after shadows?"

"I'd take the sword too."

"Why?" Cithrin asked.

"May want to kill some priests."

"No, I mean why would you go to Camnipol? Why that?"

Marcus took a deep breath. In the street, a mule brayed.

"Did Yardem ever tell you about Gradis?"

"No," Cithrin said. "I've only heard the name when they called you the hero of Wodford and Gradis."

"All right, so this was the second year of the war between Lady Tracian and Lord Springmere. I was still dancing Springmere's tune, idiot that I was. Gradis is a keep in the middle of a mountain pass. Dragon's road runs right through it. Lady Tracian had it, and if she'd kept it, her supply lines would have been solid as stone. The thing was, she had about as many men as I did, and she had position. So I sent out a force just outside arrow's range. Not a big one, but with all the banners. Springmere rode with it. I was there. Our three greatest allies, and not just their men, but them in person. Well, Lady Tracian saw us all out there like something out of a poem, and she knew she could take us. Sent her men out after us. So we fought for bit, and I sounded the retreat. We pulled back about half a league and reformed. Her men reformed, and we did it again. Better part of a day, she beat us back and back and back. And when she was pulled far enough back, all the sword-and-bows we'd left behind poured in and took the keep. No banners. No great men. Hardly any cavalry. Just the right force in the right place at the right time to win the fight that mattered."

"I see," Cithrin said.

"I don't," Isadau said.

Marcus scratched his neck and accidentally set his cut to bleeding again. "Normal strategy is going to lose. As long as they have the priests, we're Lady Tracian winning battles and losing the war. But they have a weakness. Something that scares them. I don't know what it is. As drunk on their own stories as they are, I'm not sure they do either. But whatever they're looking for, I'm betting it's the little force in the background that actually matters."

"When," Cithrin said, then coughed. "When will you go?"

"Don't see much advantage in waiting."

She swallowed. He had known her so long, he could see the mask slipping into place, and it left him aching.

"I'm sorry," he said.

"For what?" Cithrin bel Sarcour, voice of the Medean

bank in Porte Oliva, asked him. Her tone was a thing of ledgers and contracts. Hearing her pull away from him ached, but there was nothing to be done about it.

"Nothing," he said. "Don't mind me. Just…I'll be back. When I can."

"Of course," Cithrin said, and the crispness and politeness of her voice meant, *Unless you die or something keeps you or you change your mind. Or stop caring whether you come back.*

I would never leave you, he wanted to say, except that it was what he was doing.

The last of the meeting dragged on like a dog with a broken spine. When it was done, Cithrin retreated to her room, chin high and eyebrows arched, her stride low in her hips the way Kit and Cary had taught her to look older than she was. Marcus leaned out the window and spat on the ground. He found Kit and Yardem out by the stables with two fresh horses. The green sword was wrapped in wool and strapped on behind the saddle with his bedroll. Marcus felt a small pang of regret that they wouldn't have their little Kesheti mule.

"How did it go, sir?" Yardem asked.

"As well as could be expected."

"Poorly, then."

Kit made a small sound that lived halfway between a chuckle and a groan. Marcus pulled himself into the saddle.

"It's a long way to Camnipol," Marcus said. "Most of it through the leavings of a war, and autumn coming on besides. And at the end, a city full of spider priests. And someone writing letters, but we don't know his name or what he looks like. So this should be just lovely."

"But there is hope," Kit intoned.

"Sure," Marcus said. "As much as there ever is. Yardem?"

"Sir?"

"The day I take back the company?"

"It's not today, sir."

"No. It's not. Watch after Cithrin for me."

"I will."

"And thank you for . . . Well. Just thank you."

"You're welcome, sir."

"All right, then," he said. "Kit? Let's go find some trouble."

Clara

She felt young. It was disturbing and strange and wonderful. Her body felt warmer, not as a metaphor for some spiritual truth, but actually warmer. Even as the days grew shorter, the dark pressing its advantage at dawn and dusk, even as the leaves traded their green for yellow and brown and red, she left her jacket and shawl at the boarding house. The cold winds with their promise of the coming snows felt soothing against her skin, like they were holding in check some painless and glorious burn.

She had never seriously imagined taking a lover. Like anyone, she'd admired men, been aware of them. Tempted by some in an unspoken and diffuse sort of way. But to move from that appreciation to action of any sort was impossible. She was a married woman. She loved her husband and been pleased with him. Dawson had been a thoughtful lover, and his delight in her matched hers in him. There had been neither call for another man nor the boredom or complacency that might give reason to hope for such a call. And now she had given way. If the court knew, she would be even more ruined than she had been before, though that was more because Vincen was a servant. If she'd found herself in the arms of some well-positioned widower with property, title, and slightly more years than her own, the only people to object would have been the ones who wanted to anyway.

Vincen was young, beautiful, poor, and without standing or blood. He was too good for her and beneath her station. And when she lay in the darkness of his room, the sheet her only clothing, and thought of it all, it seemed not only to do with the animal joys but also with the act of rebellion. Taking Vincen Coe, huntsman and youth, to her bed meant that anything was possible. Anything could be done.

She was rougher with him than she had ever been with Dawson. More selfish. Because that was possible too.

The danger wasn't that she would be discovered, though that would have been unfortunate. No. The greater peril was that her heart would take the wrong lessons from her experience. That she would become incautious and let the soaring sense of freedom and possibility sweep her to a place where possibilities vanished. A cell in Palliako's gaols, for instance. Or a grave.

So as the days passed, and the closing of the season grew near, she tried to think. To keep her analysis of the world cool and detached and passionless, and she flattered herself that she succeeded more often than she failed. The siege at Kiaria, like the one at Nus, was taking longer than Palliako had hoped. After Suddapal and Inentai, the war had seemed to have a kind of momentum. Opinion was divided now, some feeling that Ternigan was at fault, others that perhaps even the great armies of Antea with the blessings of their newly adopted goddess were subject to the limits imposed by exhaustion, hunger, and the legendary defenses of the Timzinae stronghold.

It was, Clara thought, probably the opportunity she had been watching for. And because her heart and her flesh were in something of a riot, *probably* was good enough.

All that remained was putting the scheme in place. And for that, there were a few preparations that needed making, and specifically one item that she would require. Because Ernst Mecilli had not been close to Clara, she had no correspondence from him, and even if she had attempted the acquaintance, it would almost certainly have been his wife or daughter who returned the letter. For a sufficiently large sample of his hand, she needed letters. Asking for them seemed dangerously candid, and so she resolved to steal them instead.

Curtin Issandrian's home had become shoddy since his fall from grace. The filigree and gilding that had brightened the façade seemed faded, chipped, and tawdry. The torches that marked his gate were old and burned out. The man himself wore the years hard, but his smile was genuine and his manner as gracious as it had ever been. Of all Dawson's enemies, Clara felt most fond of him.

"A letter from your husband?"

"It would have been just at the end of the war with Asterilhold, when he was still Lord Marshal," Clara said. "You and I had spoken about the role Alan Klin was playing in the effort, and I mentioned it to Dawson as you requested."

"For which I am still grateful," Issandrian said. "Though it seems I don't have the knack for choosing allies whose stars are on the rise."

Clara smiled and folded her hands together on her knee, pulling her shawl closer around her shoulders.

"None of us knew then what would come," she said. *Any more than we know now what may happen next*, she didn't say. "I thought he said he had written to you on the matter. And I hoped you were the sort of man who keeps his correspondence."

Issandrian laughed, and the lines around his mouth seemed deeper than they had. How odd that they should both have suffered so much, and so differently.

"Yes, as a matter of fact, I am that man. But a letter from Lord Kalliam would have been something to remark on. I can't think I'd have forgotten it."

"Would it be forward of me to ask that you check? Just to be sure."

"If you'd like," he said.

"Excellent. Thank you so much," Clara said, rising to her feet as if he had invited her to his private study and she were only accepting. To his credit, he saved her the embarrassment of being corrected and went along with the pretense. The corridors of the manor were wider than her own had been, and the red carpet that marked their center seemed faded and dusty. Through the great windows, she caught glimpses of the estate across the courtyard where Feldin Maas had lived when he lived. Where Clara and Vincen had faced the traitor's blade with Geder Palliako and Minister Basrahip at their side. Somewhere in that garden, Vincen had tried his best to bleed to death in her arms. He had kissed her for the first time there. It was Geder Palliako's now, since he'd been named Baron of Ebbingbaugh. It was where he would retire to when Aster claimed the throne.

Without knowing what would come or what shape the world might take, it struck Clara as quite unlikely that Geder would ever live in that house again.

"I hear that Ernst Mecilli is doing quite well for himself these days," Clara said. "You and he were close, weren't you?"

"I wouldn't go that far," Issandrian said. "A few philosophical debates one time and another, and an unfortunate attempt to negotiate sugar rights in Pût that we both came to regret. But I wouldn't say we know each other particularly well."

"It's just I was thinking of letters, I suppose. Dawson always said Mecilli's were awful pieces of work. Impossible to tell what the man meant."

"Really?" Issandrian said as he opened a wide oaken door. "He always seemed cogent enough to me."

Clara suppressed a smile. Mecilli had written to Issandrian.

"I suppose it might only have been Dawson's temper," Clara said. "He would sometimes see what he chose to see."

"We're all like that, one way and another."

So we are, she thought.

Issandrian's private study was a thing of beauty. If all the rest of this manor house was gone slightly to seed, this, at least, was maintained. The windows looked out on a small garden, and a stone Cinnae woman looked back, her skin the mottled texture of granite, ivy curling up her side. A whole wall was taken up with books, the leather spines in a dozen different shades. Clara sat on a divan of yellow silk and pretended to look out the window at an angle that let her watch Issandrian's ghostly reflection in the glass. He took a parquet box down from a shelf and began extracting bundles of folded paper, each wrapped in ribbon. One, she guessed, for each correspondent. As his attention was on the pages, she unwrapped the shawl and pushed it discreetly between the divan and the wall. Her heart was beating fast. Everything was going so well, it was difficult not to giggle.

"Your gardener is doing a lovely job," she said.

"Hm? Oh, yes, I suppose so. He seems a little tolerant of snails and slugs sometimes."

"I suppose they need their advocates too," Clara said.

Issandrian sighed and sat behind his desk.

"I'm sorry, but there is no letter. If there was one, it never arrived here. There was a time I pinned some not inconsiderable hope on hearing a kind word from your husband."

"Well," Clara said. "Thank you for looking. It's probably silly of me. I just hoped to find something written in his hand. We lost everything when they took the estate."

"You know," Issandrian said, "Palliako hasn't named a new baron for Osterling Fells. I've heard tell that he's only waiting until he can give the title back to Jorey. If he does, there may be things you only thought were lost."

"I can hope," Clara said.

"It's been a bad few years, hasn't it?"

"It has," Clara said. A brief pang of guilt touched her. Curtin Issandrian was an unlucky man, but he wasn't a cruel one. If anything, his errors in judgment spoke of too much compassion. To exploit him seemed...not monstrous, but rude. It wasn't a thing that a well-bred lady would do. She rose to her feet, smoothing the fabric of her skirt, and Issandrian stood as well.

"Thank you again," she said.

They walked back toward the main halls more quietly. Issandrian's expression was turned inward, and his hands clasped behind his back. Without the long, flowing hair he'd once affected, he seemed older. More worn. Clara waited until they'd almost reached the main hall, then stopped.

"Oh dear," she said. "I seem to have forgotten my shawl."

"I'll have it fetched for you."

"Oh, don't be silly," she said, turning back. "I'm still spry enough to walk. Wait for me here, I'll just be a moment."

She walked with a brisk rolling gait until she turned the first corner. After that, she ran. When she reached his study, it was the work of a moment to yank her shawl back. She plucked the box from its shelf, muttering to herself as she opened it. Her fingers flew through the bundles. Alan Klin. Mirkus Shoat. Two old-looking bundles from Sesil Veren. And there. Four thin letters on cream-colored paper bound with a white ribbon. Lord Mecilli. She wrapped her shawl around them and shoved the box back into place, then hurried out of the study. Issandrian met her halfway back to the hall, and she raised her shawl in triumph.

"It fell behind the divan," she said. "I was near to giving up when I found it."

"I'm glad the hunt succeeded without the need for dogs."

"That would be embarrassing. Setting out the hounds to help poor Lady Kalliam find her things. Too plausible, I suppose."

"Not at all."

At the door to the street, she turned to him, placing her hand on his arm as she might with an old friend. Issandrian put his own hand over hers. There was no sense of flirtation, but rather a kind of shared sorrow. For a moment they stood there, old enemies from a conflict that no longer mattered. His stolen letters were in her other hand, and she felt the urge to apologize, not for what she'd done, but on behalf of the world. That they who should somehow have been friends were not, and would not be. The moment passed, and Clara walked out into the street and turned south for her rooms, Vincen Coe at her side.

"Yes?" he asked.

"Oh, yes," she said.

Back at the boarding house, Clara untied the white ribbon and laid the letters out on her bed while Vincen retrieved two more lamps from unused rooms. Clara read over each of the letters, searching for particular words and phrases, the personal idioms that would mark a letter as coming from the man himself. There were several. He was quite fond of the phrase *in the unfortunate event that* and the word *abysmal*. Then she took note of the specifics of his hand and the way he formed his letters. She needn't match it perfectly, of course. The note she intended to write in his name was something written quickly and in a state of agitation. Even if Lord Ternigan were to have letters from the true Mecilli, it would be natural to expect some departures from the usual form.

Vincen came in behind her, a plate of stewed apples and bottle of wine in his hands. They made the room smell like a kitchen in the middle of baking sweets. Clara composed the rough draft of her letter, writing the words in her own neat hand. Then she read it to Vincen, taking breaks when he fed bits of apple between her lips and also to feed him. The wine was dry and a little harsh, and the fumes went to her head. Soon she was laughing, and Vincen with her. When he began kissing her, she pushed him away. There would be time for that later. This needed to be done quickly. If the letter reached Ternigan after Kiaria fell and he was already on his way home, the scheme would fail.

She drank water and paced until she was certain that she was sober, then drew out the pen, ink, and paper she'd prepared. She wrote the whole letter twice for practice, making note of where the loops and lines of her own handwriting deviated too far from Mecilli's. Once she was certain, she took out the thick paper she'd bought. It wasn't the cream color of Mecilli's but it would do.

Lord Ternigan,

I do not have time now to wait and consider. The council I have heard has convinced me that we must act, and act swiftly if we are to act at all. You have been away from court for all of the season leading the army, but I have no doubt you have heard of the abysmal failure that Palliako has become. As the food supplies in the city wane, his popularity among the court and the low people has begun to plummet. Half the court is laughing down their sleeves at him, but the other half—the half to which you and I belong—understand the seriousness of the problem.

I will not walk the dragon's path as Kalliam did, but myself and my allies have determined that it is time to gently remove Palliako from the Severed Throne and put the care of the empire into more seasoned and steady hands. You have led the army with distinction. Forgive me for my candor, my lord, but time is short and I feel I must speak plainly. You are the one obvious choice. We are unanimous in our decision, and if you knew the names of the men who've agreed, it would astound you. I am sometimes surprised we can agree on the day of the week or the direction of the sunrise, but we have agreed upon you.

In the unfortunate event that you are not willing to make this service to the empire, I beg you to destroy this letter and never mention it again. But if you are willing, send word to me not at my house, but addressed to Lirin Petty at the Cold Hammer stables. I have an agent there who will retrieve your word and deliver it to me.

I understand this seems sudden, but I assure you it has been building for some time. If you respond, do so quickly. Palliako grows less stable by the day, and we cannot wait much longer.

Whatever your decision, please consider me your friend and ally,

Lord Ernst Mecilli

Clara put up her pen with a flourish and blotted the ink quickly. A hasty blotting paper covered a great number of sins. Put side by side with its fellows, hers still stood out. And it wasn't only the paper stock. She had to hope that the differences would be ascribed to the rushed nature of the letter. For the composition itself, she thought it struck the right notes. Flattering but also hinting that the tide might turn without him. If Ternigan proved true to his reputation, he might not agree to conspire, but he would at least not close the matter definitively. That was enough for her purposes.

She folded the letter, sewed and sealed it. She had no copy of Mecilli's signet, so she used no wax. The money she'd saved from her increased allowance would buy a fast courier. It still might be weeks before she knew whether there was a fish on her hook.

Vincen's objection wasn't one she'd considered.

"The Cold Hammer," Vincen said. "You've spoken to them about this?"

"Not this, precisely," Clara said. "I've said that if a letter arrived under the Petty name, to hold it for me. They don't know who it will be coming from nor what it will say."

"But Clara," he said, and her name on his lips still had the strange joy of transgression, "they know it's going to you. Palliako will investigate this. If he goes there, he might track the conspiracy back to you."

"It won't happen."

"You can't be sure of that."

"The man who's watching for the message was a footman in my house. When his wife birthed their first boy, I went to visit her myself. The babe was ill, and I paid for the cunning man that saved him. The man would move the sky if I asked him to," Clara said. "Certainly, he won't balk at a few simple lies."

Cithrin

Marcus left her again, this time more explicably. There was less confusion. Less of the hollowness. Half of her was angry with him for going, but the rest of her seemed resigned. He was leaving her because he felt he had to, and looking at it coldly, she agreed. She was under her own protection now. She had been for over a year. It was only seeing her half-acknowledged hopes that it might somehow go back to what it had been—or more likely what she only imagined it had been—dashed that felt so cruel. So she took her childish sense of abandonment and added it to the list of things she had to mourn.

It was a long list.

The next Tenthday, there was no march through the streets. The occupying forces didn't respect the tradition and had sent out an edict prohibiting groups with more than four Timzinae from gathering together in public or ten in private. The temples were empty even where the priests weren't dead. So instead, Isadau had the little chapel in the compound cleaned with vinegar and soap. Candles and incense burned on the humble wooden altar. Cithrin left her shoes in her room in the morning and walked there, joining the others silently. Jurin, Isadau, and Kani knelt at the front in their finest clothing. Cithrin sat in the middle with the other guests who had taken hospitality in the compound and were now trapped there by the occupation. The servants sat at the back. There were considerably more than ten Timzinae in the room, but no one mentioned it. There weren't any Anteans either.

Still, Cithrin wondered what would happen if the spider priest came back and asked whether there had been any violations of the edict. It made her uncomfortable to risk the notice of the new authorities without need. There were so many needful risks still to take that wasting them here seemed decadent.

When the time came for the priest to arrive, Yardem Hane stepped out from the hallway. He wore a dark robe that went to his feet, and the rings in his ears looked different from the usual. He lowered his eyes, gathered himself, and brought his wide chin up.

"I am not a priest of your faith," he said, and his voice rolled through the air like a distant landslide. "Nor, any longer, of my own. I was once a holy man, though I am not now. Magistra Isadau and her siblings have asked me to speak here today, and I agreed to the request so long as I could make it clear that I am not a priest."

Cithrin smiled. She could see the discomfort in the Tralgu's wide, canine expression, even if the others couldn't. Her sympathy for him expressed itself as amusement.

"I have seen a large number of cities fall. Sometimes I've been part of the reason that they did. Sometimes I was one of the men who'd tried to protect them and failed. But for whatever reason I was there, what I've seen followed a pattern, and though I make no claim to righteousness, I hoped to share that with you here.

"Often when we gather in places of worship, it is in celebration. Celebrations of marriage or of birth. The smaller celebrations of the good in our lives. Even funerals are celebrations of lives well lived. And also we come together to mourn the evil and the sorrow and the pain in the world. Our failings and the world's. We acknowledge these to each other because, whatever our race, whatever the shapes of our bodies and the inclination of our minds, doing this makes us more human. And by more human, I also mean more holy."

Cithrin's amusement and embarrassment on Yardem's behalf had fallen away. His voice was warm and soft as old flannel. Someone behind her was weeping now, and Yardem frowned in thought. His huge hands patted at the empty air in front of him.

"When a city is taken in war, the loss to those who loved what the city had been is great. But that loss is doubled because we fear to mourn it. For good reason. There are men in Suddapal now who would beat us, possibly kill us, if they felt we were disrespectful of them. In every city I have seen that suffered what your city suffers now, there is a numbness and sense of being cut off from each other. It's a funeral where no one laughs and no one cries, and it leaves us emptier than the loss alone would have. And so, today, instead of a religious service, I was hoping we might have a funeral for the cities that we have lost. Nus and Inentai and Suddapal. And Vanai."

To her surprise, Cithrin felt tears in her eyes. She kept her chin high. She might weep, but she wasn't going to snivel. Yardem spoke for a few moments more about Suddapal and when he had come to the city as a younger man. How it had changed in the years since, and how he had, and how the differences in them both had given him a sense of kinship with it. Then he asked Magistra Isadau to stand, and she spoke about the innate conflict of being a woman of business with her first loyalties to power and profit, and at the same time a citizen of the five cities. And her favorite places within them.

Then Jurin spoke about showing his son the cavern at the center of the commons for the first time, and walking with his grandmother to the marketplace the last time she went. He talked of the fear he felt for the children taken by Antea. And soon, Cithrin was making no pretense of dignity, nor was anyone else. One by one, the people stood and spoke or else only sobbed, and Cithrin wept with them.

She didn't see Yardem come to her side. His hand was simply on hers, and then without knowing how it had happened, he was leading her up to the altar. The faces looked up at her, waiting for her to speak. *I can't do this*, she thought, and from the back of her mind a small voice replied, *Yes, I can.*

"Suddapal wasn't my city," she said. "That was Vanai. The Antean army took it...took it from me. And they took the people who raised me and loved me, if anybody did. There was a place by the canal by the bank house where there was a little boy who sold coffee with his father, and they... they took them too. They took everything there and they burned it."

A sorrow she hadn't known was there opened in her, vast as oceans, and she hung her head for a moment and Yardem stepped toward her. She put out a hand to stop him, gritted her teeth, and raised her head.

"I haven't cried. I haven't mourned. I haven't let myself be angry for that loss. I never felt it because feeling it would have broken me. And now, with all of you here as witness, I am broken. I am broken, but I'm not dead. And I am not *finished*."

The hand that touched her shoulder wasn't Yardem's. Magistra Isadau turned Cithrin to her, wrapped her arms around Cithrin's shaking body, and pulled her close. Cithrin wept, and more than wept. She howled like a baby who'd lost her mother and her father, which she also was. She screamed into the older woman's flesh, and she did it with half a hundred men and women watching her do it, and she felt no shame.

"Good girl," Isadau murmured. "Oh, good, good girl. You'll be fine. Your heart isn't going to die. You're fine."

Cithrin held the Timzinae woman close and would not let her go.

It's going to fall apart," Yardem said. "All respect, the network was dangerous when it was only standing up against soldiers, bureaucrats, and cunning men. These tainted priests make it impossible."

"I know," Isadau said. "Two of the people who agreed to work with me have already missed meetings. I was able to get word out that if the priest questions you, not to answer any questions. They aren't lying if they don't speak."

Yardem grunted like he had taken a blow. Isadau raised her eyebrows.

"Not speaking can be made difficult," he said.

The courtyard had turned from lush green to leathery brown as if overnight. Autumn had come to Suddapal, and the crispness of the air said that winter would come quickly behind it. Isadau sat on a wooden stool, her body rigid and tense. Yardem stood at ease, a soldier again instead of a priest. Cithrin's pacing contrasted with their stillness, but she couldn't help it. Movement made her thoughts feel clearer and the knot in her belly less likely to lead to vomiting again. Fallen leaves crackled under her feet and skittered away from her toes where she kicked them.

"We have to make contingency plans," Isadau said, "in the event I am detained by the new magistrate."

"Why?" Cithrin asked.

"Because she's going to be detained by the new magistrate," Yardem said.

"She doesn't have to be," Cithrin said. "She can go to Carse."

"I won't abandon my city," Isadau said. "I know that I can't help for much longer. But so long as I can, I will. If anything, it's you who should leave. I've written to Komme. He agrees that losing two of his magistras is worse than losing one."

"I won't leave you," Cithrin said. "I won't go while you're here."

"Then I'm afraid Komme is going to have a very unpleasant year," Isadau said. Jurin stepped into the garden and nodded to Isadau. The magistra rose to her feet. "Please excuse me," she said, and followed her brother out.

Cithrin kicked a small pile of leaves. Her mind felt like a cat in a cage, pacing, looking for a pathway out because she wanted it to be there more than from the expectation that it would be.

"She's doing exactly what Marcus said," Cithrin said. "She's fighting battles and losing wars."

"She knows she's doomed. She's made that choice. Her informants are already being caught up. I'll be surprised if they don't come for her by next Tenthday."

"God damn that woman," Cithrin said. "That stubborn, senseless—"

"If she can save one more child before she falls, it will have been worth it to her. And there's no one else who can do what she's doing. She knows the city. She knows the people. It's the only advantage she has, and in most conditions, it would be significant."

"It's going to get her killed."

"It is."

Cithrin said something obscene, then she stopped. Yardem's ears went flat.

"Magistra?"

"I know people too," she said.

Dear Geder—

I'm sorry I haven't written to you sooner. At first it was that I was so busy with the business of the bank that even though I kept meaning to, I never seemed to find the time. And then, after it had been so long, I started feeling awkward about it having been so long. I know it sounds stupid, and I suppose it is. But there you have it. I didn't write, and I'm sorry for it, and I'm writing you now.

And, to make matters worse, I'm writing to ask a favor. Since last we saw each other, I've been reassigned within the bank. I am now the voice of the Medean bank in Suddapal, which I believe technically makes me one of your subjects. And while I understand the need for security, I've found some of your commanders here a bit difficult to work with. They have military minds, which is all well and good for what they're doing, but difficult for someone trying to run a business. I was wondering if you could put in a good word for me? If you could even just assure them that I'm not involved in any devious conspiracies against you, I think it would make things better all around, and not only for me.

Tell Aster I miss him, and you, and that terrible cat-piss stinking hole we lived in. Who would ever have guessed those would be the good old days?

Your friend, Cithrin bel Sarcour

"You. Are. *Mad*," Isadau said as she sat at her desk, the draft of the letter in her hand. Her face had gone ashen.

"It's a better plan than yours," Cithrin said. "I didn't put together your network. I can say that without lying, and so I can talk around any hard questions better than you. And if Geder does this, his people will think twice before they come too near to the bank. None of those are advantages you have, and they aren't ones you can get. These are mine. Your advantages are that more people know your role and are in a position to betray you; you're Timzinae, and Geder's decided to hate the Timzinae; and...well? What else? That may be all you have to bring to the table."

"Cithrin, you must not do this."

"How long is it going to be before your network collapses? Weeks? Days? I can keep some version of it running for months at least. Maybe more. I can do it better than you can. Forget about me. Forget about the bank. If your work falls in a week, who will help the people a month from now? If you leave and leave now, there will still be help for them. If you stay, you're condemning them. You're condemning every person that I could have helped if you had let me."

Isadau folded the page and put it on her desk as gently as if it might shatter. Or she might. Cithrin waited.

"Reckless without being stupid," Isadau said.

"Is that a yes?"

"It would work better with both of us present," Isadau said. "Send your letter. Give me the cover to work. I will stay here with you."

"No," Cithrin said. "On one hand, you're genuinely guilty and I'm not. And on the other, this is my price. You give me the bank. You leave. I help as many people get out from under the occupation as I can, and if the chance comes to do the empire some damage, all the better. But in return, you're my first client. You and whoever else you pick will leave the city now for Birancour or Herez or Northcoast. I don't want to know where you're going. Only that you're gone, and that I can't call you back. It's important that I be able to not lie about that."

Isadau bent forward slowly, her hands at her belly. She looked as if she were laughing or in pain, but she only rested there a moment, bent half over, her eyes closed and her lips in a smile that looked like pain. When she opened her eyes again, she was herself.

"I had resigned myself to dying, you know," she said.

"I did," Cithrin said, and the tears threatened to come back. "It was fucking annoying."

"I accept your proposal," Isadau said. "But not for me. You took the negotiation when you held the lives of the children you could save that I couldn't."

"Attacking at the base. You were justifying your plan to yourself because it was selfless," Cithrin said. "I undermined that by pointing out that it left innocent lives on the table when my plan recovered them. And since you only had one overwhelming argument, it all came down. If you'd wanted to win, you'd have needed to show that the bank would lose less capital if you stayed or that the cost of your leaving was significantly greater than staying here and being caught."

"Only you'd have had arguments prepared against them."

"Still do, if you're tempted," Cithrin said.

"Imaniel taught you well," Isadau said.

"So did you."

Magistra Isadau left the next day, going overland with Jurin, Kani, and almost half the household. They left a few minutes apart so that they might be mistaken for several unrelated groups and to keep within the dictates of the laws against assembly. Isadau was in the last group to go. She wore a simple traveling gown with a split skirt for riding and a hood she had plucked up to hide her face. Astride her little mule, she looked more like a hardland farmer than the voice of the most powerful bank in the world. Cithrin walked beside her to the gate. In the street, four Antean soldiers were laughing and kicking stones down the road like boys. One looked over when the gate opened, but his expression was bored.

"Thank you, Cithrin," Isadau said. "Please save what you can, but don't die here. Not for me."

"I'm in this war to win," Cithrin said. "If you see Pyk or Komme, tell them what we discussed about putting up a bounty system. I'll see you again when I see you."

Isadau urged the little mule on, and Enen closed the gate behind her. Cithrin turned to look at the compound. When she'd come here, it had been a strange, threatening place. Now it was in fact a thousand times greater threat to her life, and she didn't fear it at all. This was her place now. Her word was the word of the bank, and it had the force of gold and Komme Medean behind it.

"Nicely done, ma'am," Yardem said.

"Thank you. Now let's go about not regretting it, shall we?"

"Yes, ma'am. There's the matter of the letter to the Lord Regent."

"I know. Call for a courier and we'll send it. But I need to write one other first."

"Yes, ma'am."

In Magistra Isadau's office—Cithrin's office now—she sat at the desk and gathered her thoughts. The breeze through the windows was chilly, and she kept her cloak on. The flames from the lamp only warmed the air a little. The refugees Isadau had taken in still made music that carried through the afternoon air. The kitchens still filled the world with the scents of baking bread and roasting meat. One might almost imagine it had always been like this, and that it would always be.

She took a clean sheet of paper, a brass-nibbed pen, and a jar of ink. When she wrote, it was directly into the bank's cipher, as if it were her natural language.

Komme—

I regret to find myself with somewhat awkward news to report. It seems I've taken over another of your banks.

Marcus

The fastest route to Camnipol was west to Orsen in the Free Cities, and then following the dragon's road north through the eastern reaches of the Dry Wastes. The first danger was the Antean army camped before the massive gates of Kiaria. Holding to the south would avoid the soldiery, but the siege was going on too long. The Anteans would be pulling food out of the countryside as quickly as they could, and that meant Kit and Marcus were going to be two travelers in a countryside filled with desperate people. While they had the poisoned sword and Kit's spiders, neither one would be much good against an unexpected arrow. Then there were the mountains that divided Elassae from the Free Cities. They'd spent more than their fair share of time among mountains in the Keshet, but winter was coming on, and an early snowstorm would also negate all their advantages, though Marcus would sometimes imagine Kit shouting, *You shall not snow* at the low grey clouds. Those, at least, were the extraordinary dangers. Bandits, hunting cats, snakes, and fevers barely warranted mention.

"It seems to me you've been quite cheerful," Kit said.

"I suppose I am," Marcus said.

"Not having as many nightmares either."

"They'll be back. They always are. But it was good seeing Cithrin and Yardem again."

"Mmm," Kit said with an amused smile.

Orsen was the easternmost of the Free Cities, and the best defended. It was built on a high, flat-topped mountain that stood in the center of a plain. Marcus had traveled a fair part of the world and never seen another detail of geography to match the flatness of the landscape interrupted by the massive stone. The mountain was also odd in that its stone was ruddy granite that seemed more in place in Borja or Hallskar. Coming into the valley, the thread of red soil radiating from it showed where centuries of rain and wind had begun to erode the mountain down into the more familiar soil. It seemed to Marcus that something immense and strange had happened here, long ago, and no one knew what it might have been. But there was a dragon's road and a defensible patch of land, and that was all humanity needed to make itself at home.

Rather than take the time to follow the narrow, switchbacked roads up to the city itself, Marcus and Kit stopped at an inn at the mountain's foot. The groom, a young and painfully thin man, took their horses. A woman perhaps a decade older than Marcus and still young enough to be vital welcomed them as they entered the dim warmth of the common room. The knot of Antean soldiers at the table nearest the fire looked up at them with flat and empty expressions. Marcus nodded and took a seat not far enough to seem like he was avoiding them, and not so near that his murmurs to Kit could be easily heard.

The lady of the house brought them mugs of good cider and plates of gristly pork with a pepper sauce that kept Marcus from knowing whether the meat had started to turn. He watched the soldiers out of the corner of his eye. The five of them hunched close to each other, talking low. Every few seconds, one or another of them would glance over at Marcus.

No, not at him. At Kit.

"Interesting," Marcus said.

"What?" Kit asked, drinking his cider and ignoring his meat.

"Our friends at the next table there. I do believe they're deserters."

"Really?" Kit said, and began shifting on his bench to glance at them. Marcus put a hand on his shoulder to stop him.

"Think so," Marcus said. "And I think they recognize you as looking as if you might be one of the priests. Because ever since we stepped in, they've been jumpy as mice that smell a cat. And seeing how they outnumber us more than double, I'm thinking we're in a position that—"

The Anteans rose in a group, drawing their blades. The benches they'd sat on clattered to the ground as Marcus drew his own blade and put himself between the attackers and Kit. The lady of the house screamed and ran out the door. The chances she'd be back with timely help seemed thin.

"There's no need for violence," Kit said, and his voice filled the space. "You can put down your—"

"Shut up, you bastard!" the nearest of the Anteans shouted. "One more word out of you, and I swear we'll cut you down and burn whatever comes out."

Five men, Marcus thought, was a damned lot of people. But they hadn't attacked yet. If anything, they seemed more frightened. He backed up slowly, pushing his table with the backs of his legs as he went, trying to clear a path for the men to leave if they wanted to.

"They followed us," a dark-skinned one at the back said. "Lani, they followed us."

"Well, and if they didn't you just told them my name," the man at the front said. "And thanks for that."

"Lani?" Marcus said. "My name's Wester. We don't need to—"

The attack was fast and disorganized. Lani jumped forward, his blade swinging high. Marcus blocked and made a low counterstrike by long habit. Lani grunted with pain, falling half a step back and preparing for Marcus to press the advantage, but by then two of the others had stepped to their leader's side. Marcus could see them preparing to attack in unison. He couldn't block them both.

Kit's cider mug came from behind him in a low, fast arc and shattered against the nose of the man on Lani's right. Marcus thrust at the one on the left, who fell back, cursing.

"I don't want this," Marcus said. "We're not hunting you."

"We're not going back!" Lani shouted, and then as if on a signal, all five men turned and bolted for the yard, leaving Marcus and Kit alone in the common room. Marcus moved forward carefully. Retreating to the next room to set up an ambush was an idiot's plan when you already had five blades to the opponent's one, but working with the assumption that his enemies weren't idiots would have had its drawbacks as well. Keeping the blade at the ready, he moved forward step by careful step. The sound of hooves pelting away down the road left him feeling a little more certain, and when he reached the yard, the thin groom's confused expression and the cloud of dust in the west were enough that Marcus sheathed his blade. Kit's familiar footsteps came up behind him.

"Well," Marcus said. "That's not good."

"Don't you think so?" Kit asked. "It seems to me it might be quite a hopeful sign. Men are beginning to abandon the Antean army. And did you hear what they said to me? Cut me and burn whatever comes out? That sounds to me as if

some other people within the enemy forces have begun to
see that something odd is going on, and they aren't celebrating it."

"That's true," Marcus said. "It's not what I meant,
though."

"No?"

"I'm fairly sure they stole our horses."

"Ah," Kit said. "That's not good."

"Isn't. You think you might be able to use those uncanny
powers of yours to find us some replacements?"

"I assume we can walk up to the city. It might take some
time to earn enough to buy horses, but we can try."

"I was thinking more along the lines of walking up to
someone on a nice horse and asking them to let us use it."

Kit made an uncomfortable kind of grunt and Marcus
looked over at him.

"I believe the power—her power—can become a path of
corruption. An opportunity, as it were, to lose what is most
valuable about ourselves."

"Yeah. Saving the world here, Kit," Marcus said. "Let's
keep focus on that."

The old actor sighed.

"Let me see what I can do."

O<small>NCE</small> they'd reached the dragon's road, they moved as fast
as a courier, changing for fresh horses twice a day. The fields,
farms, and wild places of Antea spread around them like a
vast grey-brown cloak. The trees were shedding their summer green. In the fields they passed, Firstblood farmers rode
on mules with whips at their sides while Timzinae men and
women harvested the last of the autumn crops—pumpkins
and gourds and winter wheat. Whenever they passed a low
temple, the banner of the spider goddess flew from its roof.

And even with all this for warning, Marcus was surprised when at last they reached Camnipol.

Coming from the south meant that the great city stood on an escarpment above them. They went up the trails to the southern gate with only the massive walls to see. Within them, Camnipol might have been empty for all Marcus could tell. It was only when they passed through the tunnel in the wall and emerged into the wider city that the full extent of the place became clear. All around him, buildings rose two and three and four stories high. The streets were thick with people, Firstblood mostly, but Tralgu and Jasuru and Dartinae faces as well. None of those were what stopped him. There was something he couldn't quite explain—a grandeur and a weariness and sense of terrible age—that seeped through the city itself. He'd known many cities in his life, and until he walked into Camnipol for the first time, he would have said that he understood what it meant for a city to have a personality; that every gathering place of humanity had its own customs and idiosyncrasies, that the coffee in Northcoast came with honey and in Maccia with cardamom. Camnipol was something else again. Here the personality of the city wasn't just the contingencies and customs of the people in it. It was something that grew out of the stone, that scented the air. Camnipol was a living thing, and the people in its streets were parts of it the way that skin and ligaments and muscles made up a body.

And what was strangest of all, it wasn't a secret. It was as obvious as the sun the moment he stepped inside the walls. Kit reined in beside him.

"Your first time in Camnipol, then?"

"They didn't hire many mercenary companies when I was in the trade," Marcus said. "I spent more time at little garrisons. God. I'm gawking at the place like a child."

"Wait until you see the Division," Kit said. But it wasn't the great chasm of the Division that caught them up next. When they turned a corner into a wider square, the Kingspire came into view, rising into the sky higher than any human structure should. In the midday sun, it seemed almost to glow. And high up, almost at its top, a vast banner flew.

When he'd been a boy, Marcus had seen a spider's egg crack open and thousands of tiny animals with delicate pale bodies no larger than a grain of millet spin out thread into the breeze. He'd watched them rise up in the sun, thick as smoke and tiny. And later in the summer, his father had showed him a vast web at the edge of the garden where a massive yellow-and-black beast of a spider had made its home. The thing had been big as a fist, and its web strong enough to catch sparrows. Marcus still remembered the chill of understanding that had come to him. Each one of those tiny grains floating on the wind had gone out into the world and grown into a monstrosity like this one. And like that, each little banner they had seen, dyed whatever red the locals could manage, painted with the eightfold sigil, and hung from the temple's eave, had been a grain. And the massive cloth that floated in the air over Camnipol was the beast they would grow into.

The grimness in Kit's expression told Marcus that the old actor understood and was thinking along the same track.

"All right," Marcus said as they rode across the square to a public stable with the inexplicable sign of an ice-blue mallet over the gate. "What's the plan, then? Start asking people if they know who's been sending letters to Carse and wait for someone who tells us no to be lying about it?"

"It sounds inelegant when you put it that way," Master Kit said, chuckling. "I have spent some time in Camnipol, and I have some ideas where we might begin."

"Well, you can be the one who's wise in the ways of the city," Marcus said. "I'll be the one that hits whoever needs hitting."

"That seems a fair division of labor."

Rather than pay for stabling, Kit sold the horses at a decent profit, though Marcus suspected it was nowhere near what he could have gotten, and they began their walk through the city. A nail maker greeted Kit by name, and they stopped to talk for the better part of an hour. Then a butcher's stall run by a Jasuru woman with scales more green than bronze and three missing fingers. Then an old man at a tavern who called Kit "Looloo" for reasons that Marcus never entirely understood. Everyone they met was happy to see Kit, but the stories they told of life in the city were eerie. The Lord Regent, they said, was a brilliant man with powers more subtle than a cunning man's. Food was growing short, in part because the farms hadn't worked at capacity since the war with Asterilhold and in part because so much was still being sent to feed the army in Elassae. The cult of the spider goddess was a blessing for the city, and since it had come, everything was going well. The streets weren't safe after dark. Too many people were hungry. Camnipol had become more violent and dangerous because of the Timzinae and their agents. Twice, Kit's friends told of a secret ring of Timzinae who'd been stalking the streets at night and stealing away Firstblood women. In one version, they'd been taken to a secret temple under the city and slaughtered as offerings to the dragons. In another, they'd been found in a secret room in the manor house of the traitor Alan Klin, which only served to show that Klin had been as much a tool of the Timzinae as Dawson Kalliam.

It was almost night when they reached the Division. The great chasm ran through the city's heart like a river. Marcus stood at the center of a span and looked down. The depth of it left him breathless.

"I've never seen anything like this. How many bodies would you guess go into that in the course of a year?" Marcus said. Then, "Kit?"

Kit's face had gone pale. Marcus followed the man's gaze to the far side of the great canyon. A building four floors high and painted the yellow of egg yolk loomed on the farther side of a common yard. A stable stood off to the south with carts and horses enough to mark the place as a wayhouse and a tavern. Kit began to walk toward it in a drunken stagger, and Marcus followed, confused until he saw what Kit was walking toward.

The cart looked much the same as it had when Marcus and Kit and the others had hauled it as part of the last caravan from Vanai half a decade before. Two of the boards on the stage had been replaced recently, and the new wood stood out brightly from the old. Kit put a trembling hand to it. A tear tracked down his cheek.

"Hey, you old bastard," a rough voice called from behind them. "Watch whose cart you're feeling up."

The woman, thin across the shoulders with dark hair pulled back in a braid, swaggered across the yard. Two men walked behind her. When she reached them, she fell into Master Kit's arms. The two men wrapped arms around the pair until all four were in a tight knot of affection and humanity. The larger of the men turned his head to Marcus.

"Good to see you too, Captain," Hornet said.

"Always a pleasure."

Hornet pulled back an arm, inviting him into the huddle, but Marcus declined with a smile.

"Cary?" Master Kit said, half choked with sobs. "What are you...how did you come back here?"

"You made an assumption there," the other man, Smit, said. "You see how he made that assumption?"

"I did," Hornet said, grinning. Cary only looked up at Master Kit with a smile of defiance and pleasure. She looked like a child whose father had come home from a journey of years.

"You've been here all this time?" Kit said, disbelief in his voice. "This same yard for ... ? How can that be?"

"Cithrin came by with a little side work," Cary said. "Brought us enough money we could sit tight for a time."

"Been pretty much playing to dogs and pigeons the last six months, though," Smit said. "Nothing like being in one place seasons in a row to take the novelty off a production."

"We're all still here, though," Smit said. "Sandr left for about two weeks once, but the girl caught on to him and he reconsidered."

"Why did you do this?"

"So you could find us when you came back," Cary said. Her eyelashes were dewy. "Because you were coming back. You couldn't leave us behind."

"But I had no way to know that..." Kit said, and then ran out of words.

"You see? That's the problem with always playing the wise-old-man roles. You start taking them off the stage with you and thinking you're Sera Serapal with all the secrets of the dragons in your purse and acting like it's miraculous every time you're wrong about something. I always knew you'd rejoin us. I only made it easier for you. *And*," Cary said before he could object, "I was right."

Master Kit laughed and spread his arms. "How can I argue against that?" he said. "Thank you. This is the sweetest gift the world has ever given me. Thank you for it."

Cary nodded once, soberly. "Welcome home," she said.

Geder

The first group of Anteans to be initiated into the mysteries of the spider goddess stood in the great hall of the
new temple. The pearl-white ceiling arched above them all,
and fine chains with crystal beads flowed down from the
top like dewdrops on a spider's web. Three walls of the hall
were glowing with lamps fashioned from shells that glowed
soft gold, but the south was open, and Camnipol stretched
out below them. The carts in the streets were no larger than
Geder's thumbnail, the heads of the people as small as ants.
It had taken him the better part of an hour just to walk up
to the hall, and his thighs ached a little from the effort.

The dozen initiates knelt in two rows of six, their heads
bowed. Their robes were simple ceremonial white. For once,
Basrahip was the center of attention with Geder sitting at the
side. The huge priest stood at the dais with the open sky behind
him. A smaller banner with the eightfold sigil hung behind him,
and the light coming through the cloth made it seem bright.

"The life you once knew is over," Basrahip intoned. "The
veil of deceit will soon fall from you. In this time, you will
be lost and vulnerable, but we, your brothers, will stand at
your side. You will hear the truth in our voices, and we will
lead you to see the world as it truly is."

"We accept this gift," the twelve initiates said as one.
They bowed their heads to the floor.

Basrahip lifted his hands and began to chant ancient syllables. Geder felt the terrible urge to cough and swallowed
hard to try to keep the sound from interrupting. As he wasn't
an initiate, he wasn't strictly speaking supposed to be there,
but Basrahip had given permission for him to be present for
the welcoming. After that, things became private and mysterious, but from what Geder had read that was true of any
cult. He didn't take the exclusion personally, though he did
wish Basrahip had been a bit more forthcoming about the
details of what the men would be going through. It was only
curiosity, though.

Geder's interest in the theology and practice of the priesthood was real, but it had its limits. The history of the world
as the spider goddess knew it was endlessly fascinating, but
when he came to asking more practical questions—who
would be the best candidate to become a priest, what were
the trials the initiates would go through, how long did the
process require—it became more like another ceremony in
a life that had become thick with them. When he'd asked
Basrahip why women didn't serve as priests of the goddess
and the answer had hinted broadly at something to do with
menstruation, Geder stopped pursuing the questions.

When the chanting was ended, four of the minor priests
came forward with a ceramic cup, offered a drink from it to
the first of the initiates, then led him away into the depths of
the temple. This they repeated eleven more times, and by the
time the last young priest had been taken back to discover
whatever secrets there were to discover, Geder was secretly
getting bored. When Basrahip came to him to say that the
welcoming was done, Geder was happy to hear it.

"My thanks again, Prince Geder. As her power spreads
through the land, so will your glory."

"Good," Geder said as they walked back toward the

stairways that led down into the more commonly used levels of the Kingspire. "Because as far as I can tell, my glory is stuck fast in the north of Elassae."

"The stronghold of the enemy," Basrahip said, frowning. It was rare to see him look so disturbed. It occurred to Geder, not for the first time, that the rise of the spider goddess had, in a sense, come at the worst possible time. True, without the plot against Aster and King Simeon, he wouldn't have had reason to spend a summer tracking rumors of the Righteous Servant back to the hidden temple, but it seemed that since then, Antea had been drawn into one battle after another. Basrahip would say that it was the lies of the world pained by the arrival of truth, but Geder could still wish that it had happened at a gentler moment in history.

"I'm sure we'll take it before long," Geder said, starting down the stairs. His personal guard waited at the foot, not being quite so deeply in the good graces of the goddess as Geder was.

Basrahip shook his massive head. Somewhere far in the distance above them, someone started screaming, but Basrahip took no notice of it. Geder put it down as being part of the ceremony.

"The battle against the lies of the world must be fought. Long or brief, costly or not, it does not matter. She will prevail, and we with her."

"It's just that they won't come to parley," Geder said. "Ternigan says he's tried calling it eight times now, and they won't come down. And the walls at Kiaria are too high for speaking trumpets to reach the men at the top."

Basrahip paused, and Geder went down a couple more steps before he realized it and turned back and looked up at him.

"Is there something you are asking me, Prince Geder?"

"Well," Geder said. "I don't want to...I mean. I was only

wondering if there were any other gifts that the goddess had that might help with this particular problem?"

"There is one other," Basrahip said. "Patience."

Geder nodded. The screaming from the temple was getting louder, and there were more voices now. Basrahip looked back toward them, then turned to Geder and sat on the stair.

"We will be tested many times. The world will resist her truth because the world is a thing of lies. But she cannot be beaten and all who stand against her will be ground down. The world is entering into her, and we are her bearers. You and I."

A particularly high and sustained shriek caught Geder's attention. Basrahip chuckled and put a hand on Geder's shoulder and pointed up the stairway with a gesture of his chin.

"Them as well," he said. "All of us are her creatures. And those who are not will be, or they will be erased from all places under the sky."

"But it's going to take patience."

"Yes."

"I'm sorry. It's just that after Nus fell and Inentai, I thought..." He waved the thought away. "I've kept you long enough, though. Take care of your new initiates, and let me know if there's anything more I can do to help."

"I will, Prince Geder," Basrahip said, then rose and ascended again. At the bottom of the stair, a massive bronze door had been cast in the image of a huge lion. Geder walked through it, and two priests closed it behind him. The thick metal rang with a sense of finality and the sounds of human voices went silent. Geder sighed and began the long descent to his own rooms. He was beginning to regret putting the temple at the top of the spire. It was wonderful for the symbolism and security, but it was such a long walk.

Another decision he was beginning to regret was having the reports from the expeditions brought directly to him. When he'd given the order, he'd thought it would be interesting. Diverting. He'd read book-length essays about adventurers before, and as near as he could recall he'd expected the letters from the field to be similar. And also that this way, he would have the feeling of being part of it. An adventurer himself. In practice, it felt like reading any other report on the small functions of the empire.

But he'd asked to do it, and to turn it away now would make him seem unreliable and petty. So when the aged servant delivered his personal correspondence in a silvered box, it was stuffed with things he didn't actually want to read.

"Will there be anything more, Lord Regent?" the old man asked, his bow a model of obsequiousness that bent him almost double.

"No," Geder said. Then, "Yes, bring me some food. And coffee."

"Yes, my lord," the man said. With a sigh, Geder pulled out the first letter. Emmun Siu was in the back country of Borja. He had lost one of his men when they came to an obscure village near the foot of a strange mountain and the man had fallen in love with a local girl, married her, and refused to continue with the expedition. He had found three different sites where there had once been buildings, but thus far there had been nothing of interest apart from a particularly well-preserved wall with an image that appeared to be a pod of the Drowned circling a complex device. In Lyoneia, Korl Essian was apparently being very careful in how he went about buying provisions for his two teams, and his descriptions of them filled twenty pages on both sides. Dar Cinlama, who had started this whole mess in the first place, was interviewing Haaverkin along the coast of Hallskar concerning their different social orders, which in this case appeared to be something between extended family and gentleman's club. Cinlama went into some detail about the different rituals and their significance—one order would set small stones to match the positions of the stars, another enacted a complex play involving eels and a man in a bear's skin that appeared to be a retelling of an ancient war between Haaverkin and Jasuru and also very possibly the origin of the Penny-Penny stories that had spread through the whole world by now. They were the most interesting reports, and they were from the man Geder liked least of all the explorers. He read the letter through to the end, though, and took what pleasure he could from it.

Then there were the other letters. Most were disposed of by his staff, but invitations from the highest families were still presented to him directly out of courtesy to the nobles. The end of the season was almost upon them, and with it one last paroxysm of fetes and balls, feasts and teas. There were five marriages he'd been asked to speak at. The last wedding he'd been to had been for Jorey Kalliam and Sabiha Skestinin.

Another letter lay at the bottom of the box. It was written on decent paper, but not the thick near-board of the others. It wasn't a hand he recognized. He tore off the thread it was sewn with, and unfolded it. All the air went out of the room.

Tell Aster I miss him, and you, and that terrible cat-piss stinking hole we lived in. Who would ever have guessed those would be the good old days?
    Your friend, Cithrin bel Sarcour

It wasn't a long letter, and he read it ten times over. All he could think was that she had touched this page. Her hand had been against it. She had made this fold in the paper. He held it to his face and smelled it, looking for some trace of her scent. Cithrin bel Sarcour. *Tell Aster I miss him. And you.*

The servant came back, a plate of delicately spiced eggs in one hand and a cup of coffee in the other.

"Get me a courier," Geder said. "Get me the fastest courier we have."

"Shall I call for pigeons and a cunning man as well?"

"All of them. *Everyone*," Geder shouted. "I need word to reach Fallon Broot *tonight*."

He canceled all of his plans, rescheduled the meetings. And the word went out to Suddapal by every means he had. The Medean bank in Suddapal was not to be interfered with in any way. Its agents were to have total freedom of the city to conduct any business they saw fit. They were not to be questioned or detained. If there was any concern regarding the activities of agents of the bank, they were to be referred to Cithrin bel Sarcour at the bank, and her judgment on the matter was to be considered final. This by order of the Lord Regent himself.

When it was done, he took Cithrin's letter in his pocket, called for his private carriage, and rode for Lord Skestinin's little manor house as if chaos itself were after him.

Jorey seemed surprised to see him, which was fair. He hadn't seen anywhere near as much of Jorey as he'd meant to when the court season started. Things had just piled one upon another until all the days were full. Sabiha made her greetings in the drawing room, and then left the two of them alone. Geder gave the letter to Jorey with trembling hands and Jorey read it soberly. When he was done, he read it again, then, frowning, handed it back.

"What do you think I should do?" Geder asked.

"Well, I suppose that depends on the situation in Suddapal. If you think that the bank—"

"Not about that," Geder said. "About writing back to her. About...maintaining relations. With her."

Jorey leaned forward, his elbows on his knees. He looked older than he had just a couple of years before. He looked like a man grown, and Geder still felt like a boy. At least in matters like this.

"I'm not sure I understand what you're asking me, my lord."

"*My lord*," Geder said. "It's only us here. You don't have to do that. But Cithrin is a singular woman. She's smart and she's beautiful and she's powerful in her way. And once I'm not Lord Regent anymore, I'm only going to be Baron Ebbingbaugh, and even then, I don't know that she'd care to be a baroness. And of course there would be a scandal because she isn't of the noble class, and Aster would have to induct someone with Cinnae blood—"

"You're asking," Jorey said, "how to *woo* her?"

"I am," Geder said. "I don't know. You're my only friend who's ever won a woman. How did you make Sabiha love you?"

Jorey blew out a long breath and sat back in his chair. His eyes were wide and he shook his head like a man trying to wake from a dream. "Geder, you never fail to surprise me. I...I don't think what happened with me and Sabiha will help you. The situation was so different from what you're saying."

"I don't need you to write letters for me," Geder said, with a laugh meant to lighten the mood. "It's just I've never done this before. And I'm afraid...I'm afraid she'll laugh at me. Isn't that silly? Here I am, the most powerful man in the world, for the time being, and I am so desperately afraid she'll think I'm funny."

"You aren't," Jorey said. "You're a thousand different things, but funny isn't one."

"Thank you," Geder said. "What...what can you tell me? How do I write to her? What do I say?"

A servant's footsteps came down the corridor, paused, and then trotted away quickly. Sabiha was keeping the world at bay. Geder felt a little warmth in his heart for her, just for that.

"What did I do? I talked to her. And I listened to her. I don't know, Geder. It wasn't a campaign of war. I didn't draw battle plans. I saw her at some function. I don't even recall what, and I thought she was handsome and smart and had twice the soul and spine of anyone else in the room. I wanted to know her better, and I asked for the pleasure of her company."

"And then it just happened," Geder said.

"Well, no. There was a time she thought I was just looking to get her skirts up for a few minutes and then never speak to her again, and that took some getting past. And I wasn't always my best self then either. But we came to understand each other. Trust each other." Jorey raised his hands, helpless.

"And the other?" Geder asked.

"The other?"

Geder looked down. His skin felt like it was burning in the sun. He wanted nothing in the world more than to leave now. Walk away and pretend the conversation had never taken place. Except he needed to know, and there was no one else he could ask. When he spoke, his voice was low and steeped in shame.

"How do you tell a woman that you...want her?"

"Oh," Jorey said. And then, "God."

"I shouldn't have asked."

"No, it's not that. It's just...I don't know. I'm vaguely

grateful and amazed every time Sabiha comes to my bed, and we're married. How do you tell her? Honestly? Gently. With humor or soberly. Howl it at the moon. I don't know."

Relief flooded Geder's heart like water on a fire.

"I thought I was the only one," he said.

"No," Jorey said. "I think men have been trying to find the way to say that for all the generations there have ever been, and the fact that there are generations at all means we must get it right sometimes."

"Thank you, Jorey," Geder said. "I should get back to the Kingspire, I think. I have a letter I need to write."

"Yes," Jorey said. Just as Geder reached the door, he spoke again. "Good luck, my lord."

The carriage drove through the night, wheels clattering against cobbles, horseshoes striking stone. Geder leaned against the thin wood and looked out through the window.

"Cithrin," he said under his breath, "I think men have tried for all the generations there have been to say what I am trying to say now, and that there are generations means they got it right sometimes."

He could do this. And if he stumbled and got some things wrong, it would be all right. She would understand. It was Cithrin. He closed his eyes and remembered her.

Cithrin

Cithrin:

I don't care how long it took you. I'm just so happy you wrote. Finding your letter there among all the others was the best moment of my day or week. Maybe of the year, and I helped win a war this year, so that's even better than it sounds. I thought at first I was only dreaming or that I'd made a mistake. I miss you too. More than I ever thought I would. I know you're a woman of trade and that the bank has its duties for you, but I was so disappointed when you left Camnipol without our getting to spend more time together.

I am so sorry that the army has been bothering you. I've given orders that you and the agents of the bank aren't to be bothered. If there is any question, Broot will bring it to you and whatever you tell him will have the force of law. I've gotten a bit of a reputation as a danger-ous man to cross, more through luck than anything I've really done, so I don't think he'll give you any problems, but if he does, write to me, and I'll have it taken care of. There are some real advantages to sitting a throne, along with all the unpleasant parts.

And also, I wanted you to know how much I miss you too. Even with all the time we spent together, I felt like we hardly got the chance to explore who and what we are to each other. The last night—the one night...

Oh, this is so much harder to write about than I thought it would be. Jorey says I should be honest and gentle, and I want to be. Cithrin I love you. I love you more than anyone I've ever known. All this time that I've been running Aster's kingdom and fighting to protect the empire, it's been a way to distract myself from you. From your body. Does that sound crass? I don't mean it to be. Before that night, I'd never touched a woman. Not the way I touched you. Since I had your letter, I can't deny it anymore. I want you back with me. I want to sit up late at night with your head resting in my lap and read you all the poems we didn't have when we were in hiding. I want to wake up beside you in the morning, and see you in the daylight the way we were in darkness.

I love you, Cithrin. And it's such a relief to say it here, I feel lighter and purer and better already. I believe in you. I don't need to ask if you've been as true to me as I have been to you. I know in my heart that you have.

Please, dear, when you can, come back to Camnipol. Let me shower you with roses and gold and silk and whatever else crosses your mind. I am well on my way to bringing peace to the whole world, and there is nothing I want to do with my power more than make you as happy as your letter made me.

And Aster! You should see him, dear one. He already looks like he's halfway to manhood. When he ascends to the throne, and I'm not Lord Regent anymore, I will be free to—

"Magistra?" the courier asked again.

Cithrin looked up. The man stood in her office like a ghost from a dream. His hair was still damp with sweat from his ride, and he stank of horse and the road. She tried to draw a breath, but her lungs felt like they'd been filled with glass.

"Yes," she said. "I'm here."

"Orders were I wait for your reply," he said.

"There isn't one. Not now," she said. "This will…take some time."

"Yes, Magistra."

He hesitated. She was on the edge of shouting at him to get out when she realized he was waiting for a coin. She fumbled with her purse, her fingers awkward and numb, drew out a bit of metal, and gave it over without looking to see what it was. The man bowed and went out. Cithrin sat on the divan, the leather creaking under her, and put her head in her hands. She felt trapped in the moment between being struck and feeling the pain of the blow. Everything had taken on a lightness and unreality. Her stomach was slowly, inexorably knotting itself, the anxiety settling deep in a way she knew meant sleeplessness for weeks to come. Months.

Geder Palliako thought he was in love with her. Love, like something out of the old epics. He'd spilled a little salt with her, and now they were soul mates. She went back to the letter. *See you in the daylight the way we were in darkness.* Yes, she knew what he meant by that.

"Well, *shit*," she said to no one.

But, on the other hand, *I've given orders that you and the agents of the bank aren't to be bothered.*

She tucked the letter away and pulled herself to her feet. The world still felt fragile, but she could walk and speak, and if she could manage that, she could do anything. She stepped out of her office and down to the guard quarters. Low clouds pressed, threatening an early snow. Enen and Yardem were sparring in the yard, blunted swords clacking against each other. Their focus on each other was intense, and she had to call their names before they stopped.

Yardem strode over. In his leather practice armor, he looked like a showfighter. His ears twitched, his earrings jingling. Enen pulled off her vest. She'd taken the beads out from her otter-slick pelt, and it was dark with sweat.

"Is there a problem, ma'am?" Yardem asked.

"Several," Cithrin said, "but they aren't at issue right now. Where do we stand on the evacuation?"

Enen scowled. It wasn't something they talked of openly. At least it hadn't been.

"It's progressing," Yardem said. "We had half a dozen children and their mothers out last week."

A crow called from the wall of the yard, as if offering its opinion.

"I'm going to have orders soon," Cithrin said. "I'll want the two of you to carry them."

"Orders for what, ma'am?" Enen asked.

"I want to get a hundred more children out this week."

Yardem and Enen exchanged a glance.

"Not sure how we can do that without asking for trouble," Yardem said.

"We have an advantage," Cithrin said. "It seems we're above the law."

The snow began in the middle of the afternoon, small hard dots that tapped against the stone streets and blew in little whirlwinds about her ankles. Cithrin had sent word to Magistra Isadau's network that the work had been compromised and never to speak of it, even to deny it had existed. Word of what the spider priests could do was making its way through the city in whispered conversations and ciphered notes. Giving the information out as widely as she could had been her only defense until now.

But even as the network quietly collapsed, some information still came to her. Seven families had gathered together to hide their children from the Antean forces. They were secreted away in a shed behind a dyer's yard. A woman and her twelve-year-old son had taken refuge in the crawlspace beneath the house of a minor merchant, and the merchant was starting to get uncomfortable with the prospect of keeping them there. A tanner at the edge of the city had sent a message that he had people in need of help, but without any other details. Suddapal was rich in desperate people.

They started with a single cart with half a dozen large closed crates in it. Yardem drove the team with Cithrin beside him. Enen sat in the cart proper, her blade at the ready. The horses walked through the snowy streets, their breath blowing cold and opaque as feathers. Cithrin tried to bury herself in the grey wool coat she'd worn. The first stop was the merchant's house. Yardem carried one of the crates on a wheeled pallet, striding to the servant's entrance with the bored air of a man who did this every day.

When the door opened to them, a nervous-looking Timzinae man stared out.

"I'm Magistra Cithrin. We're here to accept delivery."

"Oh, thank God," the man said, and ushered them in. The runaway Timzinae woman and her son both fit into the crate, though there wasn't much space to spare. For seven families' worth of escaped children, they'd need a larger cart.

"God bless you, miss," the mother said. "Thank you for doing all this for me."

"You're welcome," she said, but she thought, *Thank Isadau. I'm doing it for her.*

Yardem hauled the crate back out with a bit of help from one of the merchant's servants. Then it was off to the tanner's. Six people ranging in age from eight years to seventy were warming themselves in the stinking sheds. Cithrin saw them safely bundled into the cart. The others would have to wait a few hours more.

As the cart trundled back toward the center of the city, torchlight marked where Antean soldiers blocked the road before them. Cithrin's breath came shorter and she lifted her chin. She had the sudden bone-deep certainty that trusting in Geder's words had been a terrible mistake.

"Hold!" the guard captain cried.

Yardem pulled the team to a halt. Cithrin thought she heard someone weeping in one of the crates behind her. *Please be quiet,* she thought. *You'll get us all killed.* The guard captain rode forward. He was a broad-shouldered Firstblood, axe and dagger at his side. Snow clung to his hair and beard. Cithrin's heart fluttered and she fought her body's sudden need to move—fidget or worry her hands or bite her tongue. She smiled coolly. The captain's gaze lingered on the crates and he stroked his thin beard. Before he could speak, Cithrin did.

"Do you know who I am?"

The captain blinked. He'd expected to be the one controlling the conversation. His eyes narrowed and a hand fell toward his axe. Cithrin didn't see Yardem shift in his seat so much as feel him.

"What are you hauling?" the guard growled.

"Don't change the subject," Cithrin snapped. "I asked you a question, and I expect an answer. Do you know who I am?"

A nervous pause followed. Cithrin raised her eyebrows.

"Why should I?" the captain asked at last, but his voice had lost some of its power. She'd put him on the defensive, which was either a good thing or the beginning of a terrible cascade.

"Because I am Cithrin bel Sarcour, voice of the Medean bank in Porte Oliva and Suddapal, and you are under specific orders from the Lord Regent that neither I nor anyone in my employ are to be bothered. And yet you are bothering me. Why is that?"

"We had word there were rebels," the captain said. "Man said they were hiding in a house near here. We're to check anyone going in or out."

"You aren't to check me," Cithrin said.

"I'm sorry, ma'am," the guard said. "But I got orders. It's just a look in them crates and under your cart to see—"

"Where's Broot?"

"Ma'am?"

"Where is Broot? The protector Ternigan named. Where is he?"

"At his house?" the captain said, his discomfort making it a question.

"Yardem, drive us to the protector's manor," Cithrin said. "You. What's your name?"

"Amis, ma'am?"

"You can follow us."

"I...I can't," he said. His hand wasn't by his axe anymore. "I've got to stay and check carts."

"Well, you have a choice, then. You can come with us to the protector and we can clarify that you, Amis, have gone against the express orders of the Lord Regent, or you can let us by and stop wasting my time and interfering with my business. And then, when you and your men go back, you can ask what would have happened to you if you *had* chosen to take me before the protector."

He knew he was being toyed with. Even in torchlight, it showed in his eyes. But he wasn't certain. Cithrin sighed the way the woman she was pretending to be would have. Her belly was so tight it hurt.

"Wait here," he said. "You and yours don't move. I'm sending a runner."

"That was a mistake," Cithrin said, and leaned back to wait. The captain rode back to his men, and a moment later one of the torches detached from the group and sped off into the city.

Despite the snow and the wind, the cold wasn't as bitter as she'd expected. The autumn hadn't given up its hold. Yardem's breath and hers ghosted, and the horses on the team grew bored and uncomfortable. In the back, Enen paced, her footsteps making the cart sway slightly. All along the street and out along the spread of the city, the falling snow gave buildings and water a sense of half-reality. Sound was muffled and distant, but she still caught the drone of strings for a moment from somewhere not so far away.

"It's a prettier city than I thought when we came here," Cithrin said.

"Has its charms," Yardem agreed.

"Are we going to live through this, do you think?"

Yardem shrugged.

"Couldn't say."

"I'll wager a fifty-weight of silver that we do," she said.

Yardem looked over at her. His face was damp from the snow and his expression the mild incredulity of not knowing whether she was joking. Cithrin laughed, and Yardem smiled. It seemed to take half the night, and was hardly more than half an hour, before the torches came back. Ten of them. Cithrin leaned forward. Her toes and fingers were numb and her earlobes ached.

The new torches mingled with the old, and she heard the bark of voices. A moment more, and five men were galloping toward her. The one who didn't carry a torch was the impressively mustached Fallon Broot, Protector of Suddapal, wearing a dining shirt and no jacket.

"Magistra Cithrin," Broot said, "I am so terribly sorry this has happened. I told my man to spread the word, but some half-wit bastard wasn't listening. I swear on everything holy this will not happen again."

He bowed deeply in his saddle, as if he were speaking to a queen. Cithrin wondered what Geder had said in his orders that would bend a baron of the Antean Empire double before a half-Cinnae merchant woman. She felt a brief tug of sympathy for the man and his terror.

"Anyone can make a mistake," she said. "Once is a mistake."

"Thank you, Magistra. Thank you for understanding."

"Twice isn't a mistake. This was once."

"And never again. You have my word. I'll have Amis whipped raw as an example to the others."

Cithrin looked down the street at the fluttering flames. Any of them—all of them—would have pulled the children out of the crates behind her. Would, at best, have driven them through the streets. At worst, the Timzinae would have died here on the snow-damp street of their home. She thought of Isadau and, for a moment, smelled her perfume.

"Do that," she said, with a smile. "Yardem? I think we've lost enough time already."

"Yes, Magistra," the Tralgu said and made a deep clicking in his throat. The cart lurched forward, and the line of torches parted to let them through. Cithrin caught a glimpse of Amis as she passed, his face a tragic mask. She smiled.

At the dock, a small ship stood at anchor. The captain was a Yemmu, the bulk of his body making do instead of a jacket. He trundled forward to meet the cart, his eyes narrow.

"You're late," he said. "Another hour, we'd have missed the tide entirely."

"There was some business that needed to be done," Cithrin said.

"Doing what?"

"Establishing precedent," she said. "We have the cargo here now. Are you still taking the contract?"

"You're still paying it?" he said, and his tusks made his grin into a leer.

"I am."

Yardem, Enen, and half a dozen sailors carried the crates across to the gently rocking deck. Cithrin watched as they disappeared. Each crate was a life or two that wouldn't end here. A child who wouldn't sleep in an Antean prison, a mother or father, brother or sister who wouldn't be parted. And one less hold that the empire would have over its newly conquered lands.

Yardem and Enen walked back down, and with the calls of the sailors, the planks rose up. The anchor line rose and the ropes holding the ship to the land cast free. Slowly, the ship moved away into the grey of the snow. It was dangerous weather for sailing and worse for staying on land. Cithrin waited until the ship vanished entirely. The melted snow had turned all her clothes wet as if she'd jumped in the sea, but she couldn't leave until she saw it gone.

Yardem laid a blanket across her shoulders. She didn't

know where he'd gotten it from, but it smelled of wet animal and it was warm.

"Seems that worked," he said.

"It did," she said. "And it will work better next time. And they've seen you and Enen, so they'll know to be careful of you as well. It isn't a promise that things will go well, but it makes our chances a thousand times better."

"Suppose that's true," he said. "So a hundred this week?"

"I think so," she said. "This can't last long, and we'll regret missing the chances we don't take."

"Fair point," Yardem said. He put his hand on her shoulder for a moment, a silent approbation, then turned back to the cart. Cithrin waited another moment, then followed him with dread thickening in her throat. When she got back to the office, she would have to write back to Geder.

Marcus

Winter came to Camnipol. There was little snow, but the winds that blew across from the northern plains and highlands were bitter. The birds in the city departed until all that seemed to be left were crows and sparrows. The citizens of the city wrapped themselves in coats and cloaks, scarves and mittens, until they all seemed part of a single unified race of the chilled.

For weeks, Marcus and Kit had wandered the streets, striking up conversations with whomever they could. A rag seller's daughter sitting on the stoop of her mother's shop. A guardsman at the Prisoner's Span. Footmen of the wealthy spending their wages at the taproom. Anyone. Everyone. They might begin anywhere—a scar on the back of someone's hand, the weather, what kind of horses pulled best on a team—and edge the conversation around until they could ask, for whatever reason, *Do you know anyone sending messages to Carse?*

Most often the answer had been no, and the people had been telling the truth. A few times every week they found someone who said yes. Then they would use some pretext to talk about the bank in Carse, and the trail would run to stone. Three times they'd found someone who said that no, they didn't know anyone doing that, and lied. Each time that happened, Marcus felt a rush of excitement and the sense that they were about to discover Cithrin's mysterious informant.

The first had taken five days to run to ground, a man whose wife hated his brother. He had been sending messages to his brother in Carse and hiding the fact to avoid fighting about it at home. The second was a courier who had a lover in Northcoast and would send messages to him to arrange assignations. The third and most promising had been a minor nobleman trading correspondence with a counterpart in the court of King Tracian. For that one, Marcus and Kit had been forced to corner the man's personal servant in the street and pepper him with questions like children throwing pebbles. They discovered that the man had been trying to buy a particularly impressive carriage without his social rival finding out and offering a higher price for it.

In the evenings, they retired to the stables by the Yellow House and slept in the company of the players. Marcus had the poisoned sword in among the props and costumes, and Kit made all the others understand the peril it represented. Even Sandr seemed wary of it. Marcus's dreams became less disturbing and vivid and his shoulders hurt less when he wasn't carrying it. And the days had taken on a kind of rhythm and the grim taste that consistent disappointment brought.

The hunt went on, striking blind and hoping, but the contact had been so discreet that no one seemed to know of him. And eventually, winter came to Camnipol, and the game changed again.

"Cary's been approached by Lord Daskellin to be part of a revel," Kit said, hunched over his cup of coffee. "Many of the most powerful men in the court will be there. And their servants."

"Sounds like a thing we should do, then," Marcus said. In the yard, half a dozen children were playing a complex game that involved kicking stones off the Division's edge. Marcus watched them, envying the energy they had and the freedom of their play. The stables were full of horses and the grooms and the farrier had pushed the players to the edge of the space, where they sat together in a clump, like sheep in a rainstorm.

"What do you think she'll put on?" Hornet asked from behind them.

"Something darker this time," Charlit Soon said. Of all the players, Marcus knew her least, but her fair hair and round face made her seem more open and naïve than she'd turned out to be. "We've been playing the farces until you can see all the threads."

"I believe farces are good in wartime," Master Kit said. "There seems to be a hunger for laughter when times are bleak."

"What we need to do is find what plays best in a famine," Smit said thoughtfully. "You think The Tailor's Boy and the Sun?"

"Why would that be good?" Mikel asked. "It's got nothing to do with a famine."

"That's my point," Smit said.

"When she and Sandr get back from the market, we can ask her," Master Kit said. "But it poses a more immediate problem for our project, Captain."

"I know," Marcus said.

The court season ran from spring to the start of winter. Within days, the migration would begin. The men and women of the court would pack up their households and retreat from the city to their various holdings throughout Antea, and now Asterilhold, Sarakal, and Elassae besides as the conquered lands were divided up among the powerful and favored. Whoever they were looking for might be going anywhere. And then the King's Hunt would begin, and a collection of the higher noblemen would track around the face of the world with the Lord Regent and Prince Aster killing deer. The court wouldn't reconvene until spring, and by then the world might be a very different place.

Charlit Soon cursed mildly and flicked a beetle off her arm. One of the boys in the yard kicked a stone that sailed past his friends and companions out into the empty air of the Division, then lifted his arms in triumph. Kit sipped his coffee.

"If we can't find him in Camnipol with everyone living in each other's laps," Marcus said, "we won't find him in winter."

"It seemed to me that it might be more of a challenge," Kit agreed. "That leaves us, I think, with a question."

"Several."

All around them, the other players went quiet. Marcus could feel the glances and gestures being exchanged behind him and had the courtesy not to look back, but the tension was in the air all the same. Cary and Sandr appeared from around the corner of the house, each with a sack over their shoulder. Food, already expensive, was growing scarcer in the city, though from what Marcus could see, the higher classes still looked well fed. Kit rose to his feet, and Marcus followed him. The time had come to have the hard conversation.

Marcus saw Cary notice them waiting for her. Her steps didn't falter so much as change the authority with which they struck the ground. Sandr was in the middle of some anecdote or argument, talking and gesturing with his free hand. Cary took the sack from around her own shoulder and handed it to him. Sandr took it, looking confused, then saw Marcus and Kit approaching. Cary stopped, and Sandr walked on.

"Cup of cider?" Marcus asked.

"Why not."

The interior of Yellow House was comfortable and familiar. Cary lifted her hand to the keeper and pointed toward the back. He lifted his chin. The gestures were a full conversation in themselves. Cary led the way to a small room where casks of wine and tuns of beer lined the walls. A lamp hung from the ceiling with smoke-darkened tin plate above it reflecting the light down onto a thin wooden table. Cary sat first, then Master Kit. Marcus got stuck in the chair with its back to the door. A moment later the keep poked his head in.

"Cider all around," Cary said. "Captain's paying."

"Pleased someone is," the keep said, and a minute later three earthenware cups of cider sat on the table before them, steaming and filling the air with the scent of apples. Marcus took a sip and was a little surprised by both the sweetness and the bite.

"Good," he said.

"They get it from an orchard in Asterilhold," Cary said. "The stuff they had before wasn't as good. So. Leaving Camnipol, then?"

"Seems that way," Marcus said. "But the shape of it's not clear. We were hoping to find someone who could give us information about some expeditions that the Lord Regent sent out into the world. What they were looking for, say. And where they were looking. Only that hasn't worked. I think we've put in as much time as we can."

"All right," Cary said. Master Kit looked pained. To leave so soon after finding his family again was hard. Marcus knew that from recent experience. It was why he'd made the decision he had.

"I'm going north. The man leading the group in Hallskar's

named Dar Cinlama. Cithrin's dealt with him before, and she thought he was the true gold. My guess is that whatever it is he's looking for, he kept the best prospects for himself."

"Seems wise," Cary said.

"I will be going with him," Kit said at the same moment that Marcus said, "I'm leaving Kit behind."

Kit's eyes went wide with surprise and Marcus leaned in toward the table, speaking quickly to take the floor before Kit wholly recovered.

"If you're willing, Cary, you can take the company to the holdings of the nobility. You can follow the King's Hunt. Kit knows how to sniff out the man we're looking for. I'll head for Hallskar by myself and try to find Cinlama and his people along the coast. It gives us two chances where we only have one otherwise."

"I think that would also double the risk," Kit said. "Traveling through Hallskar alone in winter, any number of things might go wrong."

"Makes it a larger problem if I get a fever or break a bone," Marcus said. "Also makes it less likely I'll draw attention. I figure that makes it about even either way."

"No," Kit said. "You don't."

"You know, that's really annoying."

Cary slapped the table with an open palm. The report made both men jump. A strand of her hair had come loose from its braid and she pushed it back over her ear like a carpenter holding chalk.

"You know what I'm not hearing?" she said.

"Ah. I suppose I don't," Marcus said.

"I'm not hearing anyone say, 'What do you think, Cary?'"

Marcus glanced at Kit.

"What do you think, Cary?" Marcus said.

She nodded curtly. "I think whatever this thing is you're trying to find and being so closemouthed about—"

"Well, we don't know what it is, and—" Marcus began, then Cary lifted her eyebrows. "Sorry."

"I think whatever this thing is, a bad storm in Hallskar in the winter wouldn't be good no matter how many people were on the road with you. The captain here knows it and wants us out of harm's way. Add that he knows"—Cary turned toward Kit—"which apparently you don't, that the company goes where Master Kit does." Kit started to object and then stopped himself. "So all of this lip-flapping and masculine self-sacrifice will play just fine on the stage, and the stage is going to Hallskar. I'll tell the others, send Hornet to buy some horses, and get the rest packing up. It's about damn time we left this city anyway."

Cary stood up from her chair, drank down her cider in one swallow, and marched out toward the main rooms of the house and, beyond them, the yard. Kit sipped his own cider more slowly and looked over at Marcus.

"You did give her control of the company," Marcus said.

"I did. That's true."

"I'm thinking she has a taste for it."

The journey was long, and they didn't wait for the end of the court season to begin it. The company spent the last of its money on a team of horses to pull the cart and a couple more for the people to rest on when they got tired of walking. Even with the long stay in Camnipol, years of wandering made the company a model of efficiency. Aided by good weather, the journey to Sevenpol took hardly more than a week; they arrived just about the same time they would have been playing at Lord Daskellin's party if they'd stayed.

They made Estinport a week after that. The half of the fleet that hadn't stayed in Sarakal was in winter port there, and the steep, narrow streets of the city were full with sailors spending their season's wages and the prize money from the blockade of Nus.

Warships crowded the piers, empty for the most part, and the docks were fragrant with hot tar and fresh sawdust. Most ships flew the banner of House Skestinin below the royal pennant. And below them both, the red field and pale eightfold eye of the goddess.

Cary guided the cart into the yard of a taphouse that stood not a hundred paces from the sea. The air was cold and humid and the cries of the seagulls were louder than the human voices nearby. Master Kit negotiated with the taphouse keeper and got them decent terms for a three-night run. There wasn't time enough to tailor any of the plays to the local situation or incorporate personalities, so they chose a well-known story where everyone knew the lines. While the players brought down the sides of the cart and prepared the props and costumes, Kit went to scout out boats that might be hired to ferry them across the water to Rukkyupal.

The players knew their business well enough that Marcus would only get in the way. For the better part of a day, he wandered the streets of Estinport with only himself for company. When he stopped in a taphouse for a length of garlic sausage and a mug of beer, he sat apart from the larger crowd.

A singer with a drum sat at the front of the common room, his reedy voice working through a long cycle that Marcus had heard before: the sea captain who went to war and was caught in an ancient magic that took him out of the world so that when he returned, all the people he had known were gone, all the places he had lived had changed. It was a sad song, with the dry beat of the drum carrying it along like a heartbeat. Marcus listened with half an ear, and watched the faces of the men and women in the room. They all looked young. Fresh and untried. These were sailors in a martial navy, and tradesmen, and women with households and market stalls and children of their own, and they all looked as if they were playing dress-up. More even than the players.

He had been that young once, that sure of himself and his ability to remake the world in the shape he chose. And it had been true, within bounds. It seemed like something that had happened to someone else, except when it seemed like it had all happened a week before. When he finished his beer, he walked back out in the cold, the singer's drum still throbbing behind him.

At the yard, Kit was in the back of the cart in a robe of yellow silk, his arms held out to his sides while Mikel and Smit, needles in their mouths, sewed long, quick stitches at the seams.

"It appears I lost a bit of weight in the last year," Kit said as Marcus pulled himself up to sit beside them.

"Rewards of a vigorous lifestyle," Marcus said. "Any luck with the boat?"

"Yes," Kit said. "We have passage two days from now. It won't quite break our little bank, but we have a few plays we can rehearse on the way that tend to do well with Haaverkin. The sense of humor in Hallskar tends to run to puns, I'm afraid, so we have to make sure we have the lines precisely."

"Shouldn't be a problem," Mikel said around a mouthful of pins. "This is what we do, right?"

"Apparently so," Smit said pleasantly. "Try not to turn there, Kit. Changes the drape of the thing."

"I'm sorry. I'll try not to."

The afternoon passed quickly, the low northern sun

dashing for the western horizon. The keep brought torches and braziers out to the yard, and as the sunset stained the clouds rose and gold, Marcus stood out in the crowd to guide the laughter and applause or help to remove the hecklers that popped up, one or two at every show. Charlit Soon joined him. The play wasn't one she'd done before, and since there hadn't been time to memorize all the lines, Hornet would be taking the nursemaid's role and playing it in a high comic falsetto. Marcus nodded to her and she smiled back.

"Don't believe I thanked you for bringing Master Kit back to us," she said.

"Didn't know I was doing it at the time," Marcus said. "But you're welcome all the same. It's good to see him back among family."

"What about your family?" she asked.

He was on the edge of saying that they were dead. Alys and Merian, gone except in his nightmares. Only he didn't.

"Suddapal. They're in Suddapal for the time being. If things grow too dangerous there, I expect I'll meet them again in Porte Oliva."

"Cithrin, you mean?"

"And Yardem. And the company," Marcus said. "They're what I have. I got to see them for a time on the way north, but I couldn't stay. They had their job. I had mine. But when the jobs are over..."

"When they're over," Charlit Soon agreed, and Sandr leaned out from behind the cart, his face painted red and white and his arms flowing with green ribbons.

"Oh. It's time," Charlit Soon said, and trotted to the far side of the yard.

Kit came out, stepping onto the stage, and the yellow silk of his costume seemed like cloth-of-gold in the firelight. He strode forward, the stage shifting a bit under his weight. At the edge, he paused. For a long breathless moment, Marcus saw not an actor, not King Lamas the Gold, but Kit. His friend Kit. And he saw the satisfaction in the old man's face, the happiness and the belonging. The moment passed, and Kit began hectoring the crowd, declaiming, and bringing them close despite the darkness and the cold, with the promise of miracles and of joy.

Clara

When the season's end came, Clara was not invited to any of the great parties, but Jorey and Sabiha were. Vicarian had not reappeared since the initiation at the top of the Kingspire, and there was no indication of when he would come back down. And so when the feasts and revels that marked the year's end came and the streets and courtyards of the great houses filled with slave-drawn carriages and ornate palanquins fighting for positions and rank, Clara found herself outside of all of it. Last year, when Dawson had been newly dead, she'd stumbled through her days like a woman half asleep. Now she walked the edge of the Division or looked out over the southern plains, visited the Prisoner's Span and the taprooms and the fresh markets. The increase in her allowance meant that even as the others around her struggled, she was able to keep herself near to the daily life to which she'd become accustomed. Things did change around her. The market for day-old bread had become competitive, and she gave up the practice of handing it out as charity. The price of tobacco dropped, though, so she could afford something that was actually worth smoking.

They were small examples of something larger. Years of war had changed Camnipol, and the changes weren't yet done. Small pleasures went away and new ones appeared, and Clara found that so long as she paid attention to the new, mourning the old wasn't so bad. If anything, it had become the way she lived her life.

After the last of the great parties, there were a handful of small occasions. Winter teas held in drawing rooms while the servants of the house packed the summer's things away. A knitting group where several fallen women of the court, herself included, were taught a novel way of making shawls by an ancient Jasuru man with half his teeth missing, one blind eye, and an exquisite talent for lacework. There were farewells and promises that the next year would come and it would be different. As if any were ever the same.

She gathered what gossip and information she could for her letters, though the exercise had taken on an almost formal feeling. She wrote her letters, she sent them out, and nothing ever came back. Not that she'd given anyone a way to reach her. Sometimes she thought that she should. She could give them a false name to send to at the boarding house or direct them to Cold Hammer stables much as she had Ternigan. She never did, though. Part of that was concern for not being caught, but part was also that she liked the way things were now. Sending letters into nowhere and with no response was strangely calming. Like prayer, now that she thought of it.

As for her plan to undercut Lord Ternigan, she'd all but given up hope. Weeks passed, and though Kiaria hadn't fallen, Ternigan didn't reply.

Until, one day shortly after the last of Clara's old friends had left the city, he did.

The morning had begun late, dawn creeping in later and later until it seemed that before long darkness would take the world entirely. Clara had extracted herself from the bed without waking Vincen, washed and dressed herself, and escaped into the grey streets. Frost crept along the bases of the buildings, and the horses in the streets walked slowly in order to keep their footing. At the bakery, she bought an apple tart and a cup of coffee, sitting by the doorway and watching the traffic in the street. It was her day to visit Sabiha's unmentionable son and the family that was raising him, and had it been any other errand, she would have postponed it and gone back to the comfortable warmth of the boarding house. But children came with a different set of rules, and when she had drained the dregs of her cup and licked away the last of her tart, she bought a sugar bun for the boy and made her way to the house.

When she left, near midday, she meant to walk directly back to Vincen. Nothing more was required of her, and an afternoon smoking by the fire and reading poems either to herself or aloud to him sounded more than perfect. But her path was going to take her only a few streets from the stables, and she hadn't bothered checking in there in days. She turned toward the southern gate.

She was still half a block from it when her former footman stepped out from the front gate and waved her to come closer. Clara's heart beat a bit faster, and she walked more quickly without breaking into a run. When she drew up to him, he put a hand on her arm and leaned in close enough that his breath was warm against her ear.

"It's come," was all that he said. "Lirin Petty's got a letter."

The stables themselves were dark and hot in comparison to the street. While the sunlight didn't warm them, the bodies of the horses in their stalls and the warmth radiating from the manure pile were as good as a brazier. Glancing furtively to be sure they were not being watched, he led her to the back and drew a folded and sealed page from beneath a bale of hay. Clara took it gently, as if it were spun glass.

The thread was simple, the knot work undistinguished. If a letter had been made to seem unremarkable, it would have been like this. The hand, however, was one she had seen many times before. Ternigan, Lord Marshal of Antea, had formed those letters with his own hand. She had to restrain herself from ripping the thread then and there. Instead, she tucked the page away for when she got back to her rooms.

"Thank you very much," she said.

"Anything, m'lady."

"Let's just never mention this," she said.

"Not ever," he said.

All the way back to the house, the world seemed brighter and warmer, and her body felt buoyed up with the presentiment of victory.

My dear friend—

I have thought long about what you wrote, and though I am not present in court, do not believe that I am unaware of the sentiments you speak of. The siege of Kiaria is going as well as might be expected given that the men have fought through the swamps of Asterilhold, the streets of Camnipol, and all along the vast stretch of Timzinae-infested Sarakal and Elassae. The instructions I have received from Palliako have become increasingly frustrating. When I tell him the situation, he cites stories written in history books or the assurances of his pet cultists. My patience is wearing thin with his cheap buffoonery.

You have known me many years, and you know that my admiration for and loyalty to King Simeon were unmatched. Like you, I have come to the conclusion that the empire is in grave danger, but everything will rest on how we proceed. Without the support of the full court, I am afraid we would risk another summer like the last, and to be honest I fear that prospect more than I fear Palliako.

Your faith in me is flattering, and I appreciate your confidence more than I can say, especially in these dark hours. Would I accept the regency if it were presented to me? My loyalty to the Severed Throne and Prince Aster would require it. But to seek it out is another matter. Before I can commit to that, I would need to know much more. Who is it that you have recruited to your side? What are your plans to overthrow Palliako cleanly and neatly, for whatever action we take, it must be swift and unequivocal and, unlike Kalliam, it must strike true. The Timzinae threat is real, and I fear that without a steady hand at the wheel, the empire's opportunity to take its rightful place in the world may be squandered.

I understand that this is not the full-throated acceptance that you might have hoped to have from me, but do not doubt that my appreciation and sympathies are entirely with you. In the future, I suggest that you address your correspondence to a Ceric Adom of Nijestae Town. It is a hamlet not far from my encampment, and Ceric Adom is a creature entirely within my service. Through him I may discreetly retrieve your letters.

I look forward to hearing what state your plans have evolved to and how I may aid them from here. Give my regards and my good faith to the like-minded patriots with whom you serve the interests of the throne. And be assured that I will do anything in my power to safeguard Prince Aster and the empire.

And I agree. Time may be short.

Your loyal friend

"Ternigan hasn't signed it," Clara said, "as if the discussion of the state of the army were not identification enough." She snorted her derision.

Vincen had given the only chair in his little room to her, and sat instead on the edge of the bed. His hair was still unruly from the pillow. He scratched his cheek, fingernails against the roughness of his two-day beard.

"He sounds like he's agreed," Vincen said.

"Oh, he's not so dim as that," Clara said. "If he's taken, he will claim that he was drawing the conspirators into the open so that Geder can destroy them before they act."

Vincen's forehead furrowed.

"He might actually be doing that. He might have sent word to the Lord Regent already. And the letter that we sent. If Ternigan is loyal to Palliako—"

"Then no harm done," Clara said. "Geder will have the conspiracy exposed from both sides, and while it may confuse him, he won't know who we are, and he may very well distrust Mecilli and Ternigan just a bit because the question was raised and the players aren't obvious. But, my dear, if you knew Ternigan, he's loyal to whatever direction the wind is blowing. I have very high hopes for this."

"Still. It's odd that he took so long to answer, isn't it?"

"I expect he was hoping things would progress without him. There's nothing more charming than having all the heavy work done before you offer to lend a hand, don't you think? Then you get all the goodwill of having offered without out the bother of actually doing anything."

"I suppose that would be the most pleasant mix," Vincen said with a chuckle. Clara dropped Ternigan's letter onto the bed beside him and put her hand on his leg just above the knee. Vincen leaned close and kissed her.

With practice, they had become better at it. At first, she

had expected that all men would be identical to Dawson, and so discovering the ways that the little differences in the length of an arm or the angle of a jaw made the physical act of love different was actually something of a revelation. It seemed like every time she and Vincen lay down together, she would find that something else she had thought universal had in fact been an idiosyncrasy of her husband and herself. The way that Dawson's feet would sometimes curl around her own, Vincen's did not. The small shudder that had passed through Dawson when he reached his climax, Vincen didn't show.

She had thought that her mourning was done, and for the most part, it was. Exploring Vincen Coe, and more to the point, herself in the context of Vincen, didn't leave her melancholy. Quite the opposite. But while she would never have said as much, she also felt she was coming better to know who Dawson had been by the contrast. And to learn more about him, to have that small new intimacy with her husband was a gift she hadn't expected, and all the more precious for that.

Sometime later, when she rose from the bed, she took a moment to retrieve Ternigan's letter. The page had been bent at the corner, but was otherwise undamaged. Vincen pulled himself out of bed as well, stretching like a satisfied cat.

"We'll need to have this delivered to the Lord Regent in a way that can't be followed back to us," Clara said.

"Mmm. Any thoughts on how you'd like that done?"

"Well. Do you know any couriers that you particularly dislike?"

"I can find something," Vincen said, laughing low in his throat. "Just let me find my clothes."

"Don't hurry," she said, and then waved away his leer. "I

only meant that I have some work still to do here. You may dress if you wish."

She turned up the lamp and took out her paper, ink, and pen. She held the pen in her left hand, which muddied her letters and made the script look unlike her own, yet still, she thought, passably legible.

Lord Regent Palliako

For reasons I cannot at present reveal, I am passing on to you now two letters which have come into my possession. First is the copy of a message covertly sent by Ernst Mecilli to Lord Marshal Ternigan. The second is his reply. I trust you will take the actions needed to protect yourself and Prince Aster.

A friend

She waited for a long moment to let the ink dry. It wasn't until she went to fold the letters together that she realized she'd used the same paper for her own letter and the alleged message from Mecilli, but after consideration, she let the matter pass. She'd said that the message was a copy, so one might expect it to have been copied on the same paper.

She sewed all three pages together with a blank sheet at the back on which she wrote, *Exclusively for the Eyes of Lord Regent Geder Palliako* with her left hand. By the time she was done, Vincen was dressed and his hair combed. Clara gave him the packet and three silver coins from her purse.

"Well, then," she said. "Shall we bring down a tyrant?"

"Anything, my lady," Vincen said, and his voice made the words only half a jest. "So long as it's with you."

*   *   *

Will you be going on the King's Hunt again this winter?"
Clara asked as she and her son walked through the house
toward the winter garden. All around them, the servants
were bustling through the halls and corridors. It made her
realize again how small Lord Skestinin's manor really was.
Sufficient for a man who spent most of his summers with
the fleet, but if he were ever to retire from the position, he'd
need to expand. Or else find other rooms for his daughter
and son-in-law.

"No, not this year," Jorey said. "We talked about it,
Sabiha and I. I think it would probably help my standing at
court more to winter with her and her father."

"Ah," Clara said nodding. "So how far along is she, and
when were you going to tell me?"

Jorey had the good sense to blush.

"Almost two months, and I was just working up to it," he
said. "If you'd given me until we actually reached the garden, we were going to tell you together."

"That's sensible," Clara said. "I'll pretend not to know a
thing."

"Mother, I love you, but you are the worst woman in the
world at keeping a secret."

"I suppose I am," Clara said as they reached the doorway.
"I'll do my best."

The winter garden made her miss her own solarium. The
glass roof and walls had been designed to let in light and
hold what little warmth the sun could offer. In the depths of
winter, it was as unlivable as any room, but it gave a week
or two in the winter and another in the early spring when
she could have the illusion of sitting comfortably in the out-
doors. It struck her for the first time how decadent it was

to have an entire room made for such a small span of time. And still, she missed it.

Sabiha sat under a bench beneath a willow. The wall crowded the tree, but the effect was still lovely. For all her tarnished reputation, Sabiha Skestinin really had been a fortunate match for Jorey. When she stood, there was no mistaking her condition. Second children always did show earlier. Clara looked at the girl's belly, then at her eyes, and then they were both grinning and weeping. Clara folded the girl into her arms and they stood there for a long moment while Jorey shifted his weight from foot to foot.

"Well done, my dear," Clara said. "Oh, well done."

"Thank you," Sabiha said.

Clara drew her back down to the bench, but kept her hand. Jorey used a wide block of granite as a stool. He looked proud and content. The darkness wasn't gone from his eyes, but it was lessened. Clara couldn't help recalling Dawson strutting through the house when she'd first been sure that she was pregnant with Barriath. The memory held no sting.

"So Jorey tells me you're going north for the winter," Clara said. "I assume this is why."

"Father will insist anyway," Sabiha said. "This way he won't have to come down and pry us away from the hunt."

"Would he really do that? How wonderful of him."

"So I'm afraid we're going to come back next spring with considerably less court gossip," Jorey said.

"I'm sure there will be more than enough of that. It never does seem to be in short supply."

"I know," Jorey said. "But I know you enjoy it. But we were wondering if you'd want to come with us? Estinport is, as I understand, a single block of ice and salt from now until sometime after the opening of the season, but I'm sure Lady Skestinin would find rooms for all of us. And you could..."

She could. She could be nearer to the sources of power. She could hear what there was to hear concerning the navy and its plans for the coming year. All of it the kind of thing that might be usefully put in an anonymous letter to Carse. And all she would have to leave was everything.

"That's terribly kind of you, dear," she said. "But it isn't time."

Geder

The mysterious letters found Geder halfway to the estate of Lord Annerin, four sheets, three of them written in different hands. The night after they'd come, Lord Regent Palliako had given the hunt to Prince Aster, taken his closest advisors—Flor, Emming, Daskellin, Mecilli, and Minister Basrahip—in the fastest carriages in the caravan, and sped for the south without word or explanation. It would be the scandal of the season. He'd shown no one what the letters said, he'd explained himself to no one, though for different reasons. He didn't care. He didn't care what they said about him.

Except that wasn't true. It wasn't the hard beds that kept him awake at night. It wasn't the loss of comforts or the soft music he'd been able to command in the Kingspire. What kept Geder in motion was embarrassment that he had ever trusted these high and mighty lords, and rage. Well, soon enough, the truth would be revealed. Soon enough.

They left before dawn and rode until after nightfall. At each wayhouse and taproom, they traded their blown teams for fresh and began again as soon as the horses were in harness. Lord Emming complained, but Geder had pointed out that the sword-and-bows they'd brought were all his own personal guard, and if Lord Emming preferred not to travel, they could raise a cairn over him with relative ease. There hadn't been any more complaints after that.

They rode past the free city of Orsen like a plague wind and made their way through the pass into Elassae despite snow and ice. The locals all told them that the danger was too great, but Geder ordered them on. They lost three men and two pack mules, but after five days of painfully slow progress, they reached the southern slopes. The dragon's road cleared, and they began the last leg of their journey.

The fortress of Kiaria was cut deep into the living stone of the mountains. The brass gates to the first wall stood two hundred feet high and moved on gigantic mechanisms that had lain deep within the walls since the dragons. They stood broken now, the testament to almost a full season of Antean power. The only testament, because the second wall stood intact, and the third and fourth and fifth ones beyond that. At the base of the mountains on either side of the great gates was the Antean army. Geder's army. The ground all around was a churn of ice, snow, mud, and shit. Hide tents fluttered in the wind that came down the mountain, and where there had been trees to break its power a year ago, there were only stumps now. Everything that would burn had been burned. Everything that could be eaten had been eaten. The army, according to the reports, needed three tons of food a day to stay alive, all of it coming overland from Suddapal and Inentai. Three tons of food every day for months turned to three tons of shit by the morning. The glory and power of Antea was living in its own latrine while the Timzinae sat in their caves and laughed.

And the man responsible for the war, the man whom Geder had already had to correct once, squatted in his tent scratching his balls and plotting treachery. The night before they reached the Lord Marshal's encampment, Geder could hardly sleep.

When the sentries tried to stop them, Geder made them

bow down until their noses touched their knees and stay in that position still as stones until he'd ridden past. Lord Ternigan's tent looked much the worse for wear. Dark marks along the sides showed where the leather was starting to break down from the pressures of sun, rain, and wind. The Lord Marshal stood before the doorway in his dress armor, his own guards arrayed about him. The months had treated him no more gently than his tent. Ternigan's beard was greyer than it had been in the summer, his cheeks thinner. He watched the carriages arrive one after the next until the open space before his tent was as cramped with the transportation of power as a revel at the height of the court season. Geder's servants opened his carriage door and helped him down the steps and into the filth.

"My Lord Regent," Ternigan said, then coughed wetly. "Once again, I am honored that you have chosen—"

"Shut up," Geder said. "Get into the tent."

Ternigan blinked and grew a shade paler. His gaze darted around, settling at last on Lord Mecilli and, Geder thought, relaxing a degree. Sighting an ally in dangerous times. *If you knew the names of the men who've agreed, it would astound you.* Geder had the sudden image of being in the tent only to find himself surrounded by his enemies. The guards themselves drawing knives to strike him down. Fear cut through the rage.

"Wait," Geder said as Ternigan was about to enter the tent. "Stop. Minister Basrahip?"

The priest trundled slowly forward, making a jagged path between the still carriages. His expression was calm and serene. Behind him, two of his new initiates followed. When he reached Geder, he leaned close.

"Make sure my guards are still loyal to me. Can you do that?"

"Of course, Prince Geder," the priest said, then turned to his initiates and motioned them close. They stood outside while Basrahip went to each of the guards, and then came back. Geder felt more and more self-conscious as the pause grew longer. Daskellin, Flor, Emming, and Mecilli all stood in a clump looking cold and uneasy. At last, Basrahip finished his round and came back to Geder's side.

"They remain loyal to you," Basrahip said.

"Good. Thank you," Geder said quietly. Then, in his full voice, "Captain, disarm these men."

Ternigan started, his mouth working quietly. Of the others, Daskellin and Flor seemed confused, but not alarmed. Emming appeared to hover on the margin between outrage and fear. And Mecilli...Geder couldn't tell what was in Mecilli's expression. Dispproval, perhaps. Or perhaps a kind of cold calculation. The great men of the empire had their swords and daggers taken from them. And then, Ternigan in the lead and the others behind him, they went into the tent. Then four of Geder's guardsmen, and Geder, and Basrahip last.

When picturing the confrontation, he hadn't really taken into account the size of Ternigan's tent and how it related to the number of people who would actually be present. The camp tent was large for a man alone, or even a small group of advisors. With Geder and all of his council and the priests and the guards the proceedings had a vaguely comedic aspect that left him feeling even more ridiculous now than he had outside. Geder felt the rage that had fueled him all the way from Antea begin to falter in these last moments, and he hated it.

"Lord Ternigan? Lord Mecilli? Will you please stand here before me?"

Mecilli stepped forward, and then a heartbeat later, Ternigan followed his lead. Geder nodded and drew the letters from his wallet. Mecilli looked at the pages with curiosity, but Ternigan blanched.

"These little missives," Geder said, "came into my possession. They purport to be correspondence between the two of you. Mecilli, take this."

Mecilli accepted the page and read it slowly. After a few moments, his eyebrows rose and his face grew pale and waxen. Behind him, near the farther wall of the tent, Basrahip made his way through the press of men to take a position where Geder could see him.

"Lord Mecilli?" Geder said, letting the syllables roll gently through his mouth, willing himself back to the feelings of anger and righteousness that he'd let slip. "Do you recognize this letter?"

"No, Lord Regent. I have never seen this before."

The tent was silent for a long moment, and then, to Geder's surprise and horror, Basrahip nodded. Mecilli was speaking the truth.

"You didn't write this?"

"No."

Geder felt a lump growing in his throat. He'd pulled them halfway across the country for almost weeks for nothing. It had been a hoax. They would all go back to Antea with stories of how someone had made a joke of Geder Palliako.

"Did you write something similar to it?"

"No."

"Are you part of a conspiracy against me?"

"I am not."

With every reply, Mecilli's voice grew calmer, firmer, and more certain. And at the tent's rear wall, Basrahip certified each of them true. The goddess held her hand over Mecilli's head and exonerated him. The press of bodies and the thickness of twice-breathed air called forth sweat and a lightheadedness that felt like being sick. He'd been tricked. He'd been made fun of. All of the signs and signals between the men had been figments of his fevered imagination. Somewhere, the true author of the letters was laughing.

With a sense of dread, he held out the letter that pretended to come from Ternigan.

"Lord Ternigan, did you write this letter?"

"No, Lord Regent," Ternigan said, his voice calm and vaguely pitying.

Basrahip shook his head. No. That was not true. Geder took in a deep breath of air and let it out slowly. The anger felt like relief. Like being saved.

"Say that again," Geder said. "Tell me that you didn't write that letter."

Ternigan's eyes fluttered and he glanced at Mecilli.

"I misspoke, Lord Regent. I did write that letter, but not for the reasons it might seem. My intention was to discover whether any such conspiracy actually existed."

Basrahip scowled, and Geder understood the problem.

"One question at a time, Lord Marshal. Did you write this letter?"

"I did."

"Did you write it in hopes of taking the regency for yourself."

"No," Ternigan said. "Never that."

The faintest ghost of a smile touched the corners of Basrahip's mouth. He shook his head. No, that was not true. Geder's anger came back in its full glory now. He smiled.

"Lord Ternigan? Do you think I'm stupid?"

"No."

"Do you think you can lie to me?"

"I would never lie to you," Ternigan said, and tried to

take a step back, but Daskellin and one of the guardsmen were already in the space. Ternigan turned, looking for a path through the men to the door. Or a wall that could be pushed through. Escape.

"Have you called me a buffoon, my lord?"

"No!" Ternigan cried, but it was beyond all doubt. Geder spat on Ternigan's feet. Here was the great Lord Ternigan, war hero of Antea, cowering like a child before his angry father. Here was the man who'd thought Geder was laughable and small and stupid enough that he could wrest the throne from him. That the instigator had falsely claimed to be Mecilli didn't signify. Geder knew the truth of the betrayal from Ternigan's own living voice. That was more than enough.

"Lord Ternigan," Geder said. "I am removing you from your position as Lord Marshal of Antea."

"Y-yes, my lord. As you wish it."

"Yes," Geder said. "As I wish it. Lord Daskellin? Are you involved in a conspiracy against me?"

"No, my lord." It was true.

"My lord Flor? Are you?"

"No." True.

"Lord Emming? Are you involved in a conspiracy against me?"

"I am not." True.

Geder cracked his knuckles.

"My lords, I hereby name Lord Ternigan traitor against the Severed Throne and against my person as Lord Regent."

"No!" Ternigan cried. "You have been misled, Lord Palliako! This is a conspiracy against *me*!"

"Guards, please escort the traitor outside."

Ternigan struggled, but he had no weapons and no one to take his side. The guardsmen hauled him roughly out of the tent and sent him sprawling in the mud outside. Geder walked after him, the warmth of certainty and fury making him twice his height. His fists clenched and unclenched. The others came out behind him, one by one, until everyone from the tent stood in a rough circle. The guards hauled Ternigan to his knees.

"I demand a trial," Ternigan said through a mouthful of mud. "I demand trial by combat. God knows I am innocent."

"No," Geder said. "He doesn't. Captain. Your men should draw blades now."

The captain gave the order, and the sound of a dozen swords clearing their sheaths filled the air. The sunlight glimmered on bare metal.

"This," Ternigan said. "This is an injustice."

"No. It isn't," Geder said. And then, "So. Who's the buffoon now?"

Ternigan died quickly, the last of his blood spilling into the muck outside his tent. Geder watched him die with a sense of growing satisfaction. He wasn't going to vomit this time. He was going to maintain his dignity. All around him, Lord Ternigan's men stood slack-jawed and shocked. The wind made a soft whuffling sound like the noise of sails on a ship.

Canl Daskellin was the first to speak.

"There will need to be a new Lord Marshal. And quickly. The men are going to be disheartened by...by Lord Ternigan's duplicity."

"He was corrupted," Basrahip said. "Turned against you, Prince Geder."

"The Timzinae," Geder said. "It's their desperation."

"As you say, Prince Geder," Basrahip said mournfully.

"If you would like," Daskellin said, "I can draw up a list

of men who would make good generals for the kingdom, and we can—"

"No," Geder said, rounding on him. "No. I am done with giving power over to generals and counselors and great men. Do you see what's happened when I've done that? They turn. They all turn. I don't want any more generals."

His chest was working like a bellows, and his face felt hot even in the winter wind. Canl Daskellin nodded as if what he'd said made perfect sense, then paused and held out his open hand, the palm up like he was offering something.

"What do you want?" he asked, and his voice was gentle, calm, and polite. To judge from it, they might have been sitting on leather couches in the Fraternity of the Great Bear rather than standing over the corpse of the Lord Marshal in the mud of a half-conquered battlefield. "If not generals to lead the armies or counselors, then who do you want?"

A friend, Geder thought. *I want a friend.*

Are you certain you won't come with us?" Daskellin asked. "There is still time to catch up with the hunt if we join them at Masonhalm."

"No," Geder said. "You go on ahead. I'll join you before the hunt's over. Only not yet."

Night made the gates of Kiaria more foreboding. The few fires that guttered in the camps seemed small in the face of the mountain that loomed above them, and the sky that rose above that. A half moon spilled its milky light over the valley. Dragons had been here once. Had fought here. Had built a massive fortress against each other that now the last remnant of their race had fled to. It made sense if the Timzinae truly weren't humans that they would fall back to the old defenses, the old strategies. It was the size of the thing that overwhelmed him. The war between the goddess and the dragons stretched back farther than history, and now he was supposed to end it. He was surrounded by false friends and duplicity, conspiracy and violence, and he was the one who was going to lead the world to peace? It seemed impossible.

But still, he had to try. What would they say about him if he didn't?

"This is still hostile country," Daskellin said.

"I have guards."

"Guards can be overwhelmed," Daskellin said. "If you must go south, take a real force of soldiers with you."

"They have to keep the siege."

"There's enough," Daskellin said. "Nothing of substance is going to happen here before the new Lord Marshal comes."

Geder leaned back in his chair. A falling star streaked through the sky, bloomed briefly, and was gone. A servant came and quietly spirited away the remnants of their dinner.

"All right," Geder said. "If it will make you happy."

"Thank you," Daskellin said. "Who do you think sent those letters?"

"I don't know," Geder said. "But whoever it was, they didn't have to. It's something to have an ally, even if I don't know who they are as yet."

"Well. That's one way to look at it, I suppose," Daskellin said.

Geder felt the urge to ask what he meant by that, but the effort seemed too much. The violence of the day was weighing on him, and he knew he wouldn't sleep. Or not easily, at least.

"I think it's time I retire for the night," Geder said, drawing himself up. His fingers were numb and his nose was running from the chill. And the army had been keeping its place out here for months. Geder knew it was uncharitable of him, but he couldn't help being grateful that he got to leave while they stayed on. But at least the cold had frozen the mud. He took a few steps, then paused and looked back.

"Thank you," he said.

"You are always welcome," Daskellin said. "Would it be rude to ask what exactly you were thanking me for?"

Geder shrugged.

"Not betraying me, I suppose."

Inside the warmth and comfort of the tent that had recently been Ternigan's, Geder called for paper and pen and sent for a courier. The servants brought him blankets and pillows and a butter lamp with a tall flame that filled the room with the scent of smoke. For a long time, he stared at the page, uncertain how to proceed.

Cithrin—

I know you have not written back to me, and I understand. You're busy, and I am too. But I am weary, my love. I am tired to my bones, and I find I need the company of someone who cares for me. Someone I can trust. I am writing you now from the siege camp at Kiaria, but in the morning I will begin on my way south to Suddapal and, my dear, to you.

Cithrin

Neither Komme Medean nor Pyk Usterhall made any mention of Isadau or of the steady stream of refugees that Cithrin helped flee from Suddapal. The only overt sign that anything about the operations of the bank had changed was the name to which the bank reports were addressed. Without any formal acknowledgment, they simply began to act as if Cithrin were the voice of the Medean bank in Suddapal, and so it became true. It was like a cunning man turning water to wine or a stone to an orange. She was transformed by the act of their collective will.

Still, there were some details in the ciphered reports that carried more implications than others. Pyk Usterhall's report listed a significant capital outlay for commiserative gifts, which technically meant additional payments from insurance policies that covered deaths but was also the common euphemism for bribes. Komme also recommended that all branches call in loans made to the Free Cities, Borja, and Northcoast, and that they avoid making any loans into those territories without extraordinary returns. Cithrin didn't know whether the lives of people displaced by war fell under the heading of extraordinary returns, but thought they might.

From a financial perspective, her own reports back were the collapse of an incompetent. The branch was losing money like a slaughterhouse pig bled. Ships hired for unspecified cargo. Caravan masters employed for half a dozen off-season trips into the Keshet. Cithrin gave out loans on almost any pretext with expectation of repayment to other branches and no way to track the borrower.

Which is to say that the bank's mechanism had reversed. What had been an engine designed for the accumulation of wealth had become a system for wealth's application. She could imagine herself as some sort of half-divine fairy changing the world where she wished to by the careful dispensation of gold and silver, contracts and letters of credit. The difference she made was measured not in weights of precious metal, but in some number of lives and in children living outside of prisons. And she could go on with this until the coffers ran dry, and even past that, working on deficit until even the reputation of the Medean bank wasn't enough to keep her boards from being broken.

Some nights, she would stay up late and try to calculate her efficiency. How many hundred refugees had fled danger under her watch, and how much she had spent to do it. It occurred to her more than once that the Antean Empire had placed a low price on Timzinae lives, and that she had been the one in position to buy. Those were the best nights. The worst, she thought of other things.

The logic of the world had been inverted. Cheap lives were good. Money was there to be lost. Even the opportunities that came to her were suspect.

I don't think it's a good idea," Cithrin said, shaking her head at the list of names on the page before her. "Look at these. Tamar Sol. She's that old woman who lives beside the trading house, isn't she?"

"I believe so," Yardem said.

"What could she plausibly be doing for the bank? Darning

our socks? And this one—Witan Adada? He's the one with the missing leg who begs at that taproom."

Yardem sat on the divan, nodding, his ears canted forward and his hands clasped on his knees.

"Many of them are vulnerable people," he said. "Isn't that what we're here for? To extend the protection we have to as many people as we can?"

"Our privilege isn't built on stone," Cithrin said. "When we give this list to the protector, it will be a list of people immune to his authority. But it can turn into a list of people to be singled out for persecution without folding a corner. The bank is a protection as long as we're in Geder's good graces. I'd no more single Tamar Sol out to the protector than I'd point a wolf toward a baby. I won't list anyone as working for me who isn't willing to be killed because I did it."

Yardem grunted.

"Not the best recruitment speech," he said. "Let me take that back, and I'll see what I can do about revising it."

"I'm sorry," Cithrin said, holding out the page.

"No reason to be," the Tralgu said.

The report had come in the day before. Cithrin's scheme for an anonymous bounty board appeared to be moving forward. Komme Medean had included a list of prices being offered for a variety of crimes against the sovereign powers of Antea, the escape of slaves, the death of soldiers from common sword-and-bows to nobles. There was even a massive reward listed for Geder's death. They were reported as rumors with a request that all the branches reply with whatever similar schemes they were hearing of. Even if the letters went astray or Cithrin found herself being questioned by one of the tainted priests, she could truthfully say that she didn't have knowledge of the bounties being offered by the bank or anyone else in particular. Komme's reports said that the prizes were to be collected in Herez from a shadowy figure named Callon Cane, and she could truthfully say that was all she knew for certain. She was cultivating her own ignorance. It was just another way in which the normal logic of her world had been reversed.

Yardem walked out to the compound's central yard, and she accompanied him. The compound was still full of the refugees and guests that Isadau had welcomed in, or else the ones who had taken their place. There were men and women and children. The stables were empty, though. The grass on which the horses had grazed was brown and dry. There was less music than there had been when the buildings had been a home for Isadau and her family. It made the place seem empty, even though it was full.

The sky was pale and strangely opalescent, and the wind carried the threat of storm without the promise of release. Yardem walked off to speak with Enen and the other house guards, leaving Cithrin to make her way out to the gate and the street. Suddapal was not her city. However long she stayed, the roads would always feel a bit too wide, the land a bit too open. She missed glazed windows and negotiations conducted in private. And still, she would have paved the seafront in silver if it would protect the people there.

She saw the protector's men coming along the street, dark uniforms marching in a square. Not quite a threat of violence, but ready for it at any moment. And in the center of the square, the brown robes of the priest. She felt the dread in her gut, but only waited for them patiently. They might not be coming for her.

They were coming for her.

"Magistra bel Sarcour," the priest said, bowing slightly. "I hope the day is treating you kindly."

"It will do, I suppose," Cithrin said through her smile. "Unless you have another one on offer?"

The priest smiled back uneasily. She'd spoken with him three or four times now. Less than she'd expected, since she'd made herself one of the more important people in the city. She couldn't help wondering if Fallon Broot was keeping them apart out of his own unease with the priesthood. She had noticed that the friendly nonsense of banter seemed to bother the priest, so she employed it liberally.

"There was a fire last night," the priest said.

"I didn't know that," Cithrin said, telling the truth.

"It was near the prison. While the protector's men were dealing with it, someone threw a rope ladder over the back wall and almost seventy prisoners escaped."

"Really?" Cithrin said.

"Several were the children of people in the employ of your bank."

"And I'd imagine several weren't," Cithrin said. "And in any case, it wasn't anything the bank had a hand in, so I don't believe I can help you with that."

The priest tilted his head and bobbed up and down on the balls of his feet in a way that made him look like a sparrow.

"You don't want to know which of your employees' children were part of the attack?"

"I don't," Cithrin said. "Was there anything else you wanted to ask about, or shall I return to my business?"

The priest held out a letter.

"A message came for you by military courier," the priest said. "From the Lord Regent."

"Oh," Cithrin said. "Perhaps I mistook small talk for interrogation."

She took the letter as if it were a normal thing, and not the chance that Geder had changed his mind about her and was about to have her thrown into prison. She kept her smile pleasant and her gaze locked on the priest's. Making him look away first was a petty thing, but she didn't care. She couldn't be a politician in everything, and the man frightened her. She turned back to the compound. Later, she would need to go to the trading house and at least make some pretense at the normal business of the bank, but correspondence from Geder was her first priority. She went to her office and closed the doors. She put the letter down on the desk. The address on the outer fold was written in his hand. Twice, she reached toward it and pulled back. She put a book over it to keep it from blowing under a desk, went to the kitchen, and came back with a bottle of wine and no cup. The alcohol soothed the anxiety knotting her gut, and when she was a little over halfway through, she was ready to open the letter.

...I need the company of someone who cares for me...
I will begin on my way south to Suddapal and, my dear,
to you.
    Remembering the peace that I took from your touch,
from your body, has been the only thing that—

It was like a letter written between people she'd never met. It was love and sex and a kind of raw vulnerability. If she'd only happened upon it, she would have thought it was sweet and touching. She would have imagined the woman to whom it had been written and the man who'd put pen to paper, and she would have envied them. Only she was the woman, and the man was Geder Palliako. And worse than that, she could see where this unreal version of her had grown from. She remembered feeling fond of Geder, the frightened little man who was trying to protect the boy put in his charge. She remembered watching them working puzzles with complex stories about Drakkis Stormcrow and sleeping dragons. She remembered kissing him, and more than that, wanting to kiss him.

Only now he was coming here thinking that he was still the man he'd been that summer, and she was the woman he imagined her to be.

"Well," she said, softly and to herself. "Fuck."

The scratching at the door startled her back to herself. The last of the wine had gone, though she didn't remember drinking it. There was more in the kitchens, and she badly wanted another bottle. The scratch came again.

"Come in," she said, her words perfectly sharp. One bottle wasn't enough to leave her drunk. Tonight, three might not suffice.

Enen opened the door. A Timzinae man she didn't know was at the woman's side. He wore the rough cotton of a dockworker.

"Someone asking to see you," Enen said, her voice soft and gentle in a way that told Cithrin of the fear that had brought this man, whoever he was, to her. Cithrin willed herself to sit up a little straighter. There was room enough in the chair for her and Geder's lover; there would be enough for Magistra Cithrin bel Sarcour too.

"Come in," she said.

The man stepped in. His nictitating membranes were clicking open and closed and he held his hands in fists tight against his sides.

"I'm sorry for bothering you," he said. "Only I heard about you from Kitap, and I thought...I thought..."

"Kitap?" Cithrin said, and the man's face fell. Then, "You mean Master Kit?"

"Yes. You might have called him that. He used to live

with my family, back before he was anything in particular. My name's Epetchi. Maybe he talked about me? Or Ela?"

"He may have," Cithrin said. "Now that I think of it, he may have." She didn't remember him saying a thing, but she knew from someone that there had been a café run by friends of his down near the docks.

"He said you might be able to help people. That you were a good person. A friend."

Cithrin smiled the way she did in any negotiation and nodded toward the divan.

"Tell me what's going on, Epetchi," she said.

His niece had been one of the children taken from the prison, only she'd been hurt in the flight. He was hiding her in his storeroom, but she had a fever and it was getting worse. He didn't dare go for a cunning man for fear that they'd be turned in to the Anteans. As he explained himself, the high whine of anxiety faded from his voice and a deeper, lower kind of fear came in. One more like despair.

Cithrin listened carefully. The fumes of the wine faded quickly, and her mind danced over the problem. Epetchi was right, of course. The protector's guard would be watching the cunning men. The priest would be questioning them and anyone else whose work it was to give aid to the desperate and in need. When he shrugged and went silent, she pressed her fingertips to her lips and thought.

"Come with me," she said. He followed her out to the guard room. Yardem and Enen were both there.

"Yardem, do you know of any cunning men willing to die because I put them on a list?"

"Know one I could ask."

"Do that," Cithrin said. "Then get him to this man's café. He's a friend of Kit's."

"My sympathies," Yardem said seriously, and then broke into a grin. Epetchi laughed.

"You know him too, then?"

Cithrin stepped back. Yardem would see to it now. She walked through the corridors, back to the kitchen for two more bottles, and then to her room. She'd done enough of her business for the day, and if she went there, she would only read the letter again. She didn't want to do that.

The plant that Isadau had given her that first day still sat on her sill. Its small, thick needles hadn't gone brown with the autumn. Cithrin sat on her bed and watched it quiver in the breeze. Another good night, then. Maybe another life saved. She wondered who had engineered the escape of the prisoners. It was reassuring to know that there were others in the city who were taking action, but it was not surprising. This was their home. These were their children. If the whip ever came to their hand, Geder's soldiers would suffer and die, she didn't have any doubt.

She wondered how much was enough. She had already managed an order of magnitude more than Isadau could have. She had immunity for the bank that no one else in the world could have acquired, and she'd used it as best she could. But she couldn't say it was enough. Her own argument circled back. One more day would save another few people, and how could she tell herself that the ones she would have saved were less important than the ones she already had? And one more day after that, and after that, and after that until Geder came to her door expecting a lover to fall into his arms.

And then? What were the lives worth that she could still save after that? If she fell as she was expected to, if she became the woman the letters were for, how many more refugees could she spirit out of Suddapal?

It was an exchange, just as anything was. She could maintain her branch and its immunity. She could get information about the Antean army and the spider cult. And all it would mean was becoming Geder Palliako's lover. She tried to imagine what it would be like, standing naked before him now that she knew he'd ordered the death of Vanai, now that she'd watched him slaughter a man, now that she'd lived in a city that had been broken by his will and the will of his priests. Unpleasant, yes, but her body was only a body. Access to it was something he wanted and that she was in a position to give. And what she would gain from it couldn't be had for any other price. This wasn't a new equation. She'd had the same essential decision with Sandr and with Qahuar Em. Once, it hadn't been a good trade. Once, she'd thought it was and had been wrong. Neither of those had killed her heart.

The plant shivered. Cithrin pulled the cork from her bottle and sat with her back to the cool, rough wall. The taste of grapes and the bite of the alcohol were like old friends come to commiserate. Isadau would have died for her city, and Cithrin had bought her absence with a promise. A promise to save as much of Suddapal as she could. So in a sense, if she took up with Geder Palliako again, if she sat at his table and laughed at his jokes and permitted herself to be used by him in his bed, it would still be from love. Her love for Isadau. She drank from her bottle. She knew from long experience it would take at least one more for her to sleep tonight.

"Fine," she said.

Marcus

The north coast of Hallskar in the depths of winter was a cold kind of hell. Marcus had known from stories he'd heard told by other mercenaries and wanderers that the storms could be vicious and sudden, that the land was harsh and unforgiving. He'd lived in Northcoast most of his boyhood, and the little cruelties of winter were nothing new to him.

He had underestimated.

"We're all going to die!" Sandr wailed.

"Die walking, then," Marcus shouted and leaned harder into the storm. Before them, the cart swayed in the wind. A layer of ice was forming on the left side, and Hornet had given up trying to break it off. The horses' heads were low, their manes glazed as they pushed on. Marcus was more worried about them than about Sandr. If the actor collapsed, they could load him in with the costumes and the props. If the horses fell, they would have to stop. And if they stopped, the chances were good they wouldn't start again.

The morning had been clear and cold enough to freeze piss when it hit the ground. The sky had given no particular sign of trouble until trouble descended. In the space of an hour, the day went from calm to blustery and from blustery to a howling gale. Dar Cinlama and the Antean expedition had been rumored to be just ahead of them somewhere along this road, but Marcus didn't care about them any longer. Or about the spider goddess or anything other than the thought that freezing to death on a icy track in Hallskar wasn't the way he'd hoped to die, but it also wasn't the worst.

"Your turn," someone said, but Marcus wasn't sure who. He tried to blink but his eyes felt raw. Cary tugged at his shoulder again, pushing him toward the cart. "It's your turn. Get in."

"Right," Marcus said. With numb blocks for arms and legs, he clambered up the back of the cart. The wind wasn't so bad here, though the cold was cutting. There was frost on the costumes. He inched forward until he was nearly at the front. Kit sat on the bench, his body made nearly round by the cloaks, jackets, and blankets that wrapped him. Snow and ice were sticking to him like he was a stone.

"We have to find shelter," Marcus shouted over the voice of the weather.

"Yes," the snowball-lump that was Kit shouted back.

"Are you sure we're still on the road?"

"No."

Marcus paused for a moment, trying to think what he could do about that.

"All right," he said. "I'm going to rest."

"You should."

Marcus turned back. A gust of wind shook the cart, and he felt the jarring when the wheel fell back to the ground. The tiny glass lamp that hung from the top of the folded stage didn't go out, and he cupped it in his hands, letting the warmth of the little flame thaw his fingers. They were all taking turns resting in the cart except for Kit with the team and Smit who wouldn't stop leading the two riding horses. It was only their second week out of Rukkyupal, and the fantasy Marcus had built of going from town to town putting plays on for the Haaverkin and uncovering hints about the whereabouts of Dar Cinlama was dead.

Someone shouted. Charlit Soon, Marcus thought, but it could have been Cary. He had the image of someone fallen in the snow and unable to rise. He fought the weariness, focusing his eyes, then went out to help them back up.

Only no one had fallen.

Charlit Soon was standing off to the side of the road, pointing out into the grey-white gloom of the world. Marcus fought his way toward her, slipped on the ice, and rose again. When he came close enough to hear individual words, she was shouting, "Light! There's a light."

And to Marcus's amazement, there was. It was faint and inconsistent, but somewhere close, a fire was burning brightly enough to penetrate the storm. And Charlit was standing on a side track that seemed to lead toward it. They had very nearly walked right by it.

"Stay here," he shouted. "I'll get the others."

It seemed to take hours to stop them all, to turn them, then find Charlit again and start off. The wind blew against their backs now, shoving them forward. And slowly, a darkness rose up before them: a massive structure of black wood logs woven one atop the other into a wall. More trees were laid over the top, and a load of snow as tall as all the rest towered above it, higher than clouds. A great pitch-stinking torch fluttered in the wind like a lighthouse in fog, and a thick wooden door stood beside it.

Marcus struggled forward and slammed a numb fist against the door, hoping that someone would answer him and planning how to break it down when they didn't. The door swung open on a Haaverkin woman. Her vast body was covered in light wool and fur. Her face was complicated by swirling tattoos in red and blue, and her expression was like a mother whose child has just hauled home a basket of puppies.

"Who in hell are you people?" she asked.

"Marcus," Marcus said. "Kit over there. Some others. Make plays. Wondering if we could come in."

The woman sighed, shook her head, and turned to call over her shoulder.

"Kirot! We've got more idiots." She turned back to Marcus. "I'm Ama of Order Murro. This is our lodge house. You there. Just leave the horses. We'll get them. You'll only cock it up."

Marcus nodded, then stumbled past her into the warmth.

The lodge house was a single massive room with a fire burning in a stone grate at the far end. The air was sooty and thick. Great tables ran along the walls with benches made from split trees. The Haaverkin at the tables—twenty, perhaps thirty of them—turned to watch him with amusement and curiosity. Marcus raised a hand in greeting, but kept stumbling forward toward the light and the promise of warmth. As he drew near the flames, he saw thinner figures at the hearth. A half dozen Firstblood men, and a leather-skinned Dartinae man with eyes so bright it seemed like his head was hollow with firelight blazing through empty sockets.

Oh, Marcus thought, then collapsed on the furs and blankets before the fire, his body trembling from the cold and burning from the mild heat that radiated out from the flames. Sandr crawled up beside him, and then Kit and Cary and Hornet. Charlit Soon and Smit and Mikel. They curled together like animals in some deep winter den. Marcus heard someone weeping, but was fairly certain it wasn't him.

A massive old Haaverkin loomed above him. The ink of his tattoos and the lines of his face swam together in a complexity that Marcus couldn't follow. His teeth were the grey of stone, and the rolls of fat that enveloped his body made him seem larger than he was. And strong. A bone pipe appeared in his hand.

"What's your name, then?"

Marcus didn't have the wits left to lie. "Marcus Wester."

"And these others? They're yours?"

"They're mine," Marcus agreed.

"Well, then, Marcus Wester and his brood. Kirot of Order Murro is my name, and this is the lodge house of Order Murro. We extend you our hospitality because if we didn't, you'd die out in the weather like a bunch of fucking half-wits."

"Thank you for that."

"Don't mention it," the old Haaverkin said sourly and marched off into the gloom shaking his head at the fragility and stupidity of southern races.

"You know there's a mercenary captain with that same name," a pleasantly raspy voice said. Marcus levered himself up to sitting. The Dartinae man had come to sit near to him, legs more tied together than crossed. If Marcus had taken the same pose, he'd have popped his knees loose, but Dartinae were usually a bit more supple than the other races.

"Did, actually," Marcus said.

"You get mistaken for him?"

The man wore a leather vest with a dragon on it in faded and cracking paint.

"Almost constantly," Marcus said. His senses were almost back, but not quite. He felt drunk from the cold and his toes were still numb. Soon he'd have to pull his boots off and check for frostbite, but his fingers hadn't blackened, so maybe he'd avoided the worst of it. "And you, cousin? What's your story?"

"Dar Cinlama," the man said, dispelling the last remnant

of doubt. "Citizen of the world, but lately from the court of the Lord Regent in Camnipol."

"You must have pissed him off badly for him to send you out here."

Dar laughed. "No, this is where I picked to be. Searching for hidden things in the lost corners of the world."

"Seems you've come to the right place." Marcus looked over at the Firstblood men sitting apart at the near table. There was no mistaking them for anything but Firstblood, but though their skins were the full range from pale to dark, none had the wiry hair or brown robes of a spider priest. "Those yours?" he asked, nodding to them.

"I have the loan of them. Not a bad bunch. More than I've usually had for company."

Cary groaned and curled away from their voices. Sandr appeared to be asleep, snoring lightly, his face as slack as a child's. Marcus's awareness was still broadening slowly. Along the walls, he saw the Haaverkin shields and spears interspersed with images of dragons and the skeleton of a monstrous fish, its head twice as wide as a man's shoulders, with three rows of viciously curved teeth. The Haaverkin in the room were ignoring them, talking among themselves, laughing or scowling. Even though Marcus couldn't feel the wind, and the fire in the grate drew steady and calm, the rage of the storm outside was oppressive as a hand on his shoulder.

Kit stirred, rising from the rugs. His expression was mild and amazed, as if he thought perhaps he'd died and this was where souls went to wait for judgment.

"Kit," Marcus said. "This is our new friend. His name's Dar Cinlama."

Kit's eyes took a moment to focus, but then comprehension slipped into them.

"I'm very pleased to meet you, Dar," Kit said.

"And what brings you to the warm hearth and happy home of our northern brothers?"

"We are a theater company," Kit said. "Seeking new audiences."

"Well," Dar Cinlama said, "this is a place to find them. This is likely the most Firstblood any of these orders have seen in years."

"And perhaps the last," Kit said. "I can't say we've found quite as many audiences as we'd hoped."

"Should have come in summer," Dar Cinlama said. "Bugs the size of your fist trying to drink you dry, but at least the sky isn't trying to kill you."

"Been here since then, have you?" Marcus asked, trying to keep his voice casual.

"Yes, I have," Dar Cinlama said, "and likely I'll be coming back next summer. But once the weather clears, we're going down to Borja. Winter in Tauendak or Lôdi."

At the far end of the lodge house, the door opened, and the woman who'd saved them from the cold came back in. From a distance, her cloak looked no heavier than something Marcus might have worn on a cool day in spring. She brushed the snow and ice out of her hair and walked over to Kirot. As they bent their heads together in conversation, the draft of cold air finally reached them, and Marcus shuddered.

"I think we may follow your lead," Kit said. "We were thinking of following the King's Hunt in Antea, but the company has been there a little too long, and we chose to come here."

"Bad, bad decision," Sandr said weakly, so maybe he wasn't asleep after all.

"Is your work in the north finished as well?" Kit asked,

and Marcus could feel the edge in the question. He couldn't help feeling a small thrill of excitement.

"Work's never finished," Dar Cinlama said expansively. "The world's too big and too old for that. I was following the story that a giant was buried in the north with a sword of flame that could slaughter armies."

"Really?" Marcus said.

"There's really a story," Dar Cinlama said. "And maybe there's a giant and a sword to go with it, but we haven't found it yet. I've found other hints. Part of it mentions a lake where the stars come to die, and I've found an inlet about three days from here where the fish take on a glow. Get a whole school of them, and it could be what the story meant."

At the far end of the lodge, Kirot nodded his head once sharply, then started coming down toward them. Marcus watched him without seeming to. Better for now if Kit could pull information from the Dartinae without interruption, but that was looking unlikely.

"That's what you do, then?" Kit asked. "Find old stories and match them to bits of landscape?"

"It's part," the Dartinae said. "I'll chase rumors and old tales, or I'll just head off to places where no one looks and look there. Can't know what you'll find."

"That's truth," Marcus said. Kirot was almost upon them. "No luck this time, though?"

"There were a few times I thought we were close. Old stories that made it seem like we were close to something, but nothing came of it. Next time, I'm going further inland. Takynpal, maybe."

Kirot loomed up behind.

"We put your cart and your horses in the deep stables," he said to Marcus. "Tradition is you give the host a gift for our kindness. We were thinking one of the horses would be good."

"Seems fair," Marcus said.

"Do you truly think there is something to be found?" Kit said, his attention still on the adventurer.

"There's not," Kirot said. "No such thing as giants, much less magical fire swords."

Kit's eyebrows rose and his head shifted up to Kirot.

"No?" the old actor said, his voice all innocence.

"Not a goddam thing," Kirot said. "Only thing that comes of your kind coming up to Hallskar is a fat load of bones when the drifts melt."

"There are always secrets waiting to be found," Dar Cinlama said, sounding wounded.

"Not here there aren't," Kirot said. "But you go on killing yourself trying to chase whatever it is down. We'll keep your things safe once you're dead."

The old Haaverkin turned and trundled away, puffing at his pipe.

"Kirot's bad-tempered," Dar Cinlama said, "but harmless if you don't cross him. Seems like that's the way for all the Orders. Sour. Your people should come with me. When the storm breaks we can all go down to Borja together. Lôdi's a real city. You'll draw real crowds there."

"I think we'll stay a bit," Kit said. "We've only just come here after all. You should go on without us."

The Dartinae shrugged. "Your choice. If you're warm enough now, you should ask old Kirot for some soup and beer. You're paying a horse for it."

"Cheap at the price," Marcus said.

The evening was spent talking with the Antean men and bringing the players back to themselves. Once they were recovered, Sandr and Kit put on a mock poetry competition that drew a bit of a crowd. Marcus sat by the fire drinking his beer and watching. The Haaverkin laughed at different times than Marcus expected them to, and watching Sandr and Kit respond to that, shaping their performance as they went, had a kind of beauty to it. Dar Cinlama, apart from being a little more impressed with himself than Marcus was with him, seemed a decent man. Eventually the fire burned low and the Haaverkin started bedding down on the floor of the lodge house. Dar Cinlama and the Anteans did the same, and before long the players were also in a little group, curled up under blankets together for warmth and comfort in strange surroundings. With the voices all gone quiet, Marcus could hear the storm still shrieking and ripping at the walls of the place. The glow of the embers and low flames in the great hearth threw ruddy shadows across the ceiling and along the walls.

He waited until he was almost certain that the others were asleep, then took himself through a short passage to a latrine that had been hacked out of the frozen ground. When he came back, rather than pulling the blankets over himself, he went to find Kit. As he'd expected, Kit's eyes were open and bright.

"Well," Marcus said. "Seems our friend may not have found the thing he was looking for."

"No, he hasn't," Kit said. "And more, I think he's close to giving up the chase. At least so far as this part of the world goes."

"Think he's wise in that?"

"No," Kit said, his voice so low it was hardly audible even inches from his lips. "No, I think he's being kept from it. Kirot was lying when he said there was nothing to be found here."

"Seems we've sung that song before," Marcus said. "Are you up for another verse?"

"Give us a week in Kirot's company, and I think I can manage something."

"Good that we have the powers of chaos and madness on our side sometimes. Still, I don't know what we're going to do with another damned magic sword."

Cary muttered something, turned and stretched out one leg toward the dying fire.

"It isn't a sword," Kit said. "And it isn't a giant."

"What, then?"

"I don't know," Kit said, his eyes bright and merry. "But I believe I can find out."

Cithrin

Cithrin lay in bed, her eyes focused on the ceiling. Focused on nothing. The pale ceiling looked blankly back down. The cracks in its plaster made shapes and faces. The pillow was too warm or else too cold. Another night without sleep. What did she need it for, anyway?

At last she pulled herself up and went through a rough parody of her morning ablutions. When she came out into the corridor, she was as nearly herself as she was likely to become. And in truth, very few people if anyone would notice how poorly she felt. It was the advantage of living a life of professional deceit that she could choose how much to show and how much to keep to herself. It was one of her primary skills. No one would see how she felt. Or that, at least, was the thought.

"You all right, Magistra?" Enen asked as soon as Cithrin stepped into the dining room. The smell of eggs and fish and peppers assaulted Cithrin's nose, but she didn't gag.

"Fine," she said, sitting across from the Kurtadam woman. "Just didn't sleep well."

"Anticipating the Lord Regent's arrival."

Cithrin's smile felt painted on and chipped at the edges.

"I suppose I am," she said amiably.

The runners said that Palliako was still a day and a half away, and on the march. He was being accompanied by three hundred sword-and-bows detached from the siege at Kiaria for the sole purpose of seeing that he arrived safely on her doorstep. She didn't know whether to feel flattered. Every day since she'd had Geder's letter from Kiaria had been a little harder than the one before, but she told herself that once he had arrived and she could fall into the role she'd prepared for herself, it would be better.

"Where's Yardem?" Cithrin asked, more as a way to postpone getting food than from any genuine curiosity.

"Off doing a little last-minute work," Enen said. "Making the rounds of all the people we've worked with to let them know not to expect anything from us for a time at least. We figured that with the extra soldiery and Palliako himself and his priests lurking in the doorway, it'd be better to wrap up any outstanding business."

"Probably true," Cithrin said. It was the kind of thing that she should have thought. There were enough times in her past for her to know when she was drinking too much, and she was drinking too much. The knowledge made her feel slightly more in control of things, though it wasn't going to have any particular effect on her actions. She would go right on drinking too much.

When her body finally felt it could stand the idea of food, she ate a sliced apple in cream and drank a cup of coffee, and afterward, she kept it down. She felt an unwarranted pride. She was the voice of the Medean bank in two cities. She was responsible for saving hundreds if not thousands of Timzinae from the occupation. And as her crowning glory, she didn't puke up her food like a newborn babe.

There were fewer guests in the compound now. The courtyards were empty. The quarters where refugees had slept and eaten and talked and led their lives were abandoned, with only their old straw mattresses and rag-worn clothes left behind. The day before had been taken up with that.

She'd dreaded going to all the refugees who had accreted around the compound and asking them to leave. She knew as well as they did that there was no place to go, and so she'd expected grief and recrimination. Not her best prediction, since for the most part she got as far as explaining that the Lord Regent of Antea and a force of soldiers protecting him were very likely to come to the compound. Almost before she'd finished the last syllable, they were packing up their meager belongings and their confused children and heading out into the winter. They might die of cold in the streets. They might try walking to the Keshet or Orsen without food or water enough to make it two days. Cithrin wished she could go with them.

The only solace she had was the books. Reviewing her ledgers and logs distracted her a bit from what was going to happen next. Something about the flow of income and expenditure soothed her in any case, but now it was also her justification. Leaning heavily on her desk, she could trace her fingers down all the work she'd done in Suddapal. Here were the payments she'd made to the ship captains who'd stolen away with a hold filled with humanity instead of cargo. Here were the reimbursements for drink and food that she'd granted to the men and women who'd agreed to seek out the taprooms and public spaces, moving from group to group and telling about the bounties available in Herez. Here were the loans she might as well have listed as gifts that were to be repaid at other branches. It was an account of all her sins against commerce and profit, and she took as much pride in it as she could.

She wished that Komme Medean were there. Or Paerin

Clark. Someone she could talk with about her time commanding the branch. She thought it had all been the right thing, but what if there had been some better way to do the things she'd done, and some way to build on it moving ahead? Geder wouldn't be able to stay in Suddapal forever. Perhaps he'd only come for a few days, and then go back to Antea and his court. Certainly it wouldn't be longer than the winter. When he left, she would go back to her work. Unless he wanted her to go with him. Would he insist? She imagined herself living in Camnipol, sleeping and eating in the Kingspire, and wondered what it would be like to leave the books and the bank behind. It seemed that it would leave very little room for her.

The compound of the Medean bank was also far from the only place in the city preparing itself for the arrival of its master. The protector's guards were driving teams of enslaved Timzinae through the streets, cleaning away the winter-killed plants and paving roads that had never known stone. The houses and temples that had burned in the sack were finally being torn down or rebuilt. The few times that Cithrin went out into the city, she felt a sense of dislocation seeing the changes and improvements. It was as if the real city had been spirited away in the night and replaced with the Antean image of what Suddapal should be. It would have been comic if it hadn't meant that the city as it had been was gone. That a thing once changed could only change again, and not live backward.

That afternoon she was in her room wearing a silk shift and trying on dresses in which she could meet Geder Palliako. A long-sleeved green velvet was her favorite at present, but there was a butter-yellow one with a more Antean cut that displayed her figure better, even though the color was fairly hideous. The scratch came at the doorway as she held the yellow to her chest and tried to decide whether there was a scarf she could add that forgave its failings.

"Come in," she said, half aware that she wasn't, strictly speaking, dressed and she didn't know whom she'd just invited in. It wasn't something she cared about.

Yardem entered. He was wearing leathers much like his training armor, only with touches of green at the throat and shoulders. Cithrin wondered what Geder would make of it if he arrived to find her encased in armor. The idea was almost funny.

"Magistra," Yardem said. "How are you?"

"Debased and horrified," she said lightly, making a joke of it. "And you?"

"Well enough. I needed to speak with you for a moment about the Lord Regent."

"Speak away. But first, look at these. Which do you think would be the better one to wear when he comes?"

Yardem flicked a jingling ear and sat on the bed.

"Green," he said. "It's warmer. The Lord Regent's forces will be here in the morning."

"They will," Cithrin said.

"The plan is you make yourself into Palliako's bed slave."

"I prefer the term consort," Cithrin said, putting down the yellow and picking up the green. The color really was much better. Green it was, then.

"I'm going to ask you to reconsider."

"What? You mean about Geder?"

"Yes."

The Tralgu looked up at her. His dark eyes were unreadable. Cithrin felt a knot in her throat and coughed to clear it.

"I can't," she said. "It's the right thing to do."

Yardem nodded, but his frown undercut the motion. "Walk through that with me?"

Cithrin started undoing the pearl buttons that ran down the green dress's back, her fingernail clicking against the hard little spheres. The third one was a degree larger than the others, and she had to force it through its hole.

"I have something Geder Palliako has decided he wants. In exchange for it, I can help more people. If I can just play the role, the rewards in information alone will be beyond any normal price."

"If," he said.

"You think I can't maintain the subterfuge?" Cithrin said with a grin as she stepped into the dress and pulled the sleeves onto her arms.

"I don't," Yardem said. "A year ago, I think you could have. But not now."

"You don't give me credit," she said. "Button this for me, would you?"

Yardem rose with something like a sigh and began fastening the stays and buttons up her back. It was possible that the green wasn't elegant enough for the occasion. Cithrin wasn't certain of the etiquette of giving herself over to the role of Geder's lover. Maybe a dress wasn't called for at all. Maybe she should greet him in a little rouge and a smile. She scowled at the thought and pulled the sleeves a bit straighter.

"Well, I think you're mistaken," she said. "And considering the good we can do, it's the obvious risk to take."

"It's only a risk if you don't know the outcome, ma'am," Yardem said, fixing the last and highest of the buttons. His knuckle brushed the nape of her neck as he finished. "I'd like you to take a moment to pray with me."

"What?" Cithrin asked, turning toward him. Yardem held out his hands to her, palms up. She hesitated for a moment, then took them. Yardem closed his eyes and lowered his head, and she followed his example. As soon as her eyes were closed, the chaos of her mind whipped at her. She tried to gather herself enough to pray or think kind thoughts or whatever it was she was intended to do, but it was as much as she could manage just to keep from opening her eyes, pulling away, and finding some other small task to distract her. She felt a brief but intense resentment of Yardem for imposing on her this way. She had enough to carry without the additional burden of thinking too closely about it.

Yardem let out a calm breath, and she opened her eyes as he looked up.

"Change your mind, ma'am?"

Sorrow bloomed in her and she moved in, hugging the Tralgu close for a moment before letting him go. "Thank you for trying. I can't tell you how much I appreciate it that you care. But this is what I have to do. I don't like it and I don't want it, but this war is what we have. You were the one who told me sex is a woman's natural weapon."

Yardem's ears shot forward.

"I never said that," he said.

"You did. You've just forgotten. It was when we were first going from Vanai to Porte Oliva. We were training, and I kept asking what was a woman's natural weapon. You said sex was."

"No, ma'am, I didn't. We were talking about fighting, and I made the point that on the average, men have longer reach and stronger arms, and weapons are based on reach and strength. A woman who wants to fight has to train harder to come even. I can't recommend using sex in a melee."

They were silent for a moment. Something was shifting in Cithrin's chest. Unwinding like tie rope on a spool losing its tension.

"But," she began and then wasn't sure where to go.

Yardem scratched his chin reflectively. "Sling, maybe. Or a short sword. Not sex."

"But you said—"

"No. I didn't."

"Then who did?" Cithrin asked.

"Believe that was Sandr."

"Oh," Cithrin said. Then a moment later, "Sandr's kind of a pig."

"I've always thought so."

Cithrin looked down. The unwinding sensation in her chest intensified. Something in her was releasing, opening. It felt nauseating and it felt like relief. She pressed her lips together and looked up into Yardem's face. His expression was as placid and calm as ever.

"Yardem?" she said. "I can't do this."

"No, ma'am. You can't. There's a ship waiting. I've given word to everyone that we're leaving, so they won't be caught unprepared. Enen's packed up all the books and ledgers from the office. We can get whatever else you'd like, but we should hurry. The tide's going out in two hours."

Cithrin looked around her room. Her heart was beating fast and strong and true. She plucked the little plant from off her windowsill.

"I'm ready," she said. "Let's go."

The ship was small with a shallow draft and wide sails. It slipped away from the dock seeming to go faster than the wind that carried it. Cithrin stood on the deck. She still had the green dress, but Enen had given her a thick cloak of leather lined with wool that she'd wrapped around her shoulders. The sea was choppy with a million tiny waves jittering and seagulls wheeling in the high air. They didn't have the weight to smooth the swell and drop of the sea, and one of the house guards that Yardem had brought with them was being noisily sick over the side. Cithrin's stomach, on the other hand, felt more solid and calm than it ever had. She was even hungry.

Suddapal receded. The great dark buildings greyed with distance. The great piers that pressed so far out into the water shrank to twigs and the tall ships became small enough to cover with her outstretched thumb. When she looked down into the water, she was surprised to see dark eyes looking up at hers. A pod of the Drowned had grabbed on to the ship, coasting with it like an underwater tail. Cithrin smiled at them and waved. One waved back, and before long, they had let go and fallen back into the depths of the water. By the time the sun fell into the sea, the city was gone.

And if she ever went back there, it would still be gone.

She felt Yardem come up behind her more than heard him. When she glanced back and up, he was standing there placidly, looking out at the pale white wake drawn out behind them and the darkening water.

"Well," she said, "I'm afraid I'm about to disappoint the Lord Regent. I don't imagine he'll take it well."

"To judge from his past, likely not," Yardem said.

"Perhaps I should have left him a letter."

"Saying what, ma'am?"

"I don't know. That I'm sorry. That I didn't mean to hurt him."

"Not sure that matters, ma'am."

"It does to me. He's a terrible person, you know. But he's also not. I don't think I've ever known anyone who managed to make himself so alone."

Yardem grunted, then cleared his throat. "I've known hermits, ma'am. Very few of them burned down cities."

"Fair point," Cithrin said. "Still, I wish there was some way to talk just with the best parts of him."

"Could wish that of anyone," Yardem said.

The boat rose and fell gently. Rose and fell. It would be weeks yet before she reached Porte Oliva and home. She wondered what it would be like, hearing Pyk Usterhall's rough, angry voice and sitting with Maestro Asanpur with his single blind eye and his perfect coffee and all the familiar faces again. She wanted to believe that she would fit back into the same place she had before, that she would find them as they had been, but she doubted it would happen.

She saw now that she had changed, though she still didn't quite understand what she'd become. There was a contradiction in it, because Yardem was right. A year before, she would have been able to go through with it, and now she couldn't. She had become capable of fewer things, and yet she felt freed. She wondered if Magistra Isadau was waiting in Porte Oliva. It was the sort of question that she could answer if anyone could.

"If I'd stayed," she said. "If I'd been his lover, do you think he *might* have changed?"

Yardem stood silently for a long moment, his arms crossed and his ears canted forward.

"No," he said.

Clara

Well, it's mostly the bits the butcher usually throws away, but there's enough salt in it, anyway," Aly said, putting the soup bowl in front of Clara.

"I'm sure it's fine," Clara said, picking up her spoon.

"I'm sure it's not," the other woman said, laughing. "But the company makes it better, eh?"

Aly lived in a small apartment on the fifth story of a narrow building. Her table was small enough that it was cramped even just with the two of them. The weak winter sunlight pressed in through dingy curtains and made the place seem warm and cozy, even though it was in fact almost as cold as the street.

With the court gone from Camnipol and the winter turning the black-cobbled streets to grey, Clara had given more time to the friends she'd made at the Prisoner's Span. Ostin Soukar, the odd little man who kept forcing his way into homes that weren't his, and being caught by the magistrates' men because he'd fallen asleep there. Ishia Man, who was sweet as honey sober but fought like a bull when he got drunk. Aly Koutunin and her son Mihal. They were criminals, and some of them violent. There were many, many people she had met and spoken with whom she'd not choose to be in a room alone with, but taken as a whole, they were not particularly better or worse than the noblemen who debated at the Great Bear and fought in the dueling yards.

"Did you hear about Sasin?" Aly said.

"No," Clara said, sipping at the weak, watery soup. "And I don't dare to ask what's happened this time."

"Tried to take the begging cup from that one-legged Tralgu sets up by the northern gate. You know the one? Well, the one-legged bastard hopped up on his one foot and beat poor Sasin blue with his cane. Now they're both in the pens with all those roach babies."

"Well, warmer than the cages, at least," Clara said.

"Don't know," Aly said. "I'd rather take my chances with the wind than live around Timzinae. I think it's wrong to put them in gaols with real people. Animals live in a menagerie, and they're all just a kind of dragon that got made short and stupid. I say put 'em where they belong. Bread?"

"Please," Clara said. "And…wait, where's my bag? Ah, here. I've brought my own contribution to the meal."

Aly's eyes brightened as Clara pulled the little jar from her bag.

"No. Really? You've got butter?"

"Just a little bit," Clara said. "But enough to share. Here you go."

Aly grinned and began spreading the soft cream on the dark crust of bread.

"You know," Clara said, "the Timzinae weren't any part of what Dawson did."

"Yeah?" Aly said. "Well, not what I've heard, but I suppose you'd be in a better place to know. Still, there's no question that they've been conspiring against the throne. If not your man, then the others. And really, dear, you might not have known it. They had their little hooks into Lord Ternigan, after all, and who would have thought that?"

"I suppose," Clara said, taking back the butter jar.

After their little meal, Aly walked down the street with

her and east, toward the Division. Vincen was huddled by a smithy along with a dozen other people, watching the smith hammering away at his anvil, drawn by the warmth of the forge. Aly took her leave with a half-mocking curtsey, and Clara kissed her cheek. When she put her hand on Vincen's elbow, he turned and smiled.

"Anything interesting?" he asked.

"Not today," she said. "It's astonishing how little palace intrigue changes when one takes away the palace."

The news of Lord Ternigan's death had come first from a cunning man in Camnipol who shared dreams with one on campaign in Kiaria. At first, of course, no one believed it. The dreams of cunning men were swift, but they weren't particularly reliable. Then the birds came with little notes that confirmed it. Lord Ternigan had been plotting against the Lord Regent and Prince Aster, and only Geder Palliako's brilliance and uncanny ability to root out corruption and purify the court had saved the kingdom from another battle on its own soil.

Within hours of the birds' arrival, guardsmen were closing Ternigan's mansion in the city. Granted, there was less to do with the season over and Ternigan off on campaign before that, but what there was—tables, beds, silver—was hauled in carts to the Kingspire. Before the night was through, vandals had broken into the abandoned house and put it to the torch. By morning, Lord Ternigan had gone from the hero of the nation to a loathed traitor and puppet of the Timzinae.

Seeing it play out that way fascinated Clara. She had seen the story of Geder Palliako take form. From his unmasking of Feldin Maas and King Lechan, to Dawson's rebellion, and now to a second Lord Marshal's betrayal. That the facts in each case were utterly dissimilar didn't matter; it was the story that remained the same. A dark conspiracy threatened the kingdom, and Geder Palliako, blessed by the goddess, brought it to light. And while she had expected that there would be a growing sense of fear in the city when Lords Ternigan and Mecilli fell, she'd been wrong on several counts.

First, Mecilli's name hadn't been mentioned, and his house and honor remained intact. But beyond that, and more interesting, was the sense of comfort that the news seemed to bring. As if by repeating the form of last year's betrayals, they had become familiar, and the story's end always left the throne safer and more secure, the dangers lessened. There was even, she thought, a sense of anticipation. A looking ahead to the next traitor, the next betrayal, and the next act of redeeming violence. In one way, she thought the general willingness to embrace stories with that shape and pattern might ease her work of driving Geder's best advisors away from him. But in another, she found herself complicit in the growing legend of Geder Palliako.

"Clara?" Vincen said.

"I'm sorry, dear," she said. "My mind wandering."

"Shall I take you home?"

Clara smiled and tugged on his arm. They walked together through the streets arm in arm. It was a small indiscretion. Even the last stragglers of the court were gone by now, and any who were there on winter business would likely be as pleased not to be seen as she would. Among her new acquaintances, an older woman with a younger lover was hardly cause for comment. Crows called from the eaves and sparrows darted down into the depths of the Division. She had the sudden memory of Dawson looking at Geder in his black leather cloak and the priest in his brown robes. Crows and sparrows, he'd called them.

As they walked, Clara began planning her next letter to

Carse. She could, of course, give a great deal of information about what had happened to Lord Ternigan, but she wasn't certain that would serve her well. Perhaps it would suffice if she could simply repeat what she'd heard on the streets along with an additional fact or two that was private to her. She could also report on the levels of food in Camnipol, and the miserable state of things in Palliako's prisons.

She felt Vincen's steps falter before she knew what was wrong. He drew his arm free from hers and stepped to her side. She followed his gaze. There before the boarding house, a grand carriage sat with footmen and drivers at the ready. The device on the side announced House Skestinin. Clara felt the air leave her body. Something had happened to Jorey. Or Sabiha and the new babe. She walked faster, not running. Not quite.

Jorey sat in the common room like an emerald on dirt. His jacket was a pure white with silver buttons and his cloak was black leather. When she stepped through the doorway, he rose, smiling.

"Jorey?" she said, fighting a bit for air. "What's happened? Where's Sabiha?"

"Sabiha's with her father by now," her son said, stepping forward to take her hands. "And I've come to take you home."

The first taste of fear came to her. Vincen came in behind her, taking his place as a servant, and Abatha behind him, her mouth pinched and distrustful. Clara felt her face grow pale.

"Home? I don't understand. I am home. I live here."

"Not anymore. It would cause a scandal for the Lord Marshal's mother to live in a rented room."

Clara sat down slowly, her head light. Jorey sat on the bench at her side, taking her hand in his own.

"I don't understand."

"You've heard what happened with Lord Ternigan," Jorey said. "A messenger bird caught us at Sevenpol. After all that's happened, Geder decided he wanted someone he trusts as Lord Marshal. And apparently he's been waiting for the moment to help me redeem myself with the court."

"You? After all that Dawson did?"

Jorey's smile lost some of its brightness.

"I repudiated my father in front of the court," Jorey said. "And Geder...considers me his friend. Apparently that's enough. He's given me the army. I'm going to take control of the siege at Kiaria. And what's more, I'm bringing Vicarian with me. Minster Basrahip has given permission for him to come and study under the priests in the field."

"My God," Clara said, pressing her fingers to her lips. "This can't...this can't be right."

"It's a gift, Mother," Jorey said. "It's everything we were hoping for."

She felt as though her heart were dying. A little hole had opened in her chest, and everything was flowing out through it like water draining from a basin. *I don't want to go. I'm happy here. I can't be the woman I was before. Don't go. Don't do this.*

And then, *Get a hold of yourself.*

She smiled and lifted her chin. Jorey wrapped his hand tightly around hers.

"The last time you went to war with Geder Palliako, it ended badly," she said. "Are you certain this is what you want?"

Jorey kissed her hand. His smile was gone now, and the beautiful jacket and cloak seemed more like a costume than the clothes of the Lord Marshal of Antea.

"It doesn't matter what I want, Mother. It's what I worked

for, and it's what I have to do," he said. "Can you under-stand that?"

In the doorway, Vincen Coe stood with his eyes down-cast, his expression empty. The nights of sleeping in his arms were over. The mornings waking up beside him. In Lord Skestinin's house, there would be no more walking arm in arm. He would call her *my lady* again, and not Clara. The injustice of it was exquisite.

It's what I worked for, and it's what I have to do. She had raised him in her image after all.

"I understand," Clara said. "Let me gather my things."

Lord Skestinin's manor had been closed for the winter, and setting a house in order wasn't a simple task. When Clara stepped down from the carriage, she could already hear the voices leaking out to the street. Inside, the dining room was still draped in dustcloth, and the pale halls were damp from having only just been scrubbed. Three maids were turning down her new room for her. A widow's room with beauti-ful view of the winter-dead gardens and a narrow bed. She sat on it as she might have on the creaking frame that she'd become used to. The mattress was so soft, she felt as though she were sinking into it. As if it were devouring her.

"Will there be anything else, my lady?"

Vincen stood in the doorway, and his face looked grey as stone. His hair was pulled back and he stood stiff and straight. He would have rooms in the servants' quarters now. A bunk and maybe a small stove. A box for his things. *I didn't choose this*, she thought. *Forgive me.*

"Not at the moment, Vincen," she said. "Thank you."

"Always, my lady," he said, and the tone in his voice made one of the maids look up in surprise. So not even that much was permitted. Clara watched him walk away. She waited for the space of two breaths, then rose, pretended to brush dust from her skirts, and strode out to the corridor as if she owned the house and everything in it. Vincen was walking slowly, his hands clasped behind him.

"Coe?" she said. "Might I have a word with you?"

He turned as if stung and stood there silently. She raised her eyebrows.

"C-certainly," he said.

"Excellent. This way, please."

She walked toward the gardens, but instead of opening the iron and glass gate that led into the yard, she turned left into the gardener's alcove. As she'd suspected, it was empty.

"Close the door, please," she said.

"My lady..."

"Stop that, Vincen. Stop it now."

He hesitated. There was fury in his eyes.

"Clara," he said.

"Much better. Now close the door."

"It will ruin you," he said. "*I* will ruin you. When you were disgraced, it was different. You were like us. But you're rising again, and if we're—" He stopped, and began again, his voice hushed. "If we're seen alone together, it will destroy you."

"I have been destroyed," she said. "It didn't kill me."

"It will hurt your sons. Your daughters. Your standing in court. I won't risk you. I can't do that."

"Do you really think I would be the first woman in court to have an affair?"

Vincen closed. She saw it happen.

"I'm sure many women in places of power have had affairs with servants," he said. And there it was. The gulf she could not cross. He was a servant again, and she was a woman of standing.

"You said you would follow me anywhere," she said. "Perhaps you meant anywhere but back."

"I will go find my quarters, m'lady. With your permission."

She stepped over to him, reached past him, and pushed the door closed. His mouth was hard and unresponsive at first. But only at first.

"I have not changed," she said. "I am the same woman I was this morning. It's only circumstances."

"I know, Clara," he said. "And I'm the same man. It's just... it's just that I'm having a terrible day."

"I am too. But it won't be the last day there is."

He kissed her again, and there was a real hunger in it this time. She put her arms around his shoulders and pulled him close. They stood there for a long moment and then stepped back from each other.

"Find your rooms," she said, "and then explore this house from the basement to the roof. Know it as well as you would a hunting ground. Learn everyone's name and their place and, as best you can, their schedules. I will do the same. I don't know how we can make this work, but we will."

"And your letters to Carse?"

"Those too," she said. "Though it seems I won't be trying to alienate Geder from his new Lord Marshal. Which is a pity as it went so well last time."

A distant voice caught her. A man's voice calling *Mother!*

"Vicarian's come," she said, opening the door again and pushing Vincen out before her. "Go. Now. I will find you later tonight."

She listened to Vincen's footsteps fade and turned to look at the ghostly reflection of herself in the windows of the gate. The woman who looked back seemed almost unfamiliar. She smoothed her hair.

"Well, then," she said, and the woman in the glass looked

back at her with a gentle smirk. She turned back to the main part of the house, slipping again into the guise of noble-woman and baroness, and followed her boy's voice to the main part of the house. She found Jorey and Vicarian stand-ing in the front hall grinning at each other. Vicarian's robes were the brown of the spider priests, and his face looked thin-ner than when she'd seen him last, but also oddly bright. She had the sense that if she touched him, he would feel fevered.

"Mother," Vicarian said, catching sight of her.

"No, stay there," she said. "Let me look at you."

Vicarian laughed and took a pose. The initiation hadn't changed him so much, then. She came forward and embraced him, and there was no strange heat, no sense that he had changed. It felt good having her boy back in her arms. Two of her boys.

"So," she said. "You've studied the cult of the spider god-dess. Has she made you pious at last?"

"You know," Vicarian said, taking her arms in a way uncomfortably similar to Vincen, "I think it actually may have."

He led Clara down the corridor toward the drawing room. The servants scurried around them like mice.

"A pious priest," Jorey said. "That's a miracle to begin with."

"No," Vicarian said, his voice becoming serious. "No, really. There was nothing I learned in any of the studying I did before this that compares. The goddess isn't just a set of stories we've gathered up and decided to guide our lives by. She's real."

"I would have said thinking God was real was obligatory for a priest," Clara said, stepping into the room. The dust covers had been removed and a fire set in the grate. Vicarian shook his head.

"You would, wouldn't you? But the seminary isn't like that. We talk and we read and we pray, but it's corrupt. It's all empty and corrupt, because you only have to say that you believe. With the goddess, it's not like that at all. It's... hard sometimes. But she opened the *world* for me."

Clara smiled and nodded.

I've lost him too, she thought.

Geder

Until he was set to travel across Elassae with three hundred sword-and-bows as his personal guard, Geder hadn't understood how exhausted his men had become. They pulled themselves up in the morning, thin-faced and ash-skinned. They broke down camp, loaded the carts, and moved across the fields and hills where no dragon's road led. Even the mounted men seemed to sag down in the saddles. They looked to Geder like the spirits of the dead that were supposed to ride with his armies. The short days and cold weather meant stopping to make camp when it hardly seemed past midday, and then long nights in his tent. Geder was torn between the tugging impatience to be with Cithrin in Suddapal and a horrified sympathy for the men, brought to this sad state by Ternigan's mismanagement.

"Do you think he meant this to happen?" he asked Basrahip one night after they'd finished a meal of chicken and rice. Peasant food, but more than the soldiers had.

"I do not know, Prince Geder," Basrahip said. "And he is beyond all asking now."

The leather walls of the tent popped and boomed in the wind. Outside, there were no trees, but a forest of stumps. Everything had been harvested for the fires of the army months before. The farms stripped, the animals slaughtered, and the countryside left bare. Even the low brown grass of winter seemed dead beyond reclaiming. It looked to Geder like the empty plates left after a feast. A world that had been eaten. He couldn't imagine how it would be coaxed to bloom again in spring. The burned farmhouses would sow no seeds, the unturned fields wouldn't raise up grain or fruit. If there had been cattle or sheep, they were dead now, or else spirited underneath the mountain at Kiaria. The war had left wounds on the body of the land that would take years to heal, and even then there would be scars. Geder found himself wanting badly to be away.

Basrahip sucked thoughtfully on the bones of the birds, stripping the last slivers of flesh from them. His plate was a pile of pink sticks in a jumble.

"I was thinking," Geder said. "It might be wiser to go on ahead. We're almost to Suddapal. If we took a dozen of the strongest men and rode fast, we'd be on the outskirts of the city in two days at most."

"If you would like," Basrahip said.

"But do you think it would be safe?"

Basrahip turned his calm gaze on Geder and smiled.

"It will not matter if we fall now. Even if we do, others will come and carry her banner. The will of the goddess is alive in the world. You are her chosen and I am her basrahip. And even we are—" He paused, looking around him. He picked up a thin, rubbery bone. "Even we are as this before her."

"Yes," Geder said. "I don't actually find that as reassuring as you might expect."

Basrahip laughed as if Geder had made a joke.

That night, Geder sat up, unable to sleep. The only sounds were the wind and the moaning of his suffering men. He'd read reports of winter campaigns, and they had all sounded unpleasant, frankly miserable, but they hadn't prepared him for this. Sitting at his camp desk with a small lantern, he watched his breath ghosting. He didn't like to think of it, but perhaps Ternigan's treachery was only partly to blame. Almost all the men of fighting age had spent most of a year in Asterilhold before they went to Sarakal, and now Elassae. Even with the will and power of the goddess working for them, there were limits to how much work a body could do. It was clear now that Ternigan, whether through incompetence or malice, had done the army terrible damage. There was a part of Geder that wanted to send them all home, to let them rest. Only that would leave the heart of the Timzinae conspiracy still safely in their stronghold.

But perhaps there would be a way to send some home, at least. If they reduced the number of men in the field to only enough to keep the forces trapped in the stronghold from escaping rather than trying to assault the inner doors again, for instance. And there were more priests now, so that if the Timzinae decided at some point to accept parley—

When he heard the first shout, he thought it was only some guardsman, drunk and overly merry. Then another came. And another. The night was alive with voices. He rose from his desk, his heart fluttering in his chest. The unmistakable sounds of weapons came through his tent walls. He grabbed his sword and ran out more from fear than courage.

Outside the tent, the camp was in chaos. To his left, down a gentle slope, the tents of his army were being knocked askew. He saw his own men flailing desperately at the dark bodies of Timzinae. To his right, a half dozen enemy soldiers were by the makeshift corral. The gate was knocked down, and they were whipping the beasts out into the night. His personal guard were all around his tent in a circle, their blades at the ready.

"What are you doing?" Geder shouted at them. "We're being attacked! Go help them!"

Someone screamed from the encampment, but Geder couldn't tell who or where. The pounding hooves of the escaping horses was growing louder. His guard didn't move.

"Didn't you hear me?" Geder screamed. "Don't just stand there! We're being attacked."

The riders came out of the darkness. Three men on horseback, barreling into the rough formation of his guard, swinging soot-black blades. Geder lifted his blade and danced away.

"That's him," one of the riders shouted. "The fat one. That's Palliako."

"To me!" Geder shrieked. "Assassins! To me!"

His guardsmen outnumbered the riders four to one, but the mounted men had the advantage of height and power. Geder kept backing away into the barren lands. There was nothing to use for cover, no stand of trees or deep-cut ditch to hide in. His lungs burned with fear and cold. He could see a group of his sword-and-bows running toward him, and he tried to get to them and the safety of their weapons, but it was too far. He heard the pounding hoofbeats coming. He turned, lifting his blade with a cry of despair. The great black beast sped toward him, the rider standing high in his stirrups, a sword in his upraised hand that seemed to blot out the stars.

The impact came from the side and sent Geder tumbling out of the path of the charge. In the moonlight, the brown robe looked like a paler shade of night. The priest stood before the attacker with no time to so much as dodge.

"Basrahip!" Geder screamed, realizing as he did that it wasn't the high priest, but one of the new initiates. The blade came down, taking the new priest in the jaw and spinning his body as he fell. Blood spattered horse and rider, and the swordsman leaped from his saddle toward Geder. The moonlight shone on tight bronze scales.

A Jasuru. Geder felt a stab of confusion and outrage. Why would a Jasuru want to hurt him? He'd only made war on Timzinae. He fumbled for his sword.

The Jasuru stopped and clutched at his eye. Behind them, the horse he had been riding began to scream and kick. Geder's sword-and-bows arrived at last, pressing themselves between Geder and his attacker, but the Jasuru had dropped his sword and started clawing at his eyes. He couldn't be certain, but Geder thought there was blood on the man's fingers. The black horse screamed again, bucked, and ran madly away into the night.

"Stand away," Basrahip said. "Do not approach. The hand of the goddess is upon him now."

"Fuck," one of the soldiers at Geder's side said. "Can she do that?"

The Jasuru fell to his knees and began to scream low in his throat. He thrashed, clawing at his arms and neck. Geder looked around. His personal guard had pulled one of the other riders from the saddle and were savaging him. The other seemed to have fled. Basrahip stood at Geder's side, the one remaining initiate behind him. The Jasuru screamed again. Basrahip raised his hands and walked toward the screaming man.

"You feel the hand of the goddess, sinner," Basrahip said. "Your days of lies are ended. Say now, who sent you?"

"Get them off of me!" the Jasuru howled. "Please God, get them *out* of me!"

"You have no hope but me," Basrahip said. "Listen to my voice. You have no hope but me. Who sent you?"

The Jasuru collapsed to the ground, and Geder thought for a moment that he'd died. Then, weakly, his voice came.

"Callon. Callon Cane."

Basrahip turned back. His eyes met Geder's, and Geder shrugged. The name was nothing to him.

"Who is Callon Cane?"

"For God's sake, kill me. Kill me."

"I am your only hope of peace. Who is Callon Cane?"

"He's some rich bastard in Herez. Put a price on the Lord Regent's head. Me and Siph and Lachor found a mess of angry Timzinae ready to help us if we made the try. Thought if we hit fast—Oh *God.* They're in me. They're under my skin! Kill me! Please, by all that's holy, *kill me!*"

"No," Basrahip said. "That will not happen. The hand of the goddess is upon you now."

The Jasuru screamed, his body arching until only his toes and the top of his head were touching the ground. Basrahip turned back to Geder.

"You must not approach him, Prince Geder. You and your men should return to your places. There is no danger now."

Geder felt a wash of relief, but he didn't sheathe his sword.

"What happened to him?"

"The hand of the goddess is upon him," Basrahip said. "He is our brother now. We will care for him as we would any initiate to her truth."

Geder's jaw dropped.

"Are you serious? Basrahip, he just tried to *kill* me."

"The goddess is upon him. He will not rebel again." The Jasuru screamed again and kept on screaming, barely pausing to catch his breath. Basrahip put a wide hand on Geder's shoulder. "The lies and sin are being burned out of him. It will take time, but he will become holy or he will die."

"You're sure about this?" Geder asked.

"I am certain."

"Well. All right," Geder said. "But this won't make it easier to sleep."

Suddapal was a strangely diffuse city. It had no wall, no defenses. Not even a solid marker to say where the city began. Shacks and low buildings became a bit more frequent. Paths crossed the wider track that Geder and his men had been following. And mile by mile Suddapal grew up around them. The spot where Fallon Broot and his men waited to greet him wasn't particularly different from any other, but they made it the edge of Suddapal by their presence. Geder gave the order to sound the halt and climbed down from his carriage.

Fallon Broot looked older than the months since he'd left with the invading army could explain. His face seemed pinched, his skin an unhealthy color. Geder felt a rush of sympathy for him. Broot was a decent man, and well-meaning, but possibly not suited for the burdens of authority.

"Lord Regent," Broot said, dropping from his saddle into a deep bow. "Welcome to your city."

Geder grinned. "You don't need to bow to me, Broot. We've known each other long enough we can afford a little informality, don't you think?"

Broot's smile was sickly. "Good of you, my lord."

"I don't want any feasts," Geder said, setting off deeper into the city at a walk. Broot followed, and Geder's personal guard behind them. "I'm not here to take control of anything. It's more private business. You understand."

"Of course, Lord Regent," Broot said.

"All going well in the city, I hope?"

"Some troubles," Broot said. "Nothing desperate so far.

We've...ah. Well, we've found some evidence of a group that was spiriting Timzinae away."

"What do you mean *away*?"

"Hide them on ships. Sneak them into caravans. Away."

That wasn't good. It was almost certain that any of the people central to the conspiracy against him would have been the first to escape. They were, after all, the ones with the most power. The most connections. They'd been able to corrupt Lord Ternigan and Dawson Kalliam. These were a dangerous people.

They reached a corner, and Geder paused, letting Broot show him the way, only instead the man stopped, laced his hands behind his back, and faced Geder like he was sizing up his executioner. Between the gravity of his demeanor and his lush mustache, Geder couldn't help thinking he looked vaguely comedic.

"Have you broken the conspiracy?" Geder asked.

"In a manner of speaking. We've reason to believe it's not operating any longer."

"I don't understand."

"We've had several people confess to the minister you sent us that they were brought into a group for this purpose by Isadau rol Ennanamet, voice of the Medean bank in Suddapal. And a Timzinae."

"Hmm," Geder said. "What does Cithrin say about it?"

"Cithrin bel Sarcour, you mean? She doesn't say much, my lord. She fled the city last night along with all her people."

Geder smiled and shook his head. Broot had spoken, but something must have distracted Geder. He hadn't heard the words.

"Well, where's the bank? We can go there now."

"She's not there, my lord. She and her guards and what was left of her staff got on a boat last night. They're gone."

Something cold was happening in Geder's chest. Some kind of thickening. He hoped he wasn't getting sick.

"No," he said. "That didn't happen. She knew I was coming. I wrote to her."

"That's as may be. But what I'm telling you is the woman left the city. She and the old magistra before her were shuffling Timzinae out of the city right under our noses. And with your grant of immunity," Broot said, an angry buzz coming into his voice, "there wasn't anything we could do to stop her."

The meaning sank in, and the coldness in Geder's chest detonated. For a moment, he couldn't hear. Then he was standing in the street, his fist hurting badly, and Fallon Broot was on the ground with blood flowing down his mustache and shocked expression.

"Take me to her house," Geder said. "Do it now."

The compound of the Medean bank stood deserted. The doors swung open and closed in the wind. Straw from the stable littered the yard, caught up in tiny whirlwinds. Geder walked through the abandoned halls and corridors, tears running down his cheeks. He'd ordered Broot and his guards to wait in the street. He didn't want anyone to see him.

She was gone. He'd come all this way for her, and she was gone. He'd told her how he felt for her, and she was gone. He loved her, and when he came to her to feed that love, to make it something that would have lived for the ages, she'd betrayed him and left. She hadn't even had the kindness to tell him to his face.

He found a small bedroom with a mattress and pillow still in place. He lay down and curled up into himself the way an animal might to guard a wound. He didn't feel sad or angry. He didn't feel anything. He was empty in a way he'd never felt before. Cithrin had emptied him. When he began to sob, it was a distant sensation, but with every breath it grew closer and harder. When the grief finally came, it was like nothing he'd felt before except once. When he'd been a boy and his mother had died, it had felt just like this. His body shuddered and tensed. His breastbone ached like someone had punched him, and tears flowed down his cheeks like a rainstorm. He was sure they could hear him in the street, sure that they knew, and he wanted to stop, but he couldn't. He'd started, and now he was too far gone to stop. He raged and he wept and he kicked the bed to pieces and ripped the pillow apart with his teeth and then collapsed on the floor, beaten and humiliated.

It was almost night when he drew the shell of his body up, blew his nose on a scrap of the ruined mattress, and did what he could to clean his face. His eyes felt like someone had rubbed sand in them, and his chest ached to the touch. His limbs felt heavy, like he was waking from too deep a sleep.

Broot and his men were still where he'd left them, standing in the street. Basrahip had joined them as well. Geder walked out to them and shrugged.

"You were right," he said. "She's gone."

Broot's nose was swollen and bruised. When he spoke, he sounded congested. "I'm sorry, my lord."

"Not your fault," Geder said. "This was my mistake. I… misunderstood."

Basrahip put his arm around Geder's shoulder, and Geder leaned into the priest.

"I'll call your carriage," Broot said, and a few minutes later Geder was rattling down the rough, wide roads past squares and marketplaces, all of them blighted and emptied by the winter cold. He thought he would never feel warm again, and he didn't care. Suddapal spun past his eyes without being seen. When the carriage stopped, he was mildly surprised to find himself at the protector's mansion. A footman helped him down. Basrahip helped him up the stairs.

"Jorey," Geder said. "I need to get a message to Jorey."

"Yes, Prince Geder."

"We have to take the army back from Kiaria. Just leave enough to keep them from getting out, take back the rest."

"As you say," Basrahip agreed.

"I need them. I need all of them. And the priests. I need them too. I need everyone."

"They are yours," Basrahip said. "You are blessed of the goddess, and her will can bring you all that you wish."

"Good," Geder said.

Basrahip paused in the doorway.

"Tell me," he said. "What do you want?"

When Geder spoke, his voice was rough and sharp as a serrated blade.

"I want to find Cithrin."

Marcus

In the aftermath of the storm, the sky was as wide, calm, and clear as a highwayman's smile, and Marcus put as much faith in it. With every step along the rocky shore, he was aware of the capricious power of the world around him. The clouds in the sky might be nothing or they might be the vanguard of another storm bent on wiping them all from the face of the world. And while they might be able to find their way back to the lodge house of Order Murro, they also might not. Or the Haaverkin might decide not to extend hospitality. Or, for that matter, the earth might open up and swallow them all.

Truth was, Marcus was feeling more than a little jumpy.

The stone shore stretched out before and behind them. Frozen waves cracked and shattered. Spears of ice lay white and silver in the sunlight. The air was thick with the scents of salt and cold. Even wrapped in half a dozen layers, he started shivering if they stopped for too long. It was the third day of their search along this stretch of shore, and the tide was beginning to turn already. If they didn't come across something soon, it would mean another day's waiting. Another chance for bad weather or angry Haaverkin or any of a thousand complications and dangers Marcus hadn't thought of yet. The poisoned sword was slung across his back. It wasn't useful against all threats, but it might help with some.

"Hey!" Sandr called. "Look at this!"

Marcus turned, his senses sharpening and ready for danger. Sandr stood near the high-water mark where the stones became land. He held what looked like a long, crooked stick, bent once in the middle and once at the end.

"What is it?" Cary called.

"I think it's a crab's leg," Sandr replied. "Big, isn't it? Catch one of these, it would be a good meal."

"It would or you," Cary said.

Sandr shrugged and dropped it back where it had been. Marcus walked forward. The stones grated against each other under his feet. He swept his gaze back and forth across the ground in front of him, moving slowly, his eyes a little unfocused, waiting for some detail to draw his attention. So far, Sandr was winning the prize for most interesting discovery.

"You're sure about this, Kit?"

"No," Kit said. "I'm sure that old Kirot thought there was something out here, but he may have been wrong."

Marcus stepped across a gap between two larger stones, wary of the thin coating of ice that made them slick and treacherous.

"Would have been nice if we had a damn clue what we were looking for," he said.

"Not a giant, not a sword," Kit said. "Not a weapon, not a medicine, and no sort of armor."

"How about a rock?" Marcus said. "You think any of these might be a magic rock?"

"Possibly," Kit said. "But probably not."

The storm had lasted three days, and so for three days and nights they'd sat in a the great, smoky lodge house, trading stories with the Haaverkin and playing songs. Cary and Smit had danced a number in a way that caught the attention of the Antean force and left Marcus wondering whether there was something more going on between them than he'd guessed, but the Haaverkin didn't seem impressed by it. People who weren't thick with insulating fat and heavily tattooed didn't have much erotic charge for this crowd.

When at last the weather broke, Dar Cinlama and his men packed their things, offered to travel with them one last time, and then headed south for Borja before they froze in place. Marcus had to admit that their plan had an appeal. Dar Cinlama was powerfully impressed with himself, but he told a good tale and he didn't drink more than his share of the beer. It was enough to win him some respect as far as Marcus was concerned, even with who he was working for.

"How do you think it's going out there?" Marcus asked.

"Out there?"

"In the world. Where there are people."

"I don't know," Kit said. "At a guess, poorly."

"That was my thought too." He stepped forward. A flash of yellow in one of the small tidepools caught his attention, and he leaned close. A tiny starfish clung to a stone. Probably not the source of earth-shattering magic. "Do you think Cithrin and Yardem are all right?"

"I don't know."

"That's why they call it a guess."

Kit smiled. "Well, then, since I know that they are both clever and competent, I would guess that they are fine, whatever's happened."

"But you don't know that."

"No."

They moved on, Marcus sweeping his eyes over the ground, then moving forward. Sweeping, and moving forward. Almost half an hour later, he spoke again.

"I keep thinking about the war. About how it's just like all the other wars I've seen, only it isn't."

"I'm not certain what you mean," Kit said, and squatted down.

"Find something?"

The actor reached into one of the salt puddles. When he drew out his hand, he had a thin stem of hollow bone.

"Pipe stem," Kit said. "It might been carried in by the waves."

"Or it might have been dropped by someone walking this same path. I'm going to call that a good sign."

"But you'd been talking about war."

"Right. I've seen a lot of wars fought for a lot of reasons. Pride. Fear. Power. The right to use land. Trying to keep someone else from using land. Even just the bull-blind love of winning. And I look at what Antea's been doing, and I see all of that. But the other thing—and I've always seen this no matter who's fighting and whatever they're fighting for—is once you're in a war, you want out of it. You want to win or you want to sue for peace or you want to get away from the mad bastards who are stabbing at you. Even the ones that love winning don't love the war. And that's not something I see."

"Ah. I understand. You're thinking of this as if Antea were at war."

The stone under Marcus's foot shifted and he danced back. "There's some evidence that it is."

"Consider that Antea is waging war the way that a horse leads a cavalry charge. It seems to me it is being ridden by men like myself. Perhaps Antea will rise and spread across the world with the goddess at the reins. Or it may founder and be abandoned for another champion or some number of others. When you look at Antea, you see the enemy. I see the first among victims."

"Odd kind of victim when you get all the power from it."

"I don't fear this high priest as much as I do his first enemy within the temple," Kit said.

"How do you figure that?"

"We were pure when we were in one village in the depth of the Keshet. Every day, we heard the high priest's voice. Now there are temples that are weeks to travel between. New temples being built. New initiates, I would assume. If not yet, then certainly soon. And the new initiates will bring their own experiences. Their own prejudices."

"I thought your goddess ate their minds."

Kit laughed. "Think of who you're talking with, Marcus. I am not the only apostate in history. I see no reason to think I'm the last. But the next one perhaps will understand some piece of doctrine differently. Instead of finding doubt, he may honestly and sincerely believe something that other priests in other places don't, and none of them will have a single voice to keep them from drifting apart. What the spiders do—let's not call it the goddess—is erase the ability of good men to question. They eat doubt. And when there are enough temples far enough flung from each other, and their understandings drift apart, it seems to me there will be a war of zealots and fanatics that will churn the world in blood. And I don't see how Antea or anyplace else will be immune."

"I'm not having a great upwelling of optimism about this, Kit."

"I think we are living in dark times," Kit said. "As dangerous, I would guess, as any since the fall of the dragons. But the world is unpredictable, and I take a great deal of comfort from that."

"Glad someone does," Marcus said.

The other actors—Mikel and Cary, Hornet and Smit, Sandr and Charlit Soon—were all spread along the shore from the ice-choked waterline to the edge of the land. All of them walked slowly and carefully. And by and large, they found nothing. The waves pressed slowly closer, driving them together in a smaller and smaller space. If whatever it was they were looking for was out near the low-water mark, they would walk by it and never know better. If it was lost among the stones or the caves and outcroppings near the shore, they had a better chance, and ignorance made one strategy as good as the next.

"I thought it was interesting that Dar Cinlama didn't know what he was looking for," Marcus said. "Do you think your old friends do?"

"I don't know, but I would suspect that they have some idea, even if one that's warped by time and misunderstanding."

"You don't think they just made it all up?"

Kit looked pained.

"Sorry," Marcus said. "Didn't mean to step on a sore toe twice."

"I believe that you're right that something drove them back to the temple, and that fear of it became a prison of sorts, until something happened that gave them a kind of permission to return. A story that made coming back into the world a better thing than hiding."

"But what that was?"

"I can't guess."

Near the shoreline, Smit stepped out from a small cave and put his hands to his mouth, shouting to be heard over the roar and crackle of the surf. "Think I found something."

Marcus turned and started making his way over, Kit following close behind. If it was another false find, it was still getting close enough to sundown that they'd need to decide whether to end the day's search or press on. The other players gathered around as well, until all of them were in a semi-circle by a cliff face at the shore. Marcus had the feeling of a group meeting being called, which wasn't quite what he'd been hoping for.

"What am I looking at, Smit?" Marcus said. "Apart from another hole in the ground, I mean."

"I went down a bit. The stone changes down there. Gets smooth. Like someone worked it."

Marcus eyed the darkness and sighed.

"Well, it's not as though we had a better plan," he said.

It took the better part of an hour to send Mikel and Hornet back to the cart and have them return with lanterns. Marcus went first. The first thing that surprised him was how deep they had to go in the cave before the walls changed. Either Smit had night vision like a Southling or he was braver than Marcus had given him credit for. And the second thing that surprised him was when they did. The roughness of the tunnel was smoothed, and distinct walls appeared. A slightly vaulted ceiling. A floor that would have been smooth and even if it hadn't been for generations of debris building up on it.

"Kit?" Marcus said, scraping the wall with his thumbnail. "Does that look like dragon's jade to you?"

"It does, a bit, yes," Kit said.

"Don't suppose you're at all curious what's at the end of this."

"In point of fact, I am a bit," Kit said.

They moved forward slowly. Cautiously. Marcus kept his torch high and behind him to keep the flames from spoiling his vision. After almost a hundred yards, the passage began to open and widen, and Marcus and Kit stepped out together into a great chamber. A massive black shape lay curled before them. Its snout was tucked under a massive wing like a bird in cold weather. A profound awe made Marcus drop to one knee. Awe and soul-pressing fear.

The animal was magnificent. Even covered by dust and lichen, the scales seemed almost to radiate darkness. Their torchlight fell into it the way it did into the great bowl of the night sky.

"Kit?" Marcus said in a whisper.

"Yes?"

"That's not a statue, is it."

"I don't believe it is."

The chamber the dragon slept in was massive. Images and writing covered the walls. None of it was anything Marcus could make sense of, but it was familiar all the same. The way a child knew to back away from a precipice, Marcus knew those images. They had been burned into instinct that had lasted for all of human history, and he felt himself responding to them now. Red-black streaks showed where iron sconces had been in the walls, the metal rotting away over time until there was nothing of them left but a stain.

"Follow me," Marcus said, and moved off slowly, walking the perimeter of the chamber. On the farther side, there was a small alcove with a cistern in it that looked as though it had been collecting mold and mist for centuries at the least. When they had completed their circuit of the room, Marcus sat as still as he could manage, watching the great ribcage until he was certain that the slow rise and fall wasn't the product of his imagination. It was breathing. Marcus felt himself trembling.

"Well," Marcus said, his voice low.

"Yes."

"If you have any thoughts you'd like to share about this, I'd be open to hearing them."

"When I was at the temple," Kit said, "we were taught that the dragons were an abomination. That the goddess preceded everything, including time and the world, and that the dragons, in their pride, had tried to claim the world for themselves, taking it from her. The fall of the dragons was supposed to have been the last great struggle between the goddess and the dragons."

"So the one thing we can be sure of is that whatever happened, it wasn't that."

"Yes," Kit said, "and still, there may be some grain of truth to it. The dragons, at least, were real."

"Some evidence for that, yes."

"And there was a fall. And the priests of the spider goddess disliked the dragons. Possibly they even feared them."

"So maybe that glorious bastard over there is the natural enemy of the spiders."

"Probably."

"Or maybe it's more dangerous than they are, and our best plan would be to back quietly out the way we came in and never come back here."

"That's also possible," Kit said. "But whatever we do, it would be best to do it before the tide comes in. I think the water will block our way out."

"I'd rather that didn't happen," Marcus agreed. "All right, then. So the choice is we try to wake that thing up or we leave now and never come back."

"Yes."

"And do you see us walking away from this?"

Kit was silent for a moment, and when he spoke, his voice was thick with regret and dread.

"Honestly? No. I don't."

"Me neither," Marcus said, and rose to his feet. The dragon shifted in its sleep, a slight rocking back and forth that made the whole chamber tremble a little bit. "Stay here, Kit. This is about to get interesting."

Slowly, Marcus approached the dragon. Drawing closer made the scale of the thing clear. It was as tall as three men standing on each other's shoulders, and when it uncurled, it might be as long as ten laid end to end. Marcus doubted it would be able to open its wings in the chamber. And now that he thought of it, he wasn't entirely sure how the great bastard had gotten in here in the first place. Or how it would get out.

The light of his torch glowed back at him from the dusty scales as he walked to where the massive head was tucked under its wing. Once, the books said, the dragons had been the masters of the world, and all of humanity had been their slaves. And he was about to try to wake one up.

"I hope this is a good idea," he muttered, then cleared his throat. "Um. Excuse me."

The dragon didn't stir. Marcus went closer, put his hand on the thing's head. Its skull was the size of a horse, and there was a strange beauty to it that Marcus felt himself drawn to by instinct. When he touched the scales, they flexed under his fingers.

"Excuse me. You need to wake up now."

He looked over his shoulder at Kit. The old actor held up his hands. It was fair enough. Kit hadn't woken dragons before either. Marcus sighed, then took a deep breath and shouted.

"Hey! Nap time's over! Wake the hell up!" He turned back toward Kit. "I don't think this is going to be that simple. Do you think maybe there's some sort of ritual or... I don't know. A magic drum or something?"

Kit's eyes went wide and he took an involuntary step back. Marcus felt his own blood turn cold. Slowly, he turned back to the dragon. It hadn't moved, but the one vast eye was open. Marcus saw himself reflected in the vast amber depths of it. He wanted nothing more than to run. There was no sense of threat from the vast eye. No malice. Only a danger as deep and profound as religion.

The worst it can do is kill me, Marcus told himself, and there was more comfort in the thought than he'd expected.

"It's time to wake up," he said again.

The dragon's expression shifted from annoyance to confusion with a powerful eloquence. It was as if Marcus had known dragons all his life and become familiar with the small cues of their emotions. The intimacy of it was unearned, and it disturbed Marcus to his bones.

"You need to wake up now."

The noise was low, like the rumbling of distant thunder. The dragon's vast body began to shift, and Marcus danced back, his hand reaching reflexively for his sword.

The dragon drew its head from under its vast wing and turned the near-physical weight of its attention on them both. When it spoke, its voice was perfectly clear and deeper than mountains. It was like hearing a great king's orchestra strike a single complex chord, only the sound had a meaning besides its terrible beauty.

"Drakkis?" it said.

Entr'acte

Inys, Brother and Clutch-Mate to the Dragon Emperor

Before his eyes, Aastapal fell. The great perch-spires burned, and the library of stones shrieked in its pain. Morade's soldiers held the sky to the south, ten thousand strong. Asteril's cunning slave-run craft dove through the high air, daring to stand against the force of dragons. As he watched, one of the great mechanisms dove, its blades shining in the red light of the falling sun. It caught the wing of a soldier caste, and dragon and craft fell together, joined like lovers in their violence. Somewhere among the attackers, he could smell Morade.

"We must go," Erex said, nuzzling his wing in an offer of comfort. Inys had met his lover on the feeding grounds there below them where the blood-corrupted slaves were slaughtering one another even now. "Inys, I smell him too. Your brother is coming. We can't be here when he arrives."

Inys raised his crest in acknowledgment, but couldn't bring himself to speak. The empire was crumbling. Already Morade and Asteril had shattered the fifth orb. Old Sirrick was dead, her body fallen into the sea. She had been the wisest of them all, and the violence had bested her. What could they hope for now besides a short death?

"Inys," Erex said again.

"I know," Inys said. His heart thick with grief, he turned

and launched himself toward the northern sky, leaving behind the burning city.

It had started as no more than the usual rivalry. Three clutch-mates vying for the emperor's favor. Each of them had made their great works for presentation at the fire court. Asteril had spent decades laboring on his birds of living copper. Morade built his deep-water city and the holes in the ocean through which even the widest-winged could soar to reach it. Inys had composed a poem that linked the five levels of thought to the five fallen elements. It should have been only that. Inys had only thought what he'd done a prank. Mean-spirited, perhaps, but not outside the realm of etiquette. But as soon as the waters fell in on Morade's great work, as soon as he saw the grief and rage in his clutch-mate's eyes, he knew he had gone too far. And now Morade had as well, and innocent Asteril was gone, his scales dulled forever by the poisons he poured into the culling blades for the uncorrupt. Inys mourned his brother, but then he mourned everything now.

Morade's forces outnumbered his own by a third again, and the slaves on which Inys had relied were taken from him, driven to self-slaughter and chaos by Morade's cold-eyed lust for vengeance. That the world died made no difference to his brother, so long as Great Morade was the one who killed it.

Inys rose on the wide air, speeding with Erex to the secret hold and his meeting with Drakkis Stormcrow, the last of his slave-generals. They had attempted battle and they had failed. But Inys's low cunning had begun this war. And perhaps his low cunning could end it.

The shadowed city lay buried on the barren coast, its perches and sunning grounds dug in low enough to be invisible to any but those flying directly above. Of all the strongholds the younger clutch-mates had kept, this one alone Morade and his spies had not discovered. The safety was fragile. It could not last. Inys sloped down through the cold air, blowing flame in the arranged pattern to announce his coming. Hidden deep within the flesh of the city, the great thorn-spears would be tracking him all the same. Erex followed close, riding his wake with the joy of long intimacy.

The entrance opened before them. Inys folded his wide wings and fell until the darkness of the shadows took him in. The effort of braking his descent strained the muscles of his wings and chest. The pain of it was almost pleasant. He sloped down to the lowest perch in the great hall, and Erex landed beside him. On the floor, the legions of the uncorrupt stood ready. The formation was the classical triangular units, twenty-eight slaves in a unit and twenty-eight units in a form. The strange, elongated scales that Asteril had designed, halfway between true scales and beast hide, made them seem half animal. On every back, there was a culling blade.

A slave in white walked forward, approaching the perch. Her pale hair hung down her back and her scarred face looked up at his as she made obeisance.

"All is prepared, master. Koukis has sent word that the Drowned are in their places. The island has been undermined and they await only our signal."

"And my soldiers?"

"They stand at ready."

Inys bowed his head, his wings widening in an expression of unease. Erex nuzzled him again.

"Tell the slaves to prepare themselves, Drakkis. I am sick at heart and want this ended. One way or the other, let us finish this madness now."

Drakkis Stormcrow turned, lifting her arms so that all

the signalers among the uncorrupt could see her. In each unit, her gestures were echoed. In silent array, the uncorrupt shifted. Then, trundling out of the depths of the hidden city, the dragons came. Ust and Manad were first, broadening their crests in respect before taking two of the uncorrupt in each of their foreclaws, then, beating their wings to hover, two more in each of their hind. They rose up into the distant sky, the first of his desperate and improvised army. Then Mus and Sarin. Then Costa and Saramos. Forty-eight times, his allies came and gave salute. He saw the resolve in their eyes and smelled both distress and resolve in their scents. At the last, only one dragon came out. A third-year still pale at the tips of her wings, her scales the blue white of glaciers. She flared her crest, and Erex stepped down beside the child and flared her own. The sorrow in Inys's breast was almost unbearable.

"Return to me when this is done," Inys said, his gaze locked deep with his lover's, "and I will make you the empress of the wide world."

"If being empress is the price of being at your side, I will pay it," she said. They blew flame at one another, he prayed not for the last time. And then Erex and her youngest cousin gathered the last of the uncorrupt slaves and rose to the sky. Inys stood alone in the great hall. Alone apart from Drakkis.

"We must go, master," she said. Her voice was gentle.

"Is there no other way?" Inys asked, though he knew the answer. Drakkis did not speak. She knew her place. Morade had to believe Inys destroyed or he would not return to the island. There could be no echo of him in Aastapal or in this hidden fortress. There could be no scent of him in the wind or taste of him in the water. He reached down a claw, scooping up his slave, and then rose himself. By the time he reached the open sky, his soldiers were little more than dots on the distant horizon.

The sleeping chamber stood at the side of the sea. The green of its lid called to him as he sloped through the air. He landed gently beside Drakkis's kite and let the slave loose.

"Do not fail me," Inys said.

"My life is yours for the taking, master," Drakkis said. "When the task is finished, I will return and wake you."

Inys pulled up the lid of the sleeping box. The slaves had put a bed of soft cotton there for him, and tiny torches burned in sconces set along the wall. As he stepped down into his hiding place, Drakkis Stormcrow strapped herself into the kite.

"Drakkis," he said.

"Master?"

"You are a slave plotting to kill dragons."

"I am, master."

"There are many people who would have me put you to death for that alone, Morade or not."

"If it is your will that I die, then I will die. But I beg to live long enough to see you named emperor before that."

Inys smiled. He had the impulse to blow fire at the slave, though he knew that even such small affection would destroy her. Instead, he folded his wings, pulled the lid closed over himself, and sealed the jade against all intrusion. Only a small path remained, too small for even a new-hatched dragon to pass through. The passage that Drakkis would take when the war was over and Morade defeated.

Inys settled, closed his eyes. Invoking the silence was difficult. His mind was unsettled. It kept racing ahead of him, toward the sinking of the island and the surprise attack. The legions of the uncorrupt holding formation against the madness of corrupted slaves. The final battle of generations of war, which he could win only by subterfuge and dishonor. Only by sending his lover and his friends to fight in his place. Only by using the schemes and mechanisms of his cleverer brother.

But at last, the silence came. Time became nothing. He became merely flesh. All the cycles and systems of his body passed into nothing, waiting only for the voice of his slave to recall him to himself.

The silence was not meant for dreams, and yet dreams came formless and unreal. He had the inchoate sense of being adrift in a windless openness, floating without effort on an open and empty sky with neither land nor sea below him, but only an endless expanse of air. Then the sense of a presence, alien and unwelcome that almost drove him up from the depth of the silence. He felt uneasy and restless, like a hatchling trying to sleep when it wasn't tired or else too much so.

Time passed without Inys. Even the sensation of waiting was gone. Inys surrendered to not-being.

Excuse me. You need to wake up now.

Awareness, but only the faintest prick of it, there and then gone again. Easy to ignore, easier to forget. The silence washed back in.

Hey! Nap time's over! Wake the hell up! I don't think this is going to be that simple. Do you think maybe there's some sort of ritual or...I don't know. A magic drum or something?

Awareness again, deeper. And this time, there was a sense of fear in it. He felt as if he were under a vast ocean, the weight of the water pressing him down. He had fallen too far into the silence. He had swum too near to death. Inys tried to come to himself, to reach up from the abyssal depths of his body to something else. He forced his eyes to open and had the sensation of light. He was still too deep to know what the light was or what it meant. He was not even seeing. Not really. Only he knew that somewhere, there was light.

He struggled like a drunkard to gather the pieces of his shattered mind, and felt them slipping from his grasp. Felt the silence reaching up to take him again.

It's time to wake up.

He grabbed for the voice. The words were strangely inflected, as all slave tongues were, but they existed. They were real. He could actually feel the words in the dreamed flesh of his claws, and he dragged himself along them, up into the realm of mere slumber. He managed enough awareness to know that something was wrong. He was ill or drunk or poisoned. He couldn't sleep. He couldn't let himself sleep.

You need to wake up now.

He breached from dream to the world. The light became real. A torch in a slave's hand. And another behind it. His body felt wrong, sluggish and dim. The bed he'd slept upon was gone and he felt grime and filth on his scales and in between them. The slave was wrong too. It carried a culling blade, though. The one behind it smelled corrupt. He reached out with his mind and felt Morade's weapon writhing in the slave's blood, but it didn't move to attack.

"Drakkis?" Inys managed, and his voice sounded weak and cracked in his own ears.

The nearer slave shook its head.

"I'm Marcus Wester. That's Master Kit." It was the same voice. The one that had called him back.

"Morade," Inys said. "Does Morade live?"

"No," the slave said. "I'm going to have to go with no on that."

Inys felt the relief pour into his soul. He tried to rise, but his body felt so weak. So *heavy.* The air smelled of rot and ice and the sea. He shook himself, trying to bring his mind to bear, and reared up on his haunches. Every muscle in his body was stiff, slow, and unresponsive. The sense that something was wrong grew.

"Where is Erex?" he asked. "And Drakkis? What's become of Drakkis Stormcrow?"

"Well," the slave said. "I may have some bad news about that."

Dramatis Personae

Persons of interest and import in *The Tyrant's Law*

IN SUDDAPAL

The Medean bank in Suddapal

Magistra Isadau, voice of the Medean bank in
  Suddapal
Kani, her sister
Jurin, her brother
Salan, his son
Merid Addanos, her cousin, and
Maha, her daughter
various cousins and servants of the house

Cithrin bel Sarcour, apprentice to Magistra
  Isadau
Yardem Hane, personal guard to Cithrin, also
Enen
Roach (Halvill)

Kilik rol Keston, a merchant
Samish, a rival of the bank
Karol Dannien, a mercenary captain
Epetchi, a cook

IN IMPERIAL ANTEA

The Royal Family

Aster, prince and heir to the empire

House Palliako

Geder Palliako, Regent of Antea and Baron of
Ebbingbaugh
Lehrer Palliako, Viscount of Rivenhalm and his father

House Kalliam

Clara Kalliam, formerly Baroness of Osterling Fells
Barriath
Vicarian, and
Jorey; her sons
also Sabiha, wife to Jorey, and
Pindan, her illegitimate son
and various former servants and slaves, including
Andrash rol Estalan, door slave to House Kalliam
Benet, a gardener
Alston, a guardsman
Steen, a guardsman

Vincen Coe, huntsman formerly in the service of
House Kalliam
Abatha Coe, his cousin

House Skestinin

Lord Skestinin, master of the Imperial Navy
Lady Skestinin, his wife

House Annerin

Elisia Annerin (formerly Kalliam), daughter of Clara and Dawson

Gorman Annerin, son and heir of Lord Annerin and husband of Elisia

Corl, their son

House Daskellin

Canl Daskellin, Baron of Watermarch and Ambassador to Northcoast

Sanna, his eldest daughter

Also, various lords and members of the court, including

Sir Namen Flor

Sir Noyel Flor

Cyr Emming, Baron of Suderland Fells

Sir Ernst Mecilli

Lord Ternigan, Lord Marshal to Regent Palliako

Sodai Carvenallin, his secretary

Sir Curtin Issandrian

Sir Gospey Allintot

Fallon Broot, Baron of Suderling Heights

and also Houses Veren, Essian, Ischian, Bannien, Estinford, Faskellan, Tilliakin, Mastellin, Caot, and Pyrellin, among others

Basrahip, minister of the spider goddess and counselor to Geder Palliako

also some dozen priests

And also various thugs, workers, tradesmen, and thieves, including

Aly Koutunin, mother to
Mihal, a criminal, and also
Sarai, a recent bride
Ossit, a thug with three friends

IN SARAKAL

Mesach Sau, representative of the traditional families in Nus
Abden Shadra, head of a traditional family
Silan Junnit, member of a traditional family
Sohen Bais, member of a traditional family

IN BIRANCOUR

The Medean bank in Porte Oliva

Pyk Usterhall, notary

Maestro Asanpur, a café owner

IN NORTHCOAST

The Medean bank in Carse

Komme Medean, head of the Medean bank
Paerin Clark, bank auditor and son-in-law of Komme

IN HALLSKAR

Milo of Order Murro, a young man
Kirot of Order Murro, an old fisherman and keeper of
  secrets
Ama of Order Murro, keeper of the lodge house

THROUGHOUT THE GREATER WORLD

Marcus Wester, mercenary captain
Kitap rol Keshmat, former actor and apostate of the
  spider goddess

The Players

Cary
Hornet
Smit
Charlit Soon
Mikel
Sandr

Dar Cinlama, a hunter of ancient treasures and seeker
  of lost places
also his lieutenants, Korl Essian
Emmun Siu

Merrisen Koke, a mercenary captain
also, his men

Callon Cane, a convenient fiction

THE DEAD

King Simeon, Emperor of Antea, dead from a defect of the flesh

King Lechan of Asterilhold, executed in war

Feldin Maas, formerly Baron of Ebbingbaugh, killed for treason

Phelia Maas, his wife dead at her husband's hand

Dawson Kalliam, formerly Baron of Osterling Fells, executed for treason

Alan Klin, executed for treason

Mirkus Shoat, executed for treason

Estin Cersillian, Earl of Masonhalm, killed in an insurrection

Magister Imaniel, voice of the Medean bank in Vanai and protector of Cithrin

also Cam, a housekeeper, and

Besel, a man of convenience, burned in the razing of Vanai

Alys, wife of Marcus Wester

also Merian, their daughter, burned to death as a tactic of intrigue

Lord Springmere, the Mayfly King, killed in vengeance

Akad Silas, adventurer, lost with his expedition

Assian Bey, collector of secrets and builder of traps, whose death is not recorded

Morade, the last Dragon Emperor, said to have died
   from wounds
Inys, clutch-mate of Morade, whose manner of death
   is not recorded
Asteril, clutch-mate of Morade, maker of the
   Timzinae, dead of poison
Drakkis Stormcrow, great human general of the last
   war of the dragons, dead of age

An Introduction to the Taxonomy of Races

(From a manuscript attributed to Malasin Calvah, Taxonomist to Kleron Nuasti Cau, fifth of his name)

The ordering and arrangements of the thirteen races of humanity by blood, order of precedence, mating combination, or purpose is, by necessity, the study of a lifetime. It should occasion no concern that the finer points of the great and complex creation should seem sometimes confused and obscure. It is the intent of this essay to introduce the layman to the beautiful and fulfilling path which is taxonomy.

I shall begin with a brief guide to which the reader may refer.

Firstblood

The Firstblood are the feral, near-bestial form from which all humanity arose. Had there been no dragons to form the twelve crafted races from this base clay, humanity would have been exclusively of the Firstblood. Even now, they are the most populous of the races, showing the least difficulty in procreation, and spreading throughout the known world as a weed might spread through a rose garden. I intend no offense by the comparison, but truth knows no etiquette.

The Eastern Triad

The oldest of the crafted races form the Eastern Triad: Jasuru, Yemmu, and Tralgu.

The Jasuru are often assumed to be the first of the higher races. They share the rough size and shape of the Firstblood, but with the metallic scales of lesser dragons. Most likely, they were created as a rough warrior caste, overseers to control the Firstblood slaves.

The Yemmu are clearly a later improvement. Their great size and massive tusks could only have been designed to intimidate the lesser races, but as with other examples of crafted races, the increase in size and strength has come at a cost. Of all the races, the Yemmu have the shortest natural lifespan.

The Tralgu are almost certainly the most recent of the Eastern Triad. They are taller than the Firstblood and with the fierce teeth and keen hearing of a natural carnivore, and common wisdom holds that they were bred for hunting more than formal battle. In the ages since the fall of dragons, it is likely only their difficulty in whelping that has kept them from forcible racial conquest.

The Western Triad

As the Eastern Triad marks an age of war in which races were created as weapons of war, the western races delineate an age in which the dragons began to create more subtle tools. Cinnae, Dartinae, and Timzinae each show the marks of creation for specific uses.

The Cinnae, when compared to all other races, are thin and pale as sprouts growing under a bucket. However, they have a marked talent in the mental arts, though the truly deep insights have tended to escape them. As the Jasuru are a first attempt at a warrior caste, so the Cinnae may be considered as a rough outline of the races that follow them.

The Dartinae, while dating their creation from the same time, do not share in the Cinnae's slightly better than rudimentary intelligence. Rather, their race was clearly built as a labor force for mining efforts. Their luminescent eyes show a structure unlike any other race, or indeed any known beast of nature. Their ability to navigate in utterly lightless caves is unique, and they tend to have the lithe frames one can imagine squeezing through cramped caves deep underground. Persistent rumors of a hidden Dartinae fortress deep below the earth no doubt spring from this, as no such structure has ever been found, nor would it be likely to survive in the absence of sustainable farming.

The Timzinae are, in fact, the only race whose place in the order of creation is unequivocally known. The youngest of the races, they date from the final war of the dragons. Their dark, insectile scales provide little of the protection that the Jasuru enjoy, but they are capable of utterly encasing the living flesh, even to the point of sealing all bodily orifices including ears and eyes. Their precise function as a tool remains obscure, though some suggest it might have been beekeeping.

The Master Races

The master races, or High Triad, represent the finest work of the dragons before their inevitable fall into decadence. These are the Kurtadam, Raushadam, and Haunadam.

The Kurtadam, like myself, show the fusion of all the best ideas that came before. The cleverness first hinted at in the Cinnae and the warrior's instinct limned by the Eastern Triad came together in the Kurtadam. Also, alone among the races, the Kurtadam were given the gift of a full pelt of warming hair, and the arts of beading and adornments that clearly represent the highest in etiquette and personal beauty.

The Haunadam exist to the greatest extent in Far Syramys and its territories, and represent the refinement of the warrior impulse that created the Yemmu. While slightly smaller, the tireless Haunadam have a thick mineral layer in their skins which repels violence and a clear and brilliant intellect that has given them utter dominion over the western continent. Their aversion to travel by water restricts their role in the blue-water trade, and has likely prevented military conquest of other nations bounded by the seas.

The Raushadam, like the Haunadam, are primarily to be found in Far Syramys, and function almost as if the two races were designed to act as one with the other. The slightest of frame, Raushadam are the only race gifted by the dragons with flight.

The Decadent Races

After the arts of the dragons reached their height, there was a necessary and inevitable descent into the oversophisticated. The latter efforts of the dragons brought out the florid and bizarre races: Haaverkin, Southling, and Drowned.

The Haaverkin have spent the centuries since the fall of dragons clinging to the frozen ports of the north. Their foul and aggressive temper is not a sign that they were bred for war, but that an animal let loose without its master will revert to its bestial nature. While they are large as the Yemmu, this is due to the rolls of insulating fat that protect them from the cold north. The facial tattooing has been compared to the Kurtadam ritual beads by those who clearly understand neither.

The Southlings, known for their great black night-adapted eyes, are a study in perversion. Littering the reaches south of Lyoneia, they have built up a culture equal parts termite hill and nomadic tribe worship. While capable of sexual reproduction, these wide-eyed half-humans prefer to delegate such activity to a central queen figure, with her subjects acting as drones. Whether they were bred to people the living deserts of the south or migrated there after the fall of dragons because they were unable to compete with the greater races is a fit subject of debate.

The Drowned are the final evidence of the decadence of the dragons. While much like the Firstblood in size and shape, the Drowned live exclusively underwater in all human climes. Interaction with them is slow when it is possible, and their tendency to gather in shallow tidepools marks them as little better than human seaweed. Suggestions that they are tools created toward some great draconic project still in play under the waves is purest romance.

With this as a grounding, we can address the five philosophical practices that determine how an educated mind orders, ranks, and ultimately judges the races...

Acknowledgments

I would like to thank my agents Shawna McCarthy and Danny Baror for their support in this project and for hooking me up with the amazing team at Orbit. Particularly, I owe debts of gratitude to Tom Bouman for his editorial wisdom, Alex Lencicki and Ellen Wright for their help in navigating the strange tides of promotion, and Tim Holman for giving me a port when things were stormy.

Also and always, I would like to thank my family for supporting me when things were scarce and helping me through the hard parts.

The errors and infelicities are, of course, my own.

extras

orbit

meet the author

Kyle Zimmerman

DANIEL ABRAHAM is the author of the critically acclaimed Long Price Quartet. He has been nominated for the Hugo, Nebula, and World Fantasy awards, and won the International Horror Guild award. He also writes as MLN Hanover and (with Ty Franck) James S. A. Corey. He lives in New Mexico. Find out more about the author at www.danielabraham.com.

introducing

If you enjoyed
THE TYRANT'S LAW,
look out for

THE WIDOW'S HOUSE

Book Four of The Dagger and the Coin

by Daniel Abraham

CLARA

From the time she'd been a girl, Clara had heard tales of the beauty of Birancour and the soft lands outside of Sara-sur-Mar. Its wide, grassy plains, the lush blue of its skies, and the passion of its lovers had made the backdrop of any number of small romances and ballads of youthful love. She had never made the journey herself, but the image of it that she held in her mind was as perfect and complete as the face of an old friend or a house long occupied in childhood. She could not say now whether her imaginings had been romantic fluff, or if the war had greyed it.

Low cloud pressed down until the sky seemed no higher than the treetops, and the spitting rain soaked the road, her cloak, and the coat of her horse. It thickened the air. All along the roadside, tucked back in the cover of the trees, tents and rough cobbled-together shelters huddled. Men and women watched her pass, their faces bleak and empty. The children who sat at the roadside were too hungry to play. Their faces had taken on the grey of the world.

The stink of churned earth and drowned fires clung to the

landscape as if it had always been there, as if the devastation of war had bled back through history and poisoned all that had come before. That was not true, of course. A year before, this same low road had likely been cheerful and bright as any of the old songs. That it had always been so corrupted was an illusion. But it was a persuasive one.

Clara kept her cloak tight around her and her head down. She regretted now that she'd taken so fine a horse. The nut-brown gelding stood out among the half-starved nags and exhausted plow mules that shared the road with her. The question hadn't even occurred to her. After all this time, some part of her was still the Baroness of Osterling Fells, whether she wished it or not.

A bend in the road, a grass-covered hillock to her left, and her own preoccupation hid the crossroads from her until it was too late. Five men in cloaks of undyed wool stood in the center of traffic. Their hems and boots were dark with mud and hoods covered their heads. Their blades were in scabbards, and two held unstrung bows wrapped against the rain. One of them was speaking to a thin young man, bending toward him, interrogating. The young man's head bobbed as he spoke, desperate for approval and rich with fear. An answering fear rose in Clara's throat. The hooded man nodded, waved the young man on, then stepped in front of two girls walking in the same direction as Clara.

Soldiers, then, though in this blighted space she had no way to tell which side's men they were. If they were queensmen, what would they make of an older woman with the accents of Antea in her voice and a fresh, powerful horse beneath her? And if they were Jorey's men, how could they keep from asking what errand took her into enemy territory?

Stopping now, even hesitating, would only draw further attention to herself. She wondered, if she bolted, whether the men would be able to raise an effective alarm. They let the two girls pass, and Clara was certain one of them at least was looking at her with a vague curiosity in his eyes. *Remain calm*, she thought. *Don't give them more reason to notice you.*

She might as well have stood in the stirrups and sung for all the difference it made.

"Hold there," the man in the front said, holding up his hand to her as her horse stepped into the crossroad. "Rein in, grandmother. Rein in."

Clara raised her eyebrows as she might to an impertinent servant, but she brought her little horse to a halt. One of the other men stepped in and put his hand on the reins. He managed to seem polite doing it, which she counted in his favor.

"What's your name and your business on the road?" the lead man asked. His voice had the softer cadences of Birancour, and now that she was near him, Clara could make out the green and gold of his tunic. The wet had darkened both almost to black, but there was no doubt. A queensman.

Well, at least it wasn't one of the contemptible little spider priests, she thought, and then smiled. The words might have been in her own mind, but they had been in Dawson's voice.

"Clara Osterling," she said. "I'm looking for my daughter. She was staying near here before the battle, and I haven't found her since. Her name's Elisia. She's a bit younger than you, I'd think. Brown hair? A mark on her left cheek?"

It was ridiculous. Antea was in her blood and her vowels, and there was no way of removing it from either. She could no more pass for Birancouri than she could be mistaken for a chipmunk. The man smiled.

"Can't say I have, grandmother," the queensman said.

"Then you'll excuse me. I have to keep looking."

"Not sure of that. I'm going to have to ask that you come over here with us."

"What for?" Clara asked, feigning confusion.

"Agents of the enemy all around, ma'am. Just have to be sure you're what you say."

Clara made a soft, amused sound in the back of her throat.

"Ah," she said. "It's my accent, isn't it? I quite understand."

"Then if you'd just—"

She drew her knife and slashed at the man holding her reins in a single motion. Thankfully, the blade didn't connect, but the boy started back and his grip went loose. She kicked her poor horse's flanks like he'd done something wrong, and together they leapt forward, scattering the queensmen like pins on a bowling green. She kicked again and the poor animal surged forward. Shouts rose behind her, and a woman's startled shriek. Her speed drove raindrops into her bared teeth, into her eyes. Clara bent low over the surging back and held on as tightly as she could, waiting for an arrow to pierce her back or a stone to stun her.

For God's sake, she thought, *don't kill me. I'm trying to help you.*

Leaving Vincen behind had been among the most difficult things she had ever done. Even after the wound had been cleaned and the bleeding slowed to a sickening crimson seep, the worst had not come. The cunning men moved on, tending to those among the army's wounded whom their skills could aid to health or else with their passage into darkness, leaving Clara to sit at his cot. His skin had taken on a waxen look that made her think of meat at a butcher's shop. In his fever, he kicked away the thin blankets and then, minutes later, gathered them back to himself.

She sat with him because she could think of nothing else to do. Somewhere in the camp, Jorey and Vicarian were measuring the advantages they'd won and the price they'd paid for it. She should have been there, gleaning what she could, if not farther afield, acting on what she already knew, and yet it all seemed impossible. Vincen slept in a fever and woke in it, and the two states seemed nearly the same. Near sundown, he raved for the better part of an hour about the need to find a lost dog before the hunt began, and then fell into a sleep so profound that Clara had to watch the rise and fall of his chest to assure herself that it was only sleep.

What would the men think of her attentions to a man who was, after all, merely a servant in her house? What would her boys make of it? She didn't care. She only dampened the cloth again, soothed Vincen's wounded body as best she could, and waited.

Near dawn, the fever seemed to lose its grip. The blankness left his eyes and reason returned. The terrible pressure in Clara's breast and throat eased and she felt the black exhaustion she'd spent the night ignoring.

"My lady," Vincen said, with a weary smile. "I'm afraid I haven't managed your errand yet."

"I think you may be forgiven this time," Clara said. "You have an excellent excuse."

"Thank you for your indulgence," he said, then sighed and made as if to rise. Clara put a restraining hand on his shoulder, and the weight of it alone pressed him back to the creaking canvas.

"You're not to move," she said. "Not until the fever passes."

"The message—"

"The message be damned," Clara said gently. "It's a war. Callon Cane and his agents have to know they're in danger. There's an army outside their city. It isn't as though we were being subtle. Any details we can add are only variations on the theme."

Vincen Coe frowned.

"They'll kill him," he said. "If they haven't already."

"People die. I can't save all of them," she said, and tears welled in her eyes. She felt no sorrow to match them; they simply came and she suffered their presence as if they were unexpected and unwelcome guests. "This one time, I think we can leave the enemy to their own devices."

Vincen's expression clouded, pale lips pressing together. She felt his disapproval, and her answer was rage.

"No," she said before he could speak. "No, I won't have it. We aren't responsible for the world and everything in it. Not every tragedy is our fault. Not every loss."

"We've come this far so that we—"

"Could do what we can," Clara snapped. "We came so that we could try, but there are constraints. There are limits."

"And have we reached them?" Vincen asked.

If she hadn't been so terribly tired, she would not have sobbed. Truly, staying up all night waiting for a young lover to die before one's eyes was better done at twenty. It took too much energy.

"You cannot go," she said. "And there is no one else that I trust."

"And if they kill him because we didn't warn him?" Vincen said. "If the word spreads that Palliako slaughtered him after all, can you live knowing that there was something else you could have done and didn't? Because say you can, and I'll go back to sleep."

Outside the little tent, a horse snorted. The cool morning breeze stirred the wet oilskin walls, shifting the shadows on Vincen's face as if he were an image on a banner. Could she live knowing there was something she could have done and that she hadn't?

"What do you want from me?" she asked.

"Take the message," Vincen said. "You know where to find him. That's the point, after all."

"*Me?*" Clara said, and laughed.

"Who else?" Vincen asked.

"What makes you think I could manage that?"

"You're a predator, my lady," Vincen said, and closed his eyes with a sigh. "You can manage anything."

"You're young and romantic," she said, making the words harsh and their harshness an endearment. Vincen smiled.

She could take any horse in the camp. The army wouldn't be moving before tomorrow, she was certain of that, and the city wasn't that far away. If the information was correct, she could be there and back again before nightfall. The only dangers were everyone she might meet along the way. The Anteans who might discover her, the Birancouri who would cut her down as the enemy, and the man she meant to save who could as easily turn her hostage or kill her on sight.

She said something soft and obscene. Vincen smiled.

"Sometimes doing the least necessary is still a heroic work," he said.

"When I said I didn't want to outlive another lover, this isn't what I meant."

"You won't die," he said, the words growing slushy with sleep. "You'll never die."

Everyone dies, she thought. *All of us. And usually, damn you, for things less important than this.*

*   *   *

For a long, anxious hour, Clara combed the stretch of wood, sometimes certain that she'd come to the wrong place, sometimes that the story had been a fabrication from the start, and always consumed by the fear that she would overlook the secret way and fail in her self-appointed mission. That Geder would overcome another of his enemies because she had not prevented it.

When at last she found the entrance, it was with a sense of profound relief. There, in the depths of a grey-green bush, a slightly deeper darkness. Now that she saw to look for it, a uniformity of the forest litter that spoke of being swept to look as if it were undisturbed. The thin rain tapped against the leaves and trickled down the back of her neck as she looked for a place to tie her mount. It seemed cruel to leave the poor animal out in the cold, but it wasn't as if they'd put a stable next to a smuggler's cave. She made do with a dark hollow where the canopy of trees almost stopped the wetness, and looped the reins in a branch.

"I'm sorry," she said, petting the gelding's gentle face. "I'll come back as soon as I can."

She pushed through the brush, twigs cracking against her. The darkness resolved into a sloping passage so narrow that her shoulders brushed both sides. Worn stone steps led down into the earth, and she followed them, her boots slipping a little against the dampness and grime. When the last of the raindrops had stopped, she paused to light a stub of candle. The smuggler's passage made tombs look welcoming. Streaks of slime clung to the stonework, and the walls tilted in against each other, as if on the verge of collapse. Her passage through it seemed to take hours. There was no marker to show when she passed beneath the walls of Sara-sur-Mar, when she moved from the wilderness into the city. Her little underworld was circumscribed by a single candle's light, and there might as well have been nothing outside it.

The smell of sewage was the first sure sign that she'd reached the habitation of humans. The stink of it was profound and powerful, and it grew with every passing yard she walked. The passage widened, and the stones became brick—old and weathered and alive with cockroaches. The secret passage opened into the vaulted arch of a great sewer. The rank water shone black in the candle-light, and dead things floated in it.

She followed a stone quay along the side of the wall until it turned away, up toward the light and the streets of the besieged city. She lit her pipe from the last of the candle's wick and threw the last thumb's width of wax to the gutter. It wouldn't have been enough to get her back anyway. She'd need to find a lantern. Assuming the men she was seeking out didn't kill her for her troubles.

She turned the bowl of her pipe down to keep the water from putting out the tobacco and stepped into the street. The house was a thousand times easier to find than the passage had been. The green-painted walls and yellow eaves reminded her of toys that a child might play with. She stood outside for a long moment, then sighed, marched to the bound-oak door, and rapped the iron knocker against its strike plate.

It was almost a full minute before the little viewing window squeaked open and a Dartinae woman's glowing eyes appeared.

"Who the fuck are you?" the woman demanded.

"I'm here to see Callon Cane," Clara said.

"You're off your head, then," the woman said. But she didn't laugh. There was no hesitation in her voice. Nor surprise. Any uncertainty that remained in Clara's mind evaporated in that moment and she smiled.

"I've come through danger to see him," she said. "And if you don't let me through, I can swear he'll be dead before the week's out. And likely you will too. Now open the door."

The woman blinked and slammed the window shut. Voices came from the other side. The Dartinae woman's. A man's voice, so deep he was likely one of the eastern races. Clara wished she could hear well enough to make out the words. A cart rattled by behind her, iron wheels against cobblestones. The sound almost covered the scrape of a bar being lifted.

The door opened. The rooms within were gloomy and dim. A

huge Tralgu with a bare blade in his hand stood aside and motioned her in. Clara had the sudden visceral memory of the Tralgu who'd been her own door servant, back in some other lifetime.

"I've come to see Callon Cane," she said again.

"Your thumb."

"They don't take women."

"All the same, ma'am. Your thumb."

Clara held out her hand, suffered the prick of the blade against it. The Tralgu leaned close to examine her blood, then made a satisfied grunt.

"You'll have to leave the blades," the Tralgu said. "Both of them."

Clara didn't ask how he'd known she wore two, only drew them from their sheaths and handed them over, hilt first. The Tralgu seemed satisfied with that. The Dartinae woman was gone, and Clara felt sure that she was being watched from places she didn't know.

The bare drawing room looked out over a thin courtyard, rain running down the window glass like the world weeping. The makings of a fire were laid out in the grate, unlit. The man standing at the window was little more than a silhouette. His greatcoat might have been black or brown. His battered hat sported a wide brim. He was perhaps six inches taller than Clara, perhaps six shorter than the Tralgu guard who took his place silently behind her. He could have been anyone.

Likely that was the point.

"You don't know me," Clara said. "And for reasons of my own, I won't tell you who I am. I have come to warn you. The forces of Antea know you are here, and they have a way to move soldiers into the city. You must leave at once or else..."

The man turned. His face was bloodless, pale, and aghast. Clara felt the world shift beneath her. She didn't know whether to shriek or laugh.

"Mother?" Barriath said, sweeping the wide hat from his head. "What are you *doing* here?"